Involved – by malfunctioning chance –
in the wedding festivities were:

MONICA P. FENSTERMACHER:
a journalist of female persuasion and
ultra-female endowments, she was a brewing
heiress with a mission – to expose the
masculine perfidies of government and
business, even her male-chauvinist daddy.

MATTHEW Q. FRAMINGHAM VI:
a Fellow of the Matthew Q. Framingham
Theosophical Foundation, he was in charge
of recruiting terpsichorean and ecdysiast
(known in the vulgar tongue as 'stripper')
talent for the Foundation's Wednesday
Night Evening Moral Enlightenment Group.
The fact that he mistook Monica for one
of these gifted females was understandable –
but entirely regrettable.

Also in the M*A*S*H series and available from Sphere Books:

M*A*S*H
M*A*S*H GOES TO MAINE
M*A*S*H GOES TO PARIS
M*A*S*H GOES TO LONDON
M*A*S*H GOES TO NEW ORLEANS
M*A*S*H GOES TO MOROCCO
M*A*S*H GOES TO HOLLYWOOD
M*A*S*H GOES TO MIAMI
M*A*S*H GOES TO SAN FRANCISCO

M*a*s*h Goes To Las Vegas

**RICHARD HOOKER and
WILLIAM E. BUTTERWORTH**

SPHERE BOOKS LIMITED
30/32 Gray's Inn Road, London WC1X 8JL

First published in Great Britain
by Sphere Books Ltd 1977
Copyright © Richard Hornberger and
William E. Butterworth 1975
Reprinted 1977

TRADE MARK

This book is sold subject to the condition that
it shall not, by way of trade or otherwise, be lent,
re-sold, hired out or otherwise circulated without
the publisher's prior consent in any form of
binding or cover other than that in which it is
published and without a similar condition
including this condition being imposed on the
subsequent purchaser.

Set in Photon Plantin

Printed in Great Britain by
C. Nicholls & Company Ltd
The Philips Park Press, Manchester

CHAPTER ONE

When Benjamin Franklin Pierce, M.D., F.A.C.S., chief of surgery at the Spruce Harbour (Maine) Medical Centre, arrived at his home after a rather long and tiring day in the practice of his profession, his wife, Mary, met him at the door.

'That was very nice of you, Hawkeye,' she said, giving him a wifely kiss on the cheek.

'Nice of you to say so,' he said. 'What was very nice of me?'

'Recommending Trapper John for membership in the Matthew Q. Framingham Theosophical Foundation.'

'Oh,' he said, 'that. How did you find out about that?'

'A letter came,' she said.

'The Matthew Q. Framingham Theosophical Foundation wrote you a letter?' Hawkeye asked, a touch of surprise in his voice.

'No, silly,' she said, 'they wrote you a letter.'

'Which you, naturally, opened and read?' he said, accusingly.

'Naturally,' she said, ignoring the implied accusation of invaded privacy.

'I don't suppose it would be too much to ask,' he said, a hurt tone in his voice, 'if I could have a look at my letter?'

'Of course not,' she said. 'It is, after all, addressed to you.'

She went into the living room of their house ahead of him and, as he headed for a table containing a bottle of gin, a bottle of vermouth, a jar of olives, a container of ice and another container in which all these things could be combined to make an intoxicant known as a martini, she went to the piano and took from it a crisp sheet of expensive paper.

'Won't that wait?' she asked, somewhat tartly, making reference to his martini mixing.

'It isn't every day that I hear from the Matthew Q.

Framingham Theosophical Foundation,' Hawkeye said. 'I thought a small libation was called for.'

Mary Pierce, who frankly wasn't known for her saint-like patience, fumed visibly as her mate of the past quarter century prepared his martini with somewhat more care and finesse than that lavished on prescriptions by the most dedicated pharmacist.

Finally satisfied with the mixture, the temperature and the manner with which he had rather artistically impaled two cocktail onions on a toothpick, Dr. Pierce raised his glass.

'Matthew Q. Framingham,' he said, solemnly. Then he took a generous sip, pursed his lips appreciatively and nodded his head in satisfaction. Only then did he take the letter from the hand of his wife.

It was a crisp sheet of bond paper, on which had been engraved in dignified style: 'The Matthew Q. Framingham Theosophical Foundation, Founded 1863 for the Furtherance of Philosophy, Science and Theology, P.O. Box 2131, Cambridge, Massachusetts.'

The letter, which was addressed to Dr. Pierce, was typed on an electric typewriter in a type style appropriate to the overall aura of dignity inherent in the foundation's name and purpose.

Dear Dr. Pierce,
   It is my pleasant duty to inform you that the Membership Committee, in their last regular meeting, has acted favourably upon your nomination for associate membership of John Francis Xavier McIntyre, M.D., F.A.C.S.

   As you know, associate membership is tantamount to a probationary period, during which the associate member will be afforded the opportunity of demonstrating his devotion to the principles of Matthew Q. Framingham, our revered and beloved founder. Normally, the period of associate membership ranges from one to three years, during which the associate member will be expected to contribute to the Matthew Q. Framingham Foundation archives a scholarly treatise on philosophy, theology or science, the subject to be mutually agreed upon by the associate member and the Committee on Associate-Member Theses.

This letter constitutes authority for you to inform Dr. McIntyre of his election to associate-member status in the Matthew Q. Framingham Foundation and to invite him to attend a special meeting of the foundation's Committee on Associate-Member Theses to be held in the foundation's national headquarters in Cambridge the last Friday of this month.

While the foundation is not unaware of the interest of the printed-and-electronic news media in the election of a new associate member in the foundation, and in the foundation itself, it suggests that any inquiries by such media regarding Dr. McIntyre's election be handled with the utmost discretion, bearing in mind the words of our founder: 'Many are called, but few are chosen.'

I look forward to seeing both you and Dr. McIntyre here in Cambridge.

> With kindest personal regards,
> Matthew Q. Framingham VI,
> Executive Secretary

Dr. Pierce handed the letter back to his wife. He sipped thoughtfully on his martini.

'I'm glad he made it,' he said. 'You never can tell, until after the Membership Committee meets. Many are called, but few are chosen.'

'When are you going to tell him?' Mary Pierce asked.

'I think I'll call him right now,' Hawkeye said. 'After I finish my drink, of course. Now, Mary, I don't want you spreading this all over. The foundation and its members prefer anonymity.'

'I don't see why,' Mary Pierce said. 'After all, membership in a foundation dedicated to the advancement of philosophy, science and theology is something to be proud of.'

'Modesty,' Hawkeye said, 'is the watchword.' He finished his drink. Then he picked up the telephone and dialled the home number of his friend and longtime professional associate, Dr. John F. X. McIntyre. The phone was answered before it had a chance to ring a second time by Dr. McIntyre's wife, by name Lucinda.

'Lucinda,' said Hawkeye somewhat formally, 'this is Dr. Pierce. May I speak with Dr. McIntyre, please?'

'Oh, thank you, Hawkeye!' Lucinda gushed. 'I just can't wait till my mother finds out!'

'I have no idea what you're talking about,' Hawkeye said.

'Ooops,' said Lucinda. 'I forgot. I promised Mary I'd never let on that she told me!'

'May I speak with Dr. McIntyre, please?' Hawkeye said, sternly.

'Oh, yes, of course,' Lucinda said softly, almost whispering. Then, a moment later, so loud that Dr. Pierce found it necessary to move the telephone an inch away from his ear, she bellowed, 'Trapper! It's Hawkeye! He's going to make it official!'

'This is Dr. McIntyre,' Trapper John McIntyre said. 'With whom am I speaking?'

'Dr. McIntyre,' Hawkeye said, 'this is Dr. Pierce.'

'Oh, yes, Dr. Pierce. Is there something wrong at the hospital?'

'Nothing like that, I'm happy to say,' Hawkeye replied. 'As a matter of fact, I am the bearer of some good news.'

'Is that so? And what might that be, Doctor?'

'Doctor,' Hawkeye said, 'it is my great personal pleasure to inform you that your nomination as an associate fellow of the Matthew Q. Framingham Foundation has been favourably acted upon by its Membership Committee.'

'I hardly know what to say,' Trapper John replied. 'It is a great honour, of course, simply to be nominated. I never dreamed that I would be accepted for membership the first time around.'

'Well,' Hawkeye said, without thinking, 'standards are slipping all over these days.'

'I beg your pardon?' Trapper said. 'You certainly do not mean to suggest, sir, that the high standards of the Matthew Q. Framingham Foundation have, in any way whatever, been compromised?'

'An unfortunate slip of the tongue, Doctor,' Hawkeye replied. 'I meant to imply nothing of the sort. I would venture to suggest that your election the first time your name was proposed may well be due to the unfortunate demise in the past year of three of our more distinguished longtime fellows.'

'Now that I have been elected to fellowship . . .'

'*Associate* fellowship, Doctor,' Hawkeye said. 'There *is* a difference.'

'Please accept my most profound apologies,' Trapper John said. 'I am well aware of the difference. My tongue slipped.'

'Just so that it doesn't happen again,' Hawkeye said.

'What I meant to inquire, most respectfully, was that now that I have been elected an *associate* fellow of the foundation, may I dare ask the names of the departed fellows?'

'I think, under the circumstances, that your request is in order,' Hawkeye said. 'During the last year, we lost three valued companions: The Honourable Horatio L. Potter, formerly United States Senator; Mr. Justice Waldo C. Nebbish, late Chief Justice of the Massachusetts Supreme Court; and H. Howard Budberg, M.D., F.A.C.S., Professor Emeritus of Internal Medicine, Harvard Medical School. They have all gone, in this past year, to that Great Foundation in the Sky.'

'What a tragic loss to mankind!' Trapper John said, with emotion.

'Life, as I'm sure you know, Doctor,' Hawkeye said, 'must go on.' He was aware of sniffling on the line in a duet, telling him that on each end a wife was listening in on an extension. 'I don't think I'm violating any rule or custom of the foundation by suggesting to you that you have been elected to fill the boots, so to speak, of Dr. Budberg.'

'I don't quite know what to say,' Trapper said. 'I feel wholly inadequate.'

'Man often grows to meet his responsibilities,' Hawkeye said, solemnly. 'I feel sure that eventually you will merit the hopes we all have for you.'

'That's very good of you, Hawkeye,' Trapper said. He sounded as though on the verge of tears.

'I don't really think you should, under the circumstances, be quite so informal,' Hawkeye said, rather coldly.

'Doctor, you're absolutely right. I . . . was just overcome with emotion.'

'Well, learn to control yourself, Doctor!' Hawkeye said. 'You are now an associate fellow of the Matthew Q. Framingham Foundation!'

'I'll do my level best to merit that honour, Doctor,' Trapper John said.

'I should hope so,' Hawkeye said. 'And one more thing, Doctor. It would behoove you to say as little as possible about your election to the foundation. I suggest that if anyone inquires into the reason why you will spend next weekend at the foundation in Cambridge, that you imply you have business at Harvard.'

'I understand perfectly, Doctor,' Trapper said.

'Fellows of the Matthew Q. Framingham Foundation have a reputation to uphold. Service, study and modesty! We don't like to see either the foundation or the names of its fellows bandied about in the public press!'

'I understand perfectly, Doctor,' Trapper said. 'And thank you so much for all that you've done for me in this regard.'

'I was simply and humbly serving the foundation as best I could,' Hawkeye said. 'Congratulations, Doctor, and goodbye!'

'Good-bye, Dr. Pierce, and thank you so very much.'

Dr. Pierce, who had, after all, spent a quarter of a century with the lady, was not really surprised that Mary Pierce discreetly let the Spruce Harbour *Clarion-Gazette* know not only that John F. X. McIntyre had been elected to the Matthew Q. Framingham Foundation, but that he had been nominated by her husband.

Indeed, he would have been rather disappointed if next Friday afternoon, when he and Trapper John were suitably attired in what he privately thought of as their go-to-funeral clothes, there had not been representatives of the local print-and-electronic media on hand to chronicle their departure for posterity.

Specifically, Miss Tina-Jane Cromwell, the sixty-four-year-old authoress of 'Tina-Jane's Social Notes from All Over,' a regular feature in the Spruce Harbour *Clarion-Gazette*, and Mr. Flash Paderewski, anchorman for the local television station's news programme, were on hand.

'We hear, Hawkeye,' Flash said, 'that you got Trapper John into the Matthew Q. Framingham Foundation.'

'No comment at this time,' Hawkeye Pierce responded. It was a little ploy he had learned from the Secretary of State.

Flash Paderewski rose to the challenge.

'My sources,' he said, 'which I am not at this time prepared to reveal, tell me that this story of yours – that you've got business at the Harvard Medical School – is nothing but a smoke screen to cover your real purpose.'

'I have no comment at this time,' Hawkeye repeated.

'And neither do I,' Trapper John solemnly chimed in.

'The way I hear it,' Flash went on, 'you have been a secret fellow of the Framingham Foundation for some time, and you nominated Trapper John to take the place of the late Dr. H. Howard Budberg.'

'I will say this,' Hawkeye said, carefully. 'It was my privilege to know Dr. Budberg, and I share in the opinion generally held that he was a fine physician.'

'Ah-ha!' Flash said, triumphantly. 'And do you deny that you are now, and have been for some time, a secret fellow of the Framingham Foundation?'

'As you must know, Flash,' Hawkeye replied, 'the Matthew Q. Framingham Theosophical Foundation, founded in 1863 and dedicated to the advancement of philosophy, science and theology, has a long tradition of maintaining a low profile.'

'Are you now, or have you ever been, a fellow of the

Framingham Foundation? Answer yes or no!' Flash said, rather sharply.

'No comment, I'm sorry,' Hawkeye said. 'I'm sure you know, Flash, that the names of the members of the foundation are never made public.'

'Thank you, Dr. Pierce,' Miss Tina-Jane Cromwell said, formally ending the interview.

'And thank you, lady and gentleman of the media,' Trapper John said, solemnly, 'for your courteous understanding.'

With that, the two physicians turned, kissed their respective mates and walked up the ramp of the Northeastern Airlines aircraft which would carry them to Boston, Massachusetts.

They found seats, looked out the window and waved at their mates and the press until the pilot finally got the engines started and the plane taxied away from the terminal. Neither said a word as the pilot played with the engines, making reasonably sure all the other parts of the plane were functioning. Finally, the aircraft roared down the runway and soared off into the wild blue yonder.

Then, as the stewardess came down the aisle toward them, they turned to each other, broke into wide grins and shook hands formally.

'I'd say that went rather well,' Hawkeye said.

'Couldn't have gone better,' Trapper John said. 'I think we carried it off perfectly.'

'May I offer you gentlemen a cocktail?' the stewardess asked. 'Perhaps a martini?'

'We'd hoped to have one apiece,' Trapper John said.

'But we realize that beggars can't be choosers,' Hawkeye said. 'Just make sure there are two straws.'

With something less than the warm smile and general all-around aura of charm and hospitality of stewardii in television advertisements for aerial transportation, the two were shortly delivered two miniature bottles of gin and two plastic cups full of ice.

Dr. McIntyre, who had made this flight before and

devoutly believed in the Boy Scout admonition to 'Be Prepared,' reached under his chair and took out his medical bag. He rummaged through it for a moment and then came up with a small glass bottle to the top of which was affixed a rubber bulb and a nozzle. Hawkeye held up the plastic cups filled with gin and ice. Trapper squeezed the rubber bulb twice over each cup. A mist of vermouth settled on the gin. Trapper John returned the atomizer to his medical bag and then took one of the cups.

'I give you, sir,' Hawkeye said, 'the Matthew Q. Framingham Theosophical Foundation.'

'Long may it wave,' Trapper replied, 'in respectable anonymity.'

They both then took long and obviously satisfying swallows of the drink.

CHAPTER TWO

As their Northeastern Airlines jetliner soared upward into Maine's chilly skies, another jet aircraft, this one somewhat smaller but every bit as fast, swooped downward from bright Nevada skies.

'Las Vegas Approach Control clears Learjet Double-O Poppa as number one to land,' the man in the control tower said into his microphone.

'Ah, roger, Las Vegas,' the pilot of the Learjet said. 'Double-O Poppa over the outer marker. Is there any word on the ground transportation for Mr. O'Reilly?'

'Las Vegas advises Double-O Poppa that ground transportation requested is on hand at the private aircraft terminal.'

'Roger, Las Vegas, and thank you very much,' the pilot said. 'Double-O Poppa turning on final.'

'Double-O Poppa,' Las Vegas said, 'maybe this is none of my business, but what the transportation is is two Mother O'Reilly's Irish Stew Parlors panel trucks.'

'Roger, Las Vegas,' the pilot of the Learjet said. 'That's what we asked for. Learjet Double-O Poppa on the ground at two-five past the hour. Please close out our flight plan.'

There was a scream of powerful jet engines as the pilot threw them into reverse thrust. The sleek little craft seemed to tip up on its nose as it rapidly slowed on the runway. It turned off onto a taxiway and, following the directions of a ground handler, moved into a parking position. As the sound of its engines died out, the ground handler could read the legend painted on the side of the fuselage. THE FLYING STEWPOT was painted on the nose above a four-colour painting of a bubbling, steaming pot of stew. Above the door, in somewhat more dignified gold lettering, were the words THE ROR CORPORATION and, below that, AVIATION DIVISION.

In the cockpit, the pilot went through the aircraft shutdown procedures. Then he removed the headphones from his head, unstrapped his shoulder-and-belt harness and stood up. He walked back into the passenger compartment and stripped off the yellow-and-purple, nylon, zipper-front jacket he had been wearing. On the back of the jacket, cut in flowing script from a piece of gold felt, were two legends. The larger read CAJUN AIR FORCE. Above it, in somewhat smaller letters, it said HONORARY MEMBER. On the front of the jacket, over the left breast, was a somewhat larger-than-ordinary set of pilot's wings. Instead of the federal shield (or fouled anchor of the naval aviator), the wings bore a representation of a pot of bubbling, steaming stew in their centre. Over the right breast was embroidered the word RADAR.

This was not, as most people quite naturally thought, a reference to the flight function of the wearer of the jacket. Although he was quite familiar with the operation of the R.C.A. Weather-Avoidance Radar with which Double-O Poppa was equipped, the word RADAR had nothing to do with it. It was, instead, the intimate nickname of the pilot, a moniker dating back to his service with the 4077th Mobile Army Surgical Hospital during the Korean War.

There were few people these days who would dare call J. Robespierre O'Reilly, chairman of the board, chief executive officer and sole stockholder of the ROR Corporation International, anything but 'Mr. O'Reilly'. These few included, however, Col. (Louisiana National Guard) Jean-Pierre 'Horsey' de la Chevaux, president, chairman of the board and chief executive officer of the Chevaux Petroleum Corporation, International.

It was from Colonel de la Chevaux that Mr. O'Reilly had received his yellow-and-purple flight jacket. Corporal Radar O'Reilly had first made the acquaintance of Colonel de la Chevaux when the colonel, then a sergeant, had been a patient of the 4077th MASH. After losing touch with each other, they had been reunited by coincidence in New Orleans, Louisiana, two years before[1] and immediately resumed the close personal relationship they had shared in Korea. On hearing that his old comrade-in-arms had decided to learn how to fly, to facilitate his travel between the various worldwide outposts of the ROR Corporation, International, Colonel de la Chevaux had dispatched his chief pilot (the Chevaux Petroleum Corporation operated twenty-nine jet aircraft of various sizes downward from the Boeing 747) to teach him how. Mr. O'Reilly, on being certified by the Federal Aviation Agency as a commercial pilot, airline-transport rating, multiengine jet aircraft, any power, was simultaneously named to honorary membership in the Cajun Air Force, an organization of Chevaux Petroleum Corporation pilots, and presented with the flight jacket.

Mr. O'Reilly hung up his flight jacket and shrugged into a banker-black, pinstripe suit jacket. He adjusted his tie, put on a black homburg, adjusted that, and pushed a button marked DOOR OPEN, whereupon, with a hydraulic hiss, a door unfolded from the side of the Learjet fuselage. He marched off the airplane.

---

[1] The details of the reunion were superbly chronicled for posterity in an educational, highly literate volume suitable for Christmas-giving and other such purposes, published as *M*A*S*H Goes to New Orleans* by Pocket Books, New York, 1975.

As he had been dressing, so to speak, two Ford Curbside panel trucks on which was painted MOTHER O'REILLY'S IRISH STEW PARLORS, LAS VEGAS REGION had driven onto the taxiway. Their drivers, a tall, rather skinny young man and a short roly-poly young man, both attired in standard Mother O'Reilly's Irish Stew Parlors uniforms (chef's hat, chef's whites, and red-striped apron), stood by their vehicles somewhat nervously. So far as anyone knew, this was the first time that J. Robespierre O'Reilly had ever been near Las Vegas, and no one knew what he was up to.

When he actually appeared at the door of the aircraft, they stiffened to attention.

'At ease, men,' J. Robespierre O'Reilly said, in the kindly manner of a general officer. He turned to the airport employee and spoke to him:

'Top off the tanks,' he ordered, 'and see that the floor is swept and the ashtrays emptied. These gentlemen will see to it that a supply of stew is placed aboard.' Then he turned to the Stew Technicians, Second Class. 'There's a thousand pounds of frozen New Zealand lamb aboard,' he said. 'Take it off and carry it to the warehouse. And see that the freezer is supplied with stew.'

'Yes, sir,' the Stew Technicians, Second Class, said in unison.

'I will take one of the trucks,' J. Robespierre O'Reilly said. 'I need directions to Nero's Villa.'

'Yes, sir,' the roly-poly Stew Technician, Second Class, said. 'Turn right on the highway when you leave the airport. It's about six miles down the road. You can't miss it. Just look for the statue of Nero playing his fiddle.'

'Carry on, men,' J. Robespierre O'Reilly said. 'My compliments to your Senior Stew Technician on your appearance. I have made note of your names and serial numbers.'

'Oh, *thank you*, sir,' the two Stew Technicians, Second Class, said with emotion. Their emotion was genuine. With a compliment from J. Robespierre O'Reilly himself on their service records, there was no telling how far they could rise within the Mother O'Reilly's Irish Stew Parlors hierarchy, or for that matter within the ROR Corporation itself. It was well-known that the Senior Executive Vice-President, Sanitation, had been promoted from the ranks. He had, in fact, been the dishwasher at Mother O'Reilly's Irish Stew Parlor No. 1 when J. Robespierre O'Reilly had been the Chief (and only) Stew Technician.

Mother O'Reilly's Irish Stew Parlor No. 1, a photograph of which hung next to the photo of J. Robespierre O'Reilly himself in each of the 2,108 stew parlors world-wide, was no longer open to the public. It was maintained, however, as sort of corporate shrine and as a training aid at ROR University, a wholly owned subsidiary which trained potential stew parlor managers chosen from the ranks on the basis of individual merit, without regard to race, religion, national origin or previous experience with hamburger stands.

The two Stew Technicians, Second Class, watched respectfully as O'Reilly, after first inspecting the panel truck to make sure that it was up to the rigid ROR Corporation standards of cleanliness and polish, got behind the wheel, slammed the door, started the engine and, with something of a lurch, started off the parking area and toward the highway.

'So that's him, huh?' the roly-poly technician said to his companion.

'Gee,' the tall, thin, rather skinny technician said, 'he looks just like a regular human being.'

'Who is that funny-looking little jerk, anyway?' the airport employee asked.

While there was a certain element of truth in the description of Mr. O'Reilly (he stood five-feet-three, weighed no more than 135 pounds, was mostly bald and habitually wore prescription eyeglasses in the shape favoured by aviators, a combination which some people found rather amusing), it was not the sort of thing that a wise man would say to two loyal employees of Mother O'Reilly's Irish Stew Parlors (North America), Las Vegas Region, especially two who had brand-new visions of rising high within the organization.

Three minutes later, bleeding from the nose, the first sign of what was to be a monumental shiner appearing at his left eye and with a foul taste in his mouth from the Mother O'Reilly's Counter and Tabletop Soap with which the two stew technicians had washed out his mouth, the airport employee staggered into a telephone booth and dialled a number from memory.

It was not the number of the Las Vegas police department which he dialled, however, but rather that of the Hospitality Host of Nero's Villa.

'Yeah?' that luminary growled into his telephone, in a deep-pitched and rather gravelly voice. Before being named Hospitality Host of Nero's Villa, Aloysius X. McGee had been a member of the Cook County, Illinois, Sheriff's Department. Specifically, until he resigned the day before he was to appear before a federal grand jury looking into ballot stuffing, vice-squad payoffs, and bingo-game fixing, he had been the Sergeant-in-Charge of the Vice, Gambling and Honest Elections Squad.

'I got a high roller[2] for you, Al,' the airport employee said.

'Who's dat?'

'Steve Wilson, at the airport,' he said.

'I mean duh high roller, ya little creep,' Aloysius said.

'J. Robespierre O'Reilly,' Mr. Wilson said.

'Who duh hell is J. Robespierre O'Reilly?'

'You ever eat Mother O'Reilly's Irish Stew?'

'What do you think I am, some kind of a uncultured slob? Course I eat it. What's that got to do with it?'

'That's him,' Steve said. 'He just flew in here in his private, personal Learjet.'

'Well, whaddaya know? Where's he got reservations?'

'I steered him to Nero's Villa,' Steve Wilson lied glibly. 'I told him it was the only place to go.'

---

[2] For the uninitiated, 'high roller' is the euphemism by which gentlemen of means who can be enticed to gambling tables of one form or another are known. The 'high' makes reference to their credit rating, not their gambling ability.

'O.K., ya little creep,' Aloysius said. 'T'anks. If he shows up here, I'll remember dis. If he don't, I'll remember *dat*, too.'

Aloysius hung up his telephone and turned to a small device on his desk, technically known as a computer substation. It was connected by telephone line to the National Credit Rating Information Service in New York. He typed, using one finger and frowning mightily the meanwhile, one line of characters, which appeared on the computer readout: 'J. ROBESPIERRE O'REILLY. MOTHER O'REILLY'S IRISH STEW PARLORS.' Then he found the buttons marked QUERY and CREDIT RATING. He pushed them in turn and then bent down over the device to get a good look at the readout window. In a matter of seconds, the answer appeared.

'AAAAA+.'

A look of annoyance crossed Aloysius' massive brow, which furrowed. With what this computer thing was costing them, you should be able to expect the damned thing to work. It was supposed to furnish a cash figure, the unquestioned credit rating limit of the individual whose name and company had been fed into the computer, not a bunch of A's.

Aloysius had learned, however, that the way to deal with a malfunctioning computer was not to bang it with the heel of your hand. You had to humour it. You had to keep asking questions.

He pushed the keys again, one at a time, this time spelling out 'CREDIT LIMIT IN DOLLARS' and then pushed the QUERY button again.

And again, almost immediately, the reply began to appear in the readout window. First a dollar sign appeared, then the number 1. Then, as the machine clicked steadily, a line of zeros appeared after the 1. First it read 10, then 100, then 1,000, then 10,000, and still more zeros appeared. Aloysius had just begun to smile when the numbers vanished and were replaced with 'OVERLOAD'.

Aloysius said a word that is not polite to repeat in mixed company and reached for the telephone.

'Get me dat credit bureau in New York,' he barked and slammed the phone back down. In a minute the phone rang, and he grabbed it immediately. 'Dis is Aloysius X. McGee, Hospitality Host of Nero's Villa in Las Vegas,' he said. 'I need a quick credit check on a high roller name of J. Robespierre O'Reilly.'

There was a pause.

'Duh damn thing told me "Overload",' Aloysius growled. 'Dat's how come I ain't using duh damn Handy-Dandy Instant Credit Clearer, you dumb broad! Now gimme the information!'

There was another pause as Aloysius impatiently drummed on his desk with his fingers, the smallest of which was approximately the size of a Danish salami.

'Before it tol' me "overload",' Aloysius said, his annoyance rather evident in his voice, 'it told me "AAAAA+". I don't want the crumb's report card. I want to know how much the crumb is good for in dollars!'

The frown which had creased Aloysius' face, giving it somewhat the appearance of pink sausages laid side by side, now vanished. 'Well, t'ank you very much, sweetie,' he said, his voice now dripping with charm. 'I'll do something nice for you sometime. Anytime you're in Las Vegas. . . .'

He broke the connection, suddenly remembering that his watchword was 'Business Before Pleasure'. He quickly punched a couple of numbers on the telephone.

'Front desk? Aloysius X. McGee. Got a high roller for you named O'Reilly. Put him in one of the good suites, stock it with booze and put five hundred dollars in chips someplace where he can't miss seeing them no matter how drunk he is. He'll be checking in any minute.' He broke that connection without waiting for a reply and punched the number of the doorman's telephone.

'Who's dis?' he said a moment later, as the parallel rolls of little pink sausages reappeared on his brow. 'I don't want to talk to no dum bellboy, I want the doorman!' There was another brief pause. 'What do you mean, he's having a argument wit' some deliveryman?' He didn't wait for a reply to his question. He slammed the phone down again and, moving with surprising grace for his bulk, half-ran, half-walked out of his office, which opened upon the main lobby of Nero's Villa, raced across the half-acre of lobby and to the revolving door.

The doorman (known officially in Nero's Villa as the 'Keeper of the Gate') was a dignified individual attired in a Roman toga and crown of laurel leaves and was indeed having a scrap with a deliveryman. Aloysius saw that the dumb deliveryman had driven right up to the front door (known in Nero's Villa as 'The Gate of Joyous and Triumphant Entrance') in a lousy panel truck.

Aloysius X. McGee rushed to the truck. Under normal circumstances, he would have picked the crumb up and thrown him all the way back to the highway. But these were not, he recognized suddenly, ordinary circumstances. The delivery truck was emblazoned with the world-famous pot of bubbling Irish stew, the instantly recognizable logotype of Mother O'Reilly's Irish Stew Parlors.

He could hardly give the crumb his just desserts for despoiling the peace and dignity of The Gate of Joyous and Triumphal Entrance to Nero's Villa with his lousy truck with J. Robespierre O'Reilly himself about to arrive. Not only was J. Robespierre O'Reilly the chairman of the board of the outfit, for all Aloysius knew, he was Mother O'Reilly's favourite son.

'Is dere sometin' wrong, gennelmen?' Aloysius, fixing a smile on his face, inquired as gently as he could.

'All I want to do is go inside,' Radar said. 'This guy in the sheet won't let me out of my truck.'

'Duh ting is, sir,' Aloysius said, 'we're expecting Mr. J. Robespierre O'Reilly hisself at dis very minute.'

'I am J. Robespierre O'Reilly,' Radar said. 'Who are you?'

'Welcome to Nero's Villa,' Aloysius said. 'Sound duh trumpets!'

'I beg your pardon?' Radar asked.

'I said "sound duh trumpets",' Aloysius repeated, menacingly.

'Sure, Big Al,' the Keeper of the Gate said. 'How was I supposed to know?' He turned to a yellow box mounted on one of the two, fifty-foot-tall Roman columns which flanked The Gate of Joyous and Triumphal Entrance. He pushed a small button marked TRUMPETS.

Instantly, from six fifteen-inch loudspeakers hidden within six large concrete cornucopia mounted on the wall of the villa itself, came the sound of trumpets. (What they blared, loud enough to rattle the windows in Radar's truck, was the first few opening bars of the triumphal procession from *Aida*. The most diligent research had been unable to come up with the music played by trumpets in Nero's Rome, and Caesar Augustus 'Little Augie' Finecello, resident manager of Nero's Villa, had decided that the triumphal procession from *Aida* was a satisfactory substitute.)

'Right dis way, Mr. O'Reilly,' Aloysius X. McGee said. 'Yer Roman Gladiator's Deluxe Suite awaits!'

Radar allowed himself to be led inside Nero's Villa, through a line of bellboys (known in the Villa as 'Centurion's Pages') who bowed at their passage. The trumpets of welcome were sounded only when a very important guest passed through The Gate of Joyous and Triumphal Entrance, a very important guest (or VIG) being defined as someone who was not only fond of gambling but had the wherewithal to pay his losses. J. Robespierre O'Reilly, whose credit rating in dollars had overloaded the Handy-Dandy Instant Credit Clearer, had been categorized as a V-VIG, or Very, Very Important Guest.

Mr. O'Reilly, however, was not in Nero's Villa (or for that matter, in Las Vegas) to gamble. He was here on what the French call an '*affaire de coeur*', or affair of the heart. Specifically, Radar was in love. The object of his affections was Madame Kristina Korsky-Rimsakov, a rather statuesque lady of gentle manner who was possessed of a voice (she was a coloratura soprano) which had made her the undisputed grande dame of the San Francisco Opera and world-famous and admired.

The two had met over a year before while both had been

on a trip to Paris, France,[3] where Madame Korsky-Rimsakov had been invested with the Legion d'Honneur for her vocal artistry and Mr. O'Reilly had been named to the same order for having solved the problem of excess French lamb production. (In the belief that the lamb served in the 104 French Mère O'Reilly's Stew Americaine Bistros was American lamb and thus vastly superior in every way to French lamb, the French had, in their enthusiastic embrace, so to speak, of the boiling pot simultaneously solved the excess lamb problem and made Radar even richer.)

It had been, more or less, love at first sight between the two, but with a certain problem. Both Madame Korsky-Rimsakov and Mr. O'Reilly were telepathic. That is to say, under certain circumstances they could read minds, including each other's. Indeed, it was Mr. O'Reilly's ability to read minds and to tune in on telephone and radio messages that had earned him the nickname 'Radar' during his military service. It was, further, in large measure responsible for the phenomenal success he had enjoyed in what is known as the fast food business. There had been a certain advantage in his being able to read fellow businessmen's minds and to know, for example, what a meat supplier would take for a hundred pounds (later, a hundred thousand pounds) of lamb, as opposed to what he was asking for it.

This telepathic ability, however, did not always work between Madame Kristina and Radar; they could not always read each other's minds. For all of his life, Radar had been able to read the minds of females with whom he had come in contact. While what he read, even after he achieved great wealth, was seldom flattering, there was a certain comfort to be taken in knowing what a particular lady was thinking. Since he could not always read Kristina's mind (or she his)

---

[3]The details of this rather fascinating Franco-American relationship have been described in full detail, and with a certain inimitable style, in a book entitled *M*A*S*H Goes to Paris* (Pocket Books, New York, 1975), which is available on the racks of better drug stores, bus and airline terminals and other outlets catering to the sophisticated student of international affairs.

except under certain sunspot conditions, he quite naturally was ill at ease in her presence.

He suspected, of course, that the emotion which welled up within him whenever he saw Madame Kristina was reciprocal, but he could not know for sure. The colour which flooded her face when his hand touched hers could be caused by an upset stomach as well as by a fluttering heart.

A week before, however, as he watched Kristina board an airliner bound for Las Vegas, where she was to give a series of recitals at Nero's Villa, Radar had finally bitten the bullet. Or perhaps began to really gnaw at it. It had taken him two-and-a-half days to really make the decision to fly to Las Vegas, declare his love and ask the lady to become his bride.

The decision had come to him in Lima, Peru, whence he had flown to investigate the possibility of using llama meat in his stew. He had suddenly broken off the discussion, driven to the airport and set course for Las Vegas. There was no life without Kristina. He had come to face this brutal fact when he realized that he really didn't give a damn, one way or the other, whether they put lamb, llama or water buffalo in the boiling pots of the 2,108 stew parlors worldwide.

On the way up, his mind had been beset by doubts. Why should a lovely, talented, famous singer wish to share her life with someone who really was nothing more than an unusually successful short-order cook? Radar O'Reilly was aware that he was a rather funny-looking little runt who could count on the fingers of his hands (with both thumbs and one index finger left over) his true friends, those people who liked him despite his many faults and weren't after his money.

But he realized that he had to take the gamble, had to find out once and for all if Kristina Korsky-Rimsakov loved him and would be his wife, or whether she was just being nice to him, as she was nice to small children, old women and mongrel dogs who had caught their tails in screen doors.

He had enough presence of mind to stop off at the West Coast warehouse of the ROR Corporation to load the

Learjet with a thousand pounds of frozen New Zealand lamb chunks so that the trip, no matter what happened, wouldn't be a total loss, and then he had flown on to Las Vegas.

CHAPTER THREE

Roman Gladiator Deluxe Suite No. 23 of Nero's Villa occupied one-fourth of the twenty-fifth floor of the northeast wing. It consisted of a living room, identified as the Gladiator's Forum; a large bedroom with a double bed and known as the Gladiator's Pit; and a large room housing a bathtub, a shower stall, a water closet and the same strange plumbing device Radar had puzzled over in Paris, sort of a kidney-shaped footbath (or maybe wine cooler) equipped with flowing water and located between the water closet and the washbowl. All of these items were in a room labelled, naturally, The Gladiator's Spa.

Mr. Aloysius X. McGee, who had kept a firm grip on Radar's arm all the way through the lobby and up in the elevator, pointed out the facilities of the suite with all the enthusiasm of a condominium salesman.

'I'm afraid,' Radar finally said, somewhat shyly, 'that there's some sort of mistake. This is all very beautiful, but I'm sure it's dreadfully expensive!'

'Put dat thought from yer mind,' Aloysius X. McGee said, grandly. 'Youse is a guest uh duh house.'

'You mean, it's free?' Radar asked. When Aloysius nodded, he went on, 'Why, that's very kind of you. Thank you very much.'

'T'ink nuttin' of it,' Aloysius said. 'Our pleasure. I'm one of yer greatest fans, Mr. O'Reilly. Yer stew is just like me mudder used to make.'

'Is that so?' Radar asked, pleased. 'Was your mother a mess sergeant?'

'What are you looking for, a fat lip?' Aloysius replied, momentarily forgetting with whom he was speaking.

'Oh, no,' Radar said. He had tuned into Aloysius' mind and understood that Aloysius had misunderstood him. 'Mr. McGee,' he said, 'I will tell you in confidence that I learned the famous recipe for Mother O'Reilly's Irish Stew from a mess sergeant.'

'No foolin?'

'I had modified it slightly, of course,' Radar said, 'but basically, I used the recipe I learned in the mess hall of the 4077th MASH in Korea.'

'Well, whaddaya know?' Mr. McGee said. 'How 'bout dat?' He smiled at Radar and then glanced around the room. With a tone of excited surprise, he said, 'Well, look at dat! Dere's yer Gladiator's Poyce.'

'My what?' Radar asked.

'Yer Gladiator's Poyce,' Aloysius repeated. '*Poyce*,' he repeated still again when he saw the look of incomprehension on Radar's face. 'Poyce. Like ladies carry. The gladiators carry them, too, I guess. Anyway, that's what Little Augie said to call dem.'

'I'm afraid I don't quite understand,' Radar said. 'Who's Little Augie?'

'Caesar Augustus Finecello,' Aloysius explained. 'Our resident manager, which we call Nero's Ghost.'

'Oh,' Radar replied.

'What it is, see,' Aloysius somewhat laboriously explained, 'is money. Or sort of money. Ya use it to gamble.'

'Like Monopoly money?' Radar inquired, and with enormous relief, Aloysius nodded agreement.

'Right,' he said. 'When we get a V-VIG like youse in here. . . .'

'What's a . . . whatever you said?'

'It stands for Very, Very Important Guest,' Aloysius said. 'Anyway, when somebody like youse comes in here, Mr. O'Reilly, Little Augie always gives them a Gladiator's Poyce in case they'd like a little action downstairs.'

'What kind of action?' Radar asked somewhat suspiciously. He had once gone on what the army called Rest and Recuperation Leave (R&R) from the 4077th MASH to Kokura, Japan. He had stayed in a hotel room which, while much smaller than this suite, bore a strong resemblance to it somehow. The aura was the same. He had returned to Korea knowing why the GI's had referred to R&R as I&I. It stood for Intoxication and Intercourse.

'You a gambling man, Mr. O'Reilly?' Aloysius asked, man to man.

'I used to play a little poker, of course, when I was in the service,' Radar replied.

'I could tell it by looking at you,' Aloysius said. 'Poker's a man's game, right, Mr. O'Reilly?' he asked, nudging Radar in the ribs with his elbow and almost knocking him down.

'I always thought so,' Radar agreed.

'Well, we got a twenty-four-hour-a-day poker game going on downstairs,' Aloysius said. 'And you can start in by playing with the Gladiator's Poyce.'

'Well, that's very nice of you, Mr. McGee,' Radar said. 'I'll give it serious consideration.'

'Dat's all yer gonna do? *T'ink* about it?'

Radar, reading his mind, could see that Mr. McGee was very disappointed. For reasons Radar could not quite understand, it was obviously very important to him that he play poker or participate in some other game of chance.

'Actually, Mr. McGee,' Radar said, 'I am not here to gamble.'

'You ain't?' Mr. McGee's disappointment was obvious.

'I always win, you see,' Radar said, 'and that takes the fun out of it.'

Aloysius X. McGee wasn't quite sure what to make of that statement.

'If you ain't here to tempt Lady Luck,' he asked, 'what exactly did you have in mind?'

'Actually, I came here to see Madame Kristina Korsky-Rimsakov,' Radar replied, 'on a personal matter.'

'That figures,' McGee said.

'It does?' Radar asked.

Mr. McGee was privy to certain problems in the Executive Suite of Nero's Villa involving Madame Kristina Korsky-Rimsakov. Her presence at the villa had, in fact, shaken Mr. McGee's lifelong faith in the established order of things.

The situation, as well as he understood it, was this. The establishment itself was owned by the Sicilian-American Friendship and Burial Society of Chicago, Illinois. The Executive Director of the S-AF&BS of C was Mr. Caesar Augustus Finecello, Sr., fondly known to his blood and business families as 'Big Caesar'. Because of the press of his many other business responsibilities, Big Caesar had entrusted the operation of Nero's Villa to his eldest son and namesake, Caesar Augustus Finecello, Jr., known as 'Little Augie'. Little Augie was cast in his father's mould. That is to say, he was a hardheaded businessman who understood the business he was in and how it should be operated.

Little Augie was one of Big Caesar's eight children. Seven of the children were male. Five were also businessmen, engaged in directing the far-flung business enterprises of the S-AF&BS of C, which included such divergent things as insurance companies, real estate development, advertising agencies, garbage collection services and the Sicilian-American Travel Agency, or SATA.

The seventh son was the Rev. Father Giuseppe Verdi Finecello, a Jesuit priest stationed in New Mexico who had virtually nothing to do, in a business sense, with his family. The eighth child, the baby, was Carmen Finecello Wiecnewski, known to one and all as 'Carmen-Baby'. She was the apple of Big Caesar's eye, and it was generally accepted that what Carmen-Baby wanted, Carmen-Baby got.

(This included Mr. Wiscnewski. Carmen-Baby had first seen Mr. Wiscnewski on the football field, where he had been a linebacker for Notre Dame. It had been love at first sight, and Carmen-Baby had immediately confessed her feelings to her father. Big Caesar had been, at first, not entirely happy with his daughter's choice, but had, rather predictably, given in to Carmen-Baby in the end. Mr. Wiscnewski, who had planned a career in professional football, had received an offer he couldn't refuse from Big Caesar: Carmen-Baby and the presidency of the Sicilian-American Sanitation Service, which had the garbage-removal concession for Newark, New Jersey.)

Their union, some twenty-three years before, had been blessed with a son, christened Stanislaus Caesar Augustus Finecello Wiscnewski by Father Giuseppe Verdi Finecello in what was still talked about as the most ornate christening bash ever to occur in the Italo-Polish community of Hamtramck, Illinois.

Little Stanislaus, the only blond grandchild, enjoyed in the first decade of his life almost as much favour in his maternal grandfather's eyes as did his mother. He was, truth to tell, something of a disappointment to his father. At the age of sixteen, he told his father that he thought football was a 'revolting game.' By the age of twenty, he had developed a manner of speech, a rather peculiar gait and a fondness for the company of his own sex that would have, had he not been the Grandfather's Grandchild, caused some talk.

(In Aloysius X. McGee's secret heart of hearts, he thought of 'Stanley August', the name the lad had taken at twenty-one, as a flaming faggot.)

Stanley August had, some four months before, finally found, he announced, his role in life. He was, he told 'Chère Mama', going to enter the world of the theatre.

Chère Mama (a/k/a Carmen-Baby) thought that darling Stanley's idea to form an all-male ballet company was splendid and told him that she felt sure Grandpa would be more than willing to subsidize the operation once it was explained to him.

Carmen-Baby, however, was aware that for some reason (probably advancing senility) Grandpa had in recent years grown somewhat cool to darling Stanley. For that reason, she went to him alone to discuss the idea.

For the first time ever, there were harsh, unkind words between Big Caesar and Carmen-Baby. Big Caesar said unkind things about people of Polish ancestry generally and about Stanislaus Wiscnewski, his son-in-law, in particular. Carmen-Baby responded with unkind words about the crude, boorish crassness of certain Sicilian-Americans and how she was ashamed of the family. There were shouts, tears, recriminations and more tears and finally Father Giuseppe Verdi Finecello was brought (via long-distance conference call) into the matter.

Father Gus agreed with both sides. In other words, he agreed with Big Caesar that it wouldn't be wise to send Little Stanislaus off to New York with a blank check, but that, on the other hand, Carmen-Baby was right in her belief that Little Stanislaus would be far better off, far happier in an artistic milieu, so to speak, than he would be either throwing garbage cans on one of his father's trucks or engaged, for example, in his Uncle Pasquale's collection agency, which would also require the muscle Little Stanislaus obviously didn't have.

The solution, Father Gus said, seemed to suggest itself. Little Stanislaus should be sent to his Uncle Little Augie in Las Vegas. Nero's Villa had a large showbusiness operation (there were three dinner theatres in the villa) on which Little Stanislaus, so to speak, could cut his teeth. If he proved to have a genuine flair for the theatre, then he could be bankrolled with his all-male ballet company.

Little Augie had not, frankly, been beside himself with joy when Big Caesar called him on the phone with orders to fire the incumbent entertainment director and turn his responsibilities over to what he described as the 'Polack Lily.'

'I don't want no argument, Augie,' Big Caesar said. 'For one thing, it'll make Carmen-Baby happy, and for another, your brother the Jesuit priest tells me it's our duty to a member of the family.'

And so it came to pass that Little Stanislaus, under his stage name, Stanley August, was installed as entertainment director of Nero's Villa. At first, putting aside what Uncle Little Augie thought was an extraordinary interest in certain of the lifeguards, Little Stanislaus didn't do too badly. He had a certain flair for the spectacular, which was a good thing since most of those who came to watch the shows in Nero's Villa's Dinner Theatres (which were called 'Nero's Circi Numbers One through Three', plus the largest operation, The Roman Orgy Room) were generally pretty smashed and needed a lot of noise and bright lights to keep them awake during the show and to send them out again afterward to the gambling tables.

But then, on a talent-seeking trip to San Francisco, California, Little Stanislaus was exposed for the first time to opera. He met another young man of exquisite grace and delicate demeanour in the San Francisco Museum, where both were admiring replicas of a Michelangelo statue, sans fig leaf.

The other young man simply insisted that Stanley August accompany him to the opera, where the star of the evening was Madame Kristina Korsky-Rimsakov. 'Madame Kristina,' the young man said, 'has everything that Judy Garland ever had, and then some!'

Little Stanislaus was quite as taken with Madame Kristina as his new friend thought he would be. She reminded him, he said, of what a mother should be, what women generally should be and were not. That is, gentle and kind and utterly without menace.

She was, he decided, just what Nero's Villa needed to give the place a little class. Uncle Little Augie's idea of class began and ended with long-legged, monstrous bosomed chorus girls attired in a few strategically placed sequins. Why anyone should wish to spend an hour watching scantily clad, long-legged, big-bosomed women cavorting around a stage was more than Stanley August could comprehend.

Once Uncle Little Augie realized what prestige Madame Korsky-Rimsakov would lend to his hostelry, Little Stanislaus could again dare to bring up the subject of the male ballet troupe, an idea which, so far as Little Augie was concerned, was one whose time had not come. He had been so *firm*, actually, about that that Stanley August had decided that he would not consult with Uncle Augie before engaging Madame Korsky-Rimsakov. It would be his little surprise. Uncle Augie might be a little annoyed, but Stanley August knew he could handle that by calling up *Chère* Mama and crying a little. *Chère* Mama would thereupon go to Grandpa, crying a little, and Grandpa would thereupon telephone Little Augie and settle his hash.

Madame Korsky-Rimsakov had been engaged the very next day. Stanley August had called her agent. The agent, in the belief that the call regarding Madame Kristina's services was an elaborate practical joke (Madame Kristina Korsky-Rimsakov did not customarily perform in towns like Las Vegas, generally, or places like The Roman Orgy Room of Nero's Villa specifically), had quoted a frankly ridiculous price for her services.

Stanley August, who had no idea what opera singers cost, had accepted it without argument, which baffled Madame Kristina's agent no end. For the same price, Stanley August could have engaged Frank Sinatra and a troupe of twelve performing elephants with Dean Martin and Don Rickles thrown in for the intermissions.

On his return to Las Vegas and Nero's Villa, Stanley August had decided that discretion was the better part of valour in describing the new artiste to Uncle Little Augie. He didn't lie. He said that she was female and that she had packed the 'last house' she played. He didn't mention it was the San Francisco Opera House. He was able, moreover, to truthfully reply in the affirmative to Uncle Little Augie's rather crude question about her bust development. Madame Kristina Korsky-Rimsakov did indeed have a splendid pair of knockers, although this was probably the first time they had been referred to in quite those terms.

As it happened, Uncle Little Augie was summoned to Chicago on family business two hours before Madame Kristina Korsky-Rimsakov gave her first performance (a programme of Schubert lieder) in The Roman Orgy Room. It was not until his return six days later that he came to fully understand what Little Stanislaus had done to him.

It was enough, Little Augie had confided to Mr. Aloysius

X. McGee, in a rare confidence, to try the patience of a saint. With an eye to one day hosting a national political convention, the architect who had designed Nero's Villa had designed Nero's Circi Numbers One through Three and The Roman Orgy Room in sort of a fan shape. Each was separated from the other by substantial-looking walls which in fact were collapsible, turning the four rooms into one enormous auditorium.

Reminding the hotel engineer that he was not only the official entertainment director but also the nephew of Mr. Little Augie Finecello and grandchild of Big Caesar Finecello as well, Little Stanislaus had ordered the conversion. The three circi and the orgy room were now one large auditorium.

Because they were not marching to the sound of the same drum as Madame Korsky-Rimsakov, the comics, jugglers, monologists, jazz bands and magicians originally scheduled to perform in the circi were paid off and sent packing. Nero's Nubiles, the fifty-girl-strong Corps de Hoofers, had been hastily recostumed and retrained. Instead of birdcage hairdos, eye shadow and sequins, Nero's Nubiles were now attired in maroon choir robes, with their hair done up in buns-on-the-neck, and ordered to stand in a semicircle, their hands in an attitude of prayer, behind the Steinway grand Little Stanley had had flown in (together with tuner) from New York.

When Little Augie had walked into what had been Nero's Circi One through Three and The Roman Orgy Room and was now identified as The Concert Salon, he found, instead of the 3,560 happy revellers who would normally be inside soaking up booze and paying a nominal $13.50-per-head cover, a total of twenty-four people, eighteen of them sound asleep and six giving every indication they had been at the sauce and had no idea whatever where they were.

Whatever else could be said of Mr. Caesar Augustus Finecello, Jr. (and the possibilities were practically without limit), it could not be said that he was a fool. He realized, in other words, that in his present frame of mind, if he had a little chat with Little Stanislaus about The Concert Salon and the artiste therein performing, he would subsequently be faced with explaining to his father and Carmen-Baby why he had beat Little Stanislaus about the head with darling Stanley's own arms.

His pique was not relieved very much the next day when he sought out Little Stanislaus in his office and learned (a) how much Madame Kristina Korsky-Rimsakov was being paid per performance and (b) how much longer her unbreakable contract had to run.

While it was impossible to break the singer's contract, it was not impossible, so to speak, to break the singer. But Big Caesar, who prided himself on running a tight ship, insisted that decisions of that type be made by him. Little Augie knew that he could present Big Caesar with a *fait accompli*; it would be necessary for him to confess all and leave the decision to him.

Big Caesar listened patiently, and with understanding, to his son's recital of the problems caused by Little Stanislaus.

'Ordinarily,' Big Caesar said, 'getting rid of the broad would be handled in the normal way. But this ain't a normal situation, Augie, if you get my meaning.'

'Because of Carmen-Baby, Poppa?'

'Her, too,' Big Caesar said. 'But I was talking with your brother Leonardo da Vinci just yesterday.' Leonardo da Vinci Finecello, Little Augie's next younger brother, was in charge of West Coast operations. Eighty-two per cent of waterborne cargo arriving in the United States was offloaded by members of the longshoremen's union, of which 'Little Lenny' Finecello served as president.

'What's he got to do with it?' Little Augie asked, in exasperation.

'Well, Augie,' Big Caesar said, 'lemme put it this way. Little Lenny said he was sorry he couldn't make the meeting because he 'specially wanted to see you and thank you.'

'Thank me for what?'

'For getting Josephine-Marie into the Opera Guild.'

'Poppa, I don't know what the hell you're talking about.' Josephine-Marie was Little Lenny's wife.

'Josephine-Marie's been trying to get into the San Francisco Opera Guild for years. I'd hate to tell you how much money it's cost Little Lenny trying to buy her in. She's almost as bad as Carmen-Baby when she can't have what she wants.'

'So what?'

'So she didn't come close, that's what,' Big Caesar said, 'until the word got out that her brother-in-law ... you, Augie ... was the guy what hired their head warbler to sing in his hotel. Now she's been *asked* to join the damned Opera Guild.'

'What are you trying to tell me, Poppa?'

'I'm telling you you can't go break the singer, that's what I'm telling you.'

'What am I supposed to do, then, Poppa?'

'You're a bright boy, you figure something out,' Big Caesar said. 'I don't care what you do, Augie, just so long as Josephine-Marie gets to stay in the Opera Guild and you get that dame out of my hotel.'

'Poppa!' Little Augie said, entreaty in his every syllable, but he was speaking to a dead telephone. He hung up, shaken, ashen-faced. There was only one path open to him, that of going to Madame Korsky-Rimsakov and begging her to let him out of the contract. He was used to giving orders, not begging. The prospect was frightening.

The telephone call with Big Caesar had taken place as Double-O Poppa was landing at Las Vegas. As Radar was driving toward Nero's Villa in the Las Vegas Region panel truck, Mr. Finecello had steeled himself, picked up the telephone and asked to be connected with Madame Kristina Korsky-Rimsakov.

'What a pleasant coincidence,' the singer said to him. 'I was just about to telephone your office, Mr. Finecello, to see if you could spare me a few moments of your time.'

'You was?' Little Augie asked, surprised.

'I'd like to talk to you about the balance of my contract,' Kristina said.

'You does?'

'I was just about to take my daily constitutional swim,' Kristina said. 'Would you be good enough to meet me for a few minutes by the pool?'

'I think I could probably work that in,' he said. 'Which pool is that?'

'I've been using The Pool of the Vestal Virgins,' Kristina said. 'I've found that the forty-foot diving board there is superior to the one in The Pool of Nero's Handmaidens.'

'I'll meet you there in ten minutes,' Little Augie said. He broke the connection with his finger, punched the number of the Chief Centurion of the Centurion Guard and, when that luminary came on the line, barked out an order:

'Get every last crumb-bum guest out of The Pool of the Vestal Virgins,' he said.

'How am I to do that, sir?'

'Tell them a man-eating shark's in it! I don't give a damn how you do it, just do it. I got business with a lady in ten minutes, and I want to be alone.'

'But, sir, won't people be able to look out their windows and see?'

'I mean business, you damned fool, not monkey business. Now get those creeps out of the damned pool!'

'Hail, Nero!' the Chief Centurion said, remembering his oath was not to reason why, just to do what he was told.

CHAPTER FOUR

Within a matter of minutes, the 132 Nero's Villa's guests of assorted sizes, shapes, races, creeds and national origins who had been enjoying the somewhat heavy-on-the-chlorine water of The Pool of the Vestal Virgins had been encouraged to transfer their aquatic activities elsewhere. Mr. "Little Augie" Finecello appeared at poolside and ordered the Chief Centurion to make sure that no one, save the broad what was chasing the paying customers away, was given access to the pool. Then he seated himself at a poolside table and, contemplating the large diamond ring he wore on his pinky finger, began to prepare himself mentally for the ordeal of having to ask the lady to shove off.

Twenty-five floors up in the northwest wing, Mr. Radar O'Reilly tuned in at that moment on the mental thought processes of Mr. Aloysius X. McGee. Mr. McGee's thoughts came in, in military parlance, loud and clear:

'Maybe, if I play my cards right,' he was thinking, 'we can get this ugly little twerp to the poker table and cheat him out of enough dough to make up for what that screeching, screaming broad has cost us.'

'What,' Aloysius X. McGee asked aloud, 'is yer relationship wit' duh lady?'

'You might say,' Radar replied, 'that we are good friends.'

'Yeah,' Mr. McGee said, 'I'll bet you are. Tell you what I'm going to do for you, friend,' he went on. 'I'm going to see if I can find out where she is for you.'

As he said this, he was thinking: 'Little Augie'll want to know about this guy right away.' Radar heard this quite as clearly as he would have had Mr. McGee shouted it in his ear.

'What,' he asked, 'is the relationship of Little Augie to Madame Kristina Korsky-Rimsakov?'

'You might say,' Aloysius replied, with a little chuckle, 'that he thinks about her a lot.' There was some interference at that moment with the radiation of Mr. McGee's thought processes, possibly caused by a sunspot. Mr. McGee had had a mental image of Little Augie with both his hands around Madame Kristina's neck, choking her. The image came through, but badly garbled. Radar misread it. What he thought he saw was his beloved Kristina in Little Augie's affectionate embrace. He was badly shaken.

'Tell you what, pal,' Aloysius said, 'I got a good idea. Why don't you go downstairs and get in a little game in The Roman Poker Parlor, and I'll go see if I can't round up the lady for youse?'

'Perhaps later,' Radar replied. 'I need a few minutes to collect my thoughts.'

'Well, O.K.,' Aloysius said. 'Whatever you say.' The interference with his thought radiations cleared up. What he was thinking came through again, loud and clear: 'I'll go tell Little Augie about this guy. We can sucker him into a poker game later.'

As Mr. McGee left Roman Gladiator Deluxe Suite No. 23, Madame Kristina Korsky-Rimsakov walked across the Astroturf beside The Pool of the Vestal Virgins to meet Mr. 'Little Augie' Finecello.

She got right to the point. 'I'll get right to the point, Mr. Finecello,' she said.

'Do dat,' Little Augie replied.

'I feel that my performances here have been something less than successful,' she said. 'The fault is obviously mine.'

'You feel dat, do you?' Little Augie replied.

'Yes, I do,' Kristina said. 'And I feel it would be better, all around, if we negotiated the premature termination of my contract.'

'You want to go over that again, in English?' Little Augie said.

'Please don't take offence,' Kristina said, 'but I have begun to feel that the guests of your hotel are not, generally speaking, music lovers.'

'Dat would depend on duh music,' Little Augie said.

'Probably,' Kristina replied. 'Whatever the reasons, Mr. Finecello, I think it would be best if my engagement here were terminated at the earliest possible moment.'

'You mean, you want out?'

'Exactly,' Kristina said.

'And how much is dat gonna cost me?' Little Augie asked.

'I have given the matter some thought,' Kristina said, 'and I believe it would be fair if I would return to you my entire honorarium, in exchange for being released from the balance of my contractual obligation to Nero's Villa.'

'You want to give me my dough back?' Little Augie asked.

'That is correct,' Kristina said.

Little Augie was stunned. He was, moreover, of Sicilian ancestry and given to the physical manifestation of emotional reaction common to that subspecies of Homosapiens. In other words, he stood up, wrapped his arms around Madame Kristina Korsky-Rimsakov and shouted, 'You got a deal, baby!'

At precisely that moment, twenty-five floors up in the northwest wing of Nero's Villa, Mr. J. Robespierre O'Reilly idly pushed aside the heavy window drapes and looked out the window and down at The Pool of the Vestal Virgins.

What he saw was his beloved Kristina, whom he planned to ask to be his partner on the long journey down life's twisted path, in the arms of another man. He stared just long enough to make sure that his eyes weren't deceiving him and then let the drapes fall back in place.

A half-second after the drapes fell back, Madame Kristina Korsky-Rimsakov had extricated herself from Little Augie's unwelcome embrace. She had, in fact, extricated herself with such vigour that Little Augie, $450 silk suit and all, found himself sinking in The Pool of the Vestal Virgins.

She immediately jumped in to rescue him, of course, but by that time the damage had been done. The $450 suit was ruined, and so, J. Robespierre O'Reilly thought, was his life.

He tried, and failed, to find comfort in the philosophical observation that ' 'Tis better to have loved and lost than never to have loved at all.' His world had turned to ashes.

Like countless others in similar circumstances, he felt a burning desire to lash out in revenge. Unlike others, however, he immediately saw how this could be done. Little Augie Whatsisname had stolen the one love of his life from him. In his hurt and anger it seemed entirely just and fair that Radar steal something of value from him. Aloysius X. McGee had made it quite clear that Nero's Villa hoped to entice him to a gaming table and there divest him of large sums of money by means less than honest. Well, Radar decided, we'll see about that!

As Madame Kristina hauled a soggy Little Augie Finecello out of The Pool of the Vestal Virgins, J. Robespierre O'Reilly, with determined tread, marched into The Roman Poker Parlor and sat himself down at a card table above which hung a sign reading NO-LIMIT GAME.

The dealer (known in The Roman Poker Parlor as the 'Keeper of the Treasury') had been briefed by Mr. McGee to expect 'a funny-looking little twerp with unlimited credit who's so dumb he told me he never loses.'

'You would be, sir,' the Keeper of the Treasury said, with a warm little smile, 'Mr. J. Robespierre O'Reilly?' Radar heard that with his ears, and with his mind he heard what the Keeper of the Treasury was thinking: 'It must be O'Reilly. He's a funny-looking little jerk, and if he's as dumb as he looks, I'll have him clipped like a sheep in no time at all.'

'Shut up and deal,' Radar replied.

'Your credit is fine with us, Mr. O'Reilly,' the Keeper of the Treasury said. 'How much would you like?'

'Let me have five thousand,' Radar said. 'For openers.'

Five-thousand dollars in crisp new fifties and a little IOU form were slid across the green baize to him.

'Poker, Mr. O'Reilly?' the Keeper of the Treasury asked. 'Or a little blackjack?'

'Poker's fine,' Radar said, 'but blackjack's quicker. Give me three cards.'

The cards were dealt. As someone once wisely observed, it is impossible to cheat an honest man. Radar was not faced with that problem. The Keeper of the Treasury had read all the cards he had dealt Radar and was absolutely confident that the only problem he faced was that of keeping the little twerp in the game long enough to fully scalp him. It did not occur to the Keeper of the Treasury that just as soon as he knew what any card was, including his own, and the next to be turned up in the deck, Radar knew the same thing.

At first, the Keeper of the Treasury felt that he was having a little bad luck, which was, after all, to be expected. The little twerp, by pure luck, just stood pat when the next card he should have taken would see him go bust. He didn't win every hand, of course, just three out of five. The hands he won, however, generally seemed to represent a wager of five hundred or a thousand dollars and those he lost generally involved no wager over one hundred dollars, so within a matter of minutes there was a large stack of money, neat packets of one-thousand dollars, five-thousand dollars and even two of ten-thousand dollars in front of Radar, growing with every other turn of the card.

A button was discreetly pushed with a knee, standard procedure whenever what the house referred to as a 'sucker' seemed to be winning. A floorman (known here as the Senior Keeper of the Treasury) appeared and watched with a cold, experienced eye the hands of Radar O'Reilly and the hands of the dealing Keeper of the Treasury. The little twerp was acting suspiciously, and the cute little tricks the dealer was doing with the deck of cards clearly reflected great credit upon his profession.

The neat stack of neatly bundled paper money before Radar O'Reilly grew. Spectators gathered around the table, and there were murmurs among them that they were possibly watching the man who was to break the bank at Nero's Villa, something they could tell their grandchildren.

But this was not to come to pass. The management of Nero's Villa, for one thing, was not in business to lose money at the blackjack tables. The management had no foolish notions that gambling men should actually be permitted to win.

With a practiced eye, the Senior Keeper of the Treasury examined the money in front of Radar and added it up quickly in his mind. There was $81,000 there, $75,000 in neat little bundles and $6,000 just sort of lying around.

Eighty-one thousand was six thousand dollars over the disaster figure. Under these conditions, the Standing Operating Procedures laid down by the management required that the gambler be suddenly stricken with a heart attack. But there were so many people gathered around the table watching that the Assistant Keeper of the Treasury, responsible for using the hypodermic needle, simply couldn't get close enough to Radar to let him have it.

The Senior Keeper of the Treasury, however, hadn't risen to that position at Nero's Villa without demonstrating his ability to think creatively on his feet.

'New cards!' he cried. 'New cards!'

There were, in fact, a gross of decks of crisp new cards in the drawer of the table with the green baize surface, but these were obviously unsuitable. The Keeper of the Treasury was dispatched to get more cards from the storeroom.

One of your run-of-the-mill gamblers who had just taken the house for $81,000 would just have stayed where he was, basking in the admiration of his fellows and waiting for more cards to be delivered. But Radar O'Reilly was not of that calibre.

His conscience, as a matter of fact, was bothering him. He knew, in his heart of hearts, that he really hadn't been gambling. Only extraordinary sunspot activity interfering with his extrasensory perception could have made him lose, and the sun, at the moment, was apparently rather calm.

Radar stacked the money he had won before him and did some thinking. The rage which had swept through him when he saw his beloved Kristina in the arms of another man had dissipated. He no longer felt a burning desire to lash out at the world in search of revenge. All he wanted to do, he realized, was to have the game resume so that he could lose, exactly as he won. When he was even, he would get up from the table, leave the hotel, get back in Double-O Poppa and fly off into the blue, a solitary figure doomed to saunter down life's long road alone.

He looked over his shoulder to see if the dealer was returning with fresh cards. He didn't see the dealer, but he did see Kristina, the ex-love of his life, marching through the lobby, accompanied by the man in whose embrace she had been and four bellboys carrying her luggage.

They were leaving, Radar realized. Probably eloping, probably en route at that very minute to some romantic place like Niagara Falls, New York, or the Honeymoon Heaven Hotel in Stroudsburg Heights, Pennsylvania.

Whatever else he was, Radar decided, he was not a sore loser. The least he could do as a gentleman was wish the happy couple well and incidentally let Kristina know that it mattered not at all to him, that she had just been a minor romantic interlude in a life filled with romantic interludes, most of whose names he couldn't even remember.

Moving so quickly that he was gone before any of the Assistant Keepers of the Treasury who were standing behind him could stop him, he got up from the table, absent-mindedly jammed the $81,000 in the breast pocket of his jacket and marched into the lobby of Nero's Villa on a course designed to intersect that of Kristina, his ex-love, and her gentleman friend.

He jammed his hands in his trouser pockets, fixed a smile on his face and raised his eyes to the ceiling, absolutely convinced that he now was demonstrating a devil-may-care savoir faire of which even Cary Grant would be jealous.

'Robespierre!' Madame Kristina called when she saw him. Radar pretended not to hear her. 'Robespierre!' she called again.

'Why hello there, Whatsyourname,' Radar said 'Fancy meeting you here!'

'Whatsyourname?' Kristina replied. 'Robespierre, whatever is the matter with you?'

He looked at her and met her eyes, and all his firm determination collapsed around his ankles.

And at that moment, two different gentlemen marched with purposeful step toward Kristina, Radar and Little Augie. One was the Senior Keeper of the Treasury, who had just been informed that the little twerp had walked out of The Roman Poker Parlor with eighty-one grand of Nero's Villa's money. It was desperation time, and his hand held a leather bag of lead shot, known as a sap, which he intended to apply to the base of the little twerp's skull.

As he raised his arm, however, the other gentleman, who was attired in a black suit, black shirt and clerical collar, spoke:

'That's a no-no,' he said, in a surprisingly firm voice. 'Cool it.'

'Butt out, buddy,' the Senior Keeper of the Treasury said.

'How dare you talk to my brother-the-priest that way?' Little Augie said. 'Get lost, you disrespectful crumb!'

'Gee, how was I to know?' the Senior Keeper of the Treasury said.

'Permit me to introduce myself, madam,' the priest said. 'I am Father Giuseppe Verdi Finecello, and I am one of your greatest fans.'

'How nice of you to say so, Father,' Kristina said. 'I was just having the nicest chat with your brother here.'

'I thought he might be going to have a little talk with you,' the priest said. 'And I thought it would be a good idea to pop over here to make sure it was a nice little talk.' He paused, looked at Little Augie and then went on. 'I hope it was a nice little chat?'

'Very nice,' Kristina said. 'And I was just about to leave the hotel when I ran into my dear, dear friend, Mr. J. Robespierre O'Reilly.'

'How do you do, Father?' Radar said, politely.

'A pleasure, sir,' the priest said.

'And when you walked up, Father, Mr. O'Reilly was just about to explain what he was doing here and why he forgot my name.'

'I heard about your romance,' Radar blurted, 'and since I happened to be in the neighbourhood, I just dropped by to wish you and your gentleman friend all the best from someone who once dared to hope that you would be his bride.' His voice broke toward the end, and tears filled his eyes.

'Robespierre,' Kristina said, 'have you been drinking?'

'There must be some mistake,' the priest said, glowering at his brother. 'My brother already has a wife and eight children.'

'What did you say about daring to hope that I would be your bride?' Kristina asked, before Radar could open his mouth to vehemently deny that he had been drinking.

'I said . . .' he began.

'I accept,' she replied. 'Oh, Robespierre, if you only knew how long I've waited for you to ask.'

'Huh?' Radar replied.

'Am I correct in assuming that congratulations are in order?' Father Gus asked.

'Eighty-one *thousand*?' Little Augie burst out. He had been reading over his brother's shoulder. A Centurion guard was holding up a blackboard on which some nameless artist had drawn a rather good caricature of J. Robespierre O'Reilly, together with a winged bundle of currency and the figures $81,000.

'How picturesque a compliment,' Kristina said. 'Eighty-one thousand congratulations! Mr. Little Augie, I shall forever treasure that remark.'

The priest, who was after all a member of the family even if he had gone into a somewhat different line of work, looked over his shoulder and saw the blackboard. While he did not think of himself as a cynical man, he did suspect that little Augie's crack about 81,000 had nothing to do with congratulations.

'Just leaving, were you, Madame Kristina?' he said, grasping her arm and Radar's and propelling them quickly toward the door. He jerked the door of a Gladiator's Chariot which was parked open there, installed Kristina and Radar in the back and had a word with the chauffeur.

'I am Father Giuseppe Verdi Finecello,' he said. 'Little Augie's brother-the-priest. Take these nice people where they want to go, right now!'

The Gladiator's Chariot (a 1973 Rolls-Royce sedan) roared out of the driveway. Little Augie was seen waving good-bye as his brother-the-priest watched him closely to make sure the fingers of his hand didn't close and form a fist.

Kristina Korsky-Rimsakov turned from waving back at Little Augie and faced Radar.

'You really have swept me off my feet,' she said. 'I don't even know where we're going.'

The truth of the matter was that Radar had no idea either whither he was bound. Things had been moving a little too fast for him.

'Robespierre?' Kristina pursued. 'Where are we going?'

'Actually,' Radar said, somewhat sonorously, 'what I had in my mind was this...'

'Yes?'

'I have the plane, of course,' he said. 'We could go anywhere.'

'But would that, Robespierre,' Kristina said shyly, 'be proper? We are not married yet, are we?'

Radar flushed violent red before replying. And then he had a quite clear mental image of the man to whom he had many times turned before when he didn't quite know what to do.

'Hawkeye!' he blurted.

'Hawkeye what?'

'I think Hawkeye should be the first to know,' Radar said. 'He's already married, you know. He has the experience.'

'And perhaps Mary Pierce would be good enough to help us with the arrangements,' Kristina replied. 'Radar, you always have the right answer.'

'You've noticed, have you?' he replied.

Five minutes later, Las Vegas departure control cleared Learjet Double-O Poppa for takeoff on a direct flight to Spruce Harbour, Maine. Because of the splendid sound insulation neither the pilot nor the sole passenger heard the sound of the submachines and sawed-off shotguns firing at them from a Gladiator's Chariot bearing the Nero's Villa insignia on its door, which had appeared with squealing tyres at the airport as Double-O Poppa began its takeoff roll.

As a matter of fact, Kristina was having fond thoughts about Nero's Villa and its staff.

'Robespierre,' she said, 'you and I both know that Dr. and Mrs. Pierce are generous to a fault.'

'That's right,' Radar agreed.

'And I think if they thought we hadn't made plans for our wedding, that they would want to arrange things for us.'

'Maybe they would,' Radar said. That struck him as a splendid idea.

'But we wouldn't want them to do that for us, would we?' Kristina said.

'Certainly not,' Radar said, firmly.

'So why don't we just tell them we've made our own plans already.'

'What plans?'

'I'm sure that nice Mr. Little Augie would be able to arrange for a room for us to use for the ceremony, and maybe a little plate of cold cuts, hard-boiled eggs and potato salad for a little reception afterward.'

'That's a good idea,' Radar said. 'And since his brother's a priest, maybe we could get a clerical discount for Dago Red.'

'What about Dago Red?'

'Years ago, in the 4077th MASH, Dago Red promised me that whenever Miss Right came along for me, he would do the honours.'

'Oh, that's sweet!' Kristina said. 'But, Robespierre, now that Father Mulcahy is Archbishop Mulcahy, don't you thinkit would be better if you stopped calling him Dago Red?'

'You're absolutely right,' Radar said.

'There will be room in the plane for everybody,' Radar said. 'We can have a nice, simple little ceremony.' He blushed. 'And then we can go on our honeymoon.'

'Oh, Robespierre,' Kristina said, 'I'm so happy.' She leaned over and kissed the pilot, for the first time ever, on the mouth.

Learjet Double-O Poppa, making 650 knots at 30,000 feet, described a manoeuvre known to airmen as a Double Immelman ending in a split-S, then straightened out on course for Spruce Harbour, Maine.

Behind them, the jet contrail, viewed from the ground, looked like a Valentine's Day heart.

CHAPTER FIVE

It is one of the proud claims of the American broadcasting industry that television news is absolutely immune from economic pressure of any sort. Television journalism between commercials, we are frequently told, is absolutely free to seek out and report the truth, the whole truth and nothing but the truth and to telecast same without fear or favour.

With that in mind, it must be presumed that the employment of Ms. Monica P. Fenstermacher as a research assistant to Mr. Don Rhotten,[1] anchorperson of 'The Rhotten Report'. was based on her academic record and her announcement of profound dedication to the broadcast journalism profession, rather than because she was the only child of Fritz W. Fenstermacher, Chairman of the Board of Fenstermacher Breweries, Inc., whom *Broadcasting* magazine listed as the single largest advertiser on the Amalgamated Broadcasting Network.

As a matter of fact, until a discreet word was whispered into Mr. Rhotten's ear to cool it, Mr. Rhotten had evidenced a personal interest in Ms. Fenstermacher's journalistic career. Ms. Fenstermacher was blonde, blue-eyed and, in the quaint parlance of the broadcast journalist, stacked like a brick outside sanitary facility. She was twenty-one years old and a recent graduate (cum laude in Creative Journalism) of Vassar College, Poughkeepsie, New York. Mr. Fenstermacher had learned that Vassar College had gotten its start through the generosity of a fellow brewer, and that had been enough for him to decide on the institution for his daughter's higher education.

Mr. Fenstermacher had been somewhat disappointed, it must be reported, when his beloved Monica finished four years at Vassar (a) without getting an acceptable proposal of marriage and (b) newly possessed of the belief that only Women's Lib and Television Journalism stood, a thin red line, against the wholesale overthrow of America the Beautiful by Male Chauvinist Capitalist Exploiters of the Masses, in particular the brewing industry.

Mr. Fenstermacher, further, guessed (and correctly) that Monica had sought employment with Mr. Rhotten and 'The

---

[1] Mr. Rhotten, of Serbo-Dutch ancestry, pronounces his name 'Rowten.'

Rhotten Report' primarily because she knew how deeply Mr. Fenstermacher loathed and despised Mr. Rhotten. The situation, however, was quite beyond his control. Monica Fenstermacher was not only of legal age but also of independent means, having received a rather large bequest from her late mother.

It was not that Monica Fenstermacher did not love her father. She loved him, even if he was a male chauvinist capitalist exploiter of the masses. She loved him, and it was clearly her daughterly duty to save him, and the country, from himself. The way to do this, it was quite clear to her, was to dig out and expose on the television airways the secret bastions of male chauvinist capitalism.

She had been given carte blanche in her investigation by her employer, although not quite for the reasons she believed to be the case.

The same executive assistant to the chairman of the board of the Amalgamated Broadcasting Network who had pointed out to Mr. Seymour G. Schwartz, executive producer of 'The Rhotten Report', that it might be a splendid idea to offer employment to the only daughter of their largest advertiser also pointed out, somewhat more forcibly, that it would not be especially good for business if it got back to Mr. Fenstermacher that Mr. Rhotten was breathing heavily down Ms. Fenstermacher's decolletage.

Truth to tell, Mr. Rhotten fancied himself something of a ladies' man and felt it necessary to live up to his own image of himself. He had something of a reputation within the industry as a dirty middle-aged man.

'I'll lay it out on the table for you, Seymour,' the executive assistant to the chairman of the board had said. 'While Amalgamated would like to look forward to many years of Don's service with us ... presuming he can do something about his ratings, which are, you know, down the last three weeks in a row ... the cold fact of the matter is that if we have to choose between Don Rhotten and Monica Fenstermacher, it's the product of the brewer's art over Rhotten five to one. Do you read me, baby?'

'You're not suggesting that this dumb broad is more important to the network than Don Rhotten?' Seymour G. Schwartz had countered loyally.

'You got it, baby,' the executive assistant said. 'Fenstermacher Breweries lays eight-point-seven million on us every year for advertising. We want to keep him happy. He would be very unhappy if he found out that Don Rhotten was trying to make his little girl.'

'I see your point,' Seymour G. Schwartz had replied. 'I'll have a word with Don.'

'Have several words, baby,' the executive assistant had said. 'And unless you want to go back to producing "Uncle Ralph and His Furry and Feathered Friends" in Cedar Rapids, make sure he's listening.'

This made reference to the fact that both Mr. Schwartz and Mr. Rhotten had begun their careers in television with a kiddy programme in the hinterlands. Mr. Rhotten had cut his teeth, so to speak, in television by playing Uncle Ralph's Furry Friend Big Bunny.

One Saturday morning, still a little sweaty from having bounced all over the stage for two hours in his bunny suit, Mr. Rhotten had been pressed into service reading the Noon-Time News, an emergency replacement for the regular newscaster, who had been unavoidably detained at Charley's Bar & Grill.

To everyone's profound surprise, Big Bunny, sans bunny suit, had come over quite well. There was a certain timbre to his voice that made him sound trustworthy, knowledgeable and sincere, even to his professional associates, who were quite aware that Big Bunny's Don Rhotten's entire fund of knowledge could be written inside a matchbook cover with a grease pencil.

In a very real sense, Don Rhotten was the product of Seymour G. Schwartz's genius. It had been Seymour G. Schwartz who had had the daring foresight, in the face of what at the time had looked like insurmountable odds, to buy Don Rhotten not only his first sincere tie (he had previously been given to wearing neckwear which, when a concealed button was pressed, lit up three strategically placed electric lights on a silk screen painting of Gypsy Rose Lee), but his first suit and his first wing-tip shoes as well. Seymour G. Schwartz had taken Don Rhotten to the dentist and had his rather grey, sort of free-form teeth capped; to the best ophthamologist in Cedar Rapids for contact lenses to replace the thick spectacles Don Rhotten had worn since the third grade and which had earned him the cruel sobriquet 'Fisheyes'; and equally important, taken him to Chicago and there secured for him his first hairpiece.

With Big Bunny thus transformed, Seymour G. Schwartz had invested his own money to prepare what was then known (before the development of tape) in the trade as an 'audition kinescope'. This was a 16mm motion picture film with synchronized sound. In it, Mr. Schwartz spliced together film showing Mr. Walter Cronkite, Mr. Howard K. Smith and Mr. John Chancellor delivering the news, together with film of Mr. Don Rhotten reading the same news.

It was the unanimous conclusion of the Board of Directors of the Amalgamated Broadcasting Network that Mr. Rhotten's delivery of the news had a certain quality, a certain *je ne sais quoi*, that made you *believe* what he was saying even when you knew full well he hadn't the foggiest idea what he was talking about.

Rhotten was immediately engaged as the anchorperson for the ABN Evening News. ABN, traditionally last in the Neilsen Ratings, had gone through seven anchormen (and even two anchorwomen) in the past two years. Two weeks after Rhotten had taken over, ABN surged ahead to second place and remained there. It was admitted, privately, in the upper echelons of television journalism that nothing short of a criminal conviction for bigamy and multiple axe-murders was going to divest Cronkite of his faithful fans, and ABN was perfectly willing to settle for second place.

In addition to his duties as anchorman, Don Rhotten did frequent specials, called 'The Rhotten Report', in which he reported on things of interest in great detail. He was, in short, generally regarded as one of the most prominent television journalists, and Seymour G. Schwartz had been really surprised to learn that ABN, given the choice between him and some dumb broad, had picked the broad.

Schwartz had been momentarily tempted to tell Amalgamated Broadcasting where to head in but had thought better about it. He had never been really happy as Uncle Ralph and did not want to go back to it. Miss Wanda J. Fogarty, a young lady whom he had seen performing the Dance of the Seven Veils on Bourbon Street in New Orleans, Louisiana, was hired as a research assistant for Mr. Rhotten, and the incumbent research assistant, Ms. Monica Fenstermacher, was sent off to Moose Lake, Ontario, to look into the thickness of the ice on the lake.

This had been something of a stopgap measure, however. Ms. Fenstermacher wanted to attack Male Chauvinist Capitalism and she could hardly do much of that in Moose Lake, Ontario.

Lady Luck had smiled on Mr. Schwartz. Despite his fame, the truth was that Mr. Don Rhotten had few friends, but among these was a congressman, The Honorable Edwards L. Jackson (Farmer-Free Silver, Arkansas). Don Rhotten and Congressman Jackson, known as 'Smiling Jack', had become pals in Casablanca, Morocco, specifically in the Casablanca slammer.[2] While in Moroccan Durance Vile, the congressman and the television journalist, facing they knew not what future, had sworn a solemn vow of mutual assistance for then and for the future. To the surprise of those who knew them, they lived up to their words of honour once they had been released from their unjust imprisonment. Largely as a result of frequent references to him on 'The Rhotten Report', Congressman Jackson had become one of the most widely known solons in Congress, despite his rather anonymous position as third-

---

[2] The details of this event, for those with an interest in North African Native Customs and for students of International Affairs, may be found succinctly and rather literately recorded in *M*A*S*H Goes to Morocco*, Pocket Books, New York, 1976.

ranking member of the House Committee on Sidewalks, Subways and Sewers. Similarly, to make sure that his fellow lawmakers had the benefit of the thinking of his pal Rhotten, Congressman Jackson had made it a habit to have the scripts of 'The Rhotten Evening News' and 'The Rhotten Report' printed in the *Congressional Record*.

The congressman was a great believer in what is known as 'liaison.' In the interests of governmental-news media relationships, in other words, he stationed in New York a congressional liaison specialist (GS 13–$26,900 per annum) to make sure that 'The Rhotten Evening News' and 'The Rhotten Report' got an uninterrupted flow of news releases from his office. He had been pressing his pal Don Rhotten to station someone from his staff in the congressman's office in Washington. Rhotten had passed this request on, via Mr. Schwartz, to Amalgamated Broadcasting, who said they were in complete agreement with the idea, providing only that the cost of such a liaison officer came out of the Rhotten budget.

Seymour G. Schwartz had charge of the Rhotten budget. As a matter of fact, for a little look behind the scenes, Don Rhotten himself was an employee of Don Rhotten Productions, Inc. Don Rhotten Productions, Inc., 75 percent of which was owned by Mr. Seymour G. Schwartz, produced 'The Rhotten Evening News' and 'The Rhotten Report' for ABN for a fixed fee. What that meant was that three-fourths of any money that was spent on 'The Rhotten Report' came out of Seymour G. Schwartz's pocket, a situation he did not like.

There had been, therefore, no Don Rhotten staffer stationed with the congressman in Washington. The liaison idea now seemed, however, to be a splendid opportunity to kill two birds with one stone, or perhaps to kill one cuckoo with two rocks. Ms. Monica Fenstermacher was called back from Moose Lake, Ontario, and sent to Washington to work with Congressman 'Smiling Jack' Jackson. Ms. Fenstermacher was told that the congressman would help her in her dedicated search to root out and expose male chauvinist capitalism wherever found, and Congressman Jackson was told that Ms. Fenstermacher was the liaison officer from Don Rhotten Productions, Inc., to his office.

Since Seymour G. Schwartz had come to believe that both Ms. Fenstermacher and the congressman were bananas, and furthermore spoke in tongues, he had reason to believe that each would be so confused with the other that a satisfactory status quo could be maintained for years.

The congressman, in fact, had told Ms. Fenstermacher that he fully supported her position vis-à-vis capitalist male chauvinism, and that the full resources of his office were hers to command. (The fact that the congressman believed that Ms. Fenstermacher was for male chauvinist capitalism, rather than opposed to it, is interesting but not really germane.)

Ms. Fenstermacher had a lead. She remembered, somewhat vaguely, that her father, that archetypical male chauvinist capitalist, had for some years been a fellow of the Matthew Q. Framingham Theosophical Foundation, that he had regularly made substantial financial contributions to it, and that he had regularly (sometimes as often as three times a year) gone off on week-long, rather mysterious meetings of the foundation at its International Headquarters in Cambridge, Massachusetts.

While she was able, in various places, to find references to the Matthew Q. Framingham Foundations, she was able to find nothing whatever on what it did. This, of course, whetted what her father would have called her female curiosity and what she thought of as her journalistic nose-for-news.

With the congressman's good offices behind her, the entire governmental files on the Matthew Q. Framingham Foundation were opened to her. She learned that it had been founded in 1863 and that its membership rolls had over the years included doctors, lawyers and businessmen. She learned that its executive secretary was a man called Matthew Q. Framingham VI and that he maintained offices in the Framingham Building, in Cambridge.

Finally, after some tail-twisting by the congressman, the records of the Internal Revenue Service were made available to her. Once she saw these, she knew she was on to something. The Matthew Q. Framingham Theosophical Foundation had never sought, or been granted, tax-exempt status. It had regularly, since the income tax law been passed, faithfully paid all of its taxes, generally before they were due, and had never, despite annual audits, been found guilty of an attempt to cheat the government of its due. Quite the contrary: the foundation had habitually overpaid its taxes, and refunds had been frequently paid.

It was quite clear to Ms. Fenstermacher. Any organization, limited to males, of which her father was a member, and which regularly paid its taxes was obviously up to no good. She had heard of The Establishment at Vassar, and there was no question whatever in her mind that The Establishment existed. But no one, she knew, had ever before been able to point a finger at any one organization and proclaim, 'That Is the Establishment!'

This was to be her great privilege. Monica P. Fenstermacher would go down in journalistic history as the one who had broken the story and identified the Matthew Q. Framingham Theosophical Foundation as The Establishment, had bared it to public scrutiny and had destroyed it.

Probably nothing would have come of Ms. Fenstermacher's investigation into the Matthew Q. Framingham Theosophical Foundation, however, had not Mr. Seymour G. Schwartz taken a brief, and certainly well-deserved, two-day vacation from the press of his many duties.

What happened was that a disgruntled employee of the Amalgamated Broadcasting Network, fully aware that Mr. Don Rhotten not only never read his copy prior to reading it on the air but that he also remained wholly oblivious to what he was reading during and after reading it, had slipped into the copy for Don Rhotten's Tele-Prompter a rather scathing denunciation of certain personnel policies of ABN and the officials responsible for them.

Mr. Rhotten concluded a rather devastating commentary

on an opponent of Congressman Jackson (who had dared to question whether Congress needed a Committee on Sidewalks, Subways and Sewers at all), flashed his caps and the boyish curls of his wig at the camera and then launched into a ninety-second tirade, delivered with his customary aura of utter sincerity and integrity, against ABN's brass hats, questioning their wisdom, integrity and character and suggesting that most of them had a female canine parent.

It would have been worse had not an alert employee in the control room come to his senses (the other eleven men in the room were stunned into immobility) and punched a series of buttons which (a) cut Don Rhotten off-camera and off-mike in the middle of the sentence; (b) flashed on a TECHNICAL DIFFICULTIES sign and a standby tape recording of Liberace's rendition of the Warsaw Concerto; and (c) sounded the alarm bell in the control room, which woke the rest of the engineers and directors.

Seymour G. Schwartz was right in the middle. On the one side was Don Rhotten, who had learned that he had been cut off the air, his dulcet tones replaced by Liberace, a musical personality not high on Mr. Rhotten's list. Mr. Rhotten was furious. As he pointed out, it wasn't his fault that some sorehead had monkeyed with the Tele-Prompter copy. What he read out over the airwaves wasn't *his* responsibility. All *he* had to do was show up shaven, wig, contacts and caps in place, sober and on time. He'd done that and been cut off the air. He was prepared to offer his services to CBS. With him *and* Walter Cronkite, Don Rhotten had modestly announced, they could put the other networks out of business.

On the other side were the broadcasting executives whom Mr. Rhotten had discussed on the air. They were not used to having their character, intelligence and integrity discussed at all, and certainly not on prime time television, with the implication that their Old Folks at Home had subsisted on Kennel Ration and bones from the butcher.

Seymour G. Schwartz had met the challenge, of course, but when the battle was over he was a shaken man who needed rest. After leaving instructions that six different people were to read the Tele-Prompter copy before Don Rhotten read it over the air, he repaired to Kornblatt's Catskill Mountains Rathskeller and Health Club for a well-deserved forty-eight hours of uninterrupted rest and recuperation.

It was at this time that Ms. Monica P. Fenstermacher and Congressman Edwards L. 'Smiling Jack' Jackson appeared in Amalgamated Broadcasting's chrome, plastic and plate-glass palace in New York City.

Don Rhotten was, of course, delighted to see Congressman Jackson, whom he regarded as his comrade-in-arms after their time together in the Casablanca slammer, and he had been truly disappointed to learn from Seymour G. Schwartz that Ms. Fenstermacher was off-limits. With Schwartz taking the waters at Kornblatt's, he could have another shot at Monica.

Following 'The Rhotten Evening News', Don Rhotten took the congressman and Ms. Fenstermacher to a watering hole known as P. J. Clarke's Saloon, which was popular among TV biggies. It was Don's intention to have a few belts with his old buddy Smiling Jack, for auld lang syne, which belting would have two spilloffs: it would allow him to impress Ms. Fenstermacher with the derringdo and swashbuckling it had been necessary for him to perform in the pursuit of his career, and it would ensure that Ms. Fenstermacher would take aboard enough booze to make her receptive to the indecent proposals he looked gleefully forward to making.

The best-laid plans of mice and men, however, to coin a phrase, often go astray. Mr. Rhotten forgot that Blood Tells, and that Ms. Fenstermacher was the daughter of a brewer and the granddaughter on both sides of brewers, and that she had, so to speak, teethed on a beer spigot.

At eleven o'clock that night, two Amalgamated Broadcasting Network pages and the congressman's Congressional Liaison Specialist appeared at P. J. Clarke's Saloon in answer to Ms. Fenstermacher's summons. Don Rhotten and

Smiling Jack were peacefully asleep arm-in-arm in the sawdust. Ms. Fenstermacher was completely sober and in complete charge. Mr. Rhotten was to be carried home, she ordered in a crisp, firm manner, and the congressman was to be carried aboard the New York–Washington shuttle. She was going to Cambridge, Massachusetts, with the written permission of both the congressman and Mr. Rhotten, to carry out the fullest possible investigation of the Matthew Q. Framingham Theosophical Foundation.

Neither Mr. Rhotten nor Congressman Jackson remembered anything about this when they awoke the next morning. Mr. Rhotten simply presumed that Ms. Fenstermacher had returned to Washington with his Old Buddy, and Smiling Jack simply presumed that Ms. Fenstermacher had finally succumbed to Don Rhotten's charms and stayed in New York.

CHAPTER SIX

The proprietor of the Spruce Harbor Flying Service, 'Wrong Way' Napolitano, met Learjet Double-O Poppa with his pickup truck as it taxied to a stop.

'Welcome to Spruce Harbor,' he said, as the short, skinny little man in the homburg and the tall, statuesque lady walked down the stair-door. 'Home of Napolitano's Italian Restaurant, featuring Veal Scallopini.'

'Actually,' Radar said, 'we have just eaten, but thank you just the same.'

'I suppose you don't want no fuel, either,' Wrong Way replied.

'I'll need some fuel,' Radar said. 'But what I need most of all is directions to the home of Dr. Benjamin Franklin Pierce.'

'Never heard of him,' Wrong Way said loyally.

'How about Dr. John Francis Xavier McIntyre?' Radar asked, somewhat confused. His head was still a little in the clouds (Kristina had kissed him again just before they landed), but he was sure that both Hawkeye and Trapper John lived in Spruce Harbor.

'Never heard of him, either,' Wrong Way again stated, loyally.

'But, Robespierre,' the lady said, 'I'm sure that Hawkeye and Trapper John live here. I send them Christmas cards and birthday cards all the time.'

'Might I inquire as to your identity?' Wrong Way asked.

'I'm Kris,' Madame Korsky-Rimsakov said. 'And this is Robespierre.'

'I was in the army with Hawkeye and Trapper John,' Radar said. 'If you will kindly direct me to the nearest post of the Veterans of Foreign Wars, we will be able to get to the bottom of this matter in short order.'

'Oh, Robespierre, you are so forceful!' Madame Kristina said.

'You really was in the army with them, huh?' Wrong Way asked.

'The Good Ol' 4077th MASH,' Radar said. 'All for one, and one for all.'

Wrong Way knew that the 4077th MASH was Hawkeye's and Trapper John's old outfit. Moreover, whoever these two weirdos were, they didn't look like bill collectors.

'They ain't here,' he said. 'They live here, but they ain't here.'

'Oh, what a shame!' Kristina said. 'And we just flew here to see them specially.'

'Is that so? Where from?'

'Las Vegas,' Radar replied. 'Why do you want to know?'

'Well, I'll tell you this,' Wrong Way said, 'you don't hardly look like a professional gambler.'

For the first time, Radar remembered the stack of bills he had jammed into his pocket in The Roman Poker Parlor of Nero's Villa. He took them out now and counted them. He was shocked to see he had $81,000 in cash.

Wrong Way Napolitano, who had played a little game of cards here and there in his lifetime, stared bug-eyed at the thick wad of bills. His snap judgment of this little guy was obviously wrong. He was dealing with a man's man, and God knows, they're a dying breed.

'Tell ya what I'm going to do,' he said. 'You come with me over to my house, and I'll call Mary Pierce and tell her you're here.'

'You're very gracious,' Kristina said. 'I would like very much to meet her. I've heard so much about her, and my brother has spoken highly of her.'

'Who's your brother?'

'My brother's name is Boris,' Kristina said. 'Boris Alexandrovich Korsky-Rimsakov.'

'Well, *excuse* me!' Wrong Way said.

'Certainly,' Radar said, graciously. 'What for?'

'Me and Boris is pals,' Wrong Way said.

'Oh, isn't that nice,' Kristina said.

'Come on,' Wrong Way said, 'get in the truck! We'll go get Mary on the horn.' He looked at Radar. 'You can put that away, pal,' he said. 'I've seen it.'

Radar was staring at the money with shock and concern. While he had nothing whatever against money, this was money of another kind. Not only was there one hell of a lot of it, but he had not come by it quite honestly, or even as a result of Lady Luck smiling on him. He had 'won' it because he had read the Keeper of the Treasury's mind, and that was tantamount to stealing it.

He jammed it, with difficulty, back into his pocket and got in the pickup truck beside Kristina. It wasn't simply a question of returning the money. People who ran gambling houses were not known for their kind understanding. They would not like to learn that someone had been able to walk out with $81,000 of their money because that someone had been able to read the mind of the dealer.

They would, in fact, be very likely to make sure, simply as a business precaution, that whoever had been reading minds would not be able to read minds in the future. The best way to ensure this of course, would be to break the head of the mind reader.

He was going to have to think of some way to get rid of the money, some way that would keep him out of trouble and at the same time put the money to good use.

Mary Pierce arrived at Spruce Harbor International Airport to pick up her husband's friends with some doubts in her mind. While she recognized Boris Alexandrovich Korsky-Rimsakov to be one of the world's greatest opera singers, she also remembered him as a person and as a *person* he left, in Mary Pierce's wifely judgment, a good bit to be desired. Mary Pierce was, in a manner of speaking, the exception that proved the rule. Ninety-nine and forty-four-one-hundredths per cent of the world's females, on hearing Boris Alexandrovich Korsky-Rimsakov sing, instantly lost their minds. They instantly became willing to abandon husband, children, reputation and everything else normally held dear to know the singer, biblically speaking.

For example, when Boris had been a patient at the Spruce Harbor Medical Centre, there had been a riot in the registered nurses' lounge over who was to have the privilege of changing his bandage and mopping his brow.

Mary Pierce was not similarly affected. What she saw was a large, loud, roaringly drunk male animal who needed a bath and a shave and who had been dumb enough to hook a fish hook in his rump while on a drunken fishing party.

It was understandable, therefore, that she feared the singer's sister, and the singer's friend, would be cut from the same bolt of cloth. But when she saw Kristina Korsky-Rimsakov from the moment their eyes met, she knew that she erred, that Kristina was cut from *her* own bolt of cloth.

Within thirty seconds of meeting, they were on a first-name basis and chattering gaily like a couple of high school girls.

'If it weren't for your Benjamin,' Kristina said, 'Robespierre and I would probably have never met.' Mary Pierce's heart melted at the sound of someone using her husband's proper Christian name. Very few people did that, even his mother.

'Oh, isn't that sweet!' Mary Pierce cooed.

'And so, Robespierre and I wanted your Benjamin and Dr. John F. X. McIntyre to be the first to know that Robespierre and I are to be married,' Kristina went on.

'He'll be so touched,' Mary Pierce said, dabbing at her eyes with a Kleenex. 'I'm so sorry he's not at home just now.'

'Where is he?' Radar asked.

'Both he and Dr. McIntyre are in Cambridge,' Mary Pierce said, with deep pride in her voice, 'at the Matthew Q. Framingham Theosophical Foundation. Hawk ... *Benjamin* nominated Dr. McIntyre for membership, and he was accepted, and they went down for the official investiture ceremony.'

'What's the Matthew Q. Framingham Theosophical Foundation?' Radar asked.

'Why, Mr. O'Reilly,' Mary Pierce said, 'I'm surprised that you don't know of the foundation and its many good works.'

'Robespierre is a busy man,' Kristina defended him.

'It's a charitable foundation, is it?' Radar asked. 'Excuse my ignorance.'

'It's one of the more charitable intellectual foundations,' Mary Pierce said, 'dedicated to the betterment of mankind. Founded in eighteen sixty-three in Cambridge, Massachusetts.'

'Have you got its address?' Radar asked. His problem had just been solved, the solution dropped into his lap.

'I'm sure that anything addressed to the Matthew Q. Framingham Theosophical Foundation, Cambridge, Massachusetts, would be delivered,' Mary Pierce said.

'Mrs. Pierce . . .' Radar began.

'Mary please,' Mary said.

'Mary, I hate to be a bother, but would you stop at a bank? I have some urgent business to transact.'

'Why certainly, Robespierre,' Mary Pierce said and pulled up in front of the Spruce Harbor Fisherman's, Oysterman's and Commercial Bank.

'I'll be right back,' Radar said and walked quickly inside.

'I'd like to purchase a cashier's check,' he said to the teller.

'Yes, sir,' she said. 'May I suggest that if the amount is under twenty dollars you might consider one of our Fisherman's and Oysterman's Briny Deep Money Orders? They come in three colours.'

'I think I'd better have a cashier's check,' Radar said. 'Thank you just the same. I need one for eighty-one thousand dollars.' He took out the neat packets of money, stacked them and put them on the counter.

Mary Pierce, Kris and Radar made one more stop en route to the Pierce home. Radar mailed an envelope at the Spruce Harbor post office. It was addressed to the Matthew Q. Framingham Theosophical Foundation and contained a cashier's check for $81,000 and the following note:

Gentlemen:
    As a longtime admirer of your foundation and the noble principles on which it is based, I am enclosing a small contribution which I hope you will be able to use to defray the expenses of your many, and noble, good works.

A Friend

Five minutes after Mary, Kristina and Radar had arrived at the Pierce home, the telephone rang in the Cambridge, Massachusetts, International Headquarters of the Matthew Q. Framingham Theosophical Foundation.

'Matthew Q. Framingham Theosophical Foundation,' Matthew Q. Framingham VI said.

'Long-distance call for Dr. Benjamin Franklin Pierce,' the operator said.

'Dr. Pierce is in conference. May I have your name and number, so that he might call you back when he's free?'

There was a pause, then the operator said, 'My party will talk with Dr. John Francis Xavier McIntyre if Dr. Pierce is busy.'

'I'm very much afraid that Dr. McIntyre is conferring with Dr. Pierce,' Matthew Q. Framingham VI said.

'My party says to tell you that she is Mrs. Pierce and she demands to speak to her husband.'

'I regret, madam, that that is quite impossible,' Matthew Q. Framingham VI said. 'I will endeavour at some time in the near future to pass this information along to Dr. Pierce, but I can make no promise or guarantee. Unless, of course, this is a medical emergency?'

There was another pause. 'My party says it's no medical emergency, but that it's damned important. Ooops! *Very* important.'

'In that case, madam,' Matthew Q. Framingham VI said, 'I would not dare to disturb Dr. Pierce at this time. I will, to reiterate, make every effort to pass your message along.'

He dropped the telephone back in its cradle and turned to face Dr. Benjamin Franklin Pierce.

'Well, Hawkeye,' he said, 'it's twenty bucks to you. Fish or cut bait.'

'Your twenty and twenty more,' Hawkeye replied, sliding the appropriate number of chips to the centre of the octagonal table, which was covered with green baize.

'That's too rich for me,' Trapper John said, turning his cards over and pushing them toward the centre of the table. He raised his hand over his head in the manner of a small boy asking permission to leave the classroom. Almost immediately, a very large young man wearing a white jacket and black bow tie appeared at his side with a large mug of beer.

'Thank you, James,' Dr. McIntyre said.

'My pleasure, sir,' the young man said politely.

'I'll call,' the fourth man at the table said. 'I refuse to believe that he can be this lucky this long.'

'That makes it twenty bucks to you, Matthew,' Hawkeye said. 'Put up or shut up.'

Matthew Q. Framingham VI pushed twenty dollars' worth of chips into the pot. Dr. Benjamin Franklin Pierce, Fellow of the American College of Surgeons, and Senior Fellow, Matthew Q. Framingham Theosophical Foundation, turned over his cards.

'Read 'em and weep,' he said. 'Aces, three of them over queens. What they call a full house.'

To the obvious discomfiture of his fellows, which is to say Mr. Matthew Q. Framingham VI, Dr. John F. X. McIntyre and The Hon. DeWitt L. Canady II, formerly Mr. Justice Canady of the Vermont Supreme Court, he raked in the chips.

'That's enough for me,' Trapper John said. 'You guys are apparently used to this sort of thing, but I just got elected to the foundation. Do you realize that we have been playing since six o'clock last night?'

'Would you rather, Doctor,' Hawkeye asked, rather sharply, 'be home playing Old Maid with Lucinda? If it weren't for the foundation, that's just what you would be doing.'

'You know what I'd be doing?' Mr. Justice Canady said. 'I'd be entertaining my wife's idiot brother and their somewhat backward offspring who wants a job in my office. Thank God for the foundation!'

He and Pierce simultaneously raised their right hands above their heads. The large young man immediately delivered mugs of beer.

'I give you our founder,' Hawkeye said solemnly, getting to his feet, 'without whom we would not have this island of peace and solitude in a world full of wives, patients, clients, relatives and assorted other ne'er-do-wells.'

'Hear, hear,' Mr. Framingham VI and Mr. Justice Canady said in unison.

'I don't know if this remark will be considered out of line for a new member,' Trapper said, 'but what impresses me is how long you guys have been getting away with this.'

'Since eighteen sixty-three,' Mr. Justice Canady said. 'My granduncle Oscar was one of the charter members.'

'And you've never even been *suspected*?' Trapper asked.

'Frankly, it hasn't been easy, Doctor,' Matthew Q. Framingham VI said. 'As my great-grandfather said, "Inside every slim virgin is a fat wife desperately trying to get out and ruin things for men."'

'I feel sure,' Hawkeye said, 'that Trapper John fully realizes the importance of the oath of secrecy he took.'

'Everytime . . . nothing personal, Doctor . . .' Mr. Justice Canady said, 'we take in a new man, I quake at the prospect that he might, in a moment of weakness, expose us all.'

'You understand, Trapper, that's why we had to wait until you had been married five years. In the first five years of marriage, men are sometimes a little odd. They really do tell their wives everything.'

'I guess I was that way,' Trapper said. 'I can see now how young and foolish I was.'

'We all were,' Hawkeye said, sympathetically. 'My father told me, the night I was sworn in, that he worried for years that I might not grow up sufficiently to be nominated. I was married seven years before he thought I was worthy of the trust.'

'There are only two rules,' Mr. Justice Canady said. 'Perhaps that is the secret of our success. We never discuss our wives in here, and we never discuss the Matthew Q. Framingham Theosophical Foundation with our wives at home.'

'Speaking of wives,' Matthew Q. Framingham VI said accusingly, 'that was yours on the phone, Hawkeye.'

'I've forbidden her to call here,' Hawkeye said. 'It must really be important.'

'She said there was no *medical* emergency,' Framingham said.

'Why do you take calls at all?' Trapper asked.

'Otherwise, they might doubt that we're here,' Mr. Justice Canady said. 'Hell hath no fury like a curious wife.' He paused. 'I'm surprised you haven't learned that.'

'I suppose I'd better call her,' Hawkeye said. 'Just to let her know that I'm here, of course.'

He rose from the poker table and went to one of the three heavily insulated telephone cubicles erected so that members could take, and make, telephone calls in absolute privacy. In just a minute he was back.

'Trapper,' he said, 'I want you to brace yourself. Perhaps you'd better sit down.'

'Not bad news, I hope, Hawkeye?' Mr. Justice Canady said.

'Trapper, I must tell you that Radar and Kristina are going to get married.'

'Oh, I'm so sorry,' Mr. Justice Canady said. 'Is the situation completely beyond redemption? Is it too late for you to have a talk with him?'

'I'm afraid so,' Hawkeye said.

'I saw it coming,' Trapper said. 'I guess I just didn't want to believe it, but I saw it coming.'

'I think we both did,' Hawkeye said.

'I still have some influence,' Mr. Justice Canady said. 'If you'd like, I can arrange to have him confined for psychiatric evaluation.'

'That's very good of you, DeWitt,' Hawkeye said, 'and both Trapper and I appreciate it. But the situation is out of control.'

'I understand,' Mr. Justice DeWitt Canady said. 'These things happen sometimes.'

'Matt,' Hawkeye said, 'would you get Trapper and me on the first plane home in the morning?'

'Of course,' Mr. Framingham VI replied. 'And if there's anything else I can do, Hawkeye, please feel free to call upon me. And the foundation, of course.'

'I can't think of anything,' Hawkeye said, 'but thank you.'

'Do you know when and where, Hawkeye?'

'Just as soon as possible, I'm afraid,' Hawkeye said. 'And the whole vulgar ritual, I understand. In Las Vegas, Nevada.'

'Why Las Vegas?' Trapper John asked.

'I was so shaken I didn't think to ask,' Hawkeye said. 'Probably something to do with a reception. When somebody like Radar finally takes the plunge, you know, he often goes off the deep end.'

The conversation was interrupted by the ringing of the telephone.

'Matthew Q. Framingham Theosophical Foundation,' Mr. Framingham VI said, answering it.

'Probably my wife,' Trapper said, 'gushing over with undisguised joy at the fall of a good man.'

'I am Mr. Framingham,' Mr. Framingham VI said into the telephone. 'How might I be of service?' There was a pause. 'Miss Fenstermacher,' he said. 'Excuse me, *Ms.* Fenstermacher. *Ms.* Fenstermacher, while we are of course flattered that the Amalgamated Broadcasting Network *and* Mr. Don Rhotten are interested in the Matthew Q. Framingham Theosophical Foundation, I'm afraid we must decline. The watchword of the foundation has always been, and will always remain, dignified anonymity.'

Mr. Justice Canady and both Hawkeye and Trapper stared at Matthew Q. Framingham VI with shock and horror in their eyes.

'I'm afraid,' Matthew Q. Framingham VI said, 'that our position on the matter is firm, Ms. Fenstermacher. We do *not* wish to be the subject of a Don Rhotten White Paper, and we will not co-operate with you in any way.' At that moment, a look of shock crossed his face, and he quickly took the telephone away from his ear. He shook his head as if to clear it and then, finally, laid the telephone back in its cradle.

CHAPTER SEVEN

'Did I hear you say the Amalgamated Broadcasting Network?' Mr. Justice Canady asked.

'Did I hear the name Don Rhotten mentioned?' Trapper asked.

'Did I hear the phrase "White Paper"?' Hawkeye asked.

'My God!' Matthew Q. Framingham VI said. 'This is terrible!'

'*What* was *that* all *about?*' the other three said, in unison.

'Don Rhotten of the Amalgamated Broadcasting Network wishes to do a sixty-minute White Paper on the Framingham

Theosophical Foundation,' Framingham said, horror in his voice.

'My God,' the three chorused. 'That's terrible!'

'It could ruin us!' Matthew Q. Framingham VI said.

'It could destroy my marriage of forty-seven years come Thanksgiving,' Mr. Justice Canady said.

'Let's not get excited,' Hawkeye, who sometimes could keep his cool in times of great stress, said. 'Matt, you told her we would have nothing to do with it, didn't you?'

'Yes, I did,' Matthew Q. Framingham VI said.

'Well, then,' Hawkeye said, 'what's the problem?'

'What she said when I told her that was . . .' There was a look of pain on his face as he recalled the precise words.

'What did she say, Matt?' Trapper asked.

'She said,' he said, 'that that was precisely the response she expected, and that she really preferred the adversary relationship when dealing with male chauvinist capitalist pigs.'

'She said that?' Trapper asked.

'And she said we'd be hearing from her shortly,' Matthew Q. Framingham VI said. 'And shortly after that, we and all our wicked works would be exposed to Don Rhotten's eleven million, four-hundred-thirteen thousand, two hundred eight faithful viewers.'

'In that case,' Hawkeye said, 'there's only one thing we can do.'

'What's that?'

'Get out of town,' Hawkeye said. 'Hang a GONE OUT OF BUSINESS sign on the front door and close down for a while.'

'While there is some merit in your suggestion, Doctor,' Mr. Justice Canady said, 'there are certain problems.'

'Like what?' Hawkeye said. 'We close down for a month. She'll get tired of hanging around.'

'Matthew Q. Framingham's will, which pays the overhead around here out of the fund,' Mr. Justice Canady said, 'says that the foundation must remain open twenty-four hours a day, seven days a week.'

'I forgot,' Hawkeye said.

'So long as we provide a place where the membership may come at any time, day or night, any day of the week, and find a friendly smile, a cold glass of beer and an open poker game,' Canady went on, 'the foundation gets the income from the fund.'

'And if we don't?' Trapper John asked.

'Then all the assets of the foundation are turned over to the Massachusetts Temperance Society,' Canady said. 'Our founder believed that if the beneficiaries of his inheritance weren't willing or able to provide a friendly smile, a cold glass of beer and an open poker game, we didn't deserve his money.'

'I see his point,' Trapper John said.

'Does it say where?'

'Where what?'

'Where we have to have the friendly smile, the cold glass of beer and the poker game?'

'No,' Canady said, after a moment. 'Just that we have to have those three things.' He smiled at Hawkeye. 'Your foul imagination is at work, Hawkeye,' he said, approvingly. 'I recognize the evil glint in your eyes. I always thought you should have been a lawyer.'

'The problem is solved,' Hawkeye said. 'We just move Matt here into a motel room someplace for a month. We notify the membership that the foundation has temporarily moved. Miss Whatsername comes here and finds this place closed. In a month or so, we can move back.'

'That's a splendid idea, if I do say so myself,' Trapper John said. 'Hawkeye has saved the day!'

'How do you propose to pay for all this?' Matthew Q. Framingham VI said.

'The foundation will pay for it, of course. It's a necessary expense if there ever was one.'

'Hawkeye,' Matt Framingham said, 'the foundation's broke.'

'What do you mean, broke?'

'Until we get our annual check . . . if we get our annual check . . . we have just about enough money to pay the light bill, the phone bill, the taxes and the beer bill.'

'How could that happen?' Hawkeye asked, shocked.

'The Semi-Annual Seminar on the Role of Theology in a Changing Society done us in,' Matthew Q. Framingham said. 'Practically everybody showed up, of course. And you have no idea what it cost us to bring Miss Bonnie Blue Belle and Her Confederate Sweethearts all the way up here from Dallas.'

'Well, you have to expect to pay for quality,' Hawkeye said, defensively. 'Everybody said she was the best interpretative terpsichorean artiste we've had here since Gypsy Rose Lee.'

'And so she was,' Framingham said. 'But we had to pay for that champagne bath of hers, too. And she wouldn't settle for domestic, either. Dom Perignon sixty-four. Nineteen gallons of it.'

'You're not trying to tell me that nineteen gallons of bubbly broke us?'

'It wasn't only the bubbly. We had the clambake, too, you'll remember. Have you any idea what we have to pay for lobster these days? And everybody agreed that a Framingham Foundation clambake simply wouldn't be a Framingham Foundation clambake without a Scottish Highlands Bagpipe Orchestra. What do you think it cost to fly those guys over from Scotland?'

'I personally would have been satisfied with just one or two bagpipers,' Hawkeye said. 'There's such a thing as throwing money away. Times are changing.'

'That's the point, Hawkeye,' Matthew Q. Framingham VI said. 'It was thrown away, and there's not going to be any more until we get our annual check ... *if* we get our annual check. If this women's lib nut has her way, all we have held dear for all these years is down the drain.'

'We're not just going to throw in the towel,' Hawkeye said. 'First thing tomorrow morning, just as soon as we're sure they're in their offices and their wives won't be listening, we get on the phone and we call the membership, every last fellow of the foundation, and tell them they have to send us an emergency contribution.'

'We can try it,' Matthew Q. Framingham said, without much enthusiasm.

'We have to try it,' Hawkeye said. 'We have no other choice. I'm not sure that I could go on, without knowing the foundation is here.'

'What a terrible thought!' Mr. Justice Canady said. 'I refuse to even think about it.'

'I've got twenty-five dollars my wife doesn't know about,' Trapper John said. 'With your permission, gentlemen, I'll donate that as the first contribution to the emergency fund.'

'That's the spirit!' Hawkeye said. 'And I'll throw in my emergency fund, too. It comes to eleven dollars and fifty cents. My wife forgot to ask for her change when I went shopping for her.'

'That comes to thirty-six dollars and fifty cents,' Mr. Justice Canady said. 'With thirty-one dollars which somehow eluded my own eagle-eyed bride, that's sixty-seven dollars and fifty cents. That leaves us only two or three thousand dollars, in round figures, short.'

'Something will turn up, oh ye of little faith!' Hawkeye said. 'The foundation has faced problems before and endured.'

'I suggest that we all turn in early,' Matthew Q. Framingham VI said. 'We're going to need clear minds in the morning.'

As it happened, Dr. Benjamin Franklin Pierce was the first Framingham Foundation Fellow to awaken the next morning. He had spent the night in the Oscar F. Donnelly Memorial Suite, a two-room-and-bath affair completely refurbished with the bequest of Mr. Donnelly, who had been a fellow from 1899 to 1923. The door bore a bronze plaque:

'THE FURNISHINGS IN THIS SUITE WERE PRESENTED TO THE FOUNDATION BY MR. OSCAR F. DONNELLY IN PROFOUND GRATITUDE TO THE FOUNDATION FOR PROVIDING HIM WITH SHELTER ON 117 OCCASIONS WHEN WISDOM DECREED HE NOT SHARE THE CONNUBIAL COUCH.'

Dr. Pierce woke to the ringing of the doorbell. The sound was seldom heard. Every fellow, of course, had his own key, and large, illuminated signs reading 'Please do not feed the lions and tigers' placed on the fence surrounding the property served to discourage door-to-door peddlers.

Dr. Pierce, after hearing the bell, lay motionless in the bed, hoping that Mr. Matthew Q. Framingham VI, who occupied a suite of rooms near the front door would answer the bell. But then he realized that Mr. Matthew Q. Framingham VI's contract to operate the foundation clearly specified that he was not to be disturbed before noon or during football games on Sunday.

He got out of bed, put on a bathrobe and went down the wide staircase to the entrance foyer and pulled open the door.

It was a U.S. mailperson, of the female persuasion, who had arrived by Kawasaki motorcycle.

'Special delivery for the Framingham Theosophical Foundation,' the mailperson said. 'What is this place, anyhow?'

Hawkeye reached for the letter. It was snatched back.

'How do I know this is for you?' the mailperson asked. 'You got some identification?'

'On the other hand, how do I know you're really a mailperson?' Hawkeye replied. 'Mutual trust, detente, as it were, is sometimes necessary.'

'In that case,' the mailperson said and handed him the receipt form. 'Gee, you don't look like the Secretary of State,' she said, after carefully examining the signature.

Hawkeye put his index finger before his lips. 'I'm here incognito,' he said. 'I wouldn't tell you, either, of course, were it not for your governmental connection.'

'Your secret is safe with me. Mr. Secretary,' the mailperson said, saluting militarily and remounting her motorcycle.

Hawkeye closed the door. The envelope was addressed to the Framingham Theosophical Foundation. It was postmarked Spruce Harbor, Maine. He realized that he should, of course, deliver it to Matt Framingham, but that would mean he might have to wait till noon. And it was postmarked Spruce Harbor. He ripped it open.

It was a cashier's check drawn on the Fisherman's, Oysterman's and Commercial Bank of Spruce Harbor for $81,000. He read the note which came with it. Then he stepped to the Framingham Theosophical Foundation Memorial Gong, a brass device some eight feet in diameter, suspended from a sturdy teak frame. It had been obtained (some said stolen) from a Taoist temple in Bangkok during the 1911-1912 Far East Cultural Expedition of the foundation[1] and was normally rung only to announce the passing of a fellow; a bequest to the foundation in excess of $5,000 (cash); or on similar significant occasions.

He picked up the five-foot mallet, which had a stout, wrapped-leather head, examined (as he always did) the exquisite engraving on the gong and then swung the mallet, hitting the representation of the temple dancer right on the jewel in her navel.

The sound reverberated through the halls of the foundation building. Trapper John and Mr. Justice Canady, hair mussed and eyes wild, soon appeared at the head of the stairs. Mr. Matthew Q. Framingham VI's door was flung open.

'We're saved! Hawkeye shouted. 'We're saved!'

---

[1] The 1911-1912 Far East Cultural Expedition was funded by a bequest from J. Whitney Pierpont, Sr., a Framingham Fellow 1905-1929, who headed the expedition. Its report, consisting of some 345 folio pages, 1077 photographs, 455 drawings, and 238 artifacts (sculpture, paintings and the like), may be found in the Peabody Library, Harvard University. It should be noted, however, that as a result of litigation brought by the Watch and Ward Society of Boston, the report was determined to be 'wholly obscene, pornographic, filthy, outrageous and disgusting' by the Massachusetts Supreme Court. Because of this decision, access to the report, whose proper title is 'An Investigation Into Certain interesting Sexual Practices, Orgiastic Rituals and Religious Prostitution of the Far East; Together With an Appraisial of Same by Some Western Participants', is limited to serious scholars, psychologists and personal friends of the librarian.

'You'd better be talking about the foundation,' Mr. Justice Canady said, rushing down the stairs. 'If you've let the side down by getting religion in this time of crisis, I'll bring you before the Membership Committee, Hawkeye!'

Hawkeye extended the check to him and the letter to Trapper John. Mr. Justice Canady looked at the check, read the letter and then snatched the heavy mallet from Hawkeye's hand. 'How many times does five-thousand dollars go into eighty-one thousand dollars?' he asked, as the mallet connected with the Memorial Gong again.

Just as soon as he had dropped Dr. Benjamin Franklin Pierce and Dr. John Francis Xavier McIntyre at Logan International Airport for their return flight to Spruce Harbor, Maine, Mr. Matthew Q. Framingham VI began to search for suitable accommodations for the Temporary Home Away From Home of the Framingham Foundation.

Mr. Framingham VI enjoyed a peculiar role with the Framingham Foundation. Not only was he a direct lineal descendant of its founder and its executive secretary but the foundation's only bachelor as well. He was also, by far, at twenty-three, the foundation's youngest fellow.

Approximately eight years before, young Matt had been expelled from the Saint Grottlesex School for what the Reverend Bosco Quimby Zenon, D.D., Headmaster, had called 'undue familiarity with the members of the staff.' This was somewhat euphemistic, partly because the Reverend Mr. Zenon was always loathe to call a spade a spade, and partly because, since the founding of St. Grottlesex, there had always been a Framingham either in attendance or on the board of governors, and often both. (The St. Grottlesex Memorial Chapel was a gift of Mr. Matthew Q. Framingham III.)

At fifteen going on sixteen, Matthew Q. Framingham VI had stood just over six feet one inch in height and weighed just under two hundred pounds. (He continued growing through his twentieth year, when he reached six-four and two hundred thirty.) He had reached puberty at twelve and a half and at fifteen had a deep voice, a large chest, a full head of red hair and the characteristic deep-blue Framingham eyes.

All of these combined to make him attractive to the opposite gender, a perfectly natural and even to be encouraged reaction to a healthy young male animal. Unfortunately, this physical attraction was not limited to members of his own age group.

What happened specifically was that the Reverend Mr. Zenon, en route to Thursday afternoon vesper services, had stopped by the school dispensary in order to obtain from the school nurse some medication for his sore throat. The dispensary door was locked, and there was no answer to his persistent knocking. This was surprising, as the dispensary was supposed to be open from one to five in the afternoon. Mrs. Violetta Sanders, R.N., the school nurse, who had been widowed three years before, had earned a reputation for dedication to her duty. Previously, when it had been necessary for her to be absent from her place of duty, she had arranged for Miss Harriet R. Kellogg, St. Grottlesex's librarian, to, so to speak, hold down the fort for her until her return. Miss Kellogg and Mrs. Sanders shared living quarters in the rear of the dispensary building and were quite good friends.

Realizing that it was quite odd for both women to be gone and the dispensary unmanned, the Rev. Mr. Zenon, after a moment's indecision, had walked to the side of the building and peered through a window.

'There they were,' the Reverend Mr. Zenon told his wife that night, in the privacy of their nuptial chamber. 'All three of them in the altogether. Nurse Sanders and the Framingham boy were making the beast with two backs, while Miss Kellogg urged them on by playing Berlioz' *The March of the Trojans* on her harmonica.'

'Shocking,' his wife had said. 'And how long had this been going on?'

'The Framingham boy was quite unashamedly frank about it,' the Reverend Mr. Zenon said. 'He said that he had been "friendly" with Nurse Sanders since the beginning of last year's school session. Miss Kellogg has been a recent addition to his harem, apparently. I sent him packing, of course.'

'Of course,' Mrs. Zenon said.

'And I had a sharp word with the ladies, of course,' the Reverend Mr. Zenon said. 'I told them that if they were given to that sort of thing, they would have to go to librarians' and nurses' conventions like everybody else.'

'And you were right, Bosco,' Mrs. Zenon said. 'If something like that should get out . . .'

'Quite,' Mr. Zenon had said.

'You didn't feel it necessary to discharge either Miss Kellogg or Nurse Sanders?' Mrs. Zenon asked.

'I did not,' the Reverend Mr. Zenon had answered. 'Good nurses and librarians are hard to find, for one thing. For another, I have arranged to counsel them one afternoon a week. Remember, my dear, to err is human, to forgive divine.'

CHAPTER EIGHT

Matthew Q. Framingham VI had, understandably, been rather reluctant to walk into his Belmont, Massachusetts, home and announce to his parents that he had been given the old heave-ho from St. Grottlesex. His mother was certainly going to want to know why.

What he did was decide to break the news to his father first. To do that, he would have to arrange to be alone with his father. He knew that his father customarily spent every Wednesday evening at the Framingham Foundation in Cambridge, where he was Fellow-In-Charge of Moral Enlightenment. Moral Enlightenment had been meeting on Wednesday evenings for thirty-five years.

So instead of going home, he went to the Foundation

Headquarters, timing his arrival there to coincide, he thought, with his father's arrival. Gathering his courage, he lifted the massive brass knocker on the front door and let it fall into place. He was well aware that he was forbidden to ever go to the foundation and disturb the work of the fellows, but this seemed to him to be an emergency situation, and he had to take the chance.

'Who's there?' a voice croaked from inside.

'Matthew Q. Framingham VI,' he announced, in his prematurely deep voice.

The door creaked open and he found himself looking at a wizened little old man.

'You Framinghams are all alike,' the little old man said. 'Always forgetting your damned key. Come on in. It's already started.'

As Matthew VI entered the Framingham Foundation, he recognized the little old man. He was L. Roscoe Heatherington, Chairman of the Board of the Heatherington Shipping Company, who recently had had his picture in the papers on the occasion of his 101st birthday.

He was surprised to find the interior of the building in complete darkness. A few moments later, he found out why. A motion-picture screen had been erected in a large room. (He was later to learn the room was The Great Hall.) As he groped his way inside, looking for his father, his father revealed himself. A light went on over a small lectern. His father stood behind it, bowing his head modestly in response to a small round of applause.

'Gentlemen,' he said, 'what we are about to see comes to us through the courtesy of Framingham Foundation Fellow Ethelbert G. Moriarity, who is, as you all know, public prosecutor for the state of Illinois. It was Prosecution Exhibit Two in the well-publicized trial which resulted in the conviction of six well-known pornographers. Mr. Moriarity, who was unable to be with us tonight, sends his best wishes, and hopes that we Fellows of Moral Enlightenment enjoy it every bit as much as he did.'

The room went dark. The projector began to roll.

Thirty minutes later, the lights snapped on again. Matthew Q. Framingham VI sat stunned. He had thought that Nurse Sanders and Miss Kellogg had exhausted all possible variations, but the film had just shown him in glorious Technicolour that there really is no limit to the human imagination.

He was nowhere near as stunned, however, as was his father specifically, and the rest of the Moral Enlightenment Fellows generally, to see him sitting in the back of the room sharing a pitcher of beer with Mr. L. Roscoe Heatherington and smoking one of Mr. Heatherington's coal black Corona Gigantas.

His presence there posed certain problems. Not only was it virtually impossible to expel from the foundation a 101-year-old member with sixty-two years of honourable service for admitting an outsider, but there was also the question of how to deal with the possibility that if Matthew VI should be treated unkindly he would be tempted to tell the wife of Matthew V what went on at moral enlightenment sessions of the Framingham Foundation.

'A boy,' as Matthew had the foresight to observe as his father rushed angrily toward him, 'has no secrets from his mother.'

He also pointed out that he hadn't sneaked in. He had quite truthfully announced himself as Matthew Q. Framingham VI, and he could hardly be blamed if Mr. L. Roscoe Heatherington could not keep all the Matthew Q. Framinghams in order.

An emergency meeting of the executive committee was immediately convened, and a change in the constitution voted. While membership in the Framingham Foundation was still to be limited to males of thirty years of age or older who had been married at least five years and who were recommended by six present members, an exception would be made in the case of males who were directly descended from the founder and who, through no fault of their own, came into possession of certain normally confidential information regarding the Framingham Foundation. Males meeting this criteria could be admitted to full fellowship without regard to age or marital status or length thereof.

The very next day, Fellow Matthew Q. Framingham VI was awarded a scholarship by the Framingham foundation to the Hill School in Belmont, Massachusetts, from which he was ultimately graduated summa cum laude. His father told his mother, who was touched, that Matthew V wanted Matthew VI close to home.

During his four years at Harvard College, Matthew Q. Framingham VI had earned his pocket money by working as a beer waiter and general helper at the Framingham Foundation. Perhaps understandably, he showed a certain flair for the work of the Foundation, and on his graduation was offered, and accepted, the position of assistant executive secretary of the foundation. He held this position while attending the Harvard School of Business, and upon the retirement of the incumbent executive secretary six months before, had himself been offered the post.

His mother, who said she couldn't be prouder or happier that her boy was to be associated with the organization which had so enriched the life of his father, presented him with a box-calf attaché case with silver initials to commemorate the occasion.

There were certain drawbacks, however, to the arrangement. In keeping with the dignity and decorum of the Framingham Foundation, Matthew VI's wardrobe while at Harvard (dark suits, dark ties, white shirts, black shoes and, in his junior and senior years, a homburg) seemed to set him apart from his fellow students, who dressed rather less conservatively and among whom someone who actually wore socks was an object of suspicion and even derision.

Similarly, Young Matt (or, as his fellow students referred to him, 'that red-headed giant square') evinced little interest, compared to the others, in the opposite sex within their peer group. He didn't hang around the Radcliffe dormitories, for example. Neither could he be induced to leave town for social events of one form or another at other colleges with large female populations.

The reason for this was quite simple. Matthew VI was a practical young man. If it had been necessary for him to hang around the Radcliffe dorms, or to journey to Poughkeepsie, New York, to get that which all the others were pursuing (with, he believed, far less success than they so proudly announced), he would have done it. It was simply that he didn't have to do much running after it. After he introduced regular live entertainment at the Wednesday evening moral enlightenment sessions and the Friday evening retreats, the problem simply vanished. He was, after all, in addition to his looks, size and youth, the only bachelor in attendance.

And it was his duty to carry the entertainers to and from their hotels to the foundation in the foundation's black limousine, with drawn curtains. While it was not true, as Hawkeye Pierce half-jokingly accused, that Matthew VI conducted auditions in the back seat of the limousine, it was certainly true that he frequently conducted certain mutual explorations in the back seat with a wide variety of ladies whose ability to titillate the male had just been loudly proclaimed by the Wednesday evening moral enlightenment group and that their explorations often resulted in an invitation to breakfast with the lady.

Matthew VI, in a word, got his without running after it from the time he was fifteen, and, so far as he could judge, the supply was not about to run out.

He didn't give a tinker's damn, so to speak, that his classmates regarded him as a six-foot-four celibate who wore morticians' clothes. He *knew* that *he* got to take off *his* clothes once or twice a week in rather interesting circumstances. He rather doubted, judging from the girl friends and wives of his peer group, if those who mocked him were in any position to make a similar statement.

But, to reiterate, his life-style had left its mark on him. It was natural that his manner of speaking reflected that of his associates, and most of his associates were on the far side of fifty. He came to accept the belief held by most Framingham Foundation Fellows that the Republic had been doomed from the day universal suffrage had been made the law of the land (although he did think that women should be taught to read and write).

He had made, of course, certain forays into the social whirl of his peer group. They had all ended in disaster. He remembered rather vividly the blond from Sarah Lawrence College who had blackened his eye for suggesting that he set her up in a little apartment overlooking the Charles River. He couldn't understand why she was angry; the same idea had been proposed to him just two weeks before by Miss Fiery Blaze, whose Dance of the Dying Embers had been quite a success at the Friday Self-Contemplation Retreat.

In short, at twenty-three, Matthew Q. Framingham VI was destined, he firmly believed, for bachelorhood. Not for him the joys of marriage, children, nappies, mortgage payments or the loving attention of in-laws. He was going to go through life alone, taking what little solace he could from the perquisites of the Framingham Foundation (the rent-free apartment, chauffeured limousine, round-the-clock bar service, poker games and French cuisine) and regularly scheduled female companionship on Wednesday and Friday nights.

As a class, in other words, Matthew Q. Framingham VI had little or no active interest in females of his own age group and general social background. They were far more trouble than they were worth. This is not to say that he didn't look at them. He was as much able to appreciate a shapely thigh and a well-formed bosom on the hoof, so to speak, as he was in a Goya nude on the wall. It was just that he had learned, rather painfully, that as a practical matter both were attainable only at a high cost that he did not wish to pay.

As the doorman of the Savoy-Plaza Hotel held open the door for him, he did indeed notice the blond standing on the curb. But, until she spoke to him, it was his intention to view her safely, and from a distance, as he viewed other attractive, if dangerous, creatures of God, such as lions and tigers.

'What did he call you?' the blond said to him.

Matthew courteously tipped his homburg.

'I beg your pardon, madam?' he said.

'That gesture is insulting,' the blond said. 'Do you know that?'

'I beg your pardon?' Matthew repeated.

'It goes back to the days of chivalry,' the blond said. 'A knight raised the visor on his helmet to a lady.'

'Yes, madam,' Matt said. 'So I have been informed.'

'It symbolized that the female was a weak character, posing no threat at all to the male.'

'Quite so,' he said.

'I asked you, you big ape, what he called you.'

'If memory serves, madam,' Matt replied, 'Mr. Grogarty, the doorman, said, quote, "Good morning, Mr. Framingham. Nice to see you again, sir." Unquote. I trust, madam, that that information will satisfy what I believe is known as your feminine curiosity.'

'It's my *journalistic* curiosity, you male chauvinist pig,' Monica P. Fenstermacher said. 'And I can't say I'm surprised.'

'Whatever,' Matthew said. He tipped his homburg again. 'Good day to you, madam.' He turned and walked through the revolving door to the Savoy-Plaza.

'I'm awful sorry about that, Mr. Framingham,' Mr. Grogarty, the doorman, said to him.

'Not to worry, Mr. Grogarty,' Matthew said. 'The situation was obviously beyond your control.'

He marched up the stairs and across the lobby to the offices of the vice-president and general manager, looking neither to the right nor the left and certainly not over his shoulder, so he did not see that he had been followed into the Savoy-Plaza by Ms. Monica P. Fenstermacher.

The vice-president and general manager of the Savoy-Plaza greeted him with warmth (a warmth, to be sure, in keeping with the dignity of the Savoy-Plaza, but a warmth nevertheless). The VP & GM was aware that the Savoy-Plaza got a nice little chunk of business (especially during the Semiannual Seminars on the Role of Theology in a

Changing Society) from the Framingham Foundation. There was seldom enough room at the inn, so to speak, for all the seminarians, and the Savoy-Plaza got the overflow. Their bills were always large and promptly paid by the foundation, and it was Matthew Q. Framingham VI's signature on the check.

Furthermore, the VP & GM of the S-P was a seventh-generation Bostonian, a Harvard man, and dared to hope that one day he might be nominated for, and possibly accepted into, the Framingham Foundation.

'I have a certain delicate problem,' Matthew Q. Framingham VI said to the VP & GM after he had been installed in a comfortable chair and the sherry poured, 'involving the foundation. I hope that I may place my faith in your discretion.'

'Both personally and as VP and GM of the S-P,' the VP & GM said, 'I consider it an honour that you should come to us with any problem regarding the Framingham Foundation. How may the Savoy-Plaza generally, and myself specifically, be of service to the Framingham Foundation generally and you yourself, Mr. Framingham, specifically? Let me assure you that what is said within these office walls will stay within these walls.'

He erred. Even as he spoke, every word was reaching the ears of Ms. Monica P. Fenstermacher. She had, as a matter of journalistic routine, bribed the VP & GM's private secretary with the promise of an autographed photograph of Senator Teddy Kennedy and was now in the ladies' can of the VP & GM's executive suite, hearing all over an intercom system.

'For reasons I don't think I should get into,' Matt Framingham said, 'it is necessary for the foundation to procure suitable accommodations for a thirty-to-sixty-day period away from our National Headquarters Building.'

'I see,' the VP & GM said.

'You will not be offended, I trust, when I tell you that while I hold your establishment in the highest regard, it is not suitable for our needs. The Framingham Foundation, as you know, must have its privacy.'

'I understand completely,' the VP & GM said.

'I just had a rather chilling experience,' Matt went on. 'I went to the Harvard Square Bali-Hai Motor Hotel and spoke with the manager.'

'Is that in keeping with the traditions of the Framingham Foundation, if I may presume to ask?'

'It was my original thinking to rent one of the wings of the Bali-Hai,' Matthew said. 'As you know, the Bali-Hai seems to be geared to accommodate guests who do not wish to be seen entering or leaving.'

'Yes, I know,' the VP & GM said. 'But it didn't work out?'

'The manager seemed to understand our requirements,' Matthew said. 'I did not, of course, bring the name of the foundation into the conversation.'

'Of course not.'

'I simply told him that I would require accommodations for up to twenty unaccompanied gentlemen; that we would require round-the-clock bar and food services; and that we had only one absolute requirement, that women be wholly and totally barred from the premises we would occupy.'

'And he was unwilling to provide these services?'

'Quite the contrary,' Matthew Q. Framingham VI said. 'He told me that the Bali-Hai and its staff would be overjoyed to have us, that he would be absolutely delighted to do whatever he could to make us feel at home. Then he put his hand on my knee and tried to kiss me.'

'What did you do?'

'My first thought was to throw him into the swimming pool,' Matthew said. 'I got so far as picking him up and holding him over my head. Then reason returned. I realized that embarrassing questions might be raised if I had to explain to the authorities exactly why I had thrown him from his penthouse suite into his swimming pool.'

'Of course.'

'At that point, I decided to come to you and seek your advice.'

'You should have come here first thing,' the VP & GM said.

'You're quite right,' Matthew said. 'Will you help me?'

'I should be honoured,' the VP & GM said. 'Let me cogitate a moment.' He offered Matthew a cigar and refilled his sherry glass. He put his hands, fingers interlocked, behind his head, leaned back in his chair and whistled tonelessly. Matthew Q. Framingham VI waited patiently. He was, in point of fact, remembering the crazy lady who had accosted him on the sidewalk as he left his limousine. She reminded him, in a physical sense, of some of the more spectacularly endowed terpsichorean ecdysiasts who had enlightened the seminars and retreats and moral enlightenment sessions of the foundation. He wondered, idly, if she happened to be in the profession, and, if so, whether (a) she would be interested in a professional engagement and (b) whether there would be any place for her to perform if that horrid female from 'The Rhotten Report' could not be outwitted.

'Matthew . . . I may call you Matthew, mayn't I?'

'Of course you may,' Matt said, grandly.

'Matthew, have you considered getting out of town?'

'Frankly,' Matthew said, 'I haven't. I got as far west as Cleveland one time, and it was just as dreadful as dear old dad had led me to believe.'

'I thought, perhaps, that this might be an emergency situation,' the VP & GM of the S-P said.

'You're quite right, of course,' Matthew said. 'What do you have in mind?'

'I have an acquaintance, a professional associate whom I encountered at last month's Hotelier's Convention in Athens,' the VP & GM of the S-P said, 'who just might be able to help us. Let me knock him up.'

'I beg your pardon?'

'Oh, that's just a little British expression I can't seem to shake,' the VP & GM said. 'That's British for "call him on the telephone."'

'Oh,' Matt said.

'I did a year, you know, at Oxford.' Letting Framingham

know that he was an Oxfordian just might help in getting himself considered for the Framingham Foundation.

'I hadn't known,' Matthew said.

'I thought it would give me an insight into the thought patterns of the upper classes,' the VP & GM said. 'Essential in my calling, don't you see?'

'And did it?' Matthew asked.

'To be quite frank, Matthew, I had the same trouble at Oxford that you had at the Bali-Hai Motor Hotel.'

'God, they're all over, aren't they?' Matt said.

'I don't know what the world is coming to,' the VP & GM said. 'But let me call my acquaintance.' He reached over and flipped the switch on his intercom. 'Miss Sellingworth,' he said, 'would you please get me Mr. Caesar Augustus Finecello, Jr., at Nero's Villa in Las Vegas on the line, please?'

As he waited for the call to be completed, the VP & GM said, 'I think he'll probably be able to help. He led me to believe he has a rather unusual clientele.'

'I see,' Matt said. 'He is, of course, as they say, straight?'

'As an arrow, my dear fellow. He has eight children.'

'Pardon my asking,' Matthew said.

'I understand completely,' the VP & GM said, and then, 'Caesar, old chap! How are you?'

In three minutes, everything was arranged. The Framingham Foundation would immediately be given possession of the entire twenty-fifth floor of the northwest wing of Nero's Villa. They would have a private elevator, and the entire operation would be officially carried on the hotel register as a convention; Mr. Finecello suggested using a *nom de anonymité* of Associated Life Insurance salesmen. His experience had taught him that no one ever tried to crash a convention of life insurance salesmen.

Little Augie was delighted with the prospect of playing host to what the VP & GM of the S-P described as the *crème de la crème* of northeastern society, although of course he didn't let the VP & GM of the S-P know either that he was, or why.

Among the many subordinate business enterprises of Nero's Villa was the Acme Still and Motion Picture Photography Company. The talented photographers of the company were available around the clock in Nero's Villa to make a photographic record of weddings, bar mitzvahs and business affairs of one kind or another. That side of the business, frankly, lost money. The other side of the business, however, was a real money-maker. Little Augie never ceased to be amazed at how much travellers were willing to pay for prints (and of course, negatives) of themselves joyfully cavorting in the buff around the rooms of Nero's Villa with young women listed as their nieces on the hotel registry.

Sometimes, to prime the pump, so to speak, it had been necessary for Little Augie to provide surrogate nieces from the ranks of Nero's Nubiles, but the girls always eagerly responded to his call for volunteers, probably because he gave them a flat twenty per cent of the take from the sale of the films, plus bonuses for their acting skill. (It was necessary, of course, to keep the participants within certain areas within the bedchambers so as to keep them before the camera lenses, which could be hidden in only a few locations in the walls and ceilings.)

With just a little bit of luck, he would be able to recoup from the VP & GM of the S-P's *crème de la crème* all of the $81,000 that funny-looking little jerk had gotten away with, and if things went well, a lot more than $81,000.

'Trust me,' he said on the telephone. 'We will take care of your friends.'

The VP & GM of the S-P dutifully repeated Little Augie's remark to Matthew Q. Framingham VI.

'Please tell Mr. Finecello we are grateful,' Matthew said, 'and that I look forward to making his personal acquaintance upon my arrival. I shall leave on the next plane.'

Matthew Q. Framingham, who believed in omens, was sure as he boarded the plane two hours later that everything was going to turn out all right. The spectacularly endowed blond whom he had encountered on the sidewalk outside the

Savoy-Plaza was sitting in the first-class compartment when he walked in.

Since she didn't look like a gambler, it was reasonable to presume that she was, as her physiognomy suggested, indeed a terpsichorean ecdysiast, probably en route to a professional engagement in one of the many Las Vegas hotels which featured that sort of entertainment. When he tipped his homburg to her, she smiled at him sweetly. Matthew paused and finally decided that he would take the chance and strike up an acquaintance with her. He paused too long. A travelling-salesman type rudely shoved Matthew out of the way and slipped into the seat beside the blond.

'Hello, baby,' he said. 'First flight?'

The blond rather skillfully jabbed her elbow into his abdomen, and Matthew's disappointment at not being able to sit beside her vanished. He was, in fact, rather surprised at himself. He had never before thrown caution to the winds. He consoled himself with the thought that there would be time to make her acquaintance, professionally speaking, of course, in Las Vegas.

CHAPTER NINE

It has been said that you never know who your friends are until you ask something of them. The implication is that your good ol' buddy ceases to be your good ol' buddy instantly upon learning that you need a small loan to tide you over a rough spot.

In the case of Madame Kristina Korsky-Rimsakov and Mr. J. Robespierre O'Reilly, however, quite the reverse (perhaps proving the rule) proved to be the case.

In the kitchen of the home of Dr. and Mrs. Benjamin Franklin Pierce, Madame Korsky-Rimsakov confessed to Mrs. Pierce a somewhat embarrassing truth. She had no close female friends and no family other than her brother.

She had devoted her life to her career. Until dear Robespierre had come along, she had never suspected that she would one day marry.

'Mary,' she said, 'I don't really know what to do or where to turn. What I would like most of all is a simple, quiet, dignified ceremony with just a few of our most intimate friends present. Robespierre proposed to me at Nero's Villa, and for that reason – and because the manager is such a fine gentleman – we would like to have the wedding there. Would you help me with the arrangements?'

Tears welled up in Mary Pierce's eyes, and she laid a gentle, even loving hand on Kristina's.

'Of course, I will,' she said. 'I understand completely.'

'If dear Boris can get away from Paris . . . and I hate to ask him to come all that distance,' Kristina said, 'he can give me away.'

'I'm sure he can come,' Mary Pierce said, gently. She thought: I'll make sure that drunken ape shows up sober if it's the last thing he does on earth.

'And Robespierre seems to feel that Archbishop Mulcahy will be good enough to marry us.'

'I'll send the plane for him,' Radar said. 'He won't have to be out of Rome for more than forty-eight hours. And he promised me, when we were in the 4077th MASH, that when my time came he would marry me.'

'And if you and Lucinda would be my matrons of honour,' Kristina said.

'We would be honoured,' Mary Pierce said.

'And Doctors Pierce and McIntyre could be our witnesses,' Kristina went on.

'They would be honoured,' Mary Pierce said firmly.

'And if Colonel de la Chevaux, Robespierre's best friend, would be willing to be best man . . .'

'I'm sure I can count on Horsey,' Robespierre said. 'He's always telling me it's better to marry than to burn.' The women looked at him strangely, and he flushed.

'Who else?' Mary Pierce asked.

'Reverend Mother, of course,' Kristina said.

'Yeah, we can't leave Hot Lips out,' Radar said.

'Robespierre, darling, I wish you wouldn't call her that,' Madame Kristina said.

'Sorry,' Radar said. 'It'll never happen again. She could be the flower girl.'

'I think, Robespierre,' Kristina said, 'that Reverend Mother is a little old to be a flower girl. Perhaps she could assist Archbishop Mulcahy.'

'That would seem to be everybody,' Kristina said.

'What about Henry Blake?' Radar asked. 'He was my commanding officer.'

'I'd really like to keep it small and intimate, Robespierre,' Kristina said.

'Scratch Henry Blake,' Radar said, immediately.

'No, dear. He was your commanding officer, and if you want him to be there to watch us marry, I think he should be there. But that's all. All right?'

'Thank you,' Radar said.

'Just a small, intimate wedding,' Kristina said. 'Something I never dared hope would happen to me.'

'If I may make a suggestion, Kristina?' Mary Pierce said.

'Oh, please do,' Kristina said.

'Hawk ... Benjamin and John Francis Xavier will be here at noon. Why don't we just let them make the necessary telephone calls? That way we'll know right away who can come and who can't.'

'That's a very good idea,' Kristina said. 'And they can tactfully make it plain that we don't want any fuss at all.'

'Right,' Mary Pierce said.

Hawkeye and Trapper John arrived home from the Framingham Foundation full of good cheer which Mary Pierce and Lucinda McIntyre suspected, but could not prove, was liquid in origin.

After making what Mary and Lucinda considered absolutely disgusting and wholly unnecessary comments about certain physical aspects of marriage to Radar, the two healers took the prospective bridal couple into Hawkeye's study and picked up the telephone.

'Who first?' Trapper John said.

'Let's bite the bullet and call Boris,' Hawkeye said. 'Operator,' he said, 'person-to-person to Mr. Boris Alexandrovich Korsky-Rimsakov at the French National Opera House in Paris, France. If he's not there, try the Crazy Horse Saloon.'

'What am I going to do, Kristina, if Boris says I can't marry you?' Radar asked.

'Have courage, oh ye of little faith,' Trapper John said. 'Have we ever let you down?'

As it happened, Boris Alexandrovich Korsky-Rimsakov *was* physically in the French National Opera House on Paris' rather aptly named Place de l'Opera when the international operator called. He had just finished a dress rehearsal. He had sung the role of Pope Clement VII in Hector Berlioz' opera *Benvenuto Cellini* and returned to his dressing room.

His greatest fan and close personal friend, Prince Hassan ad Kayam, had been waiting for him in the dressing room.

'You were magnificent!' Prince Hassan said, popping the cork of a freshly chilled magnum bottle of Dom Perignon '62, as was his custom when the maestro entered his dressing room following a performance.

'Yes, I thought so,' Boris said. 'Not as magnificent as I can be, but far more magnificent, of course, than anyone else who has sung this rather unimportant role.'

'Forgive me, Maestro,' Prince Hassan said. 'Could that be because you have been neglecting your exercise of late?'

The singer, who stood six feet six and weighed exactly 285 pounds, waited until Prince Hassan had poured champagne into a glass. But as he started to pour a second glass, the singer stilled his hand. He took the bottle from the smaller (one foot and four inches shorter, exactly one-hundred pounds lighter) man and tipped the neck to his mouth. As His Highness watched with undisguised admiration, the contents of the bottle descended with a steady glug, glug, glug sound into the singer's massive body. Boris then handed the empty bottle to Prince Hassan, put his right hand, fingers extended, on his papal robes and belched. It sounded like one of the larger kettledrums in a Wagnerian opus.

'It was warm out there,' he said. 'I worked up a little sweat.'

'Another, Maestro?' His Highness said, turning to a second silver cooler, in which rested another towel-wrapped bottle of champagne.

'Not right now,' Boris said. 'Every once in a great while, Hassan, you say something that makes sense.'

'Oh, thank you, Maestro,' His Highness said.

The singer, examining himself with satisfaction in the mirror, stroked his full, heavy beard. It was not a stage, or glued on, beard. It was all his.

'What you said about me failing my obligation to my art by not exercising,' he said. 'You may be right. It's been four days. Certainly, I owe it to my fans to be in the best possible shape.'

'I would dare to suggest, Maestro, that you do,' His Highness said.

'Very well,' the singer said. 'I will exercise.'

'Right now?'

'I can hardly exercise in my papal robes,' Boris said. 'Although the idea does have a certain erotic attraction, now that I think of it.'

'And what does the Sage of Manhattan, Kansas, have to say about costume?'

The Sage of Manhattan, Kansas, was T. Mullins Yancey, M.D., with whose works Boris Alexandrovich Korsky-Rimsakov had two years before become familiar[1] and whose faithful disciple he had become.

'I don't know,' Boris said, with surprise in his voice. 'I shall have to give the doctor the benefit of my thinking. He was rather touchingly grateful for my letter on exercise in

---

[1] See 'Sex and Health Through Constant Coitus,' 235 pp., $7.95, and 'Sexual Intercourse as Exercise,' 245 pp., $8.95 (illustrated), both by Theosophilus Mullins Yancey, M.D., Joyful Practice Publishing Company, Manhattan, Kansas.

pressured aircraft cabins above thirty-thousand feet, you remember.'

'Then you could consider it both exercise in the name of your art and scientific research, couldn't you?' His Highness asked. Although they were now the closest of personal friends, in the interests of truth it must be reported that His Highness had sought the friendship of the singer after realizing that the singer's female discards were of greater number, variety and quality than those which came to an Arabian prince with an income last estimated at $35,000 daily.

'That settles it!' Boris said, as the telephone rang. 'How could I possibly refuse a dual call to artistic and philosophic endeavour? Have you anything, so to speak, laid on?'

'Shall I answer the phone, Maestro?'

'You certainly don't expect me to answer my own phone, do you? God only knows who might be calling.'

His Highness picked up the telephone. 'Maestro Boris Alexandrovich Korsky-Rimsakov's dressing suite,' he said.

'Spruce Harbor, Maine, calling for that far-out name you just said,' the operator said.

'It is Spruce Harbor, Maine,' His Highness relayed to the maestro.

'It's probably that dreadful Pierce woman,' the maestro said. 'In a moment of weakness, I agreed to sing for her PTA Musical Appreciation Society, and she shows every bourgeois sign of trying to hold me to my word. Tell her that I am indisposed . . . tell her I have gone. Just because I owe my life to her husband is no reason that she should expect me to sing on cue, and for free, like a cuckoo on one of those awful Black Forest clocks.'

His Highness told the Spruce Harbor operator that he deeply regretted that Maestro Korsky-Rimsakov was not available at the moment, and then he hung up.

Almost immediately it rang again.

'That's her again,' Boris said. 'I know. She simply doesn't know how to take no for an answer. We'll have to leave. I asked you, and you rudely refused to reply, whether you have something available? Something suitable?'

'I happened to mention, Maestro,' His Highness said, 'that we might drop by the Crazy Horse Saloon after the dress rehearsal.'

'And *whom* did you mention this to?' Boris asked, suspiciously.

'The Baroness d'Iberville and Esmeralda Hoffenburg, the ballerina,' His Highness said.

'You really do *pant* after the baroness, don't you?' Boris said. 'To keep you in your place, Hassan, I'm tempted to do her the honour and leave you with Esmerelda.'

'Esmerelda would be fine with me, Maestro,' His Highness said. 'Anything that will permit you to have the exercise your art requires.'

The phone was still ringing.

'That's Hawkeye's wife,' Boris said, eyeing it distastefully. 'I can tell by the shrill tenor of the ringing. We will go.' He swept out of the room, after first adjusting the *cappa magna* of Pope Clement VII at a suitably rakish angle atop his head.

A special platoon of the Paris gendarmerie is always stationed at the Paris Opera when the maestro (who has been declared an official national treasure of France) is in the building. Their sergeant blew a whistle, and the gendarmes locked arms and formed a human chain to protect the singer as he left the stage door and marched toward His Highness' Cadillac limousine.

Boris smiled benignly at his assembled fans, most of whom were women between twenty-one and sixty-one years of age. There was a sound of swooning as he appeared, and the air was suddenly full of roses and fluttering sheets of perfumed stationery bearing telephone numbers, as well as (he knew from sad experience) a veritable hail of hotel room keys.

Boris Alexandrovich Korsky-Rimsakov raised one hand to fend off the most threatening of the room keys and with the other made the motion he'd seen the current pope use on television.

'Bless you,' he repeated, grandly, 'bless you, my children!'

One of His Highness' bodyguards opened the rear door of the limousine and waited until His Highness and the singer were inside. Then he closed the door, jumped in the front seat beside the chauffeur and flipped on the siren and flashing lights, and the limousine began to move slowly through the screaming horde of fans.

It was actually sort of a convoy, with the limousine preceded by a black Citroën sedan and trailed by four other sedans. From the front fender of the lead Citroën, and from that of the limousine itself, flapped the flag of the Islamic Kingdom of Hussid. The Republic of France procured thirty-eight percent of its petroleum needs from the Kingdom of Hussid. The official position of the government of France toward the heir apparent to the Kingdom of Hussid could be phrased rather succinctly: *Whatever makes him happy!*

The convoy rolled with a grand disregard for stop lights, stop signs and the speed limit, down the Rue Royale into the Place Vendôme, past the Ritz Hotel, past the Hotel Continental (which housed the Royal Hussid Embassy), up the Rue de Rivoli to the Place de la Concorde and then up the Champs Élysées to the Rue Pierre Charron, where it screeched to a stop in front of the Crazy Horse Saloon, a watering place which establishment, were it located in Chicago, Illinois, would be known as a striptease joint.

Bodyguards, each armed with a silver-plated submachine gun, spilled out of the five Citroën sedans and formed a lane for the singer and His Highness to enter the Crazy Horse Saloon.

A rather stunning ecdysiast was on the stage, down, so to speak, to her waist-length red hair and three strategically placed pieces of sequined cloth with a total area of perhaps three square inches. She stopped when she saw the door open and the figure of a man in papal vestments enter the establishment.

'Carry on, my dear!' the familiar voice boomed. It could only be the voice of Boris Alexandrovich Korsky-Rimsakov, no matter how he was dressed. The ecdysiast put her fingertips to her mouth, threw Boris a kiss and resumed her performance.

(In the audience were four members of the Holy Name Society of Saint Ignatius' Church of Hoboken, New Jersey, who had slipped away from the Holy Name Society's Tour of Paris' Cultural Attractions to rest their feet in what they realized was an American-type saloon. When they reported to their wives, later that evening, that a high-ranking prelate of the church, in full vestments almost papal in richness, had been in the Crazy Horse Saloon and had loudly cheered and applauded the performers, the wives' disbelief caused several noisy confrontations.)

The proprietor showed His Highness and Boris to a table, and a squad of waiters began to dance attendance upon them. Two bottles of champagne, one bottle of Gatorade and a bottle of brandy, together with the necessary glasses, were immediately set upon the table. (His Highness, of course, was a total teetotaller and had been introduced to Gatorade by Dr. T. Mullins Yancey's article 'Afterward, Then What?' in the July 1974 edition of *Together!*, the official journal of the Yancey Clinic.) A huge tray of hors d'oeuvres followed.

The Baroness d'Iberville and Esmerelda Hoffenburg, the ballerina, who occupied a table against the wall, resisted the temptation to join Boris and Hassan at their table. Hassan had made it quite clear when they had telephoned that all he was promising was that he would suggest coming to the Crazy Horse Saloon. They understood that it was by no means certain that they would either be permitted to join *Cher* Boris Alexandrovich in the Crazy Horse or that *Cher* Boris would leave the place with them. They must, they understood, wait to be asked.

Ordinarily, women of the beauty and lofty social position of the baroness and Madame Esmerelda had few restrictions placed on their actions and movements. But they were not, with *Cher* Boris, dealing with an ordinary man, nor was their relationship with the singer the ordinary relationship between Boris and other members of their sex.

Specifically, they were sisters in a very small sorority of those who had been recalled for an encore. It was Boris' often stated belief that common decency required that he spread himself around as much as possible. It was the only fair thing to do; better that one-thousand women have an experience they could treasure in memory their whole lives than for a specially privileged five hundred women to have the same experience twice, thereby depriving their sisters of what could only be justly described as their heavenly piece on earth.

That Madame Esmerelda and the baroness had been called more than once was common knowledge (they had seen to it that the word had gotten out), and a good deal of rather imaginative speculation, much of it tinged with jealousy, had been evident. What did those two have, in other words, that I don't have?

(The resentment was, of course, deeper among those women who had been called but called only once, than among those yet to be called. The latter group were able to tell themselves that once *they* had the chance, they would demonstrate *their* worthiness to be recalled.)

The truth of the matter was not nearly as esoteric as commonly believed. The Baroness d'Iberville had had a Russian nanny, who had taught her how to make *blini* (a sort of potato pancake served cold with sour cream and chopped onions), a dish of which *Cher* Boris was fond, both gustatorily and because it had very much the same effect on him, when that effect was rarely needed, as Prince Hassan's Gatorade. Madame Esmerelda had been recalled both because she had a rather unique muscular control which had permitted *Cher* Boris to exercise when he really didn't think he was up to it and because she hadn't said a word during their first encounter. The one thing *Cher* Boris could not stand was a chattering female, either before or during and especially afterward.

Boris picked idly at the food of barbecued spareribs and a half-pound of Camembert on two loaves of bread. The truth of the matter was that his conscience was bothering him. Doctor Hawkeye Pierce, as he was well aware, had twice saved his life. The first time was in Korea, when Boris (operating under the *nom de guerre* of 'Bob Alexander'), then a Browning Automatic Rifleman in Baker Company, 223rd Infantry, in the act of carting Sgt. Frenchy de la Chevaux, leaking from a shrapnel wound, off Heartbreak Ridge, had acquired a few holes of his own.

Hawkeye Pierce, then chief of surgery of the well-known Double Natural (or 4077th) Mobile Army Surgical Hospital (MASH), had sewn both of them back together.

The second time was more recently, right here in Paris, when Hawkeye and Trapper John, in Paris on a top-level diplomatic mission for the State Department, had removed singer's nodes from the singer's throat.

By the time he had worked his way through both bottles of champagne and half the bottle of brandy, Boris Alexandrovich Korsky-Rimsakov had worked himself into something of a fret. When a distinguished surgeon has twice saved your life and thus preserved a superb and unparalleled voice for the enrichment of mankind generally, the least one could do was to speak to his wife, no matter what kind of kook the wife happened to be, on the telephone.

Tears of remorse began to trickle down from Boris' deep black eyes to lose themselves in his luxurious beard.

'Is something wrong, Maestro?' Prince Hassan asked, gently.

'Wrong?' Boris exploded. 'Wrong? Of course, something is wrong. How could you, you camel thief, refuse to let me speak to the charming wife of that distinguished healer?'

'Maestro, you said you didn't want to talk to her.'

'I said nothing of the kind,' Boris said, furiously. 'How dare you make such a suggestion?'

Esmerelda Hoffenburg, the ballerina, who had been unable to keep her eyes off Boris, was now unable to resist the maternal urge to hold that magnificent, tragic, weeping head against her womanly bosom. She jumped up from her table and ran to his.

'*Cher* Boris!' she cried. 'You are unhappy! How may I comfort you?'

'Oh, Esmerelda,' Boris said, 'you nurture one of these Arabians vipers at your breast, and the first time you need them they betray you!' He allowed the dancer to hold his head against her bosom.

'Shame on you, Your Highness,' Esmerelda said. 'You should be ashamed of yourself.'

'Yes, he should,' Boris agreed.

The Baroness d'Iberville had no intention of being left out, so to speak, in the cold. She got up and rushed to the table, colliding en route with one of the maitres d'hotel, who was approaching the table with a telephone. She thought she saw her opportunity.

'Get out of here with that telephone!' she shrieked. 'Can't you see the maestro is in pain?'

'Telephone?' Boris said, sitting up. 'Telephone?'

'Maestro,' the maitre d'hotel said, 'it is the international operator. It is a call for you from the United States. I told them you don't take calls, but they insist . . .'

'Give me that phone, you idiot,' Boris said, standing up and sending Esmerelda, who had been on his lap, sprawling. 'This is Boris Alexandrovich Korsky-Rimsakov,' he said, charm oozing from every subtle timbre of his voice. 'And with whom do I have the great pleasure of speaking?'

Four thousand miles away, Dr. Benjamin Franklin Pierce said, 'Hello, you big ape, how are they hanging?'

'Hawkeye, my dear friend,' Boris replied, 'I was just thinking of you, of the manifold contributions you have made to medical science, and of your charming wife and helpmeet. I trust you both are in general, all-around good health and spirits?'

'Boris,' Hawkeye said, 'I want to talk to you about your sister. She's right here with me.'

'My beloved Kristina is there with you, my dear friend?'

'That's right,' Hawkeye said.

'Will you be good enough to wait just one moment, please?' Boris asked.

'Yeah, sure,' Hawkeye replied.

CHAPTER TEN

Boris covered the mouthpiece of the telephone with his hand. He took in a deep breath.

'Silence!' he bellowed. The pit orchestra stopped in midbeat. Fifi de San José, nearing the completion of her act, which she called 'The Liberation of the Lovebirds', was so startled that she let go of the rubber strap which she had just pulled away from her bosom to let a pigeon escape. That, in turn, startled the pigeon, who pecked her. She yelped.

'And stop that obscene performance!' Boris screamed. 'Can't you see that I am talking to my beloved baby sister?'

The large, and usually noisy, room was suddenly stilled.

'That's better,' Boris said. He took his hand off the microphone. 'As you were saying, Doctor?'

'Are you sitting down, Boris?' Hawkeye asked.

'No, as a matter of fact, I am standing up,' Boris said. 'But if you would prefer that I sit down, your wish is my command.' He sat down on the chair which he had just recently vacated. While he had been standing, however, Esmerelda Hoffenburg had climbed off the floor and sat in it. Boris, therefore, sat on her. She yelped.

'How dare you sit in my chair?' Boris bellowed. 'God, you give them an inch and they take a mile!'

Esmerelda wiggled out from under him.

'I am now sitting, Doctor,' Boris asked. 'Is there anything else you would like me to do?'

'Brace yourself,' Hawkeye said.

'You have bad news about my baby sister!' Boris said. 'I feel it in my bones.'

'I'll let her tell you herself,' Hawkeye said.

'Big Brother?' Kristina said.

'Baby Sister!' Boris said. The tears started coursing down from his eyes again.

'Boris,' Kristina said, 'I have something to tell you.'

101

'Whatever it is, I'll handle it,' Boris said. He covered the mouthpiece with his hand again and turned to His Highness. 'Don't you sit there, you cretin!' he said. 'Call the airport. Have the engines started. My Baby Sister needs her Big Brother.'

'Boris,' Kristina said, 'Robespierre has asked me to become his wife.'

'I knew that four-eyed degenerate wasn't to be trusted!' Boris replied. 'I'll tear him limb from limb! I'll make a bowl of his own rotten stew out of him!'

'And I have accepted,' Kristina went on.

'Kristina,' Boris said, 'listen to me. You're a young and impressionable girl . . .'

'Big Brother, I was forty-two last week.'

'That's exactly what I mean,' Boris said. 'You're nothing but a baby, and that pint-sized sex maniac and child molester has taken advantage of your innocence!'

'Now shut up, Boris,' Kristina said, with surprising firmness, 'and listen to me. Robespierre has proposed, and I have accepted. We're going to be married, and that's all there is to it. The only thing you have to do with this is to give a simple answer to a simple question. Will you give me away at the ceremony, or won't you?'

There was no immediate reply. Boris Alexandrovich Korsky-Rimsakov was overcome with emotion. His massive chest heaved. A pathetic, if rather loud, gurgling noise came out of his mouth. He was weeping.

'Get control of yourself, Big Brother,' Kristina ordered. 'Will you come, or not?'

He blubbered. He tried to speak but could not. His massive head shook over his massive chest. With infinite tenderness, Prince Hassan took the telephone from his limp fingers.

'Kristina,' he said, 'this is Hassan. Boris is so overcome with joy that he can't speak. Let me assure you that nothing on earth would give him greater pleasure than giving you in marriage to Mr. J. Robespierre O'Reilly. If you will just give me the details, I'll take care of everything.'

As Hassan spoke with Kristina, Boris was comforted by the baroness and Esmerelda, who held him to their breasts, running their hands consolingly through his thick hair.

By the time Hassan had finished speaking with Kristina, Boris had regained enough control of himself so as to be able to say good-bye to her, but once he had done that and the phone had been hung up, he broke down again, sobbing helplessly.

'The wages of sin,' he said, finally. 'That's what it says in the Good Book. But I never knew what it meant before!'

'What about the wages of sin?' Esmerelda asked.

'My sins have caught up with me,' he said.

'How's that?' Hassan asked.

'My sister never asked anything from me before in her life,' Boris said. 'And now, when there is something she needs, I'm going to fail her.'

'I don't quite follow you, maestro,' Hassan said.

'I realize that you're not too bright, Hassan, but even someone with your severe mental problems should be able to see mine. My sister wants me to help her get married. What the hell do I know about marriage?'

'Maestro,' Hassan said, 'I don't think that Madame Kristina wants your help with her *marriage*. What she wants you to do is help her to *get* married, to help with the ceremony.'

'And what do I know about that?'

'*Cher* Boris,' the baroness said, 'put yourself in my hands. I have been married five times. I know all there is to know about wedding ceremonies.'

'By God, that's right!' Boris said. 'And will you help me?'

'Your wish is my command, *Cher* Boris,' she said.

'I know that,' he said. 'The question is, what should I do?'

'Perhaps we could talk this all over someplace less public,' Hassan said.

'You're absolutely right,' Boris said. 'Discussing the wedding of my innocent baby sister in this foul den of iniquity is out of the question.'

'We could all go to my place,' Esmerelda said. 'I just

happen to have a baron of beef in the fridge. And some very nice Chauteau Mouton sixty-five.'

'Bless you, my child,' Boris said. 'I will, of course, need sustenance.'

'And exercise, *mon cher* Boris?' the baroness asked.

'Of course, exercise,' Boris said. 'I've told you before that I always need exercise to be at the peak of my mental powers. And God knows, I'm going to have to be to get through this.'

Thirty minutes later, Boris Alexandrovich Korsky-Rimsakov, now wearing a silk robe and a contented smile rather than his papal robes, walked into the living room of Esmerelda Hoffenburg's apartment. Esmerelda Hoffenburg, yawning and stretching languorously, trailed him.

'God,' Boris said, 'if it weren't for the teachings of that blessed man, the sage of Manhattan, Kansas, I don't know how I'd face life's problems.'

'I'm so happy for you,' the baroness said, without much conviction.

'I'm glad everything went well,' His Highness said.

'Oh, *yes!*' Esmerelda said. 'It went divinely!'

'I have decided that Esmerelda may come with us,' Boris said. 'I will have to be in tip-top form during the whole thing, and I may need her.'

'Well, I like that,' the baroness said. 'Here I am working my fingers to the bone planning your sister's marriage, and that skinny hoofer gets to go along.'

'What is she talking about, Hassan?' Boris asked.

'The baroness has been most helpful,' Hassan said.

'In that case, she may come too,' Boris said, grandly. 'I don't wish to play favourites.'

'Thank you, *Cher* Boris,' the baroness said. And when Boris' head turned for a moment, she stuck her tongue out at Esmerelda.

'Madame Kristina said she wants the simplest possible ceremony,' Hassan said. 'With just a circle of intimate friends.'

'Of course,' Boris said. 'I will leave the details to you,

Hassan. I ask you to remember only that she is the only sister I have, and that I want her wedding to be memorable.'

'I understand completely,' His Highness said. 'Maestro, you have just an hour to get to the opera.'

'I'll drive you,' the baroness said, quickly.

'You don't have a car, darling,' Esmerelda said.

'I'll use Hassan's,' she said. 'And while I'm gone, Hassan can explain to you what we did while you were . . . in there.'

'*I've* been exercising with Boris,' Esmerelda said. 'I have absolutely *no* interest in what *you* have been doing with *Hassan*.'

'They've been planning my sister's wedding, you idiot!' Boris said.

'Oh,' Esmerelda said. 'Is *that* what you meant, darling?'

'Unless you both learn to behave,' Boris said, 'neither of you may come with me to . . . where is the wedding, Hassan?'

'Las Vegas, Nevada,' Hassan said. 'And, Maestro, your sister said that she wanted a simple, intimate wedding.'

'Then that's what she'll get,' Boris said. 'Those two can wait in the hotel rooms. You will take care of the hotel rooms, won't you, Hassan?'

'That's already been taken care of, Maestro,' Hassan said. 'I have taken the liberty, my dear friend, of arranging for the reception to follow the ceremony. It will be my little wedding present.'

'Frankly,' Boris said, 'considering our friendship and all that it's meant to you, I was thinking along the lines of an oil well or two.'

'I said my "little" present,' Hassan said. 'When there was time, I was going to ask you whether you thought an island my brother just bought off the coast of South Carolina would be appropriate.'

'How big an island?'

'I don't really know.'

'Well, find out, and then we'll discuss it,' Boris said. 'We don't want to be miserly where my baby sister is concerned, do we?'

'Of course not, Maestro,' Hassan said. 'Perish the thought.'

'We'd better be running along, *Cher* Boris,' the baroness said.

'Oh, cool it!' Esmerelda said, nastily. 'There just won't be time for you before the performance anyway.'

'Oh, I don't know,' Boris said. 'Now that I am resigned to losing my little sister ... perhaps I should say, gaining a little brother ... I am in such good spirits that there just might be time to squeeze in a little exercise before my entrance. I'm always so superb, immediately after.' He turned to the baroness. 'Bring along my papal vestments,' he ordered. 'I'll wait for you in the car.'

He walked out of the apartment toward the elevator. Halfway there, he burst into song. 'I love you truuuuuuuu-——ly,' he began. The baroness, a warm look of anticipation on her face, her arms full of Pope Clement VII's vestments, ran after him.

As the official ambassadorial limousine of the Royal Hussid Embassy to the Fourth French Republic rolled majestically toward the opera, the First Secretary of the Royal Hussid Embassy was speaking on the telephone.

Specifically, he was speaking with Mr. Caesar Augustus Finecello of Nero's Villa.

'His Royal Highness informs me,' he said, 'that he will require rather austere accommodations. Twenty rooms to take care of his staff should be more than enough. One Cadillac limousine and eight Chevrolets for transportation should suffice, although that may change. We're flying out his personal chef today to arrange for supplies and to make sure your wine cellar is adequate for a little party His Highness plans to give.'

'You don't think you could tell me whom His Highness wishes to honour?' Little Augie asked.

'Oh, no,' the First Secretary said. 'Of course not.'

'Leave everything to me,' Little Augie said.

'There's just one more thing,' the First Secretary said.

'And what is that?'

'It is entirely possible that His Royal Highness Sheikh Omar ben Ahmed of the Sheikhdom of Abzug, with a small party of no more than fifty or sixty, will also be calling for reservations. If that should happen, we would be grateful if you could give them a floor of rooms next to ours.'

'We would be delighted,' Little Augie said.

'Then good day to you, sir,' the First Secretary said and hung up.

Little Augie was wreathed in smiles. First, a large group of Yankee businessmen, sure to provide a lot of black ink for the Acme Still and Motion Picture Photography Company, had been dumped in his lap and now one, and possibly two, groups of oil-rich Arabs were coming. He would be able to recoup that lousy $81,000 practically overnight. Everything was going to work out just fine. Eventually, of course, the boys were going to find that O'Reilly creep, no matter where he was hiding out, and get the $81,000 back.

Meanwhile, the Benjamin F. Pierce study in Spruce Harbor, Maine, was practically awash in feminine tears. Slightly soggy after the telephone call to Paris and Boris' emotional breakdown, the atmosphere had really become water-soaked after the placing of the next telephone call, to the Reverend Mother Emeritus Margaret Houlihan Wachauf Wilson, R.N., Lt. Col., U.S. Army Nurse Corps, Retired, in New Orleans, Louisiana.

Madame Kristina had long felt a deep debt of personal gratitude to Reverend Mother. During the Korean War, when Big Brother had been wounded, he had been confined to the 4077th MASH, where Reverend Mother, then Major Houlihan, had been chief nurse.

Major Houlihan and Cpl. Bob Alexander had immediately reached an understanding each of the other that had immediately taken root, sprouted and blossomed over the years. It was, like many deep and enduring friendships, based on shared misery.

So far as Major Houlihan was concerned, Cpl. Bob Alexander was just one more GI with holes in him. She felt no physical attraction to him, whatever. So far as Cpl. Bob

Alexander was concerned, Major Houlihan was just one more lousy brass-hat officer, and he felt no greater physical attraction to her than he did, for example, to Major General 'Jumping Joe' Hofritz, the division commander, who bore a startling resemblance to a chimpanzee.

But she was an officer, and some nitwit officer in basic training had told him that if he, as an enlisted man, ever had a problem he couldn't handle, he should feel free to turn to an officer as he would turn to his father. He hadn't paid much attention at the time, because he had never had a problem he couldn't handle and didn't plan to have any while in the army.

The situation was now changed. He was in a heavy steel GI hospital bed, one leg encased in a massive cast suspended from an iron framework and one hand and arm similarly immobilized.

'Major,' he said, when Nurse Houlihan came near his bed, 'may I have a word with you?'

Since with one exception, every other male in the place, from the commanding officer, Colonel Henry Blake, downward to Cpl. Radar O'Reilly and all the medical staff and patients, referred to her as 'Hot Lips', Major Houlihan realized that the wounded warrior on the bed was something special. He was a gentle soldier, much like Major Houlihan's good friend, Major Frank Burns, M.C., U.S.A.

'What's on your mind, Corporal?' she had asked.

'It is a rather delicate matter,' Boris/Bob had replied.

'Think of me as a major,' Hot Lips had said, 'not as a woman.'

Boris/Bob thought about this a moment and then made up his mind and plunged ahead.

'Look, the whole idea of this place is to restore me to duty as quickly as possible, right?'

'Right,' Major Houlihan had replied.

'And the way to do that is for me to get as much rest as possible, right?'

'Right.'

'In that case, Major, do you think you could get the

nurses to leave me alone? God, with them coming in here every hour on the hour after taps, one after the other, blowing in my ear, stroking me and I'd hate to tell you what else, I'll never get my strength back. They're all sex crazy, and it's killing me.'

Major Houlihan's first reaction, truth to tell, was one of outrage. How dare this lowly enlisted man, this corporal, suggest that her nurses, commissioned officers all, officially certified by act of Congress as ladies, were engaged in post-lights out hanky panky with him.

'You don't believe me, do you?' he asked, rather plaintively. 'I should have known better than to ask for help. No one believes me, no one has ever understood what it's like to be nothing more than a sexual object, a thing, so much flesh, with no purpose in life but to satisfy the selfish lusts of the other sex.'

To her own surprise, Major Houlihan saw her hand stretch out to touch his sweaty brow in a gesture of infinite understanding and sympathy.

'I do,' she said. 'I believe you. The same thing happens to me.'

'With the nurses?' Boris replied. 'Funny, I can usually tell when they're queer.'

'No, dummy, with the doctors,' she said. 'And the dentists. And the supply officers. All of them.'

'But you're not tied down to this goddamned bed,' Boris said. 'You can run. You can defend yourself!'

'Put your mind at rest,' Major Houlihan had said.

'My mind's not what's all worn out,' he said.

'No nurse will ever bother you again,' Major Houlihan said, fervently, 'or my name's not Hot Lips Houlihan!'

'You don't have to go quite that far, Hot Lips,' Boris said. 'Maybe you could just set up some sort of a roster.'

'How odd!' she said. 'You called me "Hot Lips" and it didn't bother me at all.'

'That's probably because we understand each other,' Bob/Boris said. 'If you don't mind me saying so, aside from my beloved baby sister, you're the nicest lady I've ever known in my life.'

Major Margaret Houlihan, chief nurse of the 4077th MASH and very probably the best operating-room nurse in the regular army, a soldier's soldier, had wept.

The exigencies of the service had shortly afterward separated them, but they had kept in touch over the years.

Boris had been unable to make it to Margaret Houlihan's first wedding. Her marriage to Mr. Isadore N. Wachauf, majority stockholder of Wachauf Metal Recycling, Ltd., International (formerly Izzy's Junk Yard), had been a mad, spur-of-the-moment thing, and there had been no time. Margaret, by then retired as a lieutenant colonel from the army, had been employed as chief nurse of the Rolling Hills Rest Home, to which Mr. Wachauf had been committed by his family. Izzy had managed to convince Miss Margaret that his family was really less concerned with his mental well-being than they were with gaining control of Wachauf Metal Recycling, Ltd.

They had eloped, one moonlit night, and Margaret had looked forward to a long and happy life as the helpmeet of Ohio's largest scrap-iron tycoon. She had no sooner written Boris a long letter telling him of her newfound happiness than tragedy struck. The power company chose to reduce the electric current at the precise moment Mr. Wachauf (who had regained control of his firm) chose to step under a twelve-ton square of pressed steel suspended beneath an electromagnet.

Boris had rushed to her side from Europe, in time for Mr. Wachauf's last rites, and had consoled her in her time of sorrow.

Several years later, he had sung at her second wedding, and five days later, proving that lightning *does* strike twice in the same place, at the funeral of her second husband, the Reverend Buck Wilson. Following the second funeral, Boris had taken the distraught widow with him to Europe, where they had sailed around the Mediterranean for a month aboard the 180-foot yacht *Desdemona*, which had been placed at their disposal by His Royal Highness Prince Hassan ad Kayam of Hussid.

Margaret Houlihan Wachauf Wilson knew full well the depth of Boris Alexandrovich Korsky-Rimsakov's devotion to his beloved sister. Hearing that she was to be married, therefore, was not only news which warmed the cockles of her heart but an opportunity, she instantly realized, for her to repay in some small measure all the kindnesses and courtesies Boris had shown her over the years.

'My dear Kristina,' she said, sobbing rather loudly, 'I would be deeply honoured to assist at your wedding, and I understand perfectly your desires to keep the affair small and intimate. I'll see you in Las Vegas a week from today.'

CHAPTER ELEVEN

The call from Spruce Harbor had reached Margaret H. W. Wilson in her study at the International Headquarters of the God Is Love in All Forms Christian Church, Inc., which body had been founded by her late husband, the Reverend Buck Wilson.

When she hung up the telephone, she dabbed at her eyes with a handkerchief, blew her nose and stepped to the bookcases which lined one wall. She pushed a button, and a section of the bookcase rolled back to reveal a large and rather well-stocked bar. She poured four inches of Courvoisier brandy into a snifter, drank it down in a gulp, refilled the glass and, after closing the bar, returned to her desk.

She pushed a button on her intercom. 'Jimmy,' she called, 'would you step in here a moment, please?'

Jimmy de Wilde was her personal secretary, a tall and willowy young man with long blond locks, rings on his fingers and bells on his Gucci loafers who immediately sort of floated into her office on a cloud of My Sin.

'Yes, Reverend Mother?' he asked. He had a slight lisp.

Jimmy had been the Reverend Wilson's personal assistant long before the reverend had met the Widow Wachauf. He had, in fact, been one of the first dozen members of the God Is Love in All Forms Christian Church, Inc., when the body had been organized in San Francisco, California. Buck Wilson, who had been employed as a male model and masseur in the City on the Bay, had, according to the official history of the church, 'while meditating in Finocchio's Restaurant in San Francisco, in the company of some friends, realized that it was his duty on this earth to found a church for those children of God whom the extant religious bodies seemed to either ignore or reject.

'The first dozen members, now known as the Founding Disciples, included a fine artist, two hairdressers, a writer, two ballet dancers, a male model, an interior decorator, an antique dealer and the quarterback and two defensive tackles of the San Francisco Gladiators professional football team.

'A year after its founding, the mother church was moved from San Francisco to New Orleans, whence the Reverend Wilson had been directed by the belief that a great need for the church existed in the Crescent City.'

Although modesty kept him from saying so in the official history, which he had edited, the move to New Orleans had been financed by Jimmy de Wilde. He had just changed his name from Oscar Dunlop, Jr., and felt that a whole new blank page, so to speak, was in order.

The God Is Love in All Forms Christian Church, Inc., prospered in New Orleans, despite a number of problems. There were some purists, so to speak, who violently objected to the admission of females, but Brother Buck, as he was fondly called, had insisted that the church be open to all who embraced its principles.

The greatest challenge the church faced, of course, was the announcement of Reverend Wilson's engagement to Margaret Houlihan Wachauf, R.N., whom he had met while the lady was recuperating in New Orleans from her labours in Brazil, where she had been chief nurse of the Green Inferno Christian Medical Missionary Hospital ('Gic-Miss-Em', as it was popularly known).

Two of the founding Disciples had resigned in protest, after publishing an advertisement in the New Orleans *Picaroon-Statesman* which accused the Reverend Wilson of betraying everything the God Is Love in All Forms Christian Church stood for.

Ten of the founding Disciples, led by Jimmy de Wilde, stood fast, however. They published their own advertisement in the *Picaroon-Statesman*, formally expelling the two dissident Founding Disciples. They were guilty, the 'Loyalists' said, of the sin of pride.

That furor had barely subsided by wedding time. Boris Alexandrovich Korsky-Rimsakov, longtime friend of the bride, had flown in to sing at the wedding. It was the consensus of the remaining Founding Disciples that a woman who had a friend like that magnificent animal, a platonic friend, couldn't be all bad.

And then tragedy struck. The Reverend Wilson was called to the Last Roll Call up Yonder on the very night of his wedding. Again, the Founding Disciples were split, this time right down the middle. Five of them flatly refused to believe the coroner's verdict that the Reverend Wilson had succumbed to heart failure brought on by overexertion. They charged witchcraft, and there was a good deal of talk, some of it rather hysterical, about burning the Widow Wilson at the stake.

Jimmy de Wilde, however, saw something entirely different in the Reverend Wilson's sudden summons, as he put it, 'upstairs.' 'Brother Buck,' he said, in an impassioned address to the congregation, 'was always talking about that part of our title which says "in all forms." Those of us who knew him well . . . and I don't think that any of *you* can say you *knew* him as well as *I* . . . know what a personal sacrifice it must have been for him to marry a woman. Think about it! Buck made that sacrifice for us! I don't *pretend* to understand *why*, but it is quite clear that Brother Buck felt the church needed a woman's touch!'

That very night, a somewhat weepy delegation called upon the Widow Wilson to offer her, indeed to beg her to accept, the newly created position of Reverend Mother Emeritus to her late husband's flock.

And so it came to pass that Reverend Mother Margaret Houlihan Wachauf Wilson, R.N. (Lt. Col. U.S. Army, Retired), presided over the internment of her husband, the Blessed Reverend Buck Wilson. Working through the night, two devoted labourers in the vineyards of the Lord (who, in secular life were *haut fashion* designers) came up with suitable vestments. These consisted of an ankle length purple cassock; a chartreuse cape lined in pink, on the back of which was embroidered in gold thread the words 'Reverend' (vertically) and 'Mother' and 'Emeritus' (horizontally), so that they formed a cross.

One of the more practical Founding Disciples (in secular life an antique dealer), on hearing that Boris Alexandrovich Korsky-Rimsakov was going to sing at the funeral services, arranged for the printing and sale of tickets to the last rites. Sufficient revenue was procured from music lovers (some of whom even flew in from Europe to hear the Maestro sing 'We Will Gather at the River', 'When the Roll Is Called up Yonder' and 'Auld Lang Syne') to not only pay for a twenty-three-foot marble statue of the late Blessed Brother Wilson (pictured as Saint George slaying the dragon[1]) but for the Canberra marble tomb above which the statue was placed as well.

A defrocked Episcopal priest was engaged for the sermonizing, and the administration of the God Is Love in All Forms Christian Church, Inc., assumed by Reverend Mother Emeritus Wilson. Ably abetted by Jimmy de Wilde, Reverend Mother's administration saw the church experience a rather phenomenal growth. Missionary churches were established in Los Angeles, California; Chicago, Illinois; New York City; and elsewhere. The God Is Love in

---

[1] Officials of the God Is Love in All Forms Christian Church, Inc., refuse to discuss the rumour that a dissident founding Disciple arranged for the dragon's face to resemble that of Reverend Mother Wilson. It is known, however, that 'extra work' was performed on the statue some time after its erection.

All Forms Christian Church, Inc., a cappella male choir (which was not, as rumour had it, a twentieth-century reincarnation of the famous Vatican castrati choirs, even though it was an all-soprano choral group) appeared on national television.

'Jimmy,' Reverend Mother said to Brother de Wilde, 'I have just learned that two old friends of mine are to marry.'

'Well, each to his own thing, as I always say,' Jimmy replied. 'What has that to do with us?'

'You know as well as I do, Jerry,' Reverend Mother said, 'how much the church owes Boris Alexandrovich Korsky-Rimsakov.'

'You don't mean to tell *that* thimply magnificent *animal* has been snared?'

'His sister is getting married,' Reverend Mother said.

'You had me frightened there for a moment,' Jimmy said.

'You know how Boris has been a pillar of strength to me in my time of sorrow,' Reverend Mother said.

'So?'

'And you know how much money we make every year when he sings at the annual memorial services for my late husband.'

'There you have a point,' Jimmy de Wilde said. 'What does he want from us?'

'He hasn't asked for a thing,' Reverend Mother said. 'But I was thinking that it would be a nice surprise if the choir were to sing at the wedding.'

'At a *wedding?*' Jimmy de Wilde replied.

'At a wedding,' Reverend Mother said, firmly.

'Well, I suppose we do owe him *something*,' Jimmy de Wilde said. 'And the choir does so *love* to wear its *robes*.'

'Just the robes, Jimmy. Nothing else. No wigs. No make-up.'

'Have you thought about how we'd pay for it?' he asked. 'We have to be practical, you know. Where is it to be held, anyway?'

'In Las Vegas,' Reverend Mother said. 'You've been

talking about our opening a mission there. This would be good advertising.'

'Yes, it would,' Jimmy, who was, if nothing else, quite practical said. 'I don't suppose that you could talk that horrid de la Chevaux person out of one of his airplanes, do you?'

'Horsey de la Chevaux is a good man, Jimmy,' Reverend Mother said. 'Just because he forgets himself sometimes and says unkind things . . .'

'He called me "a lisping pansy", that's what he did,' Jimmy said. 'How can I forgive that?'

'You had no legitimate reason to pass yourself off as a new masseur in the steam bath of the Bayou Perdu Council, Knights of Columbus, Athletic Club,' Reverend Mother said, 'and you know it, Jimmy.'

'Nothing ventured, nothing gained,' Jimmy de Wilde replied. 'Let me put it to you this way, Reverend Mother. If you can get us transportation out there, I think we can swing it.'

'I don't want you to swing it, Jimmy,' Reverend Mother said. 'All I want you to do is go out there and sing.'

'I don't suppose that we could sell tickets?' Jimmy said. 'We could turn a profit that way.'

'No tickets,' Reverend Mother said.

'Well, speak to that terrible man, and let me know what he says about the airplane,' Jimmy said. He floated back out of the room. Reverend Mother drank the Courvoisier and then reached for the telephone.

'Chevaux Petroleum Corporation International,' the operator said answering the phone.

'Reverend Mother Margaret H. W. Wilson for Colonel Jean-Pierre de la Chevaux,' she said.

'I'm so sorry, Reverend Mother,' the operator said, 'Colonel de la Chevaux is in Morocco.'

'In that case, could you put me through to Communications?' Reverend Mother asked. 'Perhaps I can talk to him on the radio.'

'One moment, please,' the operator said. There was a buzzing sound.

'Communications Division,' a male voice said.

'This is the operator at Corporate Headquarters in New Orleans,' the operator said. 'How's things at the North Pole?'

'Little chilly,' the man said. 'What can I do for you?'

'I have the Reverend Mother Margaret H. W. Wilson on the line,' the operator said. 'She's on the VIP list. Can you reach Colonel Chevaux for her by radio?'

'I think so,' he said, after a moment's thought. 'I'll have to route it via the satellite and Tierra del Fuego, but I think we can get through. Hold on.' There was a pause and then the sound of static as he spoke. 'Chevaux Tierra del Fuego, this is Chevaux North Pole.'

'Go ahead, Chevaux North Pole,' a Spanish-accented voice replied.

'Tierra del Fuego, I've got International Corporate Headquarters in New Orleans on the Land Line. The Reverend Mother Margaret H. W. Wilson, who is on the VIP list, wants to get through to Colonel de la Chevaux. Can you reach him?'

'Stand by, Chevaux North Pole,' the man with the Spanish accent said. 'Chevaux Tierra del Fuego calling Chevaux Mobile One. Chevaux North Pole calling Chevaux Mobile One.'

'Ah, Roger, North Pole,' a voice with a Texas twang replied. 'Mobile One reads you loud and clear. How's things on the tip of South America?'

'A little muggy, but all right,' Chevaux Tierra del Fuego replied. 'Say, Mobile One, I got North Pole, bouncing off the satellite. They've got New Orleans on the Land Line. New Orleans has got a VIP, Reverend Mother Margaret H. W. Wilson, on the telephone. She wants to talk to Colonel de la Chevaux. Is he anywhere handy?'

'No problem,' Chevaux Mobile One said. 'I'll connect you.'

There was the sound of a telephone ringing and then another male voice.

'Annex One, Bayou Perdu Council, Knights of Columbus, Joe the Bartender speaking.'

'Joe, this is Al, in Communications. I got Tierra del Fuego on the horn. They've got the North Pole via the satellite on the horn. The North Pole's got New Orleans International Corporate Headquarters on the Land Line. New Orleans has got the Reverend Mother Margaret H. W. Wilson on the line. She wants to talk to the colonel.'

'Sure thing,' the bartender replied. 'Hey, Horsey!' he called. 'Hot Lips on the horn for you!'

It was the second time in just a few minutes that Colonel Jean-Pierre de la Chevaux (Louisiana National Guard) had been summoned to the telephone. The first call had been from Paris, routed via Chevaux Petroleum de France, S.A., and the Franco-Moroccan Oil Company to Annex No. 1, Bayou Perdu Council, Knights of Columbus, which was at the moment in the Kingdom of Abzug, in the Atlas Mountains south of Morocco.

The colonel, who had been playing pinochle, laid down his cards and walked to the telephone.

'Hey, Mam'selle Hot Lips,' he called, 'I was just gonna call you. Guess what I just heard?'

'Me first, Horsey,' Hot Lips said. 'I just spoke with Kristina on the phone. Guess what?'

'Radar finally got up his nerve and asked her to marry him,' Horsey promptly replied. 'I just a few minutes ago talked to Boris in Paris.'

'I was hoping to surprise you,' Hot Lips said, somewhat disappointed.

'You better act surprised when Boris calls you,' Horsey said. 'He said he was gonna call between the first and the second acts, if there was enough time for calling after he exercised.'

'Horsey, I need a favour,' Hot Lips said.

'Mam'selle Hot Lips, anyting dat Horsey de la Chevaux's got, you can have.'

'Thank you, Horsey,' Hot Lips said. 'You're always so generous.'

'Where you're concerned, I can't do enough,' he said.

'I want to go to the wedding, Horsey,' she said. 'Kristina wants me to assist the Archbishop of Swengchan, His Eminence John Patrick Mulcahy.'

'I'm sending a plane to Rome for Dago Red,' Horsey said. 'Tell you what I'll do, I'll have the pilot stop by New Orleans and pick you up. How's that?'

'That's very generous of you, Horsey,' she said. 'Thank you very much. Do you think there would be room on the plane for some others?'

'Why not? I'm sending a seven-forty-seven. I wouldn't want to insult Dago Red by sending a little plane, like a DC-10 for him.'

'Oh, thank you, Horsey,' she said.

'Wait a minute, Mam'selle Hot Lips,' Horsey said, suddenly. 'You should forgive my asking but you ain't thinking of bringing any of your fair . . .'

'The God Is Love in All Forms Christian Church, Inc., a cappella male choir is going to sing at the wedding,' Hot Lips said quickly.

'Mam'selle Hot lips,' Horsey, distinctly uncomfortable, said, 'you know how the boys feel about your fairies.'

'We in the God Is Love in All Forms Christian Church, Inc., don't use that horrible word, Horsey,' Hot Lips said. 'I've told you that.'

'Excuse me,' he said. 'It's a bad habit.'

Colonel de la Chevaux was indebted to few people. He felt a profound debt to His Eminence Archbishop Mulcahy. He was as profoundly indebted to Drs. Benjamin Franklin Pierce and John Francis Xavier McIntyre, the former Nurse Margaret Houlihan, and former corporals J. Robespierre O'Reilly and Bob Alexander (a/k/a Boris Alexandrovich Korsky-Rimsakov).

During the late Korean unpleasantness, Colonel[2] de la Chevaux, then a sergeant in the 223rd Infantry, had been

---

[2]Colonel de la Chevaux was commissioned into the Louisiana National Guard in that rank shortly after it was confirmed that the largest field of natural gas ever discovered had been found under the Chevaux property on Bayou Perdu, Louisiana. After at first modestly rejecting the offer by the governor, Colonel Chevaux accepted the commission after learning it entitled him to affix flashing blue lights and a police whoop-whoop-whoop on his personal automobile(s).

grievously wounded leading his patrol up Heartbreak Ridge. Cpl. Bob Alexander had carried him off the hill, suffering serious wounds of his own while doing so. Drs. McIntyre and Pierce, plus Nurse Houlihan, had saved Sergeant de la Chevaux's leg and his life in the surgical tent of the 4077th MASH, with the indispensable assistance – all concerned agreed – of what was then known as the Dago Red Supercharged Prayer Machine. Dago Red was the affectionate nickname given to then Chaplain John Patrick Mulcahy, Captain, Chaplains' Corps, U.S. Army. During all the time he had spent in the hospital, Radar O'Reilly had constantly been at his side, rendering moral support and keeping his spirits up with certain stolen potables: Drs. McIntyre and Pierce had unknowingly provided gin; Nurse Houlihan unwittingly had given bourbon; and the chaplain, who was to become a high-ranking prelate of the church, had unknowingly been dispensing well-watered sacrificial wine during his services. As Horsey de la Chevaux later put it, his voice breaking, 'Greater love hath no man than a guy who would steal a chaplain's sacramental wine to give his buddy a little jolt.'

Horsey de la Chevaux, quite literally, would have given the shirt off his back (or the entire assets of what had become Chevaux Petroleum Corporation, International) to any of these people. And here Reverend Mother Hot Lips was putting him between the frying pan and the fire.

She wanted to take her sissy choir to sing at the wedding of Boris' baby sister and Radar O'Reilly. That posed large problems. Neither Horsey nor Boris had any innate dislike for Hot Lips' exquisitely graceful and flowery smelling parishioners. (Boris, in fact, had often commented that he felt personally responsible for many of them: 'With so many women interested in me and me alone, something like that is bound to happen.')

Horsey's own reaction to them was along the same lines. If there were three ladies and three men, two of whom were *that way*, it was clear that therefore there would be three ladies for one man, and for the other man who was not *that way*, it was abundant harvest time.

Unfortunately, however, most of the members of the Bayou Perdu Council, Knights of Columbus, Marching Band and Drill Team were not so understanding or philosophical about the members of the God Is Love in All Forms Christian Church, Inc., male choir. The best Horsey could hope for was that the marching band would, as they had at the funeral ceremony for the Blessed Reverend Wilson, lapse into uncontrollable hysterics when the choir began to sing. The worst that could happen was a prospect Horsey didn't like to consider. He remembered the trouble it had caused when one of Hot Lips' flock had made a certain proposal to François Mulligan. François had washed his mouth out by repeatedly dipping him into the Mississippi River at the end of a 100-foot cable suspended beneath a Chevaux helicopter.

'Yes, it is,' Reverend Mother said, 'and I would consider it a personal favour if you wouldn't use that ugly word to describe my fair . . . my flock,' she said.

'There's going to be trouble,' Horsey said, 'if you insist on taking them out there.'

'I can't imagine why,' she said. 'The only problem would come from that collection of gorillas of yours, and the newspaper said that they were in Kyoto, Japan, marching in the Annual Parade of the Sacred Tulips.'

'I just sent a plane for them,' Horsey said.

'Oh, no!'

'Boris said that he agreed that it really wouldn't be a wedding without the band,' Horsey said. 'When Radar and Kristina come down the aisle, the marching band's going to play.'

'They are?' Hot Lips asked. The prospect was, well, intriguing. The Bayou Perdu Council, K of C, Marching Band consisted of three French horns, a tuba, six bass drums, three ukeleles, two Jew's harps, a washboard in a wash bucket and a glockenspiel.

'Yeah,' Horsey said, with pride, 'it's already in their rep-pet-whore-ey.'

'That's repertoire,' Reverend Mother corrected him, then: 'What is?'

'"There'll Be a Hot Time in the Old Town Tonight",' Horsey said, with quiet pride.

'How about Mendelssohn's Wedding March?'

'Not enough beat,' Horsey said. 'We talked about that.'

'You're simply going to have to control your men,' Hot Lips said.

'Excuse me, Mam'selle Hot Lips,' Horsey said, 'but none of my boys go around sneaking into other people's steam baths.'

'I'll have a firm word with my boys,' Hot Lips replied, 'if you do the same thing with yours.'

'I'll go you one better,' Horsey said. 'I'll have Dago Red say something to them. They'll listen to him, if they don't listen to anyone else.'

'Good-bye then, Horsey,' Hot Lips said. 'And thank you. I'll see you in Las Vegas.'

'Keep your fingers crossed, Hot Lips,' Horsey said and broke the connection. When Al, in Communications, came on the line, he said, 'Al, get me Archbishop John Patrick Mulcahy in the Vatican.'

CHAPTER TWELVE

There came a great knock at the door of the modest apartment near St. Peter's Church which the church had provided for His Eminence John Patrick Mulcahy, Titular Archbishop of Swengchan, China.

Thinking it was his secretary, Monsignor Pancho de Malaga y de Villa, the archbishop called out, 'Come on in, Pancho, I'm nearly packed.' He was in the act of packing a small black suitcase. When he heard the door open and then close again, he added, 'Be a good guy and bring me a beer, will you? There's a couple of bottles in the refrigerator.'

'I'm afraid,' a gentle voice said in Latin, 'that I don't know where your refrigerator is, John.'

The archbishop, who was normally rather unflappable, stiffened in visible shock. There was only one man in the world with a gentle voice like that. He spun around, his mouth open, and started to drop to his knees. 'Forgive me, Your Holi. . . .'

'I am here unofficially,' the small man in the white vestments said. 'As a friend of long standing, to wish you well on your journey, John.'

The Archbishop of Swengchan was speechless.

'You did say that your refrigerator had a *couple* of bottles of beer?' the small man in the white vestments said. 'Perhaps you would be good enough to share one with me?'

The archbishop stared at him. 'Your Hol . . .'

'I am here, John, as nothing more than a fellow priest . . . or at least a fellow bishop, so perhaps it would be best if you just called me "Father".'

'Yes, Father,' the archbishop said.

'I really would like a beer,' he said.

'Two beers coming right up, Father,' the archbishop said and rushed out to the kitchen.

'Don't bother with a glass,' he called after him. 'I always think it tastes better fresh from the bottle.'

When the beer had been delivered, the small man said, 'I believe the proper American expression is "Mud in Your Ear"?'

'Mud in your eye, actually,' Archbishop Mulcahy said.

'How interesting,' the small man said. 'I don't believe I've ever seen this kind of beer before, Father? American, isn't it?'

'I have a friend, Father,' Mulcahy, having partially gotten over his shock, said. 'I mentioned one time that I really missed American beer, and ever since then he has a couple of cases of Fenstermacher's Finest Old Creole Pale Pilsner flown over from New Orleans every week.'

'That would be Jean-Pierre de la Chevaux?' the small man asked.

'Yes, Father, it would.'

'The same man whose airplane sits at the airfield waiting to fly you to Nevada?'

'Yes, Father, the same man. He's a good, Catholic man.'

'So the Archbishop of New Orleans informs me. A good Catholic man. A little out of the ordinary, perhaps, but a good man. The archbishop tells me that he gave the archdiocese a two-hundred-bed hospital.'

'That's true, Father, he did,' Mulcahy said. 'Horsey is very generous.'

'And also that he is a bit overfond of the grape.'

'I'm afraid that's also true, Father,' Mulcahy admitted.

'I don't believe a word of it, of course,' the small man said, 'but there's a nasty little story circulating amongst the College of Cardinals that one of our most respected archbishops was at one time known as "Dago Red", a sobriquet which apparently makes reference to his fondness for wine.'

'I must confess, Father,' Mulcahy said, 'that isn't a nasty story. It's true. It's me of whom they speak.'

'You don't say?'

'I was a chaplain at the time, Father,' Mulcahy said. 'In Korea. I made a gross error in judgment.'

'And what was that?'

'I made the mistake of having what I thought was going to be a sociable drink with two doctors.'

'There's certainly nothing wrong with having a social drink with two practitioners of the healing arts.'

'May I respectfully suggest, Father, that you don't know the two doctors involved?'

'Only by reputation,' the small man said.

'Excuse me?'

'The Archbishop of New Orleans tells me that in the opinion of Reverend Mother Superior Bernadette of Lourdes, chief of staff of the Gates of Heaven Hospital ... the one Mr. de la Chevaux gave to the Archdiocese ... your life was saved by the skill of two distinguished surgeons she referred to as Doctor Hawkeye and Doctor Trapper John. I presume it would be the same two doctors, especially as

Reverend Mother reported that it was the first time she had ever heard anyone refer to a prelate of the church as Dago Red.'

'Yes, Father. It was they. Them.'

'That's the trouble with you Americans,' the little man said. 'You're all so busy with your bingo games and football that you don't learn your Latin.'

'Yes, Father, you're quite right. Of course. I'll work on it.'

'Enough of this beating around the bush, John,' the small man said, draining his beer. 'Right to the bottom line, I always say. The real reason I'm here is that some very disturbing rumours have reached my ears. Granting you . . . mentioning no names, of course . . . that some of the guys in the College are worse than a bunch of old women, the way they gossip, I still thought it would be wise to have a word with you. On the QT, of course.'

'Whatever you say, Your Holi . . .'

'Now, I've told you about that twice. How many times do I have to tell you?'

'Sorry, Father.'

'O.K.,' the small man said. 'First, I want to hear about this Reverend Mother Hot Lips. I gather she is not one of ours?'

'No, Father,' Mulcahy said, 'she is not one of ours. I must say, however, that I have known her for years, that she served long and well as a nurse in the army and is basically a very good person.'

'I notice you sort of skipped over her morals,' the small man said.

'Well, I'll say this,' Mulcahy said, flushing with embarrassment, 'that while I know very little, personally, about her personal life, I know that she is a friend of both His Eminence the Archbishop of New Orleans and of Reverend Mother Superior Bernadette of Lourdes. As a matter of fact, the Gates of Heaven Hospital gets most of its nurses from a nursing school that Hot Lips . . . Reverend Mother Margaret, that is . . . operates.'

'The rumour going around is that you and this lady are going to share the honours at some pagan marriage rite in a gambling den. Is there any truth to that?'

'No, sir,' Mulcahy said, righteously. 'I am going to perform the wedding. It will be the realization of a promise I made to the bridegroom in Korea.'

'She's a Catholic, then?'

'No. The bride is an Eastern Orthodox Catholic . . . she's of Russian extraction. I have the necessary permission from the Russian Orthodox Primate.'

'And how is Vasily these days?' the small man asked. 'Long time no see.'

'He asked, when I had lunch with him today, should I have the honour of seeing you, Father, that I pass on his best regards.'

'Is he still drinking that awful vodka straight?'

'I'm afraid so Father,' Mulcahy said.

'Let's get back to this wedding,' the small man said. 'She's Russian Orthodox. What's the bridegroom?'

'As a matter of fact, Father,' Mulcahy said, 'at the moment, he says he's an Existentialist Buddhist.'

'There's such a thing as carrying this ecumenical business too far, John,' the small man said. 'You know how I feel about that.'

'I feel, Father, that his backsliding . . . he was raised as a good Roman boy . . . is temporary, and that soon after he falls under the influence of this good woman, we will see him back in the fold.'

'Well, let's hope so. You say she's a good woman?'

'A fine woman,' Mulcahy said. 'I know none finer.'

'Then what's she doing marrying this self-professed heathen?' the small man asked, and then without waiting for a reply said, 'I don't suppose you've got another bottle of this? It's pretty good.'

'Yes, of course,' Mulcahy said. 'And I'll have a couple of cases sent over to the papal apartments. God knows, I've got more than I can use. Horsey is generous to a fault.'

'If you're sure you've got enough to spare . . .' the small man said and then waited until Mulcahy had returned with two more beers. 'Mud in your eye,' he said. 'Got it right that time, didn't I? What does it mean?'

'I'm afraid I have no idea,' Mulcahy said.

'So tell me why this good woman wants to marry this heathen?'

'For many reasons, I'm sure,' Mulcahy said. 'Among them a desire to see him return to the church.'

'O.K.,' the small man said. 'It's your ball game, John. I mean, if I can't trust the good judgment of an archbishop, who should I trust?'

'Thank you, sir,' the archbishop said. 'I'll try to justify your confidence in me.'

'And now I'll have to be running along,' the small man said. 'I didn't tell anyone where I was going.'

'Finish your beer,' Archbishop Mulcahy said.

'I really shouldn't,' the small man said, 'but why not? All work and no play, as I always say.'

'Even He rested on the seventh day,' Mulcahy said.

'That's what I keep telling the guys in the College,' the small man said. 'I mean, what better precedent is there? But do you think they listen to me? The way they act when I try to get a couple of hours for myself! Just between you and me, John, some of these guys won't blow their noses unless they check first with me.'

'Well, I suppose, under the circumstances,' Archbishop Mulcahy said, loyally, 'that's understandable.'

'Understandable, maybe,' the small man said. 'But I'll tell you, after a while, it gets under your skin. Before I took this job, John, I didn't realize how good I had it. Before, if I wanted to go out for a plate of spaghetti and a glass of wine, I went out and got a plate of spaghetti and a glass of wine. Now! Well, you've been around the Vatican, you've seen how things go.'

'Yes, sir,' Mulcahy said. 'I think I understand your problem.'

'It's not like it was when I was a parish priest,' the small man went on. 'Then I had some time for myself. I don't mind telling you, John, I miss those days.'

'I miss them myself,' Mulcahy said.

'What have you got to complain about?' the small man asked. 'You've got a refrigerator loaded with beer. You want a beer, you drink a beer. I want a beer, they spend two weeks in the College of Cardinals deciding what kind of beer, what kind of glass and how cold it should be.'

'I understand,' Mulcahy said, sympathetically.

The door burst open and the Rev. Monsignor Pancho de Malaga y de Villa, the Archbishop of Swengchan's personal secretary, walked into the room.

'Sorry, your Eminence,' he said. 'I didn't know you had a visitor.' Then he recognized the small man in the white vestments. 'Ooooops!'

The small man raised his hand. 'Do me a favour,' he said. 'You didn't see anything, capish? Somebody asks you, don't lie. But don't go volunteering anything. You understand me? Just think of me as a common, ordinary bishop having a glass of beer with an old friend.'

'Yes, Your Holi . . .'

'I told him, now I'm telling you: you can call me "Father".'

'Yes, Father,' Monsignor de Malaga y de Villa said.

'But speaking as a bishop to a monsignor,' the small man said, 'I want you to keep an eye on the archbishop here. From what I hear, he's going to have his hands full in the next week.'

'I'll do my very best.'

'You run into anything you can't handle, get on the horn,' the small man said. 'It's not like the old days, of course, but I still have some influence. There's a couple of Jesuits in New Mexico who owe me. I'll give you a number to call. And say what you like about the Jesuits, they're good people to have in your corner in a bind.'

'I'll remember that, sir,' the Monsignor said.

'And when you get back, you got an extra couple of minutes, send me a couple of cases of this beer. I'm telling you, Monsignor, because an archbishop's got more important things to do.'

'I understand, sir,' the Monsignor said.

'Have a nice trip,' the small man said, as he walked to the door. 'You got an extra minute sometime, send me a postcard.' He turned around at the door itself. 'And, John, don't forget what I said. There's such a thing as carrying this ecumenical business too far.'

Ten minutes later, the Archbishop of Swengchan and his secretary, the Very Reverend Pancho de Malaga y de Villa, left the archbishop's apartment by car for Rome's airport. The car was a Fiat 500, a tiny little two-seater called the 'Toppolino', or 'Little Mouse'. His Eminence was expected both by airport authorities and by the eleven-man crew of Chevaux Petroleum Number Seven, a Boeing 747. The tiny Fiat was waved through the gate in the fence by saluting customs officers, and when the Monsignor stopped by the left landing gear of the aircraft, the crew was called to attention and, on order, saluted.

'Hiya, fellas,' His Eminence said. 'I hope I haven't kept you waiting?'

'Fall out!' the aircraft commander barked (he had spent thirty years in the United States Air Force and his claim to the title 'Colonel' was somewhat stronger than that of Colonel Jean-Pierre de la Chevaux). Six members of the crew walked to the Fiat, got a good grip on the bumpers, heaved on command and, carrying the car between them, trotted up the loading stairs and inside.

'How are you, Padre?' the aircraft commander asked, shaking His Eminence's hand. The first officer and the chief flight engineer walked up to His Eminence and the Monsignor. Each carried a yellow and purple zipper-front nylon jacket. Archbishop Mulcahy removed his clerical black suit jacket and shrugged into the flight jacket. On the rear of the jacket, above the legend CAJUN AIR FORCE, was additional lettering reading OFFICIAL CHAPLAIN and on the right breast were the words DAGO RED embroidered above a set of wings.

'I see you remembered the Monsignor,' the Archbishop said. 'Thank you, Colonel.'

'Any friend of yours, Padre,' the colonel said and took the second jacket from the chief flight engineer, 'is a friend of ours.' He extended the jacket to the Monsignor. The legend OFFICIAL CHAPLAIN'S ASSISTANT had been embroidered on the back. On the breast, for lack of space, Monsignor Pancho de Malaga y de Villa's embroidered name had been shortened to fit. It now read PANCHO VILLA.

'Welcome to the Cajun Air Force,' the colonel said, solemnly.

'You're very kind,' the Monsignor said, putting on his jacket. He did not, truth to tell, look entirely comfortable.

'O.K. you feather-merchants,' His Eminence said, 'enough of this horsing around. Let's get this show on the road!' He raised his right hand above his head, in a gesture not unlike that frequently made by that segment of youth known as 'Jesus Freaks', that is, with the index finger extended. But in this case, the finger was not rigid and immobile; now it described a circle.

Three stories up, the assistant flight engineer, his head sticking out the window, shouted 'Contact!' There was a whining rumble as one by one the engines started.

The official chaplain of the Cajun Air Force ran nimbly up a ladder and made his way to the cockpit.

'You want to drive, Padre?' the aircraft commander asked.

'I'm a little out of practice,' His Eminence said. 'You get it off the ground, and then I'll steer awhile.'

'Whatever you say, Padre,' the aircraft commander said. He got in the pilot's seat, strapped himself in and turned to see that the Archbishop of Swengchan was securely installed in the flight engineer's seat, with his earphones in place. Then he picked up his microphone.

'Rome Departure Control, Chevaux Petroleum Number Seven for taxi and takeoff.'

'Rome Departure Control clears Chevaux Petroleum to the threshold of the active for takeoff. You are number two to go, behind a Pan American 707 now taking off. You are cleared to 30,000 feet, direct Victor Seven to New Orleans, report over Gibraltar. Arrivederci, Roma!'

As the enormous airplane rumbled to the takeoff runway, there was what is known in the flying game as inter-aircraft chatter:

'Aircraft commander, Chaplain.'

'Go ahead, Padre.'

'That came through a little garbled. Did I understand New Orleans?'

'Ah, Roger, that's affirmative. We have a passenger pickup in New Orleans.' There was a slight popping noise as the pilot switched from Intercom to Transmit. 'Rome, Chevaux Seven on the threshold of the active.'

'Chevaux Seven is number one to take off,' the control tower instantly replied.

The roar of the engines increased as the plane began to roll.

'Chevaux Seven rolling,' the pilot said. 'Thank you, Rome, and ciao, baby!'

His Eminence John Patrick Mulcahy, titular archbishop of Swengchan, waited patiently until the 747 was airborne, until it had taken a heading which would carry it over Gibraltar, until they passed 15,000 feet and until the aircraft commander had turned over the controls to the first officer. Then he pushed his microphone switch.

'Chaplain again, aircraft commander.'

'Go ahead, Padre.'

'Who's the New Orleans passenger?'

'Aircraft commander to Chaplain. That's passengers, plural.'

'I thought Horsey and the boys were in Morocco?'

'That's affirmative,' the aircraft commander said. 'We're picking up Reverend Mother.'

'How nice.'

'And the God Is Love in All Forms Christian Church, Inc., a capella choir,' the aircraft commander added, his reluctance audible in his voice.

'Oh, my!' the official chaplain of the Cajun Air Force said.

'They're going to sing at the wedding.'

'Oh, my!' the official chaplain repeated. There was a pause, then he went on: 'Chaplain to crew. Let us pray.'

CHAPTER THIRTEEN

Fritz W. Fenstermacher, chairman of the board and chief executive officer of Fenstermacher Breweries, Inc., Milwaukee, San Francisco, New York and eighteen other places around the world daily, faced a painful experience, which he usually faced after taking aboard a quart or two of his own product to dull the pain.

It was obviously his duty as the senior executive of his firm to watch the boob tube as very expensive, and rather well done, advertisements for his beer were televised. As a matter of fact, he really enjoyed watching his commercials and took pride in them. They promised the potential customer nothing more than a tasty and wholesome product to drink. There was no suggestion, subtle or otherwise, that those who drank Fenstermacher beer would grow rich, travel to exotic places around the world, get a good-looking blond, keep their hair or save their teeth. All Fenstermacher advertised was a cold beer on a hot day.

Fenstermacher could have, in fact, spent his days happily watching his commercials showing happy people drinking what he thought of as his happy beer. The problem, and the pain, came because he had been convinced, by people whose judgment he respected, that it was simply good business to advertise twice (two sixty-minute commercials) on each nightly 'ABN Evening news Starring Don Rhotten.' His commercial message would thereby reach an average of 11,049,211 potential beer drinkers.

But Don Rhotten, unfortunately, came with the 'ABN

Evening News Starring Don Rhotten.' Fritz W. Fenstermacher loathed and despised Don Rhotten and quite literally could stand neither the sight of his boyish curls and glistening teeth nor the dulcet tones of his voice. For years, it had been necessary for Mr. Fenstermacher to watch the ABN evening news with, alternately, his fingers in his ears and his hands over his eyes to shut out the sight and sound of Don Rhotten between Fenstermacher Breweries commercials.

And for the last eight months, it had been even a worse experience. For the past eight months, every time he saw Rhotten's beaming visage or heard his inimitable voice, Fritz W. Fenstermacher was reminded that his baby girl, his one and only child, his darling Monica, was actually employed by that grinning cretin.

It was enough to drive a lesser man up the wall and while Fritz W. Fenstermacher never went, so to speak, over the brink, he frequently teetered precariously on the edge. Those close to him in the corporate heirarchy had learned, sometimes painfully, that those who approached Fritz W. Fenstermacher an hour before, or two hours after, the ABN evening news did so at their great professional and personal peril.

And so it was with great timidity and trepidation that Miss Letitia J. Kugelblohm, Fritz W. Fenstermacher's longtime (25 years) personal secretary, entered his office ninety seconds after Don Rhotten's face had faded from the boob tube. She found her employer (and, in truth, her very, very good friend) sitting at his enormous desk, his enormous hand clutching an enormous, untouched mug of Fenstermacher's Finest Old Pilsner. Tears ran down his somewhat florid cheeks.

It was a good thirty seconds before he acknowledged her presence. He took his hand from the enormous mug of Fenstermacher's Finest Old Pilsner and rubbed the tears from his cheeks with the back of it.

'Letitia,' he said, 'I don't care what it is, it'll have to wait.'

'Mr. Fenstermacher ... Fritz ...' Miss Letitia said, compassion in every syllable, 'you know I wouldn't bother you at this time of day unless it was important ...'

'I have failed, Letitia,' Fritz said, 'as a father and a man.'

Miss Letitia threw her shorthand notebook onto the large coffee table with which the office was equipped and went to her employer. He looked up at her.

'What the hell are you doing?' he asked, just before Miss Letitia clutched him to her somewhat less than generous bosom.

'Fritzie,' she said, 'I just can't stand to see you cry!'

'I did my best, Letitia,' Fritz said. 'You know that! I tried to be both father and mother to that child.'

'I know you did, Fritzie,' she said, running her somewhat bony fingers through his sparse, practically invisible hair. 'No one could have done more than you did, after Mrs. Fenstermacher, God rest her soul, passed over.'

'Where did I go wrong, Letitia?' Fritz asked. 'What else could I have done?'

'These things happen, Fritzie,' she said. 'Things could be worse.'

'How could they possibly be worse?'

'She just works for him,' Letitia said. 'She could be, you know, emotionally involved with him.'

'My God!' he said, horrified. '*That* never entered my mind!'

Letitia Kugelblohm said nothing. She hadn't intended to say what she had said; it had just slipped out. She hoped it would pass. It did not. He pulled his head away from her bosom, stood up, grasped her by the arms and looked into her face. It wasn't that he didn't know his own strength, it was simply that he stood six-feet-three and weighed 230 pounds, and Letitia stood five-two and weighed 103 in her wellies. In order for Fritz to look into Letitia's face, it was necessary to hold her about a foot off the floor, which he was now doing.

'Letitia!' he said. 'Do you know something that I don't know?'

She didn't answer him at first.

'Letitia, answer me!' Fritz said.

'It's probably nothing,' she said.

'*What's* probably nothing?'

'Fritzie,' she said, 'I've been keeping an eye on Monica.'

'How the hell have you been doing that? With a telescope?'

'I have engaged the services of a private investigator,' she said. 'Fritzie, put me down and drink your Old Pilsner.'

He set her down.

'A private eye?' he asked, disbelief in his voice. 'You took it on your own to have my only motherless child followed around by a private detective? Some hard-eyed gumshoe is watching her every move?'

Terrified now, Letitia could not find her voice. She nodded her head, admitting it.

'Goddamn, Letitia!' Fritz W. Fenstermacher said. 'What the hell would I do without you? What a splendid idea! Why didn't I think of that?' Emotion got the best of him. He wrapped his arms around Letitia Kugelblohm and squeezed her to him.

'You're breaking my ribs, Fritzie,' Letitia said. 'Let me go!'

He set her back on the floor.

'What's the private eye got to say?' he asked.

'First, let me tell you that it is Mr. Shovel's studied professional opinion . . .'

'Who is Mr. Shovel?'

'Lemuel Shovel, head of the Shovel Secret Surveillance and Security Agency,' she explained. 'He's the best around.'

'I'll take your word for it,' Fritz said. 'What's he got to say?'

'I'm happy to tell you, Fritz,' Letitia said, 'that in Mr. Shovel's opinion, and he should know, you know, this being his line of work, that Monica's morals are above question.'

'Naturally,' Fritz said, 'she's my daughter. What did you expect?'

Miss Letitia Kugelblohm chose the path of discretion and did not reply to this interogatory.

'On the other hand,' she went on, 'Mr. Shovel reports . . . I have to tell you this, Fritzie . . . that she has been consorting with some unsavory characters.'

'Like who?'

'Mr. Rhotten, for one . . . incidentally, Fritzie, Mr. Shovel reports that he didn't change his name for television; it's always been pronounced Row-ten. . . .'

'And who else?'

'Congressman Edwards L. "Smiling Jack" Jackson. . .'

'My God!' Fritz said, stung to the quick. 'You mean that simpering idiot with the flowing silver locks and the aviation spectacles?'

She nodded.

'How far has this gone?'

'Mr. Shovel reported . . . he was quite embarrassed about it, said that it had never happened before. . . .'

'Get to the point, Letitia!'

'His operative lost Monica in a saloon . . . called P.J. Clarke's . . . in New York. She was drinking there with Don Rhotten and "Smiling Jack" Jackson. . . .'

'What do you mean, he "*lost*" her?'

'Well, to keep from attracting suspicion, he had to drink. And . . . well, he got plastered, Fritz. That's the bottom line.'

'The bottom line is that he lost my poor motherless daughter, that's the bottom line!' Fritz W. Fenstermacher shouted. 'What kind of bungling private eye did you hire, anyway?'

'The best,' she said.

'So you're telling me that you hired the *best* private eye around, and that he lost my daughter, and that nobody knows where she is?'

'*I* know where she is, Fritzie,' Letitia said.

'Where is she?'

'She's on her way to Las Vegas.'

'Las Vegas? What's she going to do in Las Vegas?'

'I don't know. All I know ... and Lemuel Shovel put every available agent on the case ... is that Monica first went to Boston and then got on a plane to Las Vegas.'

'My God! My innocent, sweet, pure, motherless babe in that sin city!'

'Monica is twenty-one, Fritzie,' Letitia said. 'She can take care of herself.'

'Huh!' Fritz snorted. He thought about it and added, 'Hah!'

'Now it may not mean anything, Fritzie,' Letitia said.

'*What* may not mean anything?'

'Before I found out that she's on her way to Las Vegas, I put in a call to her at the Rhotten Report.'

'And?'

'They said she was in Washington, as liaison to Congressman Jackson,' Letitia said.

'That's a hell of a thing to say about my poor motherless daughter!'

'And then I called Congressman Jackson's office, and they told me she was in New York with Don Rhotten.'

'And you say she's on her way to Las Vegas?'

'I found that out after I called the Rhotten Report and Smiling Jack's office.'

'So they're lying, huh? Not that I'm surprised, of course. What would surprise me would be that either of them told the truth. The question is, what are they up to with my darling Monica?'

'I thought I'd better tell you, Fritzie,' Letitia said. 'I did everything I could do.'

'And I appreciate it, Letitia,' Fritz said. 'I really appreciate it. Tell the guy on the loading dock I said it's O.K. for you to take a couple of cases of beer home.'

'Thank you, Fritzie,' Letitia said. '**What are you going to do now?**'

'I'd rather you didn't know,' Fritz said. 'You've done all that I can expect.'

'I understand completely,' Letitia said. 'I'll leave you alone now.'

'You're a good friend, Letitia,' Fritz said. 'I really mean that. Tell the guys on the loading dock I said three cases of beer.'

'Thank you, Fritz,' Letitia said. She left the office, sat down at her desk and picked up the phone. With a long, rather bony finger, she punched a number.

'Max C. Huffstadter, Local Number One-oh-three, International Order of Case, Keg and Barrel Handlers,' a male voice said. The voice had all the appealing timbre of a piece of glass being dragged across the surface of a slate blackboard.

'Miss Letitia Kugelblohm calling Mr. Huffstadter,' she said.

In a moment that luminary, in tribute to whose business acumen, case, keg and barrel handling expertise, and hamlike fists his counionists had named their local, came on the line.

'Hello, Letitia,' he said, somewhat shyly. His voice was slightly less melodious than that of the man who had first answered the phone. Max C. Huffstadter had been enamoured of Miss Letitia Kugelblohm since they had been in the ninth grade together. He had come to realize, some twenty years before, that his love was doomed to go unrequited and had married another (with some success – there were eleven little Huffstadters), but his love for Letitia had endured, burning, so to speak, with what he liked to think of as a small gemlike flame.

'Max' Letitia said, 'I need your help.'

'You just name it, Letitia,' Max said.

'Fritz has got problems,' Letitia said.

'Gee, that's tough,' Max said, without much apparent conviction or sympathy.

'With his daughter,' Letitia went on.

'That's different,' Max said. Parental difficulties obviously transcended the little differences that arise between a brewer and the union official representing those knights of labour who move the suds from place to place.

'I must tell you, Max, in deepest confidence, that Fritz's little Monica has fallen in with evil companions.'

'Now, Letitia,' Max said, 'you're a woman of the world. Just because some of the boys whistle a little when they see a little blond, that don't make them no evil companions.'

'Max, Monica has fallen in with Don Rhotten,' Letitia said.

'The boob-tube kook? *That* Don Rhotten?'

'I'm afraid so.'

'Geez,' Max said, 'that's awful. I wouldn't wish that on my worst enemy. What can I do to help, Letitia?'

'Fritz has just learned that Monica is in Las Vegas. I fear that he's going to do something drastic.'

'Like go out there and get her, huh? All by his lonesome?'

'He's a proud man, Max,' Letitia said. 'He doesn't know how to ask for favours.'

'What do you want me to do, Letitia?' Max C. Huffstadter asked.

'Max, you will recall, I'm sure, that paragraph twenty one, section C, title three, subtitle B of the last union contract provides that members in good standing of Max C. Huffstadter Local Number One-oh-three, IOCK and BH, are entitled to travel, on a space-available basis, on the *Suds Bucket*.'[1]

'Yeah,' Max said, 'I remember that. I thought ol' Fritz was gonna bust a gut when we got that.'

'I have reason to believe, Max, that the *Suds Bucket* will shortly depart for Las Vegas.'

'You're coming through loud and clear, Letitia,' Max said. 'I wouldn't want this to get back to ol' Fritz, of course, but there isn't a member of Local One-oh-three who would want to stand idly by while his little girl got herself messed up with a creep like Don Rhotten.'

'And you have somebody who can go?'

'Huffstadter's Hefties,' Max said, with quiet pride, 'Local One-oh-three's world famous weightlifting and karate team just happen to be here in the union hall.'

[1] The Beechcraft King-Aire aircraft acquired by Fenstermacher Breweries, Inc., for transport of Fenstermacher Breweries executives, in particular, the president and chairman of the board, had been somewhat jocularly named the *Suds Bucket*.

'Oh, Max, you're such a good friend!'

'Think nothing of it,' Max C. Huffstadter said. 'Always glad to be of service in a time of crisis.'

At that moment, one of the little lights on Letitia's phone lit up. She hurriedly said good-bye to Max and then punched the button so that she could eavesdrop on the call Fritz W. Fenstermacher was making.

'Fenstermacher Aviation Division,' a male voice said.

'This is Mr. Fenstermacher,' Fritz W. said. 'Prepare the *Suds Bucket* for an immediate flight to Las Vegas.'

'Yes, Mr. Fenstermacher,' the man said. Fritz W. Fenstermacher broke the connection with his finger, pushed the button that would ring Letitia Kugelblohm's telephone and waited impatiently for her to answer.

There was no answer. Angrily, Fritz W. slammed the phone into its cradle and walked to the outer office. Letitia was nowhere in sight.

'Me and my uncontrollable generosity,' he said, to no one in particular. 'If I hadn't given her those three cases of free beer, she would be at her station when I need her.'

He picked up the telephone on Miss Kugelblohm's desk and punched a number.

'This is Mr. Fenstermacher,' he barked. 'Have my car brought around immediately.'

'I'm sorry, Mr. Fenstermacher,' the security guard at the main entrance said, 'it's not here.'

'What do you mean, it's not there?'

'Miss Kugelblohm just this second rode off in it,' the security guard said. 'I think she was going home.'

'Well, then,' Fritz said, 'call me a cab.' He was disappointed but not surprised. The ungrateful perfidy of man (and woman) was something he lived with day after day. But Letitia should have known that his word was his bond. If he said she could have three cases of Fenstermacher's Finest free, she could have it. There was simply no reason for her to grab it and run the way she had.

He glanced idly at the desk. His eyes lit up. There was a heavily stamped letter lying on her desk. It bore the return address of the Matthew Q. Framingham Foundation, and it had been sent air mail special delivery, registered, deliver to addressee only.

Letitia, naturally, had signed for it, opened it and apparently read it. And then, apparently beside herself with gratitude for the three free cases of suds, had forgotten to tell him about it. He took the letter from the envelope. It was an official notification that Foundation Headquarters, for reasons that Executive Secretary Matthew Q. Framingham VI did not feel free to trust to the mails, had been temporarily relocated in Nero's Villa, Las Vegas, Nevada.

'It's an omen,' Fritz W. Fenstermacher said aloud. 'That's what it is. An omen.' He jammed the letter in his pocket and hurried out of his office.

CHAPTER FOURTEEN

At that moment, Ms. Monica P. Fenstermacher and Mr. Matthew Q. Framingham VI were arriving in Las Vegas. Mr. Matthew Q. Framingham, who like Mr. Fritz W. Fenstermacher was a believer in omens, had come to the conclusion that the presence of the well-stacked blond whom he had first met outside the Savoy-Plaza on the Las Vegas-bound plane was an omen.

He had spent most of his flight to Las Vegas stretching his neck to get a look at her, where she sat with the travelling-salesman type. All he got for his efforts was a strained neck, because the seats in the first-class compartment had been designed to block nosy eyes.

Matthew told himself that someone equipped, so to speak, like that and en route to Las Vegas was almost beyond question a terpsichorean ecdysiast. His interest in her could therefore be explained as strictly professional. He was, after all, executive secretary of the Framingham Foundation and as such responsible for providing the entertainment for the

Wednesday evening moral enlightenment sessions and the Friday evening retreats, which would be carried on as usual by the Framingham Foundation in exile.

Over his second martini on the plane, he told himself that he would have an opportunity to run into the young woman at the airport in Las Vegas. He would, he decided, meet her at the luggage claim counter. He could count on spending at least thirty minutes there, as the airline went through its standard ritual of misplacing luggage. If he didn't succeed in striking up a conversation with her at the luggage claim counter, he would arrange to stand close to her at the taxicab dispatch area. Even if he were not fortunate enough to actually share her cab, he could listen carefully as she gave her driver directions and thus learn where she was going.

Unknown to Matthew, very similar thoughts were running through the mind of Monica P. Fenstermacher. She was just as disappointed as Matthew that the travelling-salesman had jumped into the seat beside her. She wanted to strike up an acquaintance with Mr. Framingham (whom she thought of as that disgustingly large male chauvinist pig) as much as he wanted to strike up an acquaintance with her.

She knew, of course, where he was going, because she had eavesdropped on his conversation with the VP & GM of the S-P, but that really wasn't very much help. She knew that Nero's Villa was an enormous hotel, and once he disappeared inside, finding him would be very difficult. It would not be hard for her, she realized, to put on an act of utter feminine helplessness at the luggage claim counter for the benefit of the large male chauvinist pig, whereupon he would volunteer to help her carry her luggage and would, more than likely, volunteer to share his cab with her, since they were both bound for Nero's Villa.

It didn't turn out that way. Monica purposely dawdled after the plane had landed, so that the large male chauvinist pig would exit the aircraft first and she could follow him. Telling herself that any sacrifice in the name of investigative television journalism was worth it, she flashed Matthew a broad, come-hither smile as he made his way down the aisle. Then she followed him out of the plane.

But they were not to meet at the luggage claim counter. A very large Irish-looking male was standing at the foot of the stairway, calling out 'Mr. Matthew Framingham.'

'I am Matthew Q. Framingham VI,' Monica heard the big oaf say.

'Welcome to Nero's Villa,' the man said. 'Yer Coitesy Chariot awaits!'

'I beg pardon?'

'I'm Aloysius X. McGee,' the man said. 'I got yer Coitesy Chariot.'

'Are you by any chance attempting to say "Courtesy Chariot"?' Matthew asked.

'What's the matter, don't you speak English, or what?'

'What in the world is a Courtesy Chariot?'

'It's a Rolls-Royce, that's what it *is*. And what it *does* is take you from the airport to Nero's Villa.'

'How nice,' Matthew said. 'Mr. Finecello sent you, I gather, to facilitate my passage from the air terminal to his hostelry?'

'That's right,' Aloysius said. 'No offence, pal, but do you always talk like that? You sound like a fairy.'

'Odd that you should say so,' Matthew said, looking down at Mr. McGee and frowning. 'Another individual in your line of work somehow apparently formed the same misconception earlier today. To disabuse him of his notion, I found it necessary to hold him above my head and shake him. Will that be necessary with you?'

Mr. McGee was somewhat discomfited. He was accustomed to looking down upon people and making threatening statements. He was not at all used to being looked down upon by someone who was visibly capable of making good the threat to hold him over his head and shake him.

He was so shaken, in fact, that he couldn't think of a thing to say. What he did was bow deeply, open the rear door of the Rolls-Royce and gesture for Matthew to get in.

He closed the door after him and got in front beside the chauffeur.

Matthew, too, was deeply shaken. His masculinity had been questioned. That had never before happened, and now it had happened twice in one day. He was so shaken, in fact, that the Courtesy Chariot was two miles down the highway from the airport before he regained full possession of his faculties.

'My God!' he suddenly cried. 'I seem to have forgotten my luggage at the airport.' There was a short pause. 'My luggage and the broad with the big boobs!'

'Your luggage will be sent to your suite,' Aloysius X. McGee volunteered from the front seat. 'And you say you want a broad with big boobs?'

'I said nothing of the kind!' Matthew Q. Framingham VI said, righteously.

Aloysius X. McGee turned in the front seat, smiled warmly and gave Matthew a big, understanding wink.

My God, Matthew thought, summoning up the most ferocious glower of which he was capable, they're all over!

Monica P. Fenstermacher arrived at Nero's Villa thirty minutes after Matthew did. Monica was annoyed but not surprised when the staff of the hotel flatly denied any knowledge of any Mr. Matthew Q. Framingham or anybody known as the Framingham Theosophical Foundation. Their denial simply proved to her that the slimy tentacles of the conspiracy extended to the hotel management. She *knew* that Matthew Q. Framingham VI, that great big male chauvinist oaf, was in the hotel. That the hotel should deny it was simply proof that something big was afoot.

It was time, she realized, to call for reinforcements. Just as soon as the Centurion's Page had left her (somewhat reluctantly, she thought) alone in her hotel room, she went to the telephone and picked it up. Almost immediately, she had second thoughts and hung up again. The male chauvinist pigs of the Framingham Foundation were entirely capable of bugging her phone.

After first dressing in what she thought of as her investigative reporter's uniform (a high-cut skirt and a low-cut, semi-transparent blouse which seemed to produce in male chauvinist pigs a sort of semi-traumatic condition in which they would blurt out things that, under other circumstances, the most excruciating torture would not wring from their lips), she went back to the lobby and sought out a pay telephone.

She telephoned, of course, collect: Ms. Monica P. Fenstermacher would speak with anyone at Don Rhotten Productions, Inc., in New York. The operator quickly reported back that the called party was unable to accept collect calls.

'Did you give them my name?' Monica P. Fenstermacher asked, shocked.

'Yes, I did. If you wish to speak to the party on the line, please deposit three dollars and sixty-five cents for the first three minutes.'

It was necessary for Monica to leave the phone booth and get change. As she stood in line before the cashier's window, she idly looked around the lobby. Her eyes fell upon Matthew Q. Framingham VI. He was standing before an elevator, warmly shaking the hand of a distinguished-looking gentleman (it was, in fact, Mr. Justice Canady, but Monica P., of course, had no way of knowing that) and then bowing him into the elevator.

Just as soon as the door slid closed, Monica P. Fenstermacher raced across the lobby to the bank of elevators. She had seen on television (specifically, on 'Lady Fuzz', a popular boob-tube thriller featuring a lady detective who constantly showed up male cops despite the fact that she was blind, confined to a wheelchair and totally bald) a detective learn on what floor the suspect was by carefully studying the floor indicator sign above the elevator door.

She learned two things: First, that the elevator had gone directly to the twenty-fifth floor, and second, that a sign on the elevator itself announced that the elevator was reserved for the exclusive use of the International Association of Life Insurance Salesman. She had, she realized with quiet pride, in one fell swoop not only stripped the cover away from the

Framingham Foundation but also located their secret hideout.

After securing the necessary silver, she returned to the phone booth, deposited three dollars and sixty-five cents and listened as the phone rang at Don Rhotten Productions, Inc., Headquarters in the ABN Building in New York.

'Don Rhotten Productions,' an operator said, answering the phone.

'Monica P. Fenstermacher,' Monica said. 'Put me through to Don.'

'Oh, I'm so sorry,' the operator said, quickly reeling off the stock speech she gave several hundred times a day, 'Mr. Rhotten is tied up at the moment. If you will give me your name and address, I will see that a genuine Don Rhotten fan photograph, complete with facsimile signature, is sent out to you right away.'

'This is Monica P. Fenstermacher,' Monica repeated. 'I am a special investigative reporter employed by Don Rhotten Productions.'

'In that case,' the operator said, 'if you will just give me your name and address, we will send you, in addition to the photograph with facsimile signature, a paperbound copy of Mr. Rhotten's book, *Journalism As I Have Known It*, at a specially reduced price of only two dollars and thirty-five cents.'

'Listen, you dumb broad . . .' Monica exploded, 'I don't want to buy . . .'

'Thank you for calling Don Rhotten Productions,' the operator said. 'I'm sure Mr. Rhotten will carefully consider your views in future broadcasts.' The line went dead.

Fighting down a shaming urge to cry a little, Monica P. Fenstermacher secured an additional supply of quarters and placed the call again. There was more than one way to skin a cat.

'Don Rhotten Productions.'

'This is Congressman Edwards L. Jackson's office calling,' she said. 'For Mr. Rhotten.'

'Funny, you sound just like a nutty broad who called up

just a couple of minutes ago trying to mooch a free copy of *Journalism As I Have Known It*,' the operator said.

'I beg your pardon?' Monica said, in righteous indignation.

'One moment, please,' the operator said. She was aware of the close personal friendship between Mr. Rhotten and the distinguished solon. Monica was able to hear what next took place. First there was the sound of a phone ringing and then Don Rhotten's inimitable voice.

'Goddamn it!' he snapped. 'How many times must I tell you that I don't want to be disturbed when I'm meditating?'

'I'm sorry to bother you, Mr. Rhotten, but Congressman Jackson's office is calling.'

'Well, put him through, put him through!' Rhotten said.

'I'm ready with Mr. Rhotten,' the operator said.

'Jack?' Don Rhotten said. 'Is that you, buddy? How are you making out with our broad with the big boobs?'

'This is Monica P. Fenstermacher, Don,' Monica said.

'Well, speak of the devil!' Don Rhotten said. 'How's things in our national capital, baby? Old Smiling Jack taking good care of you?'

'You're talking to another woman!' a somewhat annoyed feminine voice announced from the background.

'Don't be ridiculous,' Don Rhotten said, then, sotto voce to the telephone, 'What's on your mind, baby? I'm a little tied up here at the moment, if you know what I mean.'

'I'm in Las Vegas,' Monica P. said, furious with herself for the blush that had suddenly coloured her cheeks.

'I knew old Smiling Jack would take good care of you, baby,' Don said. 'Those politicians really know how to live, don't they? Having any luck?'

'Don,' Monica said, 'I'm out here working. I've uncovered the secret hideout of the Matthew Q. Framingham Theosophical Foundation.'

There followed a long silence.

'Did you hear what I said, Don? I've tracked them down. I know where they are, and I know what cover name they're using.'

'Well, look, Monica,' Don Rhotten said, 'you've got the wrong guy, I'm afraid. I'm not exactly in that end of the business. I got a deal with the writers. They don't go on camera, and I don't go messing around in the news end. It's better that way.'

'Something must be wrong with the connection,' Monica P. Fenstermacher said. 'It sounded like you aren't interested.'

'It's not that I'm not interested, baby. But I got enough to worry about pronouncing all those big words without trying to get involved in something that's really none of my business. We got people, writers, that do that.'

'Deposit three dollars and sixty-five cents for another three minutes,' the operator said, cheerfully.

Monica, barely able to fight back the tears, started to hang up.

'Give my love to Smiling Jack, baby,' Don Rhotten said. He hung up, fixed a smile on his face and turned from the telephone to face his research assistant, Miss Wanda J. Fogarty.

'Now, Wanda, baby, where were we?' No matter what else could be said about her, and a good deal could, Miss Wanda J. Fogarty had her pride. She already had most of her clothes back on.

'Don't be that way, Wanda, baby!' Don Rhotten said.

'You're not a very nice man,' Wanda replied. 'I don't think I like you anymore.'

'How can you say that?' he asked. 'I'm Don Rhotten. Can I help it if women can't resist either the sound of my voice or my boyish curls?'

'Huh!' Miss Wanda J. Fogarty snorted. 'You were so anxious to answer the phone that your boyish curls slipped.'

Don Rhotten checked in the mirror. It was true. Furiously, he slipped his toupee back where it belonged. 'You'd think,' he said, 'that a country that can land a man on the moon could come up with a toupee sticker that would work!'

There came a knock at the door.

'Go away!' Rhotten shouted. 'I'm meditating.'

'It's Seymour,' Mr. Seymour Schwartz shouted back. 'Open up. I know you've got that broad in there.'

'Go away, Seymour,' Don Rhotten said. 'You're disturbing my psyche!'

'How dare you say something dirty like that about me!' Wanda J. Fogarty said. Before Don Rhotten could stop her, she rushed to the door and flung it open. 'See for your own self, Mr. Schwartz,' she said, indignantly. 'Do I look like someone's psyche?'

'Hi, there, Jack,' Don Rhotten said, flashing his famous grin and waving his famous wave at the Hon. Edwards L. 'Smiling Jack' Jackson, the distinguished Farmer–Free Silver Representative in Congress of the good people of Swampy Meadows, Arkansas, who stood beside Seymour Schwartz.

'Don't you "Hi there, Jack" me,' Smiling Jack said. 'I knew I should never have trusted somebody I met in jail.'

'Where is she?' Seymour Schwartz demanded.

'Where's who?' Don Rhotten replied, understandably confused.

'You know damned well who,' the congressman replied. 'Whatsername. The little blond with the ... unusually generous mammary development. The one whose father is a close personal friend of the Speaker of the House.'

'What's he talking about, Seymour?' Don Rhotten asked, helplessly.

'Monica P. Fenstermacher, that's who he's talking about,' Seymour Schwartz said. 'I warned you to stay away from her, Don.'

'I'm as pure as the driven snow,' Don Rhotten replied. 'The last time I saw her, Smiling Jack was telling her that if she played her cards right, he'd nominate her for Doorkeeper of the House.'

As this little exchange had been going on, Mr. Seymour Schwartz had hurriedly searched the room, looking into closets, the small but fully equipped rest room with the large gold star and the words DON RHOTTEN on the door and under the chaise longue on which Don Rhotten had been meditating with Miss Wanda J. Fogarty.

'I'm asking you for the last time, Four-Eyes,' Seymour Schwartz screamed, reverting in his anger to the fond little nickname by which Don Rhotten had been known in the early days of their acquaintance, 'where is Monica P. Fenstermacher?'

'Oh,' Rhotten replied, relief coming to his face. 'Is that what you want to know?'

'That's what I want to know,' Seymour said.

'Funny that you should ask,' Don Rhotten replied. 'I was just talking to her a moment before you guys came in.'

'My God, you rotten jailbird, what have you done with that innocent child and daughter of the man who is a close personal friend of the Speaker of the House?' Congressman Jackson asked.

'She's not here, if that's what you mean,' Don Rhotten said. 'Your suspicions are . . . whatdoyoucallit? . . . baseless and scurrillous.' He remembered that phrase from one of his broadcasts and rather liked the sound of it, even though he wasn't quite sure what it meant.

'Where is she?' Seymour G. Schwartz and the congressman asked in unison.

'She called from Las Vegas,' Don Rhotten said.

'Las Vegas?' replied Seymour G. Schwartz.

'Nevada?' replied Smiling Jack Jackson.

'Oh, my God!' they said in unison.

'She called up to tell me that she was working,' Don Rhotten said.

'What do you mean, working?'

'Well, you know, reporting the news. I told her, of course, that that sort of thing was none of my business.'

'What else did she say, Don?' Schwartz said.

'What's this all about?' Rhotten replied. 'I'm the star around here, you know. I can't be expected to keep up with everything all the little people around here do.'

'Now listen carefully, Don,' Seymour G. Schwartz said. 'Try to pay attention. Something unpleasant has come up.'

'Oh?'

'That is the understatement of the year,' Smiling Jack said. 'I didn't even know that the Speaker of the House knew words like that.'

'Words like what?' Rhotten asked.

BLEEP!

'He really said that?' Don Rhotten asked. He was impressed.

'And the chairman of the board of the Amalgamated Broadcasting Network wasn't restrained in his choice of words by any sense of duty to the House of Representatives,' Schwartz said. 'I don't even like to remember what he said.'

'What's the bottom line?' Rhotten asked. The gravity of the situation was finally becoming apparent to him.

'Unless you can come up with some satisfactory explanation for the disappearance of this Fenstermacher broad . . .' Seymour began.

'I think, under the circumstances,' Smiling Jack said, sonorously, 'that we should refer to Miss Fenstermacher as "that splendid young woman and hope for the future."'

'You got a point, Jack, but let me get on with this,' Seymour said. 'Unless I can come up with some sort of satisfactory explanation for her disappearance, one that both the chairman of the board and her father will swallow, it's back to being Big Bunny for you, Don-Baby. On radio.'

'And the Speaker said that when he's finished with me,' Smiling Jack said, 'not only won't I be able to run for re-election, but I won't even be able to go back to chasing ambulances.'

'So think hard, Don-Baby,' Seymour said. 'What, *exactly*, did she say on the phone?'

A look of intense concentration came to the famous visage. 'She said,' he said, in the manner of a spirit medium relaying a communication from the far side of the River Styx, 'that she had uncovered the secret hideout of the Matthew Q. Framingham Theosophical Foundation.'

'That what?'

'She said that she had tracked them down,' Rhotten went

on, 'and that she knows where they are and what cover name they're using.'

'What the hell is the Matthew Q. Framingham Theosophical Foundation?' Congressman Jackson asked.

'I'll tell you this,' Wanda J. Fogarty said, righteously, 'that theosophical part of it sounds real dirty to me.'

Seymour G. Schwartz dashed to the telephone, picked it up and barked, 'Research, and hurry.' His three companions sat staring at him in silence until he had the information he sought.

'Well?'

'God, I don't know,' Seymour G. Schwartz said. 'Research says that the Matthew Q. Framingham Theosophical Foundation is a long-established, highly respected, above-suspicion cultural outfit in Cambridge, Massachusetts, practically on the Harvard campus.'

'A dead end!' Smiling Jack said, striking his rather ample forehead with the heel of his hand. 'I'm ruined. It's back to hanging around night traffic court for me!'

'If they're so respectable,' Wanda J. Fogarty asked, 'how come they got a dirty word like "theosophical" in their name?'

'And what are they doing in Las Vegas?' Don Rhotten said.

Seymour G. Schwartz looked stunned. 'Smiling Jack,' he said, 'did you hear that?'

'So what? I think theosophical sounds dirty, too.'

'I mean what the idiot ... I mean, Don-Baby, of course ... said. I never would have dreamed it possible, but I think he's come up with something.'

'I have?' Don Rhotten replied.

'If this Matthew Q. Whatever-the-hell-it-is is so respectable, what's it doing in Las Vegas under a phony name?'

'Beats me,' the congressman said.

'It's just possible,' Seymour G. Schwartz said, 'that that little broad has come up with something. If she has been working, we can say it's been a secret assignment, and we're home free.'

'Like what?' Don Rhotten and Smiling Jack asked, in unison.

'I don't know,' Seymour Schwartz said, 'but I do know that we're going to grab a camera crew, get our asses in high gear and get out to Vegas.'

'On a donkey?' Don Rhotten replied. 'That's a long way on a donkey, Seymour. Las Vegas is way out west someplace.'

'On an airplane, stupid,' Seymour said. 'Put your pants on, straighten that goddamned wig and get ready to move out.' He turned to face Congressman Jackson. 'I feel sure that you can handle the transportation, Congressman, can't you?'

'I get your meaning,' Smiling Jack said. He grabbed the telephone. 'This is Congressman Edwards L. Jackson,' he intoned. 'Get me the commanding officer of the nearest air force base. This is a national emergency. My entire political career depends on how fast I can be flown to Las Vegas.'

CHAPTER FIFTEEN

Monica P. Fenstermacher's professionalism, it must in honesty be reported, did crack, if only briefly, during and immediately after her telephone conversation with Don Rhotten. It had been a severe blow to Monica's conception of journalistic duty to learn that Don Rhotten, when you got down to the bottom line, actually preferred hanky-panky with Wanda J. Fogarty to working at his profession.

Tears, in fact, had run down her pretty little nose, to be mopped daintily away with a lace handkerchief as Monica sort of staggered in the direction of the elevators.

'Is there something wrong, miss?' a male, somehow familiar voice inquired. Monica raised her eyes from the handkerchief and found herself staring at a Phi Beta Kappa key suspended on a gold chain between the vest pockets of a banker's black suit vest. There was something about the situation which reminded Monica of how, in the good old (preliberation) days, she had cried on her poppa's vest when the world had been cruel to her.

But Poppa didn't have a Phi Beta Kappa key, nor was Poppa quite this large. Monica raised her tear-flooded eyes to look at the face of her potential benefactor. To do this, she had to tilt her head just about as far back as the muscular structure would permit. When she had done so, she found that the reason the gentle voice had been familiar was that it belonged to the enormous male chauvinist pig oaf she had followed from Boston and whom she was going to expose to the cold scrutiny of Don Rhotten's 11,029,211 faithful viewers.

'My name, miss or madame as the case may be, is Matthew Q. Framingham, and if you will pardon my saying so, it would appear from the appearance of your red nose and that sopping wet handkerchief that you have been crying. How might I perchance be of some assistance?'

'It's nothing,' Monica said, blowing her nose furiously. That proved to be a tactical error. It was a lace, or decorative, handkerchief, rather than a solid, or nose-blowing, handkerchief.

The enormous male chauvinist oaf, of course, immediately saw her predicament. A large, spotless, white, male handkerchief was immediately snapped from its previous position in the breast of the banker's black suit and offered to her. It posed something of a problem. Her first reaction, of course, was to tell him to shove it, but if she gave into that temptation, she would be left with the soggy lace item and rather messy fingers.

'Thank you,' she said, taking the handkerchief. 'You are very kind.'

'Not at all,' Matthew said. 'Actually, despite the mess you're making of my next-to-last Irish linen handkerchief, I would say that on balance, our chance encounter may prove, in the end, to be fortuitous.'

'Fortuitous, you say?' Monica replied, hating herself for,

a moment before, being pleased that she had finally met someone who spoke like a gentleman.

'Indeed,' Matthew went on. 'At the risk of sounding unduly presumptuous, miss or madame as the case might be, perhaps you would be willing to discuss something with me over a small libation.'

'It's miss,' she said.

'How nice,' he said. 'Miss what?'

'Miss Mon,' she began and then remembered that she had given the enormous oaf her name over the telephone back in Boston. 'Miss Montague Smith,' she quickly corrected herself.

'A great pleasure, Miss Smith,' the monstrous oaf said and actually bowed over her hand and raised it to his lips. 'Enchanté, mademoiselle,' Matthew Q. Framingham said. That was the very first time anything like that had happened to Monica P. Fenstermacher, and it disturbed her greatly. After a moment, she decided that was because she could never remember being quite so close to such an enormous male.

'You're welcome, I'm sure,' she said, for no reason at all.

'Would it be reasonable of me to presume that you are a professional terpsichorean ecdysiast?' Matthew asked.

The only word Monica recognized was professional.

'That would be a reasonable presumption,' she said. 'And let me say what a great privilege, a rare privilege, it is for me to meet someone who speaks the English language with such mastery.' That had just slipped out. Monica had no idea why she was behaving so strangely.

'Harvard, don't you know,' Matthew said, pleased with the compliment. 'To return, however, for a moment, to my original interrogatory, Miss Smith. Would you do me the great honour of joining me for a small libation, over which I would presume to open a discussion leading to a possible professional engagement for you by an organization of which I have the honour to be executive secretary?'

'Oh, yes,' Monica P. said. 'I'd like that very much.'

'Splendid.' Matthew beamed, his lips curling back to

reveal a massive, perfect set of pure white teeth. Then, as quickly, the smile vanished. 'Oh, my,' he said.

'Is something wrong?' Monica asked.

'An unforeseen happenstance has occurred,' Matthew said. 'Would you be good enough to pardon me for just a moment?'

'What did you do?' she asked.

'I must have a word with two gentlemen of my acquaintance,' he said. He nodded toward the reception desk of Nero's Villa, where stood Dr. Benjamin Franklin Pierce and Dr. John Francis Xavier McIntyre, a short little man he didn't know by sight and three women.

At the moment Matthew spotted Hawkeye and Trapper John, Trapper John spotted Matthew and jabbed Hawkeye with his elbow in the ribs.

'I saw her as we walked in,' Hawkeye replied. 'About nine-point-two on a scale of ten, I would say.'

'I mean Matthew,' Trapper John said.

'What did you say?' Mary Pierce asked.

'I said that when I'm staying in a hotel, I like to have breakfast between nine and ten.'

'Hawkeye, this man says he doesn't have any room for us,' Mary Pierce said. 'I told you that we should have called and made reservations.'

Matthew Q. Framingham marched up at that moment.

'Doctors Pierce and McIntyre,' he said, 'what an unexpected surprise to find you here.' He paused and added, significantly, 'With what I presume to be your wives.'

'Why,' Trapper John said, 'as I live and breathe, if it isn't Matthew Q. Framingham VI, executive secretary of the Framingham Foundation, himself.'

'Oh, really?' Mary Pierce said, jabbing Lucinda McIntyre in the ribs. Both ladies looked appreciatively at the enormous young man in the banker's suit.

'I don't believe you know our wives,' Hawkeye said. 'Mary, Lucinda, may I present Mr. Matthew Q. Framingham VI? And this is Mr. J. Robespierre O'Reilly and his fiancée.'

'I am honoured, ladies and sir,' Matthew said, bowing and kissing the hand of each in turn. 'I had no idea,' he added significantly, 'that I would have the pleasure of meeting you ladies under these particular circumstances.'

'I have heard so much about you, Mr. Framingham,' Lucinda gushed.

'And Lucinda and I would like to take this opportunity to thank you for all the Framingham Foundation has done to enrich the lives of our husbands,' Mary Pierce said.

'How nice of you to say so,' Matthew said. 'May I ask what brings you ladies to Las Vegas?'

'Well, we really shouldn't tell you,' Mary Pierce said, 'as we're trying to keep it small and intimate, but we're here for the marriage of Kristina and Robespierre.'

'Oh, I see,' Matthew said. 'How nice.'

Hawkeye finally had an idea what Matthew was doing there.

'Matthew, have you perchance been able to arrange that little matter we discussed in Cambridge?'

'What little matter is that?' Mary Pierce asked.

'Foundation business, I'm afraid, my dear,' Hawkeye said.

'As a matter of fact, Doctor, I have met with some success in finding a solution, as it were, to that problem.'

'Right here in Nevada?'

'Yes. Right here.'

'Isn't that interesting?' Trapper John said.

'Mr. Framingham,' Mary said, 'I would presume that someone of your stature would have some influence.'

'Naturally,' Matthew said. 'Is there some way I might be of service?'

'There's no room at the inn, Matt,' Trapper John said. 'Can you fix that?'

'I feel sure that I can,' Matthew said. He turned to the desk clerk. 'Would you please inform Mr. Finecello that Matthew Q. Framingham VI would like to have a word with him?'

Little Augie Finecello was not especially pleased to be

informed that Matthew Framingham wanted to see him. He had been taking telephone reports from members of the family in strategic locations across the country about their efforts to locate J. Robespierre O'Reilly and $81,000 of Nero's Villa's money. Their efforts to locate Mr. O'Reilly had so far been unsuccessful, and this displeased Little Augie.

He told himself, however, as he rose from behind his desk, that nothing must be permitted to interfere with his plans for Mr. Framingham and his friends. The blackmail potential in twenty or thirty East Coast biggies having a stag party in Las Vegas was something that Lady Luck did not dump into one's lap every day.

Fixing a smile on his face, he stepped behind the desk clerk's counter to greet Mr. Framingham. His mouth fell open. Standing, his chin on the level of the counter, was the little jerk he'd been looking for all over the country.

'Hello, there,' Little Augie oozed. 'How nice to see you again, Mr. O'Reilly. And how may I be of service to you, Mr. Framingham?'

'Your man in the lavender sheet here,' Matthew said, indicating the desk clerk (Keeper of the Catacombs), 'informs my friends that there is no room in the villa for them.'

'He said dat, did he?' Little Augie said, kicking the Keeper of the Catacombs in the shins. 'Well, you know how hard it is to get decent help these days.'

'I may presume, then, that you will rectify the situation?' Matthew said.

'Mr. O'Reilly and his friends,' Little Augie said, 'couldn't get out of Nero's Villa if they wanted to.'

'I'm pleased to have had the opportunity to have been of service,' Matthew said. 'And now, with your permission, I will say ta-ta. Perhaps the opportunity will arise for us to have a moment or two alone, Doctors, while we're here.'

'If you have solved our little problem,' Hawkeye said, 'with your customary finesse, Matthew, you can count on it.'

'I haven't firmed up the details yet,' Matthew said, nodding in the direction of the young woman whose name he thought was Montague Smith, 'but the possibility exists that an ad hoc meeting of the Wednesday evening moral enlightenment group may be convened. Perhaps your busy schedule would permit your attendance?'

'My husband,' Mary Pierce said, remembering Hawkeye's outrageous vulgarity about the physical aspects of marriage, 'will be there, Mr. Framingham, you can count on it.'

Trapper John looked hopefully at his wife. Lucinda said nothing, and Trapper's heart sank.

'And so will Dr. McIntyre,' Mary Pierce said. 'Lucinda, you're too forgiving.'

Matthew Q. Framingham bowed and took his leave, returning to Miss 'Montague Smith'.

'Miss Smith,' he said, 'permit me to express my appreciation for your understanding. May I suggest that we now return to the matter of sharing a libation as we discuss a professional engagement?'

Monica, while watching Matthew, had regained control of herself. She was thoroughly ashamed of herself for having cracked up after talking with Don Rhotten and even more ashamed of herself for her total loss of control when in close physical proximity to the enormous male chauvinist oaf afterward. She vowed to make amends by keeping her nose to the journalistic grindstone.

She realized, once she had her thoughts back on the track, that the essence of the whole story depended on her getting inside the secret headquarters of the Matthew Q. Framingham Foundation with a camera and a tape recorder.

Steeling herself for the ordeal, Monica raised her baby-blue eyes upward toward those of Matthew Q. Framingham and batted them.

'Mr. Framingham,' she said, 'you were right. I was having a little problem when we met. I would now like the opportunity to refresh myself. Is there someplace we could meet in, say, thirty minutes?'

Matthew looked thoughtful.

'Perhaps your room?' Monica P. Fenstermacher, a/k/a Montague Smith, asked innocently.

'Splendid suggestion!' Matthew promptly replied. 'And might I suggest that it might behoove you to bring along with you what professional paraphernalia you can conveniently accommodate. If that could be arranged, you would thus be in a position to demonstrate your terpsichorean and ecdysiastical offerings, which would, of course, felicitate our discussion regarding the honorarium therefore?'

'Right you are,' Monica said. 'Shall we say thirty minutes? What's your room number?'

'I have the twenty-fifth floor,' Matthew said. 'Oh, I'm glad you brought that matter up.' He took Monica/Montague's arm and led her to the elevator reserved for the exclusive use of the International Association of Life Insurance Salesmen, before which stood two large, if somewhat effeminate, Centurion Guards.

'Permit this young lady to freely pass,' Matthew said.

'Hail, Caesar,' the two said, in sort of a falsetto duet, raising their arms in the Roman salute.

'Aren't you going up?' Monica asked Matthew.

'No, I have to send someone a message,' Matthew said. 'I'll just get a sheet of stationery and an envelope in the lobby. And then I'll go up.'

'I just want to stop by the souvenir-and-book stand a moment,' Monica said. 'And then I'll go freshen up.'

They marched back to the main lobby. Matthew bowed, Monica smiled wanly and they parted paths.

Matthew got a sheet of paper and an envelope and wrote out a cryptic message: 'Don't Pay Any Attention to the International Association of Life Insurance Salesmen Sign,' it read. He addressed the envelope to Dr. Benjamin Franklin Pierce and sought one of the Centurion Guards.

'Would you have this delivered immediately?' he asked.

'Thertainly,' the Centurion Guard said. 'I'm just a pushover for your type.'

160

My God, Matthew thought, another one. They're taking over the world!

Monica made two stops in the lobby. She went to the retail outlet of the Acme Still and Motion Picture Photography Company and rented both a 16-mm motion picture camera and a pocket-sized tape recorder. Neither the camera nor the tape recorder was what she wanted, in other words up to the high technical standards of 'The Rhotten Report', but that was all Acme had in stock at the moment. The salesclerk confided that the professional end of the business was working a big job and using all the equipment it could find.

Then Monica stopped by the newsstand and bought a dictionary. As she rode up in the elevator to her room, she looked up 'terpsichorean'[1] and 'ecdysiast'[2] in her new dictionary. She looked up terpsichorean first and smiled shyly. Maybe there was something artistic and gentle about the big oaf after all; otherwise how could he have know that she just *loved* to dance? Then she looked up ecdysiast. Her eyes widened; her mouth dropped open. Then her eyes narrowed and her mouth closed, after uttering a description of Matthew Q. Framingham that could never have been broadcast over the air, even on 'The Rhotten Report'. She stormed off the elevator vowing revenge. Matthew Q. Framingham VI, by the time she was through with him, by the time she had exposed the Matthew Q. Framingham Theosophical Foundation and all its wicked works on nationwide television, would curse the day he was born.

[1] Terpsichorean (from the Greek, pertaining to the muse). A dancer, generally female, who makes dancing an art.

[2] Ecdysiast (from the Latin *ecdysiatist*, an animal which sheds its outer covering). A stripper (sometimes 'stripteaser'), an entertainer who seeks male approval by the ritual stripping off of clothing, most commonly in public, such as a burlesque or nightclub, but frequently within a brothel (q.v.) or other such place.

CHAPTER SIXTEEN

The stories which appeared in the French press bemoaning the transfer of French cash assets to the Islamic Kingdom of Hussid in exchange for Hussidic petroleum products (thirty-eight percent of the energy consumed in La Belle France came from beneath the sands of Hussid) were, in the final analysis, somewhat unfair.

They didn't mention that much of the money the Kingdom of Hussid received for its oil was spent in France. Not only had the nomadic citizens of Hussid turned in their camels for fleets of Citroën, Peugeot and Renault automobiles and trucks, but their diet had changed. *Le Boeuf Wellington, Pâté de Foie Gras Strasbourg* and *Crêpes Suzette* had replaced camel chops, stewed lizards and fried grasshoppers in the Hussid menu. Hussid women (who did not, however, give up their veils) were now gowned, even the least (which is to say the fattest) of them in the latest creations of Paris' high-fashion designers. Air Hussid had six daily scheduled airfreight flights supplying the kingdom and its people with wine, champagne, French bread and snails, all of it, of course, paid for in cash.

The single largest recycling of what the financiers called 'oil francs', however, occurred in the aviation industry and should have been cited as a splendid example of Hussidic sympathy for French problems. The French, with some assistance from the English, had developed an aircraft designed to show up the Americans. Known as 'L'Discorde', it was designed to fly far faster and far higher than any American aircraft. It met what are known as 'design specs.' In other words, it did fly faster and higher than any other aircraft in the world. There was only one small problem, in that area known to the cognoscenti as 'operating costs.' Presuming the aircraft was filled to capacity and presuming a seat-mile charge of $1.05 (the amount each passenger is charged for each mile of the journey; on American airlines the seat-mile charge is approximately a nickel), each flight hour on L'Discorde, because of the cost of the aircraft and the cost of the fuel consumed, represented a dead loss to the owners of approximately $55,000.

This dead-loss factor understandably made the world's airlines just a little reluctant to add L'Discorde to their fleets, and sales were not what the French government had hoped they would be. They had envisioned worldwide sales of some 450 aircraft, each costing approximately $14,000,000. Actual sales had been five, one each to the governments of France and England, an Anglo-Franco showing of the flag, so the speak, and three to the Islamic Kingdom of Hussid.

The Kingdom of Hussid was not troubled with a franc shortage, so to speak, especially when the happiness of the Royal Family was at stake. His Majesty the King did not like to use the telephone, having once received a busy signal which he naturally considered an affront to his dignity, and if it was necessary to spend $14,000,000 plus $55,000 an hour to provide His Majesty with an alternate means of communication with his diplomatic staff, well then, this was the way L'Discorde would have to fly. The three Hussid L'Discordes had been assigned to the Royal Hussidic Foreign Service. One was stationed in Tokyo (Japan was another major customer for Hussidic petroleum) for the use of the Hussidic ambassador. When the king wished to confer with the ambassador, the ambassador got on L'Discorde and flew home. Since, pre-oil, the king's ambassadors three hundred miles away in Cairo had required two weeks to make the camel journey home, His Majesty was now more than pleased to get them home within two days of a summons.

The second L'Discorde was kept as a spare, since 'down time for maintenance' was somewhat greater than expected. The third L'Discorde was assigned to His Majesty's Ambassador to the Republic of France, his eldest son and apparent heir, His Royal Highness Prince Hassan ad Kayam.

Various troublemakers, most of them in the French Foreign Office, had seen to it that His Majesty learned of the use to which his son and heir put the plane, which, after all, was French and thus should be utilized in a manner reflecting the prestige and decorum of La Belle France. The interior (which had provided space for 101 passengers) had been gutted and replaced with an interior offering seats for the 16 members of HRH bodyguard; a 'concert salon' with grand piano; a 'reception room' with water bed and motion picture projector; two large, private staterooms; a compartment outfitted with a number of bunk beds, makeup mirrors and other feminine conveniences.

'It is nothing more, Your Majesty,' the French troublemaker had said, 'than a *maison tolerée aeriale*.'

'Splendid,' His Majesty had replied. 'Boys will be boys, you know.'

'In which,' the troublemaker went on, with the tenacity for which the French are famous, 'your son, Prince Hassan, zooms around the world in company of a man, an American whose morals are as low as his vocal talent is soaring.'

'I suspect you are casting foul frog aspersions on my friend Boris,' His Majesty replied, ruining the French troublemaker's whole day. 'Dear Boris sings like an angel, and he has the loins of a lion. What better example for my son to emulate?'

As Monica P. Fenstermacher, a/k/a Montague Smith, stalked off the elevator in Nero's Villa, Air Hussid L'Discorde Number Three, at 50,000 feet over Columbus, Ohio, radioed to Las Vegas Approach Control that they expected to be on the ground at Las Vegas in fifteen minutes, and would Las Vegas please give them landing instructions?'

HRH Prince Hassan walked out of the recreation room and made his way to Cabin Number One, where he discreetly knocked at the door.

'Maestro?' he called. 'Are you tied up?'

'What kind of sexual pervert do you take me for?' Boris replied. 'Of course I'm not tied up. I'm simply standing on my head.'

'We will be in Las Vegas in about fifteen minutes, my dear friend,' HRH said. 'I thought perhaps you might wish to prepare yourself.'

There came a groan and then the maestro's voice: 'You'll have to stop that, Esmerelda,' he said. 'I must get dressed now and see to my baby sister's marriage.'

Hassan, a little smile of relief on his face (The maestro would stand for having his exercise interrupted, even for good cause. It had once been necessary to hold the third act of *Boris Gudonov* at the Bolshoi for three-quarters of an hour before the maestro had sufficiently revitalized himself with Dr. T. Mullins Yancey's prescribed exercise to go on) turned and walked away. He had taken three steps when there was a bellow of outrage.

'Where the hell are my clothes?'

Hassan turned back and knocked again at the door.

'Maestro?' he called again. 'Did you call? May I come in?'

'Of course I called. And of course you can come in. Get in here, Hassan, and explain to me why I don't have any clothes to wear.'

Hassan pushed the door open. Esmerelda Hoffenburg, wearing a contented smile and in the act of shrugging into a dressing gown, was standing beside the water bed. Boris Alexandrovich Korsky-Rimsakov, wearing a frown and nothing whatever else, was lying on the water bed.

'You don't expect me to walk into the hotel where my baby sister is to be married wearing this, do you?' Boris asked, holding up the vestments he had worn while singing the role of Pope Clement VII.

'Of course not, Maestro,' Hassan said. 'Perhaps you will recall that you refused to take the time to change following your performance.'

'Nothing must stand in the way of my baby sister's happiness,' Boris said. 'Certainly you can understand that.'

'I took the liberty of having some clothing packed for you, Maestro,' Hassan said. 'You will find it in the closet.'

'Well, why didn't you just come out and say so?' the singer said. He jumped out of bed, which was an error, for

L'Discorde's cabin was some three inches under six feet tall, and the singer was some six inches over six feet.

There was a loud boom, and with a puzzled look on his face, Boris Alexandrovich Korsky-Rimsakov sank unconscious to the floor.

'My God,' Esmerelda Hoffenburg screamed. 'He's killed himself.'

Hassan dropped to his knees and put his ear to the singer's massive chest. There was a reassuring pounding of the singer's heart.

'He's not dead,' Hassan said, 'but I think he should see a doctor.' He became aware of the singer's birthday-suit attire. 'Get some clothes on him,' he ordered. 'I'll radio ahead to Las Vegas.'

He left the cabin and trotted toward the cockpit, encountering the Baroness d'Iberville en route. 'Go back to Boris' cabin and help Esmerelda put his clothing on him,' he ordered.

'Put his clothing *on* him?' the baroness asked, incredulously. 'Is he sick, or what?'

'Go!' Hassan said, somewhat dramatically. '*Cher* Boris Alexandrovich needs you!'

As a routine matter, of course, to spare His Royal Highness the indignity of having to partake of food prepared for ordinary people, an advance party headed by the royal chef and equipped with a short-wave radio, had been dispatched to Nero's Villa.

'This is His Royal Highness Prince Hassan,' Hassan said modestly to the radio operator on duty. 'An emergency has arisen. Somewhere in the hotel are Dr. Benjamin Franklin Pierce and Dr. James Francis Xavier McIntyre. You will present my compliments to them and ask them to meet me at the airport with an ambulance and whatever other necessary medical equipment they consider necessary to care for Boris Alexandrovich Korsky-Rimsakov.'

'Yes, Your Royal Highness,' the radio operator said. 'Immediately, if not sooner.'

Three minutes later, Mary Pierce gave a little yelp when she answered her hotel room door and found herself facing a small, excited Frenchman and two fully robed Arabians holding silver-plated submachine guns.

'Madame,' the excited little Frenchman said, 'I zeek Doctaire Hawkeye!'

'What for?' Mary Pierce replied, having recovered her composure. 'If this is some clever little scheme to get them out of helping to arrange for the ceremony . . .'

'Madame,' the excited little Frenchman said, 'zis is a medical emergency!'

'Just one moment, please,' Mary Pierce said. The ground rules by which she and her mate played The Game of Life made provision for every little trick ever devised by mankind with the sole exception of joking about medical emergencies. She had no reason to suspect that he would violate the rules now, even as disturbed as he was by the formal dress she had selected for him to wear at the wedding and which, at this very moment, he was trying on.

She knocked and then, without waiting for a reply, pushed open the door to the room where Hawkeye and Trapper John and Radar were standing around in their rented finery.

'Mary,' Hawkeye said, examining the rose-pink lace cuffs of his dress shirt, 'there's no way I'm going to wear this in public.'

'There's a medical emergency,' Mary said.

'Don't change the subject!'

'There's a Frenchman and two Arabs out there,' Mary said, 'asking for you.'

'I can't let them see me dressed like this!' Hawkeye said. 'I look like an escapee from a musical comedy.'

'Remember the Hippocratic Oath,' Trapper John said.

'You remember it; you go talk to them,' Hawkeye said.

Trapper John did just that, and in a moment he was back 'Hassan's plane is about to land,' he said. 'He radioed saying that we should meet it with an ambulance. Something's apparently happened to Boris.'

'He's probably got a splinter in his thumb,' Hawkeye said, but he went to the closet and came out with his doctor kit.

'I'm going,' Radar announced.

'We have to go,' Trapper said. 'Duty calls. But there's no reason you have to go out where people can see you and laugh and laugh at you.'

'He is almost my brother-in-law,' Radar said. 'Kristina would want me to go.' He drew himself up to his full five-feet-two. 'I insist.'

There were no further objections from either Hawkeye or Trapper John. They quickly left the suite and made their way to the elevator.

There was a Centurion's Page standing idly by in the corridor. His orders were clear and simple. He was to prohibit, by whatever means necessary, the departure of Mr. J. Robespierre O'Reilly from the suite. It had not been the first time he had been similarly stationed outside some sucker's room to keep him from getting away without paying his bill or his gambling debt, and he had accepted the assignment routinely. But Little Augie had not led him to believe that the guest he described as 'the little sawed-off creep' would be leaving accompanied by two bearded giants carrying submachine guns. He decided that discretion was the better part of valour, smiled warmly at the group as it passed him and then jumped to a telephone to inform Little Augie of this latest, unexpected development.

As they moved quickly through the lobby toward The Gate of Joyous and Triumphal Entry, Hawkeye said, 'What about an ambulance?'

'I have ordered that one go directly to the airport,' the Frenchman said.

At that moment, the alarm bell went off. On being advised that J. Robespierre O'Reilly was trying to make his escape, Little Augie had pressed the Deadbeat Escaping Alarm button. When he did that, a number of carefully prearranged things took place. First, all doors to Nero's Villa were closed and locked. Second, all Centurion's Pages rushed to all exits to stand guard. Third, the nearest Courtesy Chariot to The Gate of Joyous and Triumphant Entry rolled up before the door against the eventuality that it might be necessary to give the escaping deadbeat a ride witnessed by as few people as possible.

The plate-glass doors slammed shut just as Hawkeye reached them. He pushed, but nothing happened.

'Not to worry,' one of the bodyguards said. There was a short burst of submachine-gun fire. The plate glass shattered. The bodyguard bowed Hawkeye, Trapper John and Radar through the opening.

The Courtesy Chariot rolled up, as Standard Operating Procedure called for, at exactly that moment. The chauffeur, a longtime employee of the establishment, recognized the sound of submachine-gun fire. He opened the rear door with one arm and raced the engine for the getaway.

Once the three were in the back of the car, however, and the car, tyres screaming, had rolled away from The Gate of Joyous and Triumphal Entry, the chauffeur had second thoughts. Not only had he never before in his life seen such ridiculous costumes on human beings, but none of their faces were familiar.

'I don't recognize you guys,' he said. 'You're with the family, of course?'

'Friends of both the bride and groom, as a matter of fact,' Trapper John said. 'Take us to the airport, and hurry!'

'You got it, pal!' the chauffeur, reassured, said.

Little Augie and two of the largest Centurion's Pages arrived at The Gate of Joyous and Triumphal Entry on the run. He got there in time to see the Courtesy Chariot skid onto the highway on two wheels and in time to see the bodyguards, who had been left behind, summon a taxi from a waiting line by gesturing for it with the muzzles of their submachine guns.

Little Augie, too, decided that discretion was the better part of valour. It made absolutely no sense at all to become involved in a controversy with individuals armed with submachine guns when all one had for self-protection was a couple of pistols and a set of brass knuckles.

He was unable to restrain himself, however, from stepping through the hole where the plate-glass door had previously been and shaking his fist at the bodyguards.

'I'll see you guys later!' he shouted. The bodyguards jovially waved back.

As Little Augie stood there, two taxis turned off the street and rolled up before The Gate of Joyous and Triumphal Entry. From the first a large, florid-faced, rather bald man emerged, a look of determination on his face.

'Who's in charge here?' he demanded. Little Augie's ego got in the way of his discretion.

'I am,' he said.

'Where have you got her?' the man demanded.

'Where have I got who?'

'My innocent little baby daughter, that's who!'

'I don't know who you're talking about,' Little Augie replied.

'Don't make the mistake of thinking you can fool Fritz W. Fenstermacher,' the man said. 'I'll find her, or my name isn't Fritz W. Fenstermacher!' He strode purposefully through where the plate-glass window had previously been, stalked to the centre of the lobby, put his hands on his hips and shouted: 'Monica! Monica! Everything's all right, baby. Daddy's here!'

Little Augie had rather naturally followed this rather out-of-the-ordinary spectacle with his eyes. He was somewhat surprised when he was suddenly spun around by two of the largest men he could recall seeing.

'What did he ask you?' one of them demanded.

'I don't know,' Little Augie said. 'He's some kind of a nut, I guess. He thinks I've got his baby daughter in here.'

Little Augie suddenly found himself suspended at arm's length over the head of the smaller of the two men.

'It ain't nice to call Mr. Fritz W. Fenstermacher some kind of a nut!' the larger one of the two said.

'Edward,' a female voice said, 'put that man down.'

'He called Mr. Fritz some kind of a nut, Miss Letitia,' the large man said.

'In that case, you may put him down in the pool,' Miss Letitia Kugelblohm said.

Little Augie had a strange feeling, like flying. Then there came a large splash, and he realized that he was now sinking into The Roman Goldfish Pool by the side of The Gate of Joyous and Triumphal Entrance.

'Help!' he called, and with a courage that would long be remembered in the annals of the Centurion's Guards, four guards rushed to attack those who had attacked Little Augie. In moments, there were five people in The Roman Goldfish Pool.

It took Little Augie several moments to regain his composure and another full minute to divest himself of a rather large goldfish which had swum up his trouser leg, apparently in the belief that it was a submarine tunnel. His id and psyche, in the quaint cant of the shrink, had been sorely disturbed. Nothing like this had ever happened to him before in his life.

'Thay there,' a voice called him. 'Yoo hoo! Fat little man in the goldfish pool!'

'Are you talking to me, buddy?' Little Augie replied in what was only a sad travesty of his normally assured tones.

'Yeth, of courth I am. Is thith the place of the O'Reilly-Korsky-Rimsakov nuptials?'

At this point, Stanley August, who had been sort of sulking in his office after Uncle Little Augie had sent Madame Kristina Korsky-Rimsakov packing and returned Nero's nubiles to the Roman Orgy Room, appeared. He had, of course, been attracted by the noise of the submachine-gun firing and the crashing glass.

Now he could hardly believe his eyes and his good fortune. Not only had someone given Uncle Little Augie what could only be described as his just desserts for his beastly behaviour, but he had done so before the eyes of the largest collection of kindred souls. . . . a Greyhound bus full . . . Stanley August had ever seen.

'Perhaps if you would tell me who you are and what you're doing in those simply *gorgeous* robes,' Stanley said to the fellow talking to Uncle Little Augie, 'I could be of some service.'

'Oh, I *bet* you *could!*' the man said.

'Did you throw him in the goldfish pool?' Stanley asked, stepping close to finger the material in the robes. '*Very* nice.'

'Yeth,' the man said. 'We think so, too. But thank you ever so much for saying so. No, we didn't throw him in. I don't know who did. He was just sitting in there when we drove up.'

'Well, never look a gift horse in the mouth, as I always thay,' Stanley August said. 'Now, what can I do for you?'

'We're looking for the O'Reilly–Korsky–Rimsakov nuptials,' he said. 'Is this Nero's Villa?'

'Is the pope a Catholic?' Stanley August replied and a moment later could have just bitten off his tongue in shame.

'Thith is it, Reverend Mother,' Stanley August's new friend shouted. 'You and the archbishop can get off the bus!'

CHAPTER SEVENTEEN

'I'm dead,' Boris Alexandrovich Korsky-Rimsakov said, opening one eye. 'I'm dead, and I've gone to hell. There couldn't possibly be any other explanation for seeing you hovering over me dressed up like an Abyssinian eunuch.'

'You're not dead,' Hawkeye said. 'But speaking of clothes, when did you start wearing a dress?'

'That's not a dress, you demented chancre mechanic,' Boris said. 'Don't you recognize papal vestments when you see them?'

'There's an explanation, Dr. Hawkeye,' HRH Prince Hassan said.

'I was afraid of that,' Hawkeye said. 'I don't want to hear it. I've got enough troubles of my own.'

Boris looked around the cabin and saw Trapper John, Esmerelda, the Baroness d'Iberville and Radar looking down at him.

'I want to talk to you, little man!' he said, pointing a

finger at Radar. He began the sentence sternly, but as he spoke his tone lightened. At the end, he was giggling.

'What's with the rose-pink lace cuffs?' he asked. 'Have you guys joined Hot Lips' a cappella choir, or what?'

'Actually,' Trapper John said, 'it was Mary Pierce's idea.'

'That figures,' Boris said. 'I'd hate to tell you guys what you look like.'

'Of which Kristina firmly approves,' Hawkeye said. 'There's one just like it, waiting for you, at the hotel.'

'Over my dead body,' Boris said.

'That's what Kristina said,' Trapper John said. 'You'd do it just to make her happy.'

'Tell me what happened to your head,' Hawkeye said. 'Has the lump on your head got something to do with the dent in the ceiling?'

'I'd rather hear why he's wearing a dress,' Trapper John said.

'I told you, you degenerate leprechaun,' Boris said. 'These are my papal vestments.'

'Classic case of dementia,' Trapper John said. 'He thinks he's the pope.'

'Probably has something to do with the lump on his head,' Hawkeye said.

'The Maestro came directly from the opera to the airfield,' Prince Hassan said.

'I wanted, naturally, to rush to Baby Sister's side,' Boris said. 'There was no time to change out of my costume. As a matter of fact, there was barely enough time for my exercise.' He paused. 'That was, of course, before I knew Baby Sister had the weird idea that I would be willing to wear a fruit suit.'

'It's not a fruit suit,' Radar said, with surprising firmness. 'It's the Prince Dishabelli Formal Suit for Weddings and Other Occasions.'

'Who the hell is Prince Dishabelli?' Boris asked.

'The nephew of the man who runs the hotel introduced him to Kristina,' Radar said. 'I think he works mainly as an interior decorator.'

'I still would like to know how the ceiling came to be dented,' Hawkeye said.

'Hassan came in here to tell me we were about to land at Las Vegas,' Boris explained. 'So, I quite naturally rose from my bed to find my clothing and get dressed. The next thing I know, you're standing over me, in your eunuch suit, with that revolting look of concern on your face.'

There came now, filling the cabin, the strains of rather unusual music. Boris' face lit up.

'If that's what I think it is,' he said excitedly, happily, and jumped to his feet. It was obviously his intention to look out the aircraft window. Unfortunately, the cabin ceiling was still some nine inches shorter than Boris was tall. There came again the bell-like clang of the irresistible force meeting the immovable object, and again Boris Alexandrovich Korsky-Rimsakov, a bemused smile on his face, sank to the floor.

Trapper John immediately bent over him and then reached into his medical bag for a capsule of a certain chemical compound which, when held beneath the singer's nostrils, would return him to the world of the wide awake.

'Cool it, Trapper,' Hawkeye said.

'What for?'

'That noise, I'm afraid, is exactly what Boris thought it was.' He pointed out the window, and Trapper John went and looked. A Douglas DC-10 aircraft was parked some fifty yards from L'Discorde. Lined up by the stairway, in uniforms which appeared to be those of the Polish Navy, as modified by the man who stages the Folies Bergère in Paris, were thirty rather large men. The men were enthusiastically playing musical instruments of one kind or another. There was a glockenspiel, a rank of Jew's harps, six bass drums, three tubas, two fifes, six slide trombones and some other instruments.

There was a drum major and (a new addition since Dr. Pierce had last seen the musical ensemble) eight drum majorettes. They were all of apparently Japanese national origin and wearing costumes consisting of shockingly abbreviated kimonos. Four of the drum majorettes were standing side by side, arms around each other's shoulders, performing the high-kicking dance made famous by the Rockettes of New York's Radio City Music Hall. (The Rockettes, however, customarily wore less-revealing uniforms.)

The other four majorettes held two large, sequin-lettered signs between them. One sign read 'FIRST PLACE–KYOTO FESTIVAL OF THE SACRED TULIPS.' The other identified the group: 'BAYOU PERDU COUNCIL, KNIGHTS OF COLUMBUS, MARCHING BAND.'

As Hawkeye and Trapper John watched, the drum major blew a mighty blast on his whistle, made rather fascinating movements with his six-foot-long drum major's baton and the group marched away from the airplane toward two chartered buses, drums booming, fifes shrilling, trombones blaring, glockenspiels tinkling.

'Is that what I think it is?' Hawkeye asked.

'Yes, indeed,' Trapper John replied, 'the Bayou Perdu Council, K of C, Marching Band.'

'I meant the music,' Hawkeye said.

'Yes, indeed,' Trapper John replied. 'I don't think Mendelssohn envisioned it quite that way, but that's the Wedding March. They must have been practising.'

'Well, it could be worse,' Hawkeye said.

'How?' Trapper John asked, scornfully.

'The God Is Love in All Forms Christian Church, Inc., all-male a cappella choir could be here.'

'Don't even *think* that!' Trapper John said.

'Let us consider what we are to do in order to assure that Short-Stuff here can get hitched to Kristina with the least possible fuss,' Hawkeye said.

'Knock off that Short-Stuff stuff.' Radar bristled.

'Do you want our help or don't you?' Trapper John said. 'Or should we just wake Boris up so that he can join the marching band?'

'Anything you say,' Radar said.

'Problem One,' Hawkeye said, 'is to keep Boris, so to speak, on ice until it's time for him to appear, sober, shaved and in what he so aptly terms his eunuch suit, at the wedding.'

'Right,' Trapper John said.

'Problem Two is to keep him away from the Bayou Perdu Council, K of C.'

'Check,' Trapper John repeated.

'Problem Three is how to explain to Kristina that nothing is really wrong with the big ape, so that she won't worry about her darling brother.'

'Check,' Radar said.

'The only way I know to keep Boris quiet and trouble-free is to knock him out with an exceedingly strong dose of some sort of powerful drug, which would clearly be a violation of the Hippocratic Oath,' Trapper John said.

'Right,' Hawkeye replied. 'I'll roll up his sleeve, and you stick him with the large hypodermic needle.'

'What are we going to do, leave him here on the plane?' Trapper John asked, as he wiped Boris' arm with a pad of cotton soaked in antiseptic solution.

'I think it would be best if we moved him back to the hotel, so we could keep an eye on him,' Hawkeye said.

'Where can you possibly stash him in the hotel?' Trapper John asked, driving the needle, and then the plunger, home.

'I know this sounds like treason,' Hawkeye said, 'but this is a desperate situation. I think our Beloved Founder would understand.'

'Well, nobody would think to look for him there,' Trapper John added reasonably.

'Radar,' Hawkeye said, 'you go back to the hotel with Hassan. Think up some good story to tell Kristina.'

'I couldn't lie to Kristina,' Radar said. 'She's about to become my wife.'

'It'll be good practice,' Hawkeye said. 'Just tell her you have Trapper John's word that Boris will be at the ceremony and on time.'

'Why my word?' Trapper John asked, indignantly.

'Don't make waves,' Hawkeye replied. 'I have enough problems as it is.'

'I hate to bring this up,' Hassan said, 'but the Baroness d'Iberville and Esmerelda Hoffenburg, the ballerina, just happened to be on the plane.'

'Well, take them to your suite,' Hawkeye said, 'and keep them there.'

'You're right, of course,' Hassan said, a gleam in his eyes.

'Remembering, of course, that Boris will eventually wake up,' Trapper John added.

'How could I forget something like that?'

'And we'll need some of your bodyguards, six or eight of them, Hassan, to move the body,' Hawkeye said. 'I see the ambulance is out there, so they'll have a stretcher.'

'You don't want to tell me where you're going to, as you put it, "stash" him?' Hassan asked.

'Our lips are sealed,' Trapper John and Hawkeye said, together.

'I understand,' Hassan said, although, of course, he didn't understand at all.

'You get going,' Hawkeye said. 'I've got a telephone call to make.'

Matthew Q. Framingham VI was more than a little annoyed to receive the telephone call from Dr. Benjamin Franklin Pierce announcing that he was shortly going to deliver a package which would have to be installed in one of the bedrooms of the Framingham Theosophical Foundation's Home Away From Home.

Dr. Pierce turned a deaf ear to Matthew's statement that bringing anybody not a member in good standing, for whatever reason, into the foundation's quarters was clearly a violation of the foundation's constitution. Dr. Pierce replied to that by reminding Matthew Q. Framingham VI that the first stated purpose of the Framingham Foundation, clearly spelled out in the constitution, was the preservation of both the sanity of the members and of the members' marriages when either or both were placed under strain by the exigencies of marriage.

'Let me put it to you this way, Matthew,' Dr. Pierce had said. 'If this marriage does not go off smoothly and without incident, not only my marriage and mental ability but those of our new co-member, Dr. Trapper John McIntyre, as well, are very likely to be destroyed. Do you want the responsibility for that on your shoulders?'

'You say that he's unconscious?'

'Dr. Trapper John himself gave him a shot that'll keep him in dreamland for at least twenty-four hours,' Hawkeye replied. 'All he's going to do is lay there and breathe.'

'Well, since you phrase the matter in those parameters,' Matthew said, 'there is little option offered to me, as I see the situation. I would appreciate it, however, if you would accomplish the transporting of the gentleman at your earliest possible convenience.'

'What's the rush?'

'I have scheduled an appointment with a terpsichorean ecdysiast,' Matthew replied, 'of whom I have formed a favourable initial impression and whom, presuming her demonstration performance is up to the standards of the foundation, I am considering placing under contract for the Wednesday evening moral enlightenment get-together.'

'You dirty young man, you!' Hawkeye said, admiringly. 'You never do get enough, do you?'

'Doctor,' Matthew Q. Framingham said, 'I assure you that my interest in this person is entirely platonic and wholly professional.'

'Yeah, sure it is,' Hawkeye said. 'I'm just in the wrong profession, that's all.'

'To reiterate, Doctor: I have an appointment, and I would suggest that our purposes would be better served were it possible for you to install, as it were, your guest prior to the arrival of my candidate.'

'Candidate?' Hawkeye asked. 'Is that what you call her?'

'Indeed. What term would you suggest that better fits her relationship vis-à-vis the foundation and myself?'

'I wouldn't think of suggesting anything,' Hawkeye replied. 'We'll be right over.'

Matthew Q. Framingham VI's fears that Miss 'Montague Smith' would come to the floor while Hawkeye and Trapper

John were installing their nameless friend in one of the bedrooms proved groundless.

Miss 'Montague Smith', in fact, had no intention whatever of going to the Framingham Foundation's secret hideaway just yet. She had been so disturbed by the realization that Mr. Framingham VI actually took her for a terpsichorean ecdysiast that her fury did not diminish even after she had kicked the wastebasket all around her room, nor even after she had drawn a rather good, if somewhat cruel, caricature of Mr. Framingham VI on the mirror over the dresser with her lipstick. She realized that her emotional state was such that she was wholly unable to practice television journalism with anything approaching professional objectivism and detachment. She had, in fact, been right on the verge of going to her rendezvous with Mr. Framingham VI with her camera, with the intention of using the camera as a club, and had only gotten control of herself at the last minute.

In desperation, then, she had called the Don Rhotten office again from her room. This time her call had been expected, and there was a message for her:

'Mr. Rhotten, Mr. Schwartz and Congressman Jackson are at this moment in an air force jet, flying to Las Vegas. You are to give us your present location and to stay where you are without taking any action whatever until further orders.'

Monica's self-esteem returned. What had happened during her first telephone call had apparently been the result of some sort of misunderstanding. She should have known better than to think that Don Rhotten did not care about the news. For reasons that she would learn in good time, he had just said that. The fact that he was at this very moment en route, in an air force jet, to join her, accompanied by the executive producer, Mr. Seymour Schwartz, and Congressman 'Smiling Jack' Jackson, was proof positive not only that Mr. Don Rhotten was indeed living up to the finest traditions of television journalism but also that he did indeed place full faith and trust in the ability, loyalty and all-around *chutzpah* of his loyal research assistant.

'Wait till Don Rhotten gets here!' Monica P. Fenstermacher said, shaking her hand in the direction of the twenty-fifth floor and Mr. Matthew Q. Framingham VI. 'He'll grease *your* wagon, you big oaf!'

She then retired to the Roman Spa-ette (shower only, no tub) of her room and stood for a long time under the cold water. It not only calmed her down, but she remembered hearing somewhere that cold showers were good for you under certain conditions. She couldn't remember what those conditions were, exactly, and under the circumstances would have been more than a little piqued if she had been able to remember,[1] but that didn't seem to matter. Nothing really seemed to matter, now that she knew Don Rhotten himself was on the way to put the finishing touches to her journalistic scoop.

Meanwhile, in his plushly furnished office just off the lobby, Caesar Augustus Finecello was, with great relish, in the act of placing a telephone call to his-brother-the-priest, Rev. Giuseppe Verdi Finecello, S.J.

Father Gus had said some pretty strong, and generally unkind, things to Little Augie when he had last been in the hotel, and if there was one thing Little Augie liked less than a priest self-righteously running off at the mouth about people being nothing more than hoodlums, crooks, and thugs, it was a little brother who happened to be a priest calling him a hoodlum, a crook and a thug.

'I truly hope I didn't interrupt nuttin'',' Little Augie said to Father Gus. 'Like a juicy confession or something?'

'As a matter of fact, I was playing tennis,' Father Gus replied. 'What's on your mind, Augie?'

'Well, whatsamatter? Can't a brother call up his brother and just say hello?'

'There are exceptions to every rule,' Father Gus said.

---

[1] In the eleventh grade, Monica's hygiene teacher had announced that under certain conditions of close proximity to the male animal, females sometimes developed sweaty palms, palpitations of the heart and flushed cheeks, the recommended treatment for which was a long, cold shower.

'You took the words right out of my mouth,' Little Augie said.

'What's that supposed to mean?'

'The thing is, Gus . . . I can still call you "Gus", can't I?'

'I'd prefer Father Finecello, actually,' Father Gus said. 'As a priest, I have to talk to you. As your brother, I don't possess that much milk of human kindness.'

'Have it your way, Father,' Little Augie said. 'What I was gonna tell you was that we got three priests checked in here at Nero's Villa.'

'They must either have the wrong place or be part of some churchly investigation of wholesale sin,' Father Gus replied.

'Gee, you really know how to hurt a guy,' Little Augie replied. 'But just to keep the record straight, Father, they ain't in the wrong place.'

'So?'

'So two of 'em checked in with forty fruits.'

'I beg your pardon?'

'Forty fruits *and* a Reverend Mother,' Little Augie said, carefully enunciating each syllable.

'Fruits?'

'You know, like Little Stanislaus. Walking around smelling like God knows what, waving their hands.'

'Augie, so help me, if this is your idea of a joke!'

'Would I kid about a thing like that? To my own brother-the-priest?'

'How do you know they're q . . . like little Stanislaus?'

'That little freak greeted them like long lost brothers,' Little Augie said.

'I can't say I particularly appreciate the simile,' Father Gus said. 'So what are they doing now?'

'Most of them is in Roman Circus Number Two with Little Stanislaus. Two of the priests is up in the hotel room with the Reverend Mother.'

'I find all of this quite hard to believe, Augie.'

'Boy scout's honour, Gus . . . *excuse* me, Father Finecello,' Little Augie said.

'You said there were *three* priests?'

'The third one's maybe better than a priest,' Little Augie said, helpfully. 'Probably a monsignor.'

'What makes you think that?'

'Well, when the Arabs carried him through the lobby, he was wearing a white whatchamacallit.'

'Whatchamacallit?'

'You know, those robe things.'

'A cassock?'

'I thought you put your feet on a cassock.'

'You put your feet on a *hassock*,' Father Gus said. 'A white cassock is something . . . oh my God! . . . that certain high-ranking prelates of the church wear. What do you mean, when the "Arabs carried him through the lobby"?'

'I'd be the last man in the world, you know that, Father Finecello, to suggest that a priest was smashed. All I can tell you was that this guy was dead to the world and smelled of booze, and that his funny little hat kept falling off the stretcher.'

'What kind of a funny little hat?'

'The kind the Jews wear when *they* go to Mass,' Little Augie explained. 'Except this one was white and embroidered with pearls.'

'Tell me more about the Arabs,' Father Gus said.

'What can I tell you? You seen one Arab, you seen them all. They're all about seven feet tall, wearing those funny things on their heads and bathrobed down to their ankles.'

'You're sure?'

'Sure I'm sure,' Little Augie replied. 'Oh, one more thing, Father Finecello, they all had silver-plated tommy guns.'

'What do you mean, tommy guns?'

'You know, *tommy guns*,' Little Augie said. Then, by pressing his lips together and blowing hard, he came up with a rather credible mimicry of the sound of a submachine gun being fired.

'Augie,' Father Gus said, after a moment's solemn reflection, 'I believe you.'

'I should hope so,' Augie said. 'Would I lie to my-brother-the-priest?'

'I believe you because you're not smart enough to dream all this up by yourself.'

'Is that so?'

'That's so,' Father Gus said.

'Well, I just thought you would like to know,' Little Augie said, slyly.

'Why did you think so?'

'Like it says in the Good Book, Father,' Little Augie said, triumphantly, 'let him who is without sin cast the first stone.' He cackled like a hen and hung up.

Father Gus laid the telephone back in its cradle. The matter was going to require some deep thought. But as soon as the phone was back in the cradle, it rang again.

'Father Finecello,' he said.

'Gus, this is Max,' the voice said.

'Yes, Father Superior?'

'You pretty busy, are you, Gus?'

'I . . . uh . . . well, the truth of the matter is . . .'

'Good,' Father Superior said. 'Idle hands make mischief, as I always say. The thing is, Gus, I just got a call. From, well, sort of a friend of mine, a guy I owe, in Rome.'

'Is that so?' Father Gus said. 'Father Superior, the fact is that I just had a call from my brother . . .'

'That'll have to wait, Gus,' Father Superior said firmly. 'This . . . this *friend* of mine . . . in Rome? Well, I *owe* him. I owe him a *lot*. You get my meaning?'

'Yes, Father Superior, I think so.'

'That's one of the things I like about you, Gus, you're smart.'

'Thank you for saying so, Father Superior.'

'We're all smart, otherwise we wouldn't be Jesuits, right? But there's smart, and there's *smart*. You're *smart* smart, you get my meaning?'

'What exactly is it you wish me to do, Father Superior?'

'Right to the bottom line? That's what I like about you, Gus. In addition to being smart, it's always right to the bottom line with you. O.K., I'll tell you. I wouldn't want this to get out, so play it cool, but there's a certain archbishop, the Archbishop of Swengchan, China, to nail it down...'

'Is His Eminence of Chinese extraction, Father Superior?'

'Could be, I suppose,' Father Superior said, 'but I don't think so. His name is John Patrick Mulcahy. That sound Chinese to you?'

'Irish, I would say,' Father Gus replied.

'That figures,' said Father Superior, who happened to be of Scottish extraction. 'Most of them Irish are a little weird.'

'Perhaps, Father Superior, if you would explain the nature of the problem...'

'Right,' Father Superior said. 'Here it is. Get a car, Gus, and get over to Las Vegas. This archbishop is due in over there any minute now. Him and a monsignor... get this, Gus... named Pancho Villa.'

'Yes, Father Superior.'

'Some hotel named Nero's Villa. You ever heard of it?'

'Yes, Father Superior, I know it.'

'O.K., Gus. Get over there and keep your eye on the archbishop. Don't be a spoil sport. He wants to have a little fun, let him have a little fun. All work and no play, as I always say. But... my friend... says he's heard something about some Reverend Mother. And, well, you're smart, you figure it out. Keep me posted, Gus, and if you need any help, just yell.'

'I'm on my way, Father Superior,' Father Giuseppe Verdi Finecello said. With what he'd learned from Father Superior and what he'd learned from his brother the thug, hoodlum and crook, everything had become clear. Entirely too clear.

CHAPTER EIGHTEEN

One of Boris Alexandrovich Korsky-Rimsakov's most devoted fans and admirers was Sheikh Abdullah ben Abzug, absolute monarch of the Sheikhdom of Abzug, a relatively small Islamic country (geographically speaking) whose recently discovered oil and gas reserves were exceeded only by those of Saudi Arabia and the Kingdom of Hussid.

Sheikh Abdullah had come to know the singer through his art. That is to say, he had heard the singer sing through the medium of phonograph records in the possession of his grandson and heir apparent, Sheikh Omar ben Ahmed. (His son, and Omar's father, had been in line for the throne until he became enamoured of, and married, the former Ingeborg Schwartzenfuss, a Bavarian belly dancer he had met in a Beirut nightclub. The couple were now living, in sort of disgrace, in Portugal, and the very mention of his name was punishable by death in Abzug.)

From the first moment Sheikh Abdullah had heard the singer sing, he had known that he was a singer cut from his own cloth, one, in the sheikh's rather inadequate French, 'avec les boules' (roughly, one with a certain *machismo*).

When, on his very first trip to Paris, France, he had been introduced to Boris Alexandrovich Korsky-Rimsakov by their mutual friend His Royal Highness Prince Hassan ad Kayam, they had instantly become mutual admirers and fast friends.

Following a weekend spent in the company of some U.S. Marine Corps friends of the singer and their lady friends, Sheikh Abdullah had impulsively conferred Abzugian citizenship on the singer, together with a proper (that is to say, non-English) title. So far as the monarch of Abzug was (and thus all Abzugians were) concerned, Boris Alexandrovich Korsky-Rimsakov was His Excellency Sheikh El Noil Sniol, Knight Companion of the Royal Bedroom, and thus entitled to all the not-inconsiderable rights and prerogatives thereto pertaining.

It was, in fact, because of the Sheikh's affection and admiration for the singer that exploitation of Abzugian petroleum deposits had been granted to the Chevaux Petroleum Corporation, International. 'Any friend,' Sheikh Abdullah had declared, somewhat emotionally, 'of old Lion Loins is a friend of mine.'

As it happened, when word reached Colonel de la

Chevaux, chairman of the board and chief executive officer of Chevaux Petroleum Corporation, International, that the baby sister of Boris Alexandrovich Korsky-Rimsakov was to marry, the colonel was in the Sheikhdom of Abzug, personally supervising the drilling of an oil-well known as 'Penelope Quattlebaum ben Ahmed Number Three.'

Her Royal Highness Scheherezade Naomi ben Ahmed (née Penelope Quattlebaum), recent bride of grandson and heir Omar ben Ahmed, was in a family way, and her grandfather-in-law, Sheikh Abdullah ben Abzug, as a sign of both his personal affection and his royal approval, had decreed that six holes be sunk in a proven field, with title given to the blond former infidel about to present him (he was sure) with a great-grandson. HRH Scheherezade Naomi ben Ahmed would thus have a little spending money for diapers, booties and the like.

When the radio-telephone calls had come, first from Boris in Paris and immediately afterward from Reverend Mother Emeritus M. H. W. Wilson, R.N., in New Orleans, Sheikh Abdullah ben Abzug had been in Annex No. 1 of the Bayou Perdu Council, K of C, at the well-drilling site. The sheikh was in a good mood, having just beaten Colonel de la Chevaux 21-7, 21-11 and 21-7 in three straight games of electronic Ping-Pong.

Colonel de la Chevaux thus had little trouble complying with Boris Alexandrovich Korsky-Rimsakov's radio-telephone request to 'ask ol' Abdullah if he wants to come to the wedding.'

Sheikh Abdullah had immediately accepted. Not only was it only fitting that he attend the wedding of the beloved sister of Sheikh El Noil Sniol (who was, after all an *ex officio* member of the Abzugian Privy Council) but it had been the sheikh's experience (as indeed, it had been HRH Prince Hassan's experience) that where Boris went, so did hordes of willing females.

Within a matter of hours, arrangements had been completed. Troop 'C' of the Royal Abzugian Cavalry had been loaded aboard Chevaux Petroleum's 747 Number One, as had six camels (for the ritual camel slaughter) and a herd of sheep (plus the necessary shepherds and butchers) for the traditional post-nuptial feast.

The flight passed uneventfully (with the exception of a minor problem caused by one of the less-experienced shepherds, who, feeling the pangs of hunger, had attempted to build a small bonfire on one of the fuel tanks on which to roast a leg of lamb) and fourteen hours after Horsey had received the first word of the impending nuptials, Las Vegas Approach Control cleared Chevaux 747 as Number Two to land.

Prince Hassan, had of course, arranged for suitable accommodations (the twenty-fourth floor of the northwest wing) for the sheikh and his party, and he had even sent his own Rolls-Royce to the airfield to carry the sheikh to the hotel. He had had no way of knowing, of course, that the sheikh was either coming officially (that is, accompanied by Troop 'C' of the Royal Abzugian Cavalry) or that he, too, planned a post-nuptial feast necessitating a supply of sheep.

The progress of the party, thus, from the airfield to the hotel was somewhat slower than originally anticipated. Not only was it geared to the top speed of the sheep, but there were two en-route delays. The first was caused by the Las Vegas police, who rather rudely demanded to see the permit for the circus parade. To get the cops, so to speak, off their backs, it had been necessary to communicate with the Department of State and for the Secretary of State himself to assure the Las Vegas police that under international law a sovereign head of a sovereign state travelling on a diplomatic passport was immune to the laws of the land and could indeed, if he so chose, stage a circus parade down Las Vegas' main drag at any time the notion struck him as a good one.

The second delay occurred when the proprietor of a hotel which prided itself on the variety of the entertainment it offered its guests saw the procession and decided that it was just what he needed. He was not accustomed to taking 'no' for an answer, and it was only after the sheikh spoke to the commanding officer of Troop 'C' and three lancers advanced, at the gallop, on the hotel proprietor that he could be persuaded to get out of the way.

Once they reached Nero's Villa, however, things went smoothly. The sheep were turned into a rope compound hastily erected around The Pool of the Roman Goldfish. The sacrificial camels were tied to stakes on the lawn, and Troop 'C', after gathering their mounts, immediately went to work on the construction of the Royal Banquet Tent.

When he walked through The Gate of Joyous and Triumphal Entry, Sheikh Abdullah found two old friends on hand to greet him.

'Hawkeye,' he shouted, in a few words of English that Boris had taught him. 'How're they hanging?'

'How are you, Sheikh?' Hawkeye replied. 'You remember Trapper John, of course?'

'Mud in your eye, Trapper John,' the sheikh said warmly. 'Bring on the broads.'

'Thanks for coming down to meet us,' Horsey de la Chevaux said.

'I wouldn't have missed it for the world,' Hawkeye said.

'I mean,' Horsey said, 'people who don't know Abdullah don't speak English . . .'

'Speak English?' the sheikh said. 'Mud in your eye. Your mother wears army shoes. Up yours.' He beamed proudly.

'That's fine, Abdullah,' Horsey said, in Arabic. 'Hawkeye and Trapper say to tell you welcome to Las Vegas.'

'My joy at seeing them knows no bounds,' the sheikh replied.

'He says he's glad to see you,' Horsey translated.

'I have not seen such a splendid brothel,' the sheikh said, approvingly, 'since some demented female forced the Sphinx in Paris to close thirty years ago.' He looked around the lobby and spotted four members of Nero's Villa's corps de ballet, 'Nero's Nubiles', walking toward the elevator. 'I'll take all of them,' he said. 'Have them sent up in thirty minutes.'

'Horsey, tell him it doesn't work quite that way,' Hawkeye said.

'I didn't know you spoke Arabic,' Horsey said, surprised.

'I don't,' Hawkeye said. 'I read eyes.'

'Where is my beloved friend, he with the voice of the angels and the loins of the lion?'

'He wants to know where Boris is,' Horsey translated.

'Just between you and us, Horsey,' Trapper John said, 'in the interests of peace, tranquillity and a dignified wedding, we gave him a shot that'll keep him knocked out until the ceremony.'

'Boris's taking a little nap, Abdullah,' Horsey translated. 'He was a little tired.'

'In that case, I will finish anything he started,' the sheikh, his eyes lighting up, announced. 'Where is he?'

'I don't think at this time,' Hawkeye said, 'without meaning to sound like a spoilsport or anything, that that's a very good idea.'

Horsey thought for a moment. Then his face brightened.

'Come on, Abdullah,' he said. 'I got something to show you. A new toy.'

He led the sheikh to a row of slot machines.

'Somebody give me some quarters,' he said, as he put one in the machine and pulled the lever. Sheikh Abdullah's face lit up. He watched the wheels revolve and then stop with great fascination. He was even more delighted when Horsey's pull (probably by mechanical error) resulted in a payoff, and six quarters spilled into the payoff slot.

'If you think *I'm* going to give *him* gambling money,' Hawkeye said.

'Would you rather he went looking for Boris?'

Hawkeye instantly produced a ten-dollar bill and thrust it at the sheikh. 'Have a good time, Abdullah,' he said with a smile and then, to Horsey, 'how long will he play this thing?'

'For hours, I hope,' Horsey said. 'What time is the wedding?'

'Nine in the morning,' Trapper John replied. 'Radar believes in getting things going early in the day.'

'And you're sure Boris will be out all night?'

'We gave him enough to keep two people out all night,' Trapper John said.

'O.K.,' Horsey said, 'no problem with these two, then. I'll have one of these things moved onto his floor, and he'll be as happy as a pig in mud. Now tell me who else has shown up?'

'The marching band is here,' Hawkeye said. 'They now have eight Japanese drum majorettes. Did you know that?'

'I heard,' Horsey said. 'I'll worry about that later. What about Hot Lips and her fair. . . .'

'Hark, hark, a covey of larks!' Trapper John said, interrupting him, cupping his hand over his ear and nodding in the direction of Roman Circus Number Three. Horsey cocked his head and listened. Very faintly, one could make out the sounds of forty sort-of-soprano voices rendering 'Let Me Call You Sweetheart'!

'That's what I was afraid of,' Horsey said. 'Where's the marching band?'

'We installed them on the twenty-fifth floor of the north wing,' Hawkeye said, 'and threatened the elevator operator with castration if he lets any of them back down here without permission.'

'All gone,' Sheikh Abdullah said. 'I put the little coins in that thieving machine, and it has kept them!' He started to draw his scimitar.

'It's a game, Abdullah,' Horsey explained, 'like electronic Ping-Pong. You have to learn how to play. So far you've lost.'

'Oh,' Abdullah said. 'I will need more little coins, then, won't I?'

'You can get them from bellboys,' Trapper John offered.

'Bellboy' was another English word in Sheikh Abdullah's vocabulary. He reached out and grabbed one of the Centurion's Guards as he walked past and thrust a bill at him. It wasn't the ten-spot Hawkeye had given him. That was a gift from a friend, and one took care of gifts from friends. The sheikh had tucked Hawkeye's ten dollars in the purse which hung from his gold-cord belt. He now reached into his headdress, where he kept his small change, and came out with another bill. This he thrust at the bellboy, with the words 'little coins!' (In English).

The bellboy stared at it bug-eyed.

'Change that into quarters,' Horsey explained. 'And then have that one-armed bandit taken to the sheikh's suite.'

'He wants a thousand dollars' worth of quarters?' the Centurion's Guard asked.

'Little coins,' Sheikh Abdullah repeated.

'Yes, sir!' The Centurion's Guard said, enthusiastically.

'He's going to have the game taken to your suite, Abdullah,' Horsey explained. 'And he'll bring you lots of little coins.'

'And are you going with me?' Abdullah asked.

'No, I am going to see the Bride-to-be and Archbishop Mulcahy,' Horsey said. 'You remember him, from Rome?'

'Dago Red!' Abdullah said, delightedly. 'The nice little man who has nothing to do with women, but at the same time is not, how do you say, a sissy?'

'That's the one,' Horsey said.

'Ah,' Sheikh Abdullah said. 'You are a good man, Horsey! A good friend! Since his heathen religious belief will not permit him to break in the bride, you will do it for him!'

'What did he say?' Hawkeye asked.

'He said he thanks you for meeting him and looks forward to the wedding,' Horsey de la Chevaux said, blushing for the first time in a very long time.

'You have already done too much,' the sheikh said, having had a moment to think the matter over. 'As proof of *my* friendship, I will break in the bride! Where is she?'

'It isn't done that way, here,' Horsey said. 'Here the bridegroom has to do that for himself.'

'This is truly a strange place,' the sheikh said. But he pursued the matter no further. With Hawkeye on one side and Trapper John on the other, Sheikh Abdullah permitted himself to be led to the elevator. Behind them, five Centurion's Guards carried the one-armed bandit and pushed a little truck on which sat bags containing $1,000 in quarters.

It has been said that unlettered sons of the desert, and Sheikh Abdullah was certainly an unlettered son of the desert, frequently demonstrate an ability to see things as they are, rather than as they seem to be.

Unknown to Hawkeye, Trapper John, or Horsey, Sheikh Abdullah had just given a demonstration of this in the lobby of Nero's Villa. The four members of Nero's Nubiles whom the sheikh had seen walking across the lobby were indeed practitioners of the world's oldest profession, and had they known of the sheikh's interest (and ability to pay) it must be presumed that the sheikh would have spent the next couple of hours playing with something somewhat warmer and softer than the cast-aluminium handle of a one-armed bandit.

The ladies were, in fact, en route to make a sort of house call, at the express order of Little Augie Finecello.

'Take the elevator wit' duh Life Insurance Salesman's Convention sign,' Little Augie had ordered. 'Dere's already three guys up there.' In consideration of what religious feelings the ladies might have, Little Augie did not mention that one of the three was a priest, or maybe a monsignor, who had arrived in the hotel so drunk he had to be carried to his room.

'You're sure they like girls?' one of the ladies had asked.

'If I was to get the idea you were making certain allusions to any member of my family, I would be very disturbed,' Little Augie had replied. 'You get my meaning?'

'Just asking, just asking,' the lady replied.

'And this time,' Little Augie said, his voice dripping with menace, 'I want youse all to remember this ain't no screen test you're making. We want the *guys* on the film. The last time, the way you hammed it up, we could hardly see the men.'

That accusation had stung the ladies' professional pride to the quick. They glowered at Little Augie, who didn't seem at all hurt by the glowers.

'Like I said, there's three guys up there. Start out with the big one,' he ordered. 'By the time you're through with him, there's bound to be more. They got the whole twenty-fifth floor reserved.' He waited until this had time to sink in and then finished his little pep talk: 'This is a great opportunity for all of us,' he said. 'I have every confidence that youse will be able to handle it in a way which will reflect credit upon your profession.'

He took quiet pride in knowing that he had touched their hearts. They walked out of his office proudly, in step, chests out. They hadn't even noticed Sheikh Abdullah and the others more than casually in the lobby. They were out after big game, not some two-bit player of a one-armed bandit.

Gaining access to the northwest wing of the twenty-fifth floor proved to be no problem at all, mainly because Little Augie had had a word with the Centurion Guard on duty, telling him the ladies would be coming.

They got off the elevator and walked from door to door, peering in on one empty room and suite after another. They were just beginning to become worried, to suspect that they possibly had gotten off on the wrong floor, when one of them pushed open a door and then let out a low whistle.

'I've got mine, girls,' she said. 'I don't care if he is wearing a white dress.'

The others, naturally, went to see what she saw.

'I *know*,' the second one said. 'Let's all sort of warm up on this one. Little Augie said he was especially interested in the big one, and there's no way they can come any bigger than this one!'

The one who had spotted him was a little annoyed that she wouldn't have him all to herself, but reminding herself that business was business, she gave in. The three ladies tiptoed into the room.

'He's asleep,' one whispered.

'Not for long,' the second one said.

'Lights, action, camera!' the third one said, and when they heard the muted whirring sound, they advanced on the bed.

Boris Alexandrovich Korsky-Rimsakov, who had been given, in the professional medical opinion of Drs. Benjamin

Franklin Pierce and James Francis Xavier McIntyre, a sufficient quantity of a nerve-depressant drug to keep him out until eight the next morning, was laying on the bed, arms and legs spread, mouth open, not moving at all.

As the ladies approached him, however, there was movement on his face. His nose wrinkled. Then his face lapsed into repose again, only, a moment later, to have the nose wrinkle again. It wrinkled twice, this time followed by a massive inhaling of air. A smile crossed the lips. Suddenly, both eyes were wide open.

'Hassan!' he said, sitting up, wide awake. 'Wherever you are, you camel thief, you, Boris apologizes for thinking you could fail him in his hour of need.'

'Hi, there, Big Boy!' the first lady said.

'My, aren't you handsome!' the second one said.

'I find you irresistible!' said the third.

'I think I should tell you,' Boris said, as he divested himself of the costume he had worn while singing the role of Pope Clement VII, 'that the one thing I can't stand is a lot of talking!'

With that, he jumped out of bed, threw the window open, and began that calisthenic exercise known in the military as deep knee bends.

'What the hell are you doing?' the first one asked.

'Exercise, exercise, *toujours l'exercise*,' Boris announced. 'Quoting the Sage of Manhattan, Kansas, of course. Perhaps, if you feel up to it later, I might have time to tell you something of the sage's wise words. But for now, girls, why don't you draw straws or something to decide who's first?'

CHAPTER NINETEEN

The flight of Congressman Edwards L. 'Smiling Jack' Jackson and the staff, including the namesake, of 'The Rhotten Report' was not as pleasant as the congressman was used to. The air force, of course, had responded instantly to the congressman's announcement that a national crisis was at hand by providing him with an aircraft.

The jet which the air force made available, however, was a common, ordinary, run-of-the-mill air force jet, not one of the plush, highly polished, ornately equipped jets of the Special Air Missions Wing, that air force organization charged with ferrying members of Congress, the President, Vice-President, and assorted other public servants hither and yon in the public interest.

Not only was there not a private compartment for the congressman to have his traditional in-flight massage, but not even a masseuse. The crew chief, moreover, used language that congressmen were not used to hearing from members of the armed forces when Smiling Jack said that while he was willing to make reasonable sacrifices in the service of his country, he thought that being asked to make a flight all the way from New York to Nevada without in-flight movies was a bit much.

Things got worse when the plane landed at Las Vegas. Don Rhotten took one look out the window, saw the desert and somehow got the idea that the congressman and Mr. Schwartz had perpetrated a nefarious plot against him. Specifically, he suspected that for reasons he couldn't understand, Schwartz and Smiling Jack had flown him back to Morocco, a country of which he had bad memories.

'Don,' Schwartz said, 'trust me. This is Nevada. Part of the Good Old USA.'

'Then what's all that sand out there? I know a desert when I see one.'

'That's not a desert, Don. Look at the sign. What does the sign say?'

'It says "El Rancho Vegas Mobile Home Estates",' Rhotten said, reading it aloud.

'Does that sound Moroccan?'

'You bet your sweet ass it does,' Don Rhotten said. 'You forget, Seymour, that you tricked me before. You can only fool ol' Don Rhotten once.'

'Think, Don,' Seymour Schwartz said. 'If this was Morocco, wouldn't there be guys in Arab robes?'

Don Rhotten looked around the airport, found no one in Arab robes and allowed himself to be led off the plane.

He was not, however, entirely convinced. 'It's as hot here as it is in Morocco,' he added. 'How do you explain that?'

'Get in the cab, you rotten jailbird,' Smiling Jack said. 'My political career is at stake.'

'Just to keep the record straight, Mr. Congressman,' Rhotten said icily, righteously, 'you were in that slammer when I got there.'

'You guys cut it out,' Schwartz pleaded. 'We got enough to worry about without you two fighting among yourselves.'

Troop 'C' of the Royal Abzugian Cavalry, the six sacrificial camels and the herd of sheep, plus the banquet tent, of course, were spread out before The Gate of Joyous and Triumphal Entrance to Nero's Villa, but for some reason none of this rekindled Don Rhotten's suspicions that he had been smuggled, against his wishes, back into Morocco.

'I mean,' he said, 'if I can't trust you guys, who can I trust? As rotten as the both of you are, I simply can't believe that you'd do anything dirty to America's most beloved television journalist.'

'Shut up, you rotten jailbird,' Smiling Jack said, 'and get out of the cab.'

'If you call me that one more time,' Rhotten said, flaring, 'your name will never again be mentioned on "The Rhotten Report".' It was the ultimate ultimatum.

'Sorry, Don,' Smiling Jack said. 'We're all under a little strain.'

Five minutes later, the three were conferring with Ms. Monica P. Fenstermacher in Ms. Fenstermacher's room, while the sound and camera crew waited outside in the hall.

Within a matter of minutes, Seymour G. Schwartz thought that he saw a light at the end of the long tunnel. All was not lost. Fritz W. Fenstermacher, the largest single advertiser on the Amalgamated Broadcasting Network and personal friend of the Speaker of the House, would be in no position to make waves about his daughter if he had what is known in the trade as film-in-the-can of Fritz W. Fenstermacher participating in the secret rites of the Matthew Q. Framingham Theosophical Foundation.

As a practical man of the world, Seymour G. Schwartz had a pretty good idea what sort of 'recreation' was being offered a bunch of East Coast biggies having a convention under a phony name in Nero's Villa. He had seen some pretty interesting things himself just recently at Kornblatt's Catskill Mountain Health Farm and Rathskeller, and, compared to Nero's Villa, Kornblatt's was about as wicked as Vatican City.

'The problem, sweetie,' Seymour said.

'Under the circumstances, Seymour,' Smiling Jack said, 'I think it would be best if we referred to this charming young lady and daughter of a personal friend of the Speaker of the House as "Miss Fenstermacher".'

'That's *Ms*. Fenstermacher,' Monica corrected him.

'Right,' Seymour said. 'No offence.'

'Watch it,' Monica said.

'Right,' Seymour said. 'The problem, as I see it, Ms. Fenstermacher, is how do we get a camera into the secret hideaway of this outfit?'

'No problem,' Monica replied.

'All we do is put the crew on the elevator,' Don Rhotten said. 'How's that a problem?'

'Shut up, Don,' Seymour said.

'I think what Mr. Schwartz is suggesting, Don,' Monica said, helpfully, 'is the way they have things set up, they wouldn't let us just walk in with a camera.'

'God, clever devils, aren't they?' Don Rhotten said. 'What if we told them we were from CBS?'

'Shut up, Don,' Seymour repeated. 'You were saying, sweetie?'

'*Ms. Fenstermacher*, for God's sake,' Smiling Jack said. 'I told you, Seymour, her father is a *personal* friend of the *Speaker of the House!*'

'Right,' Seymour said. 'You were saying, Ms. Fenstermacher?'

'I'll tell you what,' Monica said.

'Great!' Seymour said. 'Tell me what.'

'I'll call you "Seymour" and you can call me "Monica",' Monica said. 'I mean, we're all in this together, right?'

'That's very kind of you, Monica,' Seymour said.

'Not at all, Seymour,' Monica said.

'And you can call me "Congressman Jackson",' Smiling Jack said, benevolently.

'You were about to say something, Monica,' Seymour G. Schwartz said.

'The big, arrogant, male chauvinist pig who's running the operation . . .'

'That would be Matthew Q. Framingham VI?'

'Right,' Monica said.

'What about him?'

'He told the guards at the elevator door to let me into the elevator,' Monica said.

'Great!'

'And I have a camera,' Monica said.

'Great!' Seymour repeated.

'Not great!' Don Rhotten said. 'The cameraman's union won't like that.'

'Shut up, Don,' Seymour said.

'He may have a point,' Smiling Jack said. 'In my long career of public service, I have never willingly offended our noble knights of labour.'

'Shut up, Jack,' Seymour said. 'Go on, Monica.'

'You seem to forget, Seymour,' Congressman Jackson said, angrily, 'that under that lousy constitution of ours, every last one of those union creeps gets to vote!'

'For the last time, Jack, shut up,' Seymour said.

'How would it be, Seymour,' Monica asked, 'if I just took my camera and went up there and shot the story myself?'

'I thought you said, Monica,' Seymour replied, 'that your father is up there.'

'He is,' Monica said. 'I have ascertained that fact beyond any reasonable doubt!'

'And you're willing to go up there, and not only see what's going on, but take pictures of it? Of your own father?'

'You bet I am,' Monica said.

'Monica, sweetie,' Seymour G. Schwartz said, emotionally, tears forming in his eyes. 'Let me say, in all sincerity, that I have misjudged you.'

'Oh, really?' Monica replied, suspiciously.

'Yes, I have,' Seymour said. 'I never would have thought it, let me admit that, but you just proved that you have what it takes to make it in this business.'

'Why, Seymour,' Monica said, 'how nice of you to say so!'

'Now that I see what you're thinking, Seymour,' Don Rhotten said, 'I think it's a pretty rotten . . .'

'Shut up, Don,' Seymour said. He stood up, put his hands on Monica P. Fenstermacher's shoulders and looked her in the eye. 'Go to it, Monica!' he said. 'If you carry it off, "The Rhotten Report", and television journalism generally, will be proud of you!'

With tears in her eyes, not trusting herself to speak, Monica P. Fenstermacher picked up her camera, straightened her shoulders and marched out of the room.

'Stop staring,' Seymour said, sotto voce, to Don Rhotten. 'They're still off limits to you, Don-Baby.'

'God, the sacrifices I must make for my career!' Don Rhotten said. 'If my fans only knew.'

'What you have done is a really rotten thing, Seymour,' Smiling Jack said.

'Yeah, isn't it?' Seymour said, visibly pleased. 'What would you guys do without me?'

As his high-level staff planning conference had been under way, another conference had taken place, by telephone, between Mr. 'Little Augie' Finecello and Arthur C. 'Needlenose' Hightower, Chief Photographer of the Acme Still and Motion Picture Photography Company.

'Mr. Little Augie,' Needlenose said. 'This is Needlenose.'

'I know,' Little Augie replied. 'I could tell by the way you sort of whistle when you talk.'

'We got a little problem, Mr. Little Augie,' Needlenose said.

'Let me spell it out for you, Needlenose,' Little Augie replied. '*We* don't have no problems. You may have problems, but I don't have no problems. You get my meaning?'

'Yes, sir, Mr. Little Augie,' Needlenose said. 'Could I tell you my problems, Mr. Little Augie?'

'Certainly you can, Needlenose,' Little Augie replied. 'My door is always open to my co-workers. That's a Nero's Villa policy.'

'I'm out of film, Mr. Little Augie,' Needlenose said, blurting it out all at once.

'Then you do indeed have a problem, Needlenose,' Little Augie said. ' 'Cause I remember distinctly telling you how important this job was and how disappointed I would be wit' youse if any little thing went wrong.'

'Mr. Little Augie, I brought two cameras and three hours worth of film up here with me.'

'In round numbers, how much film is that in feet?'

'I don't know in feet, Mr. Little Augie, but it's about five and a half miles.'

'The boxes were empty? The film was no good? Is that what you're trying to tell me?'

'No, sir, Mr. Little Augie. Everything worked just fine.'

'Then how come you're out of film?'

'I used it all up,' Needlenose said.

'You mean you're all finished?'

'No, Mr. Little Augie,' Needlenose said. 'I just got film of the one guy.'

'You shot five and a half miles of film on just one guy?'

'Yeah, the big one, the one they carried in on the stretcher?'

'The *great* big one?' Little Augie asked. 'The one wearing the white Jew's hat and the hassock?'

'Excuse me, Mr. Little Augie, I think that's cassock.'

200

'Hassock, cassock, schmassock!' Little Augie said. 'Whatever. I hope he wasn't alone?'

'No, sir, all three of them was there.'

'All three of them, at once?'

'Yes, sir, Mr. Little Augie.'

'And where are they now?'

'The broads is asleep. They're all sound asleep, with smiles on them,' he said.

'And the big guy?'

'You're not going to believe this, Mr. Little Augie, but right now he's doing pushups, with one hand, by the window and singing real loud and happy in some foreign language.'

'Latin, probably,' Little Augie said. 'And you've got five-and-a-half miles of film of him with the broads?'

'Yes, sir, Mr. Little Augie.'

'You done well, Needlenose,' Little Augie said. 'There'll be a little something extra in your envelope this week.'

'Thank you, Mr. Little Augie.'

'And I'll get some fresh film right up there to you.'

'Thank you, sir,' Needlenose said. 'If I may presume to make a suggestion, Mr. Little Augie?'

'Sure, Needlenose. Shoot.'

'I'd send some fresh broads, too,' he said. 'These three are all worn out. They deserve a rest. Not that they're complaining or anything.'

'Fresh broads coming right up,' Little Augie said. 'Anything else?'

'I need another camera,' Needlenose said. 'One of them burned out.'

Miss Monica P. Fenstermacher, chest thrust proudly outward, rode down in the elevator from her room, marched across the lobby and boarded the elevator reserved for the International Association of Life Insurance Salesmen. She was instantly whooshed to the twenty-fifth floor, so quickly that there wasn't really very much time for her to worry about how she was going to explain the camera to Matthew Q. Framingham VI, much less take pictures with it.

She stepped out of the elevator and paused to consider the

problem. She could say, she supposed, that she had found it in the lobby, and when she was finished with him, she was going to turn it in to lost and found.

'Over here, baby,' a man called to her, in a peculiar whistling whistle.

'And who might you be?' Monica asked.

'Shut up, for God's sake!' Needlenose said. 'You want them to hear you? Just give me the camera.'

'Why should I give you my camera?' Monica asked reasonably.

'You need a camera to take pictures,' Needlenose explained reasonably.

'Oh, you're going to take the pictures?' Monica asked. Her heart filled with admiration for the ingenious crew of 'The Rhotten Report'. They had somehow sneaked their way in here, and now the problem of how to explain the camera to the big oaf was solved.

'Here you are, and congratulations on your enterprise,' Monica said, handing over the camera.

'They're right in there,' Needlenose said, gesturing toward a door. Monica looked in the direction he indicated. 'Do what you have to, of course, baby,' Needlenose added. 'But it would be better for me if you didn't take your clothes off until the other broads show up, and then you can all take them off at the same time. That'll save film.'

Monica stopped in midstep. She shook her head. Could she possibly have heard what she heard? She spun angrily around. The funny little man with the long pointed nose had vanished. She stopped again, thinking, and finally decided that she had been paid the ultimate accolade. The camera crew of 'The Rhotten Report' had finally accepted her as a member of the team. They were joshing her as one of the boys, which meant that she had been accepted.

She walked to the door Needlenose had indicated, fixed a smile on her face and pulled it open, framing in her mind the deceptively feminine excuses she would offer for being a little late for her rendezvous.

But the moment the door was open, she could hear

familiar male voices talking. She heard the sound of her own name. No female alive, not even a dedicated television journal person who had just been accepted as one of the boys, is going to pass up an opportunity to eavesdrop on a conversation in which she is being discussed.

On tiptoe, Monica P. Fenstermacher made her way down the hall, found a closet, stepped inside and, standing on a garbage can, peered discreetly over the transom so that she could see, as well as hear, herself being discussed by her father and Matthew Q. Framingham VI.

The first thing she saw surprised her. There were three men in the room – her father, Matthew Q. Framingham VI, and a small, slight, elderly gentleman of distinguished demeanour. All three of them were, as the British so tactfully put it, in their cups.

This was clearly evident by their dress and deportment. Their neckties were askew. For the first time in her life, Monica saw her father with his vest unbuttoned and his shoes off. He was sitting in the middle of the floor, his hand wrapped around a half-gallon of Old White Stagg Blended Kentucky bourbon, tears running down his cheeks.

The slight little man of distinguished demeanour was standing by a fifty-gallon keg of Fenstermacher's Finest Old Creole Pale Pilsner with a mug in his hand and the tap flowing full bore. The stream of Old Creole Pale Pilsner, however, was not connected with the mug he held in his hand. It was, instead, and for some time apparently had been, flowing unrestrained onto the floor. The slight little man of distinguished demeanour didn't seem to notice.

Matthew Q. Framingham VI was standing up beside a strange, oriental-looking device. Monica looked closer. He wasn't standing by it, he was holding himself up with it, and what it was was an enormous brass gong, on which, highly polished, had been etched with some skill a representation of an oriental lady of rather generous mammary proportion performing what Monica knew from her Vassar courses in abnormal psychology was a lewd and lascivious dance.

'Getting back to my problem,' Matthew said, somewhat

thickly, and pausing to raise his own half-gallon bottle of Old White Stagg Blended Kentucky Bourbon to his lips for a long, gurgling pull.

'To hell with your problem,' Fritz W. Fenstermacher replied, as thickly. 'What about my darling Monica?'

'I told you, Fritz,' the small slight man said, 'that my ol' buddy, the Nevada commissioner for vice and gambling, has placed his entire force at our disposal. We'll get your little Whatsername back to you, or my name is not Mr. Justice Canady.'

'Judge,' her father said with deep feeling, 'you're a prince.'

'Getting back to my problem,' Matthew said. 'Did I tell you guys that Miss Montague Smith has a set very much like this oriental lady?' He patted the gong gently, almost reverently.

'Yesh,' the man who had called himself Mr. Justice Canady said, 'I remember you shaying that. But where, shir, I ashk you, is your proof?'

'I don't shee,' Fritz W. Fenstermacher said, 'how you guys can claim to be pals and stand there talking about some doxie Matthew got rejected by.'

'I will thank you, sir,' Matthew said, drawing himself up to his full height by sort of climbing up the stout timbers which supported the gong, 'not to refer to Miss Montague Smith as a doxie. She's a lady. Period. Do you think I don't know a lady when I see a lady?'

'I 'pologize,' Fritz said. 'Excuse me, Matthew.'

'You're 'scused,' Matthew said. 'Judge, do you think it would help if I called the desk again and asked again?'

'You've called down there sixty-five times, and sixty-five times they've told you they've never heard of a Miss Montague Smith.'

'So I have,' Matthew said, and his frame was suddenly shaken as he began to sob. 'Ships passing in the night, that's all we were,' he sobbed. 'For the very firsht time in my whole life, I meet someone, fell deeply in love at first sight, and now she's gone forever.'

'Don't be ridiculum,' Mr. Justice Canady said. 'Ridicum. *Silly*. Firsht you tell us that you're going to have this lady for the moral enlightenment session, and now you're telling us that you're in love with her.'

'He's right, Matthew,' Fritz W. Fenstermacher said. 'You couldn't marry a terpsichorean ecdysiast. They make lousy wives.'

'You just take that back, Fritz Fenstermacher,' Mr. Justice Canady said, suddenly furious, 'or you can find that female juvenile delinquent of yours by yourself!'

CHAPTER TWENTY

'I sheem,' Fritz W. Fenstermacher said, carefully enunciating each syllable, 'to have inadvertently offered some kind of offence. But on the other hand, Judge, what right do you have to call my beloved, sweet, innocent Monica a juvenile delinquent?'

'By your own admission, Fritzie, ol' pal, of who she's running around with,' Mr. Justice Canady said. 'No decent girl would associate with Don Rhotten, and you know it.'

There was no arguing with that, so Fritz changed the subject. 'Judgie, ol' pal,' he said, 'are you aware that you're pouring beer all over the floor?'

'Schertainly I am,' Mr. Justice Canady replied. 'I was just getting rid of the sediment.' He moved the mug beneath the stream of Old Creole Pale Pilsner and then watched with fascination as the mug filled and then spilled over. 'Hey, looka this,' he said. 'My cup runneth over!'

The three of them found this hilarious, and for a few moments there was general hilarity, but then, as if suddenly remembering, Mr. Justice Canady shut off the stream of beer and turned to glower at Fritz W. Fenstermacher.

'I don't know what I'm doing laughing with you, you foul slanderer!' he said.

'Me either,' Matthew said. 'I happen to think that terpsichorean ecdysiasts are simply super!'

'My boy,' Mr. Justice Canady said, 'I could tell from the first moment I laid eyes on you that you were a discerning gentleman.'

'Just between you, me and him, Judge,' Fritz W. Fenstermacher said, 'you're a little long in the tooth to be thinking about terpsichorean ecdysiasts.'

'Huh,' Mr. Justice Canady snorted. 'That's how much you know. Why don't you ask Mrs. Canady about that, wise guy?'

'What's Mrs. Josephine Canady,' Fritz W. Fenstermacher replied, thickly sarcastic, 'otherwise known as "The Unquestioned Queen of the Bluenoses of New England", got to do with terpsichorean ecdysiasts?'

'Shows how much you know, Fritz Fenstermacher,' Mr. Justice Canady replied, angrily. 'I'll have you know that as Jolly Josephine, the Viennese Jelly Roll, my little Josephine was the toast of Minsky's for years.'

'I didn't know that!' Fritz W. Fenstermacher said.

'And she's been one hell of a good wife, too, I'll have you know,' the judge said.

'I'm sure she has,' Fritz said uncomfortably.

'You think I'm just saying that,' the judge said. 'Well, I'll tell you something else, Fritz. She knows all about the foundation, too. All about it. And she's known about it for fifty years.'

'My God!' Matthew said. 'If I hadn't heard that from your own lips, Mr. Justice Canady, I would not be able to believe it!'

'That's because you're a dummy, Matthew,' Fritz W. Fenstermacher said. 'You don't know the first thing about women, and that's probably why this stripteaser got away from you.'

'I don't know anything about women?' Matthew snorted.

'That's what I said,' Fritz said. 'Only a dummy like you would believe that the women don't know about the foundation.'

'Yours, too, Fritz?' Mr. Justice Canady said.

'Almost from the beginning,' Fritz W. Fenstermacher said. 'She didn't let me know, of course. She was far too good a woman to do that and ruin things for me. But, just before she died, she let me know that she had known all along. Her last request of me was that I find a foundation fellow for our little Monica!'

'What about Matthew here?' Mr. Justice Canady said.

'Don't be absurd!' Fritz W. Fenstermacher said. 'What would a bright, charming, intelligent, sensitive girl like my darling Monica want with a dummy like Matthew?'

'And just what, Fritz,' Matthew said, his ego sorely tried, 'makes you think that I'd be interested in your demented little delinquent?'

(Monica, it must be reported at this time, heard nothing of this conversation after her father's announcement that her mother's last request of him was to find a foundation fellow for her. If Monica's late mother, whom Monica remembered fondly, approved of the Matthew Q. Framingham Foundation, then the foundation was worthy of Monica's approval as well. Besides, an organization with Matthew Q. Farmingham VI as its executive secretary couldn't be all bad. The sudden 180-degree shift in position now necessary, however, was a bit too much for Monica's already strained psyche. At that point, her reserves of journalistic stamina and determination exhausted, she climbed off the garbage can, sat in the corner and started to weep into her hanky.)

'Show him the picture you carry around, Fritz,' Mr. Justice Canady said, and since this seemed like a reasonable suggestion (a picture being worth a thousand words, as Fritz always said), a photograph of Monica was produced from Fritz's wallet and extended to Matthew.

Matthew stared at it blearily for a moment, his brow furrowing as he focused his eyes.

'My God,' he said, 'This is my Montague!'

'Your Montague my foot, you dummy,' Fritz said, snatching the photograph back. 'That's my Monica!'

'By whatever appelation that young woman is correctly

known,' Matthew said, quite sure of himself, 'she is the one who represented herself to me as a between-engagements terpsichorean ecdysiast!'

'How dare you even suggest such a thing!' Fritz W. Fenstermacher shouted, getting to his feet. That exhausted very nearly all of his vestigal strength, and when he swung his massive right fist at the young man who had blasphemed his daughter's reputation, that act took the rest of it. Fritz' right cross missed, and his fist connected instead with the large brass gong. Then he slumped to the floor.

Matthew Q. Framingham, who had expended nearly all his reserves of energy staggering over to examine the photography, similarly overdrew the account, so to speak, in avoiding Fritz' punch. He ducked backward out of the way, and there just didn't seem to be any energy left to swing back. He crashed backward onto the floor, shook his head groggily and then gave up the battle. His chin dropped to his chest, his eyes closed and he went to sleep.

The sound of the gong, while not as loud as it would have been had it been struck with the gong-striker, was still of a sufficient intensity to reach the ears of Monica P. Fenstermacher, where she was sobbing into her hanky, and to scare hell out of her. Throwing caution to the winds, she threw the closet door open and rushed into the room.

'What have you done, you dreadful little old man,' she said to Mr. Justice Canady, 'to my beloved poppa? And to my . . . that young gentleman laying there with that look of divine repose on his handsome face?'

'And who the hell are you?' Mr. Justice Canady said. 'You must have the wrong floor, sweetheart. We didn't call for any girls.'

'How dare you?' Monica replied, but her complaint fell on deaf ears. Mr. Justice Canady, who had, after all, a half century's experience in such matters, had surveyed the room, immediately seen that the party was in brief recess and decided, under the circumstances, that a short nap would be in order. He was, in other words, sound asleep on the couch.

Monica rushed to her father, rolled him over with great effort and put a pillow under his head. She bent and kissed him on the forehead. 'Oh, poppa,' she said. 'How I have misjudged you!'

Then she went to Matthew, who was already laying on his back, and similarly put a pillow under his head. She brushed a lock of his hair away from his forehead with a gesture of sweet tenderness, and then, giving in to the delightful urge, bent over him and kissed him on the forehead.

'That's very sweet and all that jazz,' a female voice said, 'but it ain't box office.'

Monica, blushing furiously, stood and turned to face the door, where stood two blondes and a redhead.

'And who might I inquire, are you?' Monica asked.

'We're three of the Vestal Virgins,' the redhead said. 'Who do we look like?'

'What are you doing here?'

'The same thing you are, sweetheart,' one of the blondes said. 'But I think we're better at it than you.'

The second blonde, giving Monica the impression she was suddenly stripped of her senses, turned and spoke directly to the ceiling.

'What do we do now, Needlenose?' she asked.

The ceiling immediately responded; 'Fake it, Lulu!'

'Gotcha,' Lulu replied, giving the ceiling the standard O.K. sign with her thumb and index finger forming a circle, the remaining three extended.

In less time than it takes to tell about it, and certainly less time than Monica, who had not had much experience in these areas, needed to respond, the blond named Lulu and her two fellow practitioners of the oldest profession had divested themselves of their clothing and had joined the three gentlemen where they rested in such positions as to suggest the gentlemen were active participants who had just momentarily closed their eyes.

Monica stared with open mouth. Then her ears heard the unmistakable whirring noise made by a motion picture camera when it is, in the cant of the trade, 'rolling'.

The ceiling spoke again: 'Ginger,' it said, 'move the big one over a couple of feet will you? The camera angle's lousy!'

That, so to speak, was the straw which broke the camel's back; there was no longer room for any doubt whatever. That rotten Don Rhotten (he must be rotten, Monica knew, because Darling Poppa didn't like him) had tricked her. For God knows what foul purposes, he was taking films of her beloved poppa, and other distinguished members of the Framingham Theosophical Foundation in compromising positions.

Monica, aware that she was outnumbered, looked desperately around the room for a suitable weapon. Her eyes fell upon the eight-foot-long, leather-wrapped gong knocker. She grabbed it and, swinging it around her head, a blood-curdling scream coming from her mouth, advanced on the ladies who had identified themselves as the Vestal Virgins.

'Out! Out!' she shouted. 'Begone!'

The ladies were prepared for just about anything but a wild-eyed young broad swinging a club at them and, grasping their discarded garments, made for the exit. Monica remained in hot pursuit. As they reached the elevator, a light came on and the door opened.

'What's going on here?' Miss Letitia Kugelblohm said. 'Monica, shame on you!'

'Shame on me? I hate to tell you what these three have been up to,' Monica said.

'Hiya, beautiful ladies,' the three men accompanying Miss Kugelblohm said, addressing the three birthday-suit gals. They were, of course, Huffstadter's Hefties, members of the Weightlifting and Karate Team of Max C. Huffstadter Local 103, International Order of Case, Keg and Barrel Handlers.

'You guys are here on business,' Miss Letitia said, firmly. 'Try to remember that.'

'Yeah,' they said in unison, and with some slight remorse. 'That's right!'

'Where is your father?' Miss Letitia asked.

'In there,' Monica said. It was on the tip of her tongue to explain that he was passed out, but she stopped herself in time. 'Miss Letitia,' she said, 'trust me!'

'Huh!' Miss Letitia snorted. 'Give me one reason why I should. The way you've worried your poor poppa!'

'That,' Monica P. Fenstermacher said, dramatically, and with obvious sincerity, 'is a dark and closed page in my past!'

'What do you want me to do?'

'Somewhere in the ceiling is a man with a movie camera,' Monica said. 'We have to get his film!'

'Don Rhotten?' Miss Letitia said. 'Is he behind this?'

'Who else but rotten Don Rhotten could be?'

'Tear the place apart, boys, if you have to,' Miss Letitia Kugelblohm said. 'But find the film. Monica and I will be in my room.' She grabbed Monica by the arm and, over her protests, led her into an elevator and pushed the DOWN button.

As all this had been taking place, the three ladies whom Monica had chased out of the foundation, demonstrating an equal facility to get dressed as rapidly as they had undressed, slipped back into their clothes as the elevator carried them to the lobby. Then they marched upon the office of Mr. Little Augie Finecello to explain to him, somewhat less than politely, that they had not bargained for being assaulted by a crazy blonde broad armed with a large stick.

'Youse must be good enough to pardon my little mistake,' Little Augie said. 'I personally, myself, just talked with Needlenose.' This was an out-and-out untruth. Little Augie had not talked to Needlenose. But he was determined to get motion pictures of the other creeps. Under these circumstances, obviously, deviating slightly from the facts was a perfectly appropriate thing to do.

'So?' the girls asked.

'And Needlenose tells me that another business lady making a house call got off at the wrong floor, and that, quite naturally, she got the mistaken idea that youse were where she was supposed to be, if you get my meaning.'

They got his meaning. The same sort of innocent misunderstanding had, at one time or another, happened to all of them.

'You mean, it's safe to go back?'

'You got my personal word of honour,' Little Augie said. 'In addition to which, I'm gonna throw in another two percent of the gross profits for youse, just to sweeten the pot. Can I rely on youse to go up there and give the old Nero's Villa try?'

'You're all heart, Little Augie,' the redhead said.

'All heart,' Little Augie agreed, 'plus an extra two percent of the gross profits.'

The three members of the Huffstadter's Hefties, Local 103, International Order of Case, Keg and Barrel Handlers had, frankly, been somewhat confused by the events which transpired before the elevator doors. They had had enough experience with Miss Letitia Kugelblohm, however (and were of course aware of the esteem in which she was held by Max C. Huffstadter himself), to know that theirs was not to reason why but to do what they were told, even if they weren't sure what that was.

They could not find (indeed, they would have been deeply surprised had they found) a motion picture camera in the ceiling. What they did find was something more in keeping with the natural order of things: Fritz W. Fenstermacher and two other drunks, snoring in various positions around a large room. One by one, Fritz, Matthew and Mr. Justice Canady were carried to empty bedrooms, undressed and tucked in.

Then, with the sense of satisfaction that comes with having done one's good deed for the day, Huffstadter's Hefties returned to the room where they had found Old Fritz and his friends for a little cheering cup.

They had barely time to mix a proper barrelmaker (equal portions of bourbon whiskey and beer) when there came a gentle knock at the door.

'Anybody home?' a female voice asked.

'Hey, youse decided to come back, huh?'

'Are you the fellas who are supposed to be in here?' the redhead asked.

'You betcherass, baby,' one of the hefties said. 'Miss Letitia Kugelblohm herself told us to come in here.'

'Would youse ladies care for a little snort?' another Heftie said.

'Don't mind if I do,' one of the blonds said.

'You getting this, Needlenose?' the second blonde said.

'Rolling!' a faint voice replied, seeming to come from the ceiling.

'Why don't we take off our clothes and get comfie?' the redhead said.

'I knowed you was my kind of broad duh minute I seen you out there by the elevator,' one of the hefties said. 'You want to feel my muscle, baby?'

'Oh, *do* I!' the redhead said. She seldom, so to speak, had a chance to mix business with pleasure, and this was obviously going to be one of those times. Not only were these the most muscular gentlemen acquaintances it had been her good fortune to meet in some time, there was also that extra two percent of the gross profits from Little Augie.

And peering through his viewfinder, Mr. Arthur C. 'Needlenose' Hightower, too, was filled with professional pride. This was going to be one of the red-letter days in his life. He already had more than five-and-a-half miles of first-class stuff in the can, and to judge from the opening scenes of the drama, so to speak, playing out below him, he would have another five-and-a-half miles of first-class film before the day was done. Little Augie would be pleased.

At that moment, wearing as a disguise a T-shirt reading 'Surfers Do it Standing Up!' in lieu of his customary black shirt and clerical collar, the Rev. Giuseppe Verdi Finecello, S.J., made his entrance to Nero's Villa by way of the boiler room. He didn't want Augie to know, just yet, that he was in the hotel. He found a house phone and managed to get the one man in the place he knew he could trust to keep his secret, Little Stanislaus, on the line.

'Stanislaus,' he said. 'This is your uncle the priest.'

'How nice of you to call, uncle Gus. What can I do for you?'

'I've got to see you, Stanislaus,' Father Gus said. 'Right away.'

'Is it important?' Little Stanislaus asked. 'I'm on my way this very minute to have a martini with Reverend Mother.'

'The good Reverend Mother will have to wait,' Father Gus said. 'Where are you?'

'Rehearsing with the choir in Roman Circus Number Three,' Little Stanislaus said.

'I'll meet you backstage right away,' Father Gus said.

'Why backstage?'

'I'll tell you when I see you,' Father Gus said and hung up.

Little Stanislaus was delighted to see him.

'What a darling T-shirt, Uncle Gus! Am I to infer that you're sort of out on the prowl?'

'Pay attention to me, Stanislaus,' Father Gus said. 'Remember that I'm the only one in the family immune to Carmen-Baby's little scenes on your behalf.'

'Sounds serious,' Little Stanislaus said.

'What is that awful caterwauling?' Father Gus asked.

'That's the choir, of course,' Stanislaus said. 'Reverend Mother's own personal choir.' He pushed the curtain aside and gave his uncle a brief look at the choir.

'Oh, my!' Father Gus said. There was no explaining that away. Things were just as bad as Father Superior's friend in Rome had suspected they were.

'I think so, too,' Stanislaus said.

'Somewhere in this latter day Sodom and Gommorah,' Father Gus said, 'there is a large ... gentleman. He was carried in here on a stretcher. I want to know where he is right now.'

'No trouble at all,' Stanislaus said. 'I don't suppose you would want to tell me why you want to know, Uncle Gus?'

'No, I wouldn't,' Father Gus said. 'And from here on in, Stanislaus, it's Father Gus to you.'

'Oh, my, you are all upset, aren't you?'

'Just get me the information, Stanislaus.'

In thirty seconds, Stanislaus had the location of the large gentleman who had been carried into Nero's Villa on a stretcher. Plus the delicious information that he had been carried in wearing what looked very much like a white formal dress.

'You didn't tell me he was wearing a dress,' Stanislaus said.

'Where is he, Stanley?'

'There's a whole floor of fun people on the twenty-fifth floor of the northwest wing,' Stanislaus said. 'You can't get on the elevator without my say-so, though.'

'You have exactly ten seconds, Little Stanislaus,' Father Gus said, quite calmly, 'to fix it. Otherwise, I will be very annoyed with you. And you would be surely very unhappy if I became annoyed with you.'

'By the time you get there, it'll be fixed,' Stanislaus said, very quickly.

'Thank you, Stanislaus,' Father Gus said. 'Now, tell me where I can find this Reverend Mother.'

'Horsey has arranged for a suite for her and the archbishop and the monsignor on the twenty-third floor of the northeast wing.'

'For her and the archbishop? And the monsignor?'

'Right. You're just going to love Reverend Mother, Uncle Gus . . . excuse me, *Father* Gus . . . she's a million laughs.'

'Where is the archbishop now?'

'I don't know. Reverend Mother told me he's been giving some kind of private counselling somewhere.'

'Not one word to anybody that you've seen me, Stanislaus. You understand?'

'I understand perfectly,' Little Stanislaus said. 'We all have our little secrets, don't we?'

Five minutes later, Father Gus got off the elevator at the twenty-fifth floor. He headed for the sound of male and female voices joined in merriment and bawdy song and, by coincidence, found himself standing on the same garbage can in the same closet in which Monica P. Fenstermacher had experienced her change of heart regarding her father and Matthew Q. Framingham VI.

Giuseppe Verdi Finecello was after all a Jesuit, and he wasn't, truth to tell, all that shocked about what he saw over the transom. It was, therefore, almost immediately apparent to him that none of the three gentlemen in the room demonstrating their weightlifting and other skills to the ladies could possibly have been a priest, much less an archbishop of the church. He had obviously gone to the wrong room.

He proceeded further down the corridors, this time homing in on the sound of male snoring. He found another closet, another garbage can and, standing on it, peered over another transom. This time he was shocked by what he saw. He was, of course, no more shocked by the sight of the enormous man naked in bed with the three naked women hanging onto him in the manner of the buxom beauties in Rembrandt paintings than he was by what he had seen in the other room. But he was shocked by what he saw in the corner of the room. There, resting against the wall, a white skullcap hanging from its top, was a curved wooden object that could be nothing else than the shepherd's staff given to bishops, archbishops and other prelates to symbolize their role as keeper of the flock.

Shaken to the quick, Father Gus rested a moment (much, in fact, as Monica P. Fenstermacher had rested after her transom peering) and considered his alternatives. He obviously could not storm in there and send the ladies packing. He obviously could not storm in there, period. Lowly priests did not lecture archbishops on morality.

He had an inspiration. It wasn't much, he realized, but Little Stanislaus had said that he would 'love Reverend Mother', that she was 'a lot of laughs'. Since they had come to this ... this ... this *place* together, maybe she had some influence over the archbishop, and possibly, just possibly, he could reason with her.

He left the twenty-fifth floor determined to do his best.

CHAPTER TWENTY-ONE

As Father Giuseppe Verdi Finecello, S.J., walked across the lobby of Nero's Villa to the other bank of elevators, en route to face down the Reverend Mother who was a 'barrel of laughs', his progress was impeded by a very large gentleman who wore both a full beard and what Father Gus recognized as absolutely authentic Arabian robes. This apparition raised his hand in the manner of a traffic cop stopping a vehicular flow.

'Up yours,' he said, with a warm smile. 'Your mother wears army shoes. Small coins.'

'Perhaps,' Father Gus said, in fluent Arabic, 'it might be better if you repeated that in Arabic.'

'I have been playing the machine with the lever,' the Arab, who was, of course, Sheikh Abdullah ben Abzug said, 'into which one puts small coins, causing wheels to revolve. I now require more small coins.'

Father Gus looked quickly around the lobby. This was no time to deliver a lecture on the evils of gambling, especially to an Arab, who probably wouldn't understand anyway.

'Over there,' he said, gesturing toward The Roman Poker Parlor. 'They have a supply of small coins.'

'Thank you,' Sheikh Abdullah said. 'Here's a little something for your trouble.' He reached into his elaborate headdress, where he kept his small change, and pressed a bill into Father Gus' hand. And then, before Father Gus could refuse, he strode off toward and into The Roman Poker Parlor.

Father Gus looked after him for a moment. Then, telling himself that the greater need was to deal with Reverend Mother about the archbishop, he continued across the lobby.

Father Gus rode the elevator to the twenty-third floor and stepped off. He started to walk down the corridor and, looking down it, saw something he thought might just be the

217

unexpected assistance that comes from On High to those fighting the Good Fight.

Coming down the corridor toward him were three people, a woman, a man and a priest. They were all smiling gently. The woman was large and comfortable looking. The man was short and dressed like a respectable member of the business community. The priest was a man in his middle years, white-haired, pink-skinned and with warm and gentle eyes. He was obviously, Father Gus realized, a parish priest, one with long years of pastoral experience.

When the priest smiled at him as they neared, Father Gus knew what he must do.

'Excuse me, Father,' he said, 'but I really have to talk to you.'

'Of course, my son,' the priest said. 'I was just about to leave these good people anyway.' He turned to the couple and raised his index finger. 'Now, Robespierre, there is just one final thing. I know what a splendid sense of humour Hawkeye and Trapper John have, and with that in mind, I would suggest to you that if they suggest a bachelor dinner, or anything like that, tonight, that you politely decline.'

'I know just what you mean,' the little man said.

'I'm afraid I don't,' the woman said.

'Kristina, I'm sure that Robespierre will be glad to explain it to you after tomorrow, when you're man and wife.'

'Oh, my!' the woman said and blushed.

'These good people, my good friends,' the nice little priest said, 'are to be married tomorrow. We have just finished a nice little chat together.'

'How nice,' Father Gus said, frankly a little impatiently.

'We'll leave you now,' the woman said. 'And thank you very much.'

'My pleasure,' the priest said. 'And Radar ... ooops ... Robespierre, you remember what I said about Hawkeye and Trapper John. We'll want to be fresh and clear-eyed tomorrow morning, won't we?'

'I won't go near them,' Radar replied. With that, he took

Kristina's arm and walked further down the corridor with her.

The priest waited until they were out of earshot and then laid a friendly hand on Father Gus's arm.

'And now, my son,' he said, 'how can I help you?'

'Father,' Father Gus said, 'I don't know how to begin this, but the bottom line is that unless I can do something about it, the church stands a very good risk of great embarrassment. Not to get into the subject of sin at all.'

'Forgive my asking,' the priest said, 'but are you in a position to judge what could embarrass the church?'

'I'm a priest myself, Father,' Father Gus said, remembering only then his 'Surfers Do It Standing up' T-shirt. 'I'm Father Giuseppe Verdi Finecello, S.J.'

'I believe you, of course, Father,' the priest said. 'But I must say, in all honesty, that I couldn't tell by the way you're dressed.'

'This is a disguise, Father.'

'Of course, Father,' the priest said. 'I knew there must be an explanation. Now, you said the church stood a great risk of being embarrassed. Could you tell me how, and what I can do?'

'Father, what would you say if I told you that right in this very hotel is a high-ranking prelate of the church who, probably bereft of his senses, is . . .'

'That's awful!' the priest said, when Father Gus had finished.

'I need your help,' Father Gus said. 'I need all the help I can get.'

'And you shall have it,' the little priest said, with surprising firmness. 'I will go directly to the scene and have a word with our backsliding brother.'

'I thought of that, Father,' Father Gus said. 'But I didn't think it was my position, as a lowly priest, to . . . uh . . . bring the matter up myself.'

'I'll have a word with him,' the little priest said. 'I'm not questioning your word, Father, but neither am I presuming sin. Judge not, as it says in the Good Book.'

'The facts speak for themselves, Father,' Father Gus said.

'In that case, of course,' the little priest said, 'I will straighten the matter out.'

'I admire your self-confidence,' Father Gus said.

'Thank you,' the little priest said, softly, self-deprecatingly. Then, shocking Father Gus with an abrupt change to the icy tone, he called out:

'I want to see you two bums!'

Father Gus looked over his shoulder and saw two rather respectable-looking gentlemen, dressed in the strangest clothes he had ever seen, coming down the corridor.

'Well, hello there, Dago Red!'

'I told you never to call me that in public!' the little man said with ice in his tones.

'Sorry,' the taller of the two said, 'it's my evil companion here. He's a bad influence.'

'Speaking of bad influences, Hawkeye,' the little priest said, 'if you've got any funny ideas for Radar tonight, forget them!'

'I have no idea what you're talking about,' Hawkeye said.

'I have my sources of information,' the little priest said. 'And you're not going to send Radar on his honeymoon with his left leg in a cast and with a set of frankly obscene instructions painted on his chest with merthiolate.'

The two looked stunned.

'Where did you ever get an idea like that?' Trapper John finally asked.

'Let me put it this way, Trapper,' the little priest said. 'You two are the worst kind of heathens, but Horsey's one of mine.'

'Horsey betrayed us!'

'I prefer to think that he chose not to lie when his priest asked him a few simple questions,' the priest said.

'I consider that unfair!' Hawkeye said. 'Taking advantage of your position.'

'You do, huh?' 'You two, either one of you, get a half-inch out of line between now and the time that Kris and Radar go off on their honeymoon, you'll find out what unfair is. I have, for example, some very interesting photographs of you two studying nature on the banks of the Imjin River that I think your wives would be rather interested in seeing.'

'I'm surprised at you!' Trapper John said.

'I've had good teachers,' the little priest said. 'You two. You two have really broadened my horizons. And I'm sure that we now understand each other, don't we?'

'I never thought you'd be a party-pooper,' Hawkeye said.

'We do understand each other, don't we?' he repeated.

'We surrender,' Trapper John said, 'our heads bloodied but unbowed.'

'And now I have something to do,' the little priest said. 'I'll see you around.' He turned to Father Gus. 'Father,' he said, 'I think it would be a good idea if you were somewhere I could reach you. I'm going to send you with Drs. Pierce and McIntyre here.'

'Can I ask where we're going?' Hawkeye said. 'You cold-hearted blackmailer and all around spoilsport?'

'Now that I have your word of honour you're going to behave,' the little priest said, 'I think it would be perfectly all right if you had a drink with Reverend Mother. A *little* drink.'

'Now you're telling us how much we can drink?'

'Right,' the little priest said. 'One of Reverend Mother's martinis should be enough for anybody. That's a word to the wise, Father,' he added to Father Gus.

'How come you keep calling this guy "Father"?' Hawkeye said. 'Or is that T-shirt the last word in clerical vestments?'

'I call him Father because he's a priest,' His Eminence John Patrick Mulcahy, Archbishop of Swengchan, China, said. 'But you have a point about that shirt. When you get to Reverend Mother's suite, tell Pancho I said to get the good father an appropriate shirt.'

'I sort of like the one he's wearing,' Trapper John said, solemnly. 'It has, I don't know, a certain *je ne sais quoi*.'

'Get going!' Dago Red ordered, and the three continued down the corridor.

'Hawkeye Pierce,' Hawkeye said, extending his hand. 'Any friend of Dago Red's a friend of mine.'

'Likewise,' Trapper John said. 'You can call me Trapper.'

'I'm Father Finecello,' Father Gus said.

'Finecello?' Hawkeye replied. 'You're the one in the movie business?'

'I beg your pardon?'

'Just before we came here, a guy named Finecello called me up, asked if I was a member of the Framingham Foundation, and when I said I had that distinct honour and pleasure, said that he would have some movies he thought we would like to buy.'

'What kind of movies?' Father Gus asked.

'He didn't say. He just said he was sure we would want to buy them, and then he laughed and hung up.'

'It wasn't me,' Father Gus said. He had, of course, a very good idea who it had been.

'Well, here we are,' Trapper John said, pushing open a door. Father Giuseppe Verdi Finecello found himself being led into a large suite. It held, in addition to his nephew, Little Stanislaus, and the purple-robed choir he had heard sing shortly before, a man in clerical vestments and what could only be Reverend Mother, although Father Gus couldn't imagine to what body of religious Reverend Mother could belong.

He knew that it was Reverend Mother because she was wearing a purple and gold robe on which had been embroidered a gold cross, stretching from the floor-length hem to the high collar. On the cross itself, embroidered in sequins, were the words 'REVEREND' (vertically) and 'MOTHER' and 'EMERITUS' (on the horizontal cross members).

She advanced on the three new entrants, her waist-length, platinum-blond hair swishing from side to side and carrying the largest martini glass Father Gus had ever seen.

'Did you bring this gorgeous hunk of a man for little me?' Reverend Mother said, handing Father Gus the martini with one hand and pinching his chest with the other.

'Cool it, Hot lips,' Trapper John said. 'He's one of Dago Red's.'

'Oh, quelle *pity!*' Reverend Mother said, with obvious

regret. Then she brightened. 'Well, anyway, he can be company for Pancho.' She looked over her shoulder and called out. 'Jimmy de Wilde! You naughty, naughty boy! Stop trying to put your arm around Pancho and send him over here.'

A man in a black suit and clerical collar, obviously relieved to be leaving the company of Jimmy de Wilde, walked over.

'Pancho,' Hawkeye said, 'say hello to Father Finecello. Dago Red says for you to get him a uniform shirt.'

'I see,' the Very Reverend Pancho de Malaga y de Villa said, rather coldly. 'If you'll come with me, Father?'

Father Gus followed him out of the crowded living room and to a bedroom, where Pancho opened a suitcase and took from it a clerical shirt and collar.

'Would it be reasonable for me to presume, from your clothing, that you're a Catholic priest?' Father Gus asked.

'A monsignor, actually,' Pancho said. 'And would it be reasonable for me to presume, since you are putting on a clerical collar that you, too, are a priest of the Catholic Church?'

'Monsignor, I am Father Giuseppe Verdi Finecello, S.J.,' Father Gus said.

'How do you do?' Pancho said. 'Would you mind telling me what you were doing in that "Surfers Do It Standing up" T-shirt?'

'It's a disguise,' Father Gus said. 'Actually Monsignor, I'm really glad to find you here. The thing is, we have a problem.'

'We do? What sort of problem?'

'Brace yourself, Monsignor,' Father Gus said. 'I must tell you that a high-ranking prelate of the church, an archbishop to be specific, is either drunk or crazy or both.'

'Is that so?' Pancho asked.

'And is, at this very moment, in bed with three ladies. I saw them with my own eyes.'

'An archbishop? What's his name?'

'Mulcahy, or something like that. He's Archbishop of Swengchan, China.'

'I find that very interesting,' Pancho replied, 'since I happen to have the privilege of being His Eminence's private secretary.'

'In that case, Monsignor,' Father Gus said, 'if you will forgive my saying so, you ought to be ashamed of yourself!'

'Sit down, Father,' Pancho ordered sternly. 'I suspect there's more here than meets the eye.'

'I'm telling you, Monsignor, that I *saw* him with *my own eyes!*'

'Sit down,' Monsignor de Malaga y de Villa repeated. 'Take a good stiff swallow of that martini, and get control of yourself. Then start all over at the beginning.'

Five minutes later the door to the Monsignor's bedroom opened again. Monsignor Pancho stood in the doorway.

'Doctor Pierce!' he called. 'Doctor McIntyre! I wonder if I might have a moment of your time?'

The two healers made their way to the room, entered and turned to face the monsignor.

'What's on your mind, Pancho?'

'Trapper, Hawkeye,' the Monsignor said, 'we have a little problem.'

'Is that so?'

'How strong an injection did you tell His Eminence you had given Mr. Korsky-Rimsakov to keep him out of trouble?'

'Enough to keep him out until tomorrow morning,' Hawkeye replied.

'I have bad news for you, Doctor,' the Monsignor said.

CHAPTER TWENTY-TWO

When Monica P. Fenstermacher did not return, as she had promised to do, with motion-picture film of the shenanigans her father and the other fellows of the Matthew Q. Framingham Theosophical Foundation were up to in the secret headquarters on the twenty-fifth floor, Don Rhotten, Smiling Jack Jackson and Seymour G. Schwartz began to worry. A good deal, after all, was at stake.

Alternate plans were necessary, although all three were agreed that the way to solve the problem was to get film of Fenstermacher and his cronies. Any kind of film would do. The film could be edited in the workrooms of 'The Rhotten Report' to show just about anything. The Rhotten film editors, under Mr. Schwartz' personal direction, enjoyed an industry-wide reputation in this regard, and indeed, a motto was hung in the darkroom reflecting their skill: 'Give Us Your Raw Film. Tell Us What You Want To Prove and Leave the Editing to Us!'

And as Congressman Jackson pointed out, the odds were that if they just burst through the door with cameras rolling, they were bound to catch them doing something embarrassing, if only changing their pants. If he had just a few feet of Fritz W. Fenstermacher changing his pants, with a little bit of judicious editing, the boys in the dark-room could easily turn it into a triple-X hard-core porno movie, which would force the Speaker of the House to disown his old buddy, Fritz W. Fenstermacher.

Seymour G. Schwartz' thought processes ran along similar lines. If he had film showing Fritz W. Fenstermacher doing anything at all naughty, that would put Fritz W. Fenstermacher in the position of either knocking off his wholly unjustified criticism of 'The Rhotten Report' or seeing his escapades (edited for television, of course) telecast all over the country.

Don Rhotten's thought processes were not nearly so complicated or Machiavellian. He was perfectly satisfied to go along with the 'break-in, cameras rolling' plan because it just might give him a chance to see Monica P. Fenstermacher in the act of changing her pants, something which had, frankly, rather occupied his thoughts since he had first seen the young lady.

The decision was made to go ahead with what Seymour G. Schwartz called 'Operation Truth'. The camera and sound crews were gathered together and briefed on the mission. Access to the elevator would be gained by subterfuge. One camera crew would appear before the elevator door, ostensibly shooting a man-on-the-street interview programme. They would interview the guards, one at a time, subtly moving them away from the elevator door in the name of good lighting and suitable backgrounds. Once they were out of the way the action team, consisting of Don Rhotten, Smiling Jack and Seymour, plus, of course, a cameraman, would rush into the elevator and ride it up.

Phase One of Operation Truth went off as planned with one minor addition. As they crossed the lobby, Seymour G. Schwartz happened to peer into The Roman Poker Parlor. He saw an Arabic gentleman with enormous stacks of chips (which he seemed to be losing almost as quickly as he could be resupplied) gambling. Reasoning that gambling was also sinful and that editing the Arab gentleman into the Fenstermacher film would pose no problem at all for his talented staff, he ordered that the cameraman get, as he put it, 'a couple of minutes of that jerk losing all his money.'

Once that had been accomplished, they crossed over to the guarded elevators and with minimal effort ('a piece of cake,' Don Rhotten whispered to Smiling Jack) succeeded in luring the guards away from the elevator doors.

With speed and finesse, they got in the elevator, pushed the button and felt themselves being hauled aloft. There were no guards outside the elevators when the doors opened, and this was generally conceded to be a good omen. Moreover, from behind a nearby set of doors, there came the unmistakable sounds of what Seymour G. Schwartz had already decided to call 'a chilling example of shocking depravity.' There was the tinkle of glasses and the sound of feminine laughter and of voices joyously raised in ecstasy of one kind or another.

On command, Don Rhotten and Smiling Jack put their shoulders to the door. And at this point, Operation Truth began to go sour. The door held, for one thing, and Smiling Jack, having painfully bruised his shoulder, began to cry.

Seymour G. Schwartz and Don Rhotten had at the door again, and again the door held.

'I'll kick it open!' Seymour G. Schwartz said and raised his foot like he'd seen the guy do on *Kung-Fu*. At the exact moment he raised his leg and kicked, the door was opened by one of Huffstadter's Hefties, who had been naturally curious about the muffled thumps at the door. He was, truth to tell, a little gassed, but not too gassed to miss what he recognized as a flying foot coming in his direction. Flying feet, were, after all, part and parcel of karate, and the reputation of the weightlifting and karate team was well earned.

Seymour G. Schwartz' foot was grabbed.

'Hieya-YA!' the Huffstadter's Hefty called, according to the ritual of karate, and threw Seymour G. Schwartz into the room. In moments, the Honourable Third-ranking Member of the House Committee on Sewers, Subways and Sidewalks, America's most beloved television journalist, and the cameraman had joined him.

'Gee,' one of the hefties said to another of the hefties, as he stood, somewhat unsteadily, over the pile of bodies, 'Miss Letitia was right about the camera after all.'

The second hefty staggered over and looked down.

'And you know what?' he said. 'If that funny-looking one had his wig on straight, he'd look just like rotten Don Rhotten, the guy what stole ol' Fritz' little girl.'

'I think,' said the third hefty, 'that maybe we better tell Miss Letitia about dis. I don't think we'd better pull his arms out by the roots until we're sure that really is rotten Don Rhotten.'

'Ladies,' said the third hefty, 'would youse mind puttin' yer clothes back on? Miss Letitia Kugelblohm is shortly going to join us, and I fear dat she might not understand why youse is, in a manner of speaking, bare-assed.'

'Maybe we just better run along,' one of the ladies said.

'Nah. We want you for character witnesses,' one of the hefties replied. 'We wouldn't want Miss Letitia to get the idea that we invited them crumbs up here.'

The third hefty was already on the telephone.

'Miss Letitia,' he said, 'we got that camera you said was in the ceiling. Only it wasn't in the ceiling. It come right through the door, with what we think is rotten Don Rhotten wit it. Could youse come up here?'

The first question that Miss Letitia Kugelblohm asked when she and Miss Monica Fenstermacher walked into the Home Away From Home of the Matthew Q. Framingham Theosophical Foundation dealt with Mr. Fritz W. Fenstermacher.

'Where's Mr. Fritz?' she demanded. 'I'll deal with those dreadful, nasty people later,' she added, pointing to the pile of Schwartz, Jackson, Rhotten & Company.

The hefties, to a man, were embarrassed. It simply wasn't fitting for them to have to betray their fallen employer with the announcement that, having passed out on the floor, Fritz W. Fenstermacher had been carried off to bed.

'Now that you mention it, Miss Letitia,' the first hefty said, 'I think Mr. Fritz said something about wanting to think about business and things like that there, and that he didn't want to be disturbed.'

'There was also, I understand,' Monica said, 'another gentleman in here, a tall handsome, muscular gentleman. Have you any idea where he is?'

'Didn't see nobody like that,' the first hefty said.

'That great big guy?' the second hefty said. 'Took all three of us to carry him.'

'Miss Monica,' the third hefty said, 'now that I think about it, I think your poppa said that he was going to talk over business and things like that with that big guy.'

'In that case,' Miss Letitia said, 'we'll just look in on them a moment.'

'I don't think that would be such a good idea,' the third hefty said. 'Why don't you, instead, just stay here and watch us while we pull rotten Don Rhotten's arms and legs off?'

'That will have to wait,' Miss Letitia said. 'I am, of course, Mr. Fritz' private secretary, and he may have need of me. Come along, Monica,' she said.

'Miss Letitia!' Monica said. She was naturally concerned

with what Miss Letitia was going to find, basing her assessment of the situation on the condition of the gentlemen in question the last time she had seen them, when her father and Matthew were sprawled, as rotten Don Rhotten and his friends were now sprawled, on the floor.

'Come along, Monica!' Miss Letitia repeated, and Monica had no choice but to obey.

Miss Letitia opened a door. Judge Canady was peacefully asleep in a bed. 'That gentleman, Monica,' she said, 'is Mr. Justice Canady, of the Massachusetts Supreme Court. Not only is he one of the nation's most distinguished jurists, but only last month he celebrated his fiftieth wedding anniversary.'

'Is that so?'

'You may well be asking yourself why I am telling you this,' Miss Letitia said.

'Yes, I was.'

'In good time, Monica,' Miss Letitia said. 'In good time.' She moved to the next door and opened it. She indicated to Monica the sleeping form of a handsome young man of Monica's recent acquaintance.

'That Monica,' she said, 'is Mr. Matthew Q. Framingham VI, scion of the Framingham Family, Harvard College and the Harvard School of Business Administration and presently employed as executive secretary of the Framingham Foundation. He is as a matter of passing interest, a bachelor.'

'You don't say?'

'You may well suspect, Monica,' Miss Letitia said, as she pulled the door closed again, 'that I am leading up to something.'

'That thought has crossed my mind,' Monica replied. Miss Letitia opened a third door, revealing Fritz W. Fenstermacher, sound asleep with the sheet tucked around his chin.

'And this, of course, is your beloved poppa.'

'So I see.'

'You will recall, Monica, that I was leading up to something.'

'Yes.'

'I trust you will not be unduly disturbed to learn that I've had it bad for your poppa for a long time. Even before your late mother passed on, but much worse, of course, since.'

'I can't truthfully say I'm surprised,' Monica said.

'You will not, I presume, be offended if I observe that your poppa is as hardheaded as a keg of Fenstermacher's Finest Old Creole Pale Pilsner?'

'That's a simple statement of fact,' Monica said.

'And you didn't really think I was going to permit those nice young men to pull rotten Don Rhotten's arms and legs out, did you? Even if he deserves it?'

'I wondered about that,' Monica said.

'Monica, have you ever wondered what makes a man propose?'

'I never even thought about it until very recently,' Monica confessed, which was perfectly true. She had been giving a good deal of thought in recent hours, however, to that very question, vis-à-vis Mr. Matthew Q. Framingham VI.

'It's quite simple,' Miss Letitia said. 'All you have to do is convince them you're a fair, fragile flower of womanhood about to perish unless they take you under their massive male machismatic protection. It's a lot of crap, obviously, but on the other hand, it always works.'

'Does it work for everybody?'

'You mean you've already decided to take the plunge with Matthew number Six?'

'Yes, I guess I have,' Monica admitted truthfully, blushing furiously.

'Well, that may complicate things some,' Miss Letitia said, 'but I think it can be arranged.' She took Monica by the arm and led her back to the room where Schwartz, Rhotten, Jackson and the photographer, having regained consciousness, were standing against the wall, guarded by Huffstadter's Hefties.

'Let the photographer go, Sam,' Miss Letitia said. 'He is nothing more than an innocent hireling.' The photographer made a mad dash for the door and was gone.

'Mr. Schwartz,' Miss Letitia said, 'when I spoke with you on the telephone, you lied to me. And it's not nice to lie to Miss Letitia Kugelblohm. My gut reaction, frankly, is to turn you over to my friends here. On the other hand, if you do exactly as I say, I may be willing to show a little mercy.'

'I'm sure that we can work out something,' Seymour G. Schwartz said.

'O.K.,' Miss Letitia said. 'Set up that camera, right over here,' she said. 'And get ready to shoot.'

'Madame,' Smiling Jack said. 'I'll have you know you are addressing a member of Congress.'

'We all have our little dark secrets, don't we?' Miss Letitia said.

'Monica,' Don Rhotten said, deciding to bite the bullet, 'forgive me!'

'Fat chance, rotten Don Rhotten,' Monica said. 'After what you tried to get me to do to darling poppa!'

'Monica, I beg you!' Don Rhotten said, getting onto his knees.

'Not only is she going to forgive you, rotten Don Rhotten,' Miss Letitia said, 'but she's going to let you put your arms around her.'

'She is?' Don Rhotten asked, a smile of delight appearing on his face.

'I am not!' Monica said, firmly.

'Trust me, Monica,' Miss Letitia said. Then she turned to the hefties. 'I want you to watch that door,' she said, indicating the door through which she and Monica had just returned to the room. 'When it opens, I want you to look scared.'

'Scared?' they said, all together.

'Scared. Like these three bums look,' Miss Letitia explained.

'Whatever you say, Miss Letitia,' they replied.

'O.K., Schwartz,' Miss Letitia said. 'Roll 'em!' The camera began to whirl. Miss Letitia stepped before Congressman Jackson and, taking his hands, put them around her waist.

'Put your arms around Monica, rotten Don,' Miss Letitia

ordered, and Don Rhotten did as he was ordered, mingled pleasure and faint suspicion on his face.

'Fritz!' Miss Letitia Kugelblohm screamed. 'Save me!'

'Matthew!' Miss Monica Fenstermacher screamed suddenly, getting the idea. 'Save me!' Miss Letitia smiled at her approvingly.

In just a few moments, the door opened. Huffstadter's Hefties feigned absolute terror on cue. Fritz W. Fenstermacher and Matthew Q. Framingham VI burst into the room, attired only in their underwear.

'Fritz!' Miss Letitia repeated. 'Save me!'

'Matthew!' Monica cried. 'Save me!'

'I daresay,' Matthew Q. Framingham VI said, excitedly, 'this gives all the appearance of a dastardly attack upon the person and purity of the woman I love!'

'I'll save Miss Letitia,' Fritz cried. 'Her attacker is visibly the more degenerate of the two. You take the other one!'

'Unhand that woman, sir,' Matthew said.

'You all have got to be kidding!' Don Rhotten said. 'This is all a great big practical joke, right? It smells like something that Howard K. Smith would set up.'

Matthew reached for Mr. Rhotten's head with the intention of holding him by the hair. The hair came off in his hands. He stared at the object in his hands for a moment in some confusion.

'Give me back my rug, you big ape,' Don Rhotten protested. 'This joke has gone far enough. My wig is sacred.'

'Matthew,' Monica offered hopefully, 'rotten Don Rhotten has just called you a big ape. Are you going to stand for that?'

'Not only that,' Matthew said, 'but he presumed to take liberties with the person I love, apparently without permission!' He pushed Monica gently to the side, grabbed Don Rhotten and held him over his head.

Meanwhile, Fritz W. Fenstermacher had grabbed Congressman Jackson by his rather acquiline nose and was twisting it rather severely. 'How dare you assault my dearest friend in the world?' he demanded.

'Fritz, what would I do without you to protect me?' Miss Letitia said.

'I don't really know,' Fritz said, thoughtfully. 'We'll have to work something out. That's clearly my duty as a Framingham Fellow and all around gentleman.'

'I accept!' Miss Letitia said. 'You can let go of Smiling Jack's nose now, Fritz.'

'Put me down!' Don Rhotten cried pathetically, as Matthew spun him around over his head. 'Television needs me!'

'Toss him to us!' the hefties cried. 'You guys are having all the fun, and that's not fair.'

'Do as the nice man says, Matthew darling,' Monica said, and Matthew complied.

Miss Letitia walked to the camera and extracted from it the film Mr. Schwartz had just shot. And at that moment, Mr. Justice Canady appeared at the door, fully dressed of course, as befitting a Justice of the Supreme Court and a Senior Fellow of the Framingham Foundation.

'Matthew!' he said. 'Fritz! Do you realize what you've done? Indeed, what you are doing?'

'I was tweaking that degenerate's nose, that's what I was doing,' Fritz said. 'And I'm proud of it, judge!'

'I mean, have you forgotten where you are?'

'My God!' Matthew said. 'This is the Home Away From Home of the Framingham Foundation!'

'And you have brought disgrace and dishonour upon it,' Mr. Justice Canady said. 'Bringing strange women in here while you cavort around in your underwear!' He waited until this had had a moment to sink in, and then he went on. 'The rules are clear,' he said, 'and you know them as well as I do. The only women allowed inside the foundation's quarters are terpsichorean ecdysiasts. Unless you are prepared to give me your words as gentlemen that these females are terpsichorean ecdysiasts, I'm afraid I must ask you for your immediate resignations.'

Matthew and Fritz looked crushed.

'I can't do this to you, Fritz,' Miss Letitia said. 'I know what the foundation means to you. I couldn't have it on my conscience that I was responsible for you losing it,' she said. 'All right,' she said. 'Let it be known that I, Letitia Kugelblohm, maiden lady of previously impeccable reputation, publicly profess that I am a terpsichorean ecdysiast.'

'Me, too,' Monica said. 'Me, too.'

'I couldn't ask that of you, Letitia,' Fritz said. 'Is there nothing else, your Honour, that can be done?'

'Only one other thing,' Mr. Justice Canady said. 'You could marry them and swear them to secrecy.'

'But that,' Fritz said, 'would mean that my darling Monica would be married to the dummy!'

'Watch it, Poppa!' Monica flared but stopped when she caught Letitia's eye.

'I admit he's not too bright,' Letitia said, 'But he did rush in here and save Monica from that rotten Don Rhotten.'

'He did that, Poppa,' Monica said. 'You know that!'

'So he did,' Fritz said.

'And Momma told you to find a Foundation Fellow for me,' Monica said, without thinking. 'Remember that, too!'

'Would you two settle for a long engagement?' Fritz demanded of them.

'Yes, sir,' Matthew said quickly. 'I always believe in long, long engagements.'

Monica glowered at him, and then softened, just slightly.

'Long enough for me to buy a dress and send out invitations,' she said, sweetly.

'Well, Fritz,' Mr. Justice Canady said. 'What's it to be?'

'All right, Judge,' Fritz said. 'I know when I'm whipped. I'll leave it up to you to arrange a quiet little dual ceremony.'

CHAPTER TWENTY-THREE

At three that morning, Colonel Horsey de la Chevaux (Louisiana National Guard) and Captains Jedda ben

Mustafa and Ali ben Babba, Troop 'C' of the Royal Abzugian Cavalry, were making their nightly rounds. Horsey, who understood the necessity of maintaining a tight perimeter guard under the circumstances, had temporarily assumed allover command. It was obviously necessary to keep the Abzugian Cavalry and the Bayou Perdu Council, K of C, Marching Band away from Nero's Nubiles. It was also necessary to keep the God Is Love in All Forms Christian Church, Inc., all-male a cappella choir from stealing, so to speak, into the tents of the cavalry, for whom the choir had already expressed a wide admiration.

At Archbishop Mulcahy's specific request, moreover, special detachments of sabre-wearing cavalrymen guards had been placed at other places in the hotel. There were, for example, six guards posted outside Boris Alexandrovich's suite in case the singer should be tempted to forget his promise to the archbishop that he would neither exercise nor partake of intoxicating spirits until after the wedding.

Another detachment was posted outside the rooms of the Baroness d'Iberville and Esmerelda Hoffenburg, the ballerina, against the possibility that those ladies would be tempted, so to speak, to grease the departure of the singer from the narrow path of righteousness.

Still other detachments were posted outside the doors and windows of the rooms occupied by Drs. Hawkeye Pierce and Trapper John McIntyre, against the eventuality that the healers might wish to play any sort of innocent little pranks against the person of Radar O'Reilly.

Even to Horsey's somewhat jaundiced eye, everything appeared to be under control. It was his intention, now that the inspection was over, to grab a little shut-eye himself. It had been a long and tiring day. But as he walked across the lobby of Nero's Villa he happened to glance into The Roman Poker Parlor. There was a large crowd of people, a very large crowd, gathered around one table.

'Up yours,' a familiar voice cried. 'Your mother wears army shoes!'

'I think we better have a little look in there,' Horsey said to the officers of the guard. They made their way inside and found a game of chance, specifically 'playing at dice', or, as it is popularly known, 'craps', in progress.

There was only one player, His Royal Highness Sheikh Abdullah ben Abzug. The dice were being played for the house, in other words against the sheikh by no less a personage than Mr. Caesar Augustus Finecello Jr., himself.

Little Augie was smiling broadly. He hadn't, he had just proven, lost his touch. He was still capable of suckering a sucker into making larger and larger bets, and he had before him what must be the Grand Imperial Royal Sucker of all time. The funny Arab (whose credit was, according to Aloysius X. McGee, who never erred in these matters, somewhat stronger than the Bank of England's) had been losing all night. Little Augie had to pinch himself to make sure he wasn't dreaming, but he had already clipped him for six million dollars, and the sucker kept coming back for more.

'How goes it, Abdullah?' Horsey asked, in, of course, Arabic.

'I like this game,' the sheikh replied. 'I am losing, but I realize I must first learn the game before I can expect to win.'

'You got the rules down pretty pat, have you?' Horsey asked.

'I think so,' the sheikh said.

'Who are you?' Little Augie demanded, angrily. 'And what are you guys talking about?'

'I just asked my friend if he knew the rules,' Horsey said.

'He knows the rules all right,' Little Augie said.

'Go on, Abdullah,' Horsey said to the sheikh. 'Tell me about the rules.'

'Well, we each have a set of little cubes with numbers on them,' the sheikh said. 'My set rolls nothing but sevens. His set rolls everything but sevens.'

'Two sets of dice?' Horsey asked.

'That's right,' Sheikh Abdullah said. 'He hides his dice in his hands sometime,' he added. 'But I expect to catch on before long, Horsey. I've only lost a few million dollars so far.'

'Captain,' Horsey said to Captain Jedda ben Mustapha, 'you know that little trick you do with the pineapple? Where you throw it in the air and cut it in six slices before it hits the ground?'

'Captain Ali ben Babba,' said Captain ben Mustapha modestly, 'can make eight slices.'

'Really?' Horsey asked. 'I don't believe it!'

'I will show you,' Captain Ali ben Babba said, and, taking a medium-sized grapefruit from a table display, he tossed it in the air. There was a chorus of oohs and aahs from the assembled spectators as his glistening scimitar flashed in the air, and the grapefruit, reduced to slices, fluttered to the ground.

'What the hell was that all about?' Little Augie Finecello said.

'That's what happens to people who palm dice on my pal,' Horsey said. 'And that's just for openers.'

'Get out of here, you butinsky,' Little Augie said. 'Before you have more trouble than you ever dreamed about.'

'Captain Mustapha,' Horsey said, 'don't you think it's about practice alert time, to see if the troops are awake and on their toes?'

'I'm playing games with this nice man,' the sheikh said. 'Can't that wait?'

'I think the nice man would like to see your boys in action, Abdullah,' Horsey said. 'Go ahead, Mustapha, blow the whistle.'

Captain Mustapha reached into his robes and extracted a sterling silver whistle. He blew on it three times. Instantly, there came the sound of a wailing siren and of trumpets, the sound of pounding hooves and tramping feet. Within ninety seconds, The Roman Poker Room held an additional thirty people, ten armed with scimitars, ten armed with sub-machine guns and ten armed with rocket launchers.

'Now can I play dice with the nice man?' Sheikh Abdullah said, waving at his troops.

'Now you can play with the nice man,' Horsey said. 'Can't he, nice man?'

'Of course,' said Little Augie, sweating profusely.

'Which set of dice would you like to play with, Abdullah?' Horsey asked.

'I think I would like to play with his set,' the sheikh said, after thinking it over.

'Give him the dice that can't crap out, nice man,' Horsey said to Little Augie.

Thirty minutes later, Little Augie rose from the table. He had one eye on Captain Mustapha, who, encouraged by applause, was slicing one pineapple in midair after another, and the other eye on Horsey de la Chevaux.

'Congratulations, sir,' Little Augie, sweating heavily, said, extending his hand to Sheikh Abdullah. 'You have just won Nero's Villa.'

'Mud in your eye,' the sheikh replied. 'Nice man.'

'Say goodnight to the nice man,' Horsey said. 'The game is over. You just won.'

'Your mother wears army shoes,' the sheikh said, smiling at the nice man. 'Up yours.'

At nine o'clock the next morning, right on schedule, the wedding ceremony began. There were now three couples to be joined in holy wedlock, rather than just one, and what was described as 'the unexpected overflow of guests' made it necessary to make other changes in the original programme.

The Roman Orgy Room, for one thing, was the site of the ceremonies, rather than the sitting room of Kristina's suite, as originally planned.

Kristina had hoped that her brother would be good enough to sing to a piano accompaniment, perhaps something from Schubert or Mendelssohn. What she got was her brother singing to the accompaniment of the Bayou Perdu Council, K of C, Marching Band, backed up by the God Is Love in All Forms Christian Church, Inc., all-male a cappella choir, who warbled softly in the background.

Each bride was preceded down the aisle by the Bayou

Perdu Marching Band Drum majorettes, in pairs. The first two carried a sign reading 'Here Come the Brides!' and subsequent pairs of drum majorettes carried signs identifying each individual bride.

The ceremony, except for Mr. Robespierre O'Reilly, who fainted immediately by upon being informed that he was now a married man with a wife, went smoothly. His Eminence John Patrick Mulcahy, Titular Archbishop of Swengchan, naturally presided, assisted by Monsignor Pancho de Malaga y de Villa, Father Giuseppe Verdi Finecello and Reverend Mother Emeritus Margaret Houlihan Wachauf Wilson, R.N.

While the male clerics, of course, wore their traditional vestments, Reverend Mother made an extra effort for the occasion. She was, with her flame-red robe with 'REVEREND MOTHER EMERITUS' embroidered on the front in sequins and 'LOVE LOVE LOVE' endlessly in the same fashion on the back, in the words of the archbishop, 'really something to see.'

Immediately after being pronounced men and wives by the archbishop and kissing their respective mates, the newlywed couples made their way back down the aisle, preceded by the Bayou Perdu Council Marching Band, who played 'There'll Be a Hot Time in the Old Town Tonight' and the all-male a cappella choir, who skipped down the aisle in their robes, scattering rosebuds along the way.

The newlywed couples naturally tried to slip away from the reception as soon as they could, but they were kept from doing this by Troop 'C' of the Royal Abzugian Cavalry, on horseback and carrying lances, at the suggestion of Colonel Chevaux, who said that a wedding reception really wasn't a reception without the bridal couples.

Eventually, of course, the newlyweds made their goodbyes and slipped away. What happened to the male choir after this is a little fuzzy. When Reverend Mother was asked what had happened to them, where they had gone to continue the celebration, her reply was a somewhat mysterious 'Don't ask.'

The Bayou Perdu Council, K of C, Marching Band was

not, it is known, with them, and neither was Troop 'C' of the Royal Abzugian Cavalry. The Marching Band adjourned to The Pool of the Vestal Virgins for water sports with Nero's Nubiles, and Troop 'C' was entertained by the showing of motion pictures in the royal banquet tent.

The archbishop somehow got the idea that the motion pictures being shown were naughty but was reassured by Dr. Benjamin Franklin Pierce who told him he knew they were nothing more than home movies showing Boris Alexandrovich Korsky-Rimsakov doing his exercises, and a second reel showing Max C. Huffstadter's Hefties doing theirs.

All in all, a good time was had by all, and especially by his Royal Highness Sheikh Abdullah ben Abzug. As a small token of his gratitude for the hospitality shown him and his affection for the archbishop, His Highness presented the archbishop with a piece of paper he had won the night before. The piece of paper was the title to Nero's Villa, and it is now known as the Archbishop Mulcahy Home for Wayward Girls.

Mr. Caesar Augustus Finecello, Jr., has not been seen from the moment he was seen rising in The Roman Poker Parlor to congratulate Sheikh Abdullah ben Abzug on his phenomenal run of luck. Anyone who has seen Little Augie is asked to contact his family in Chicago, who are known to be looking high and low for him.

CARBON CHEMISTRY
An introduction to organic chemistry and biochemistry

© 2005 Ellen Johnston McHenry
Most recent update: August 2015

ISBN 978-0-25377-2-5

**The author gives permission to the purchaser to make
copies as needed
for use with classes or homeschool groups.**

The author does not give permission for this curriculum, in whole or
in part, to be included in other publications that will be sold for profit.
If you like this curriculum and want to use some of it in your own
publication, please contact me. Thanks!

ejm.basementworkshop@gmail.com

Prerequisite:

This curriculum is designed to be a follow-up to <u>The Elements</u>, by the same author. Some previous knowledge of chemistry is helpful (and is highly recommended) but it is not absolutely essential.

Age level recommendation:

The target age group is 9-14.

Reproducible Student Booklet

CARBON CHEMISTRY

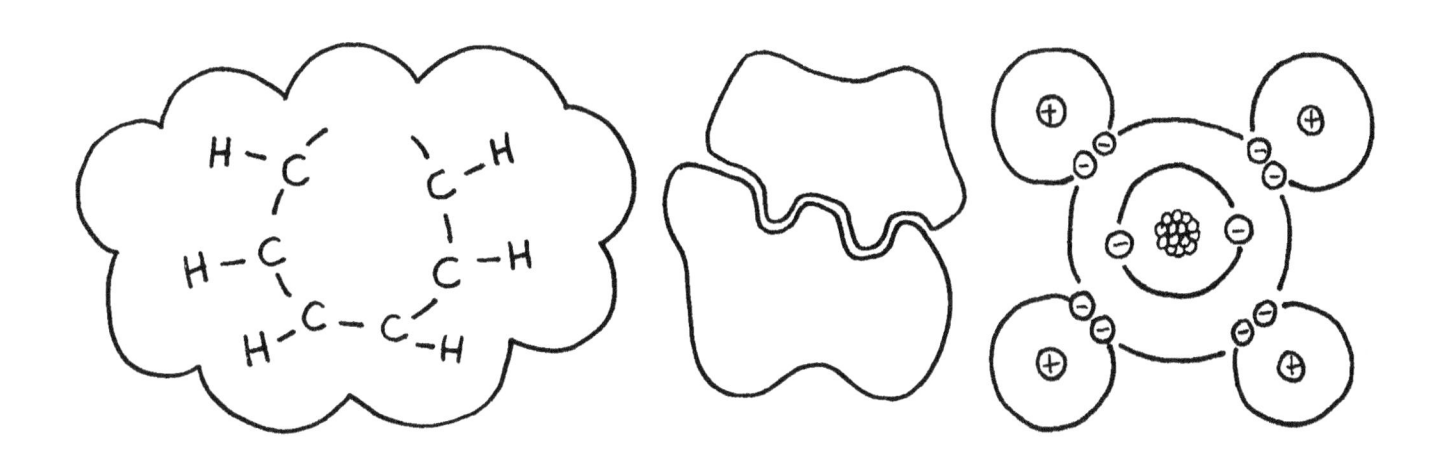

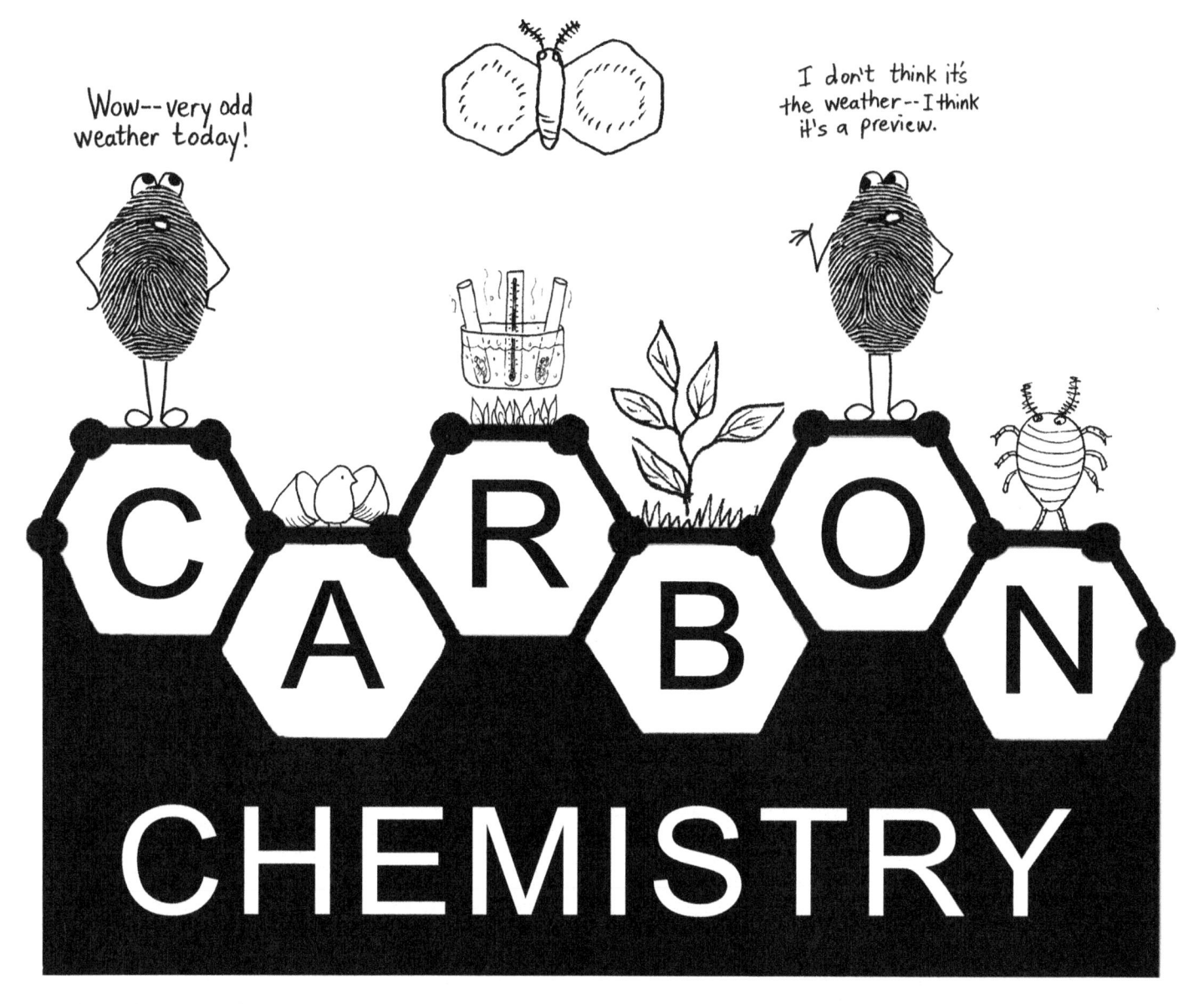

An introduction to organic chemistry and biochemistry

by Ellen J. McHenry

"Wow--very odd weather today!"

"I don't think it's the weather--I think it's a preview."

Table of Contents

Chapter One: Carbon..1
Atomic models: electron cloud, solar system, ball and stick
The carbon atom
Allotropes of pure carbon: diamond, graphite, buckyballs, coal and charcoal

Chapter Two: Alkane Hydrocarbons...7
Alkanes: methane, ethane, propane, butane, etc.
Octane, crude oil and refineries
Isomers, CFC's

Chapter Three: "-enes" and "-ynes"..15
The concept of saturated versus unsaturated
Alkenes (with double bonds) and alkynes (with triple bonds)
Benzene, toluene, naphthalene

Chapter Four: Functional Groups..21
Alcohols, carboxylic acids, aldehydes, ketones, esters, and ethers

Chapter Five: Combining Functional Groups......................................27
Sodium benzoate, nitroglycerin, soap, prostaglandins, pheromones

Chapter Six: Plastics..37
Polyethylene, polypropylene, polystyrene, PVC, Teflon™
Invention of Bakelite (celluloid)

Chapter Seven: Rubber and Silicones..47
Natural latex rubber
Cross-linking in polymers
Chewing gum and Silly Putty™

Chapter Eight: Carbohydrates..53
Simple sugars (glucose, fructose, galactose)
Glycogen, diabetes and glucose intolerance
Disaccharides (lactose and sucrose)
Starch and cellulose

Chapter Nine: Fats..63
Structure of fat molecule
Saturated and unsaturated fats
Cis fat versus trans fat
Fat's jobs in the body

Chapter Ten: Proteins..69
Amino acids, polypeptides and proteins
The three dimensional shape of proteins, and the lock and key principle
Structure of DNA

Chapter Eleven: Carbon Oxides and the Carbon Cycle....................77
Carbon dioxide, carbon monoxide, the carbonate ion
The carbon cycle

Chapter One: Carbon

The heart of carbon chemistry is, of course, the carbon atom. Like all atoms, the carbon atom is made of only three particles: protons, neutrons, and electrons. There are several ways to represent a carbon atom. Each model has strengths and weaknesses.

This is called the **electron cloud model**. It shows how the carbon atom looks under an electron microscope. It is the closest to being an actual "photograph" of the atom. However, it is almost useless when we want to study the orderly arrangement of electrons into shells and orbitals, or when we want to show chemical bonding.

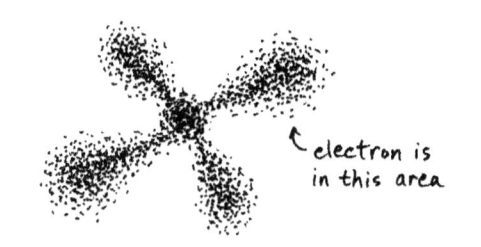

This is called the **solar system model**. It doesn't look anything like a real carbon atom, but it is a very good model to use for learning about the arrangement of protons, neutrons and electrons. It helps us to understand how the electrons orbit around the nucleus. We can show the arrangement of the electrons into shells. The weakness of this model, however, is that it is very easy to forget that atoms are really three-dimensional, not flat.

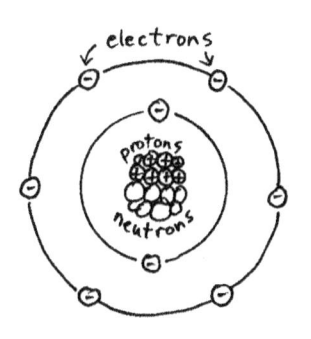

This is called the **ball and stick model**. It doesn't look anything like a real carbon atom, either. The ball in the center represents both the nucleus of the atom, and any electrons that are in "inner" shells, closer to the nucleus. The sticks represent free electrons on the outside of the atom that are available for bonding with other atoms. This model is very useful when you want to build actual models of molecules. It does not show the electrons, however; it shows only sticks where the bonds are, and this can be confusing to beginning students. You have to remember that the stick represents an electron or a pairing up of electrons.

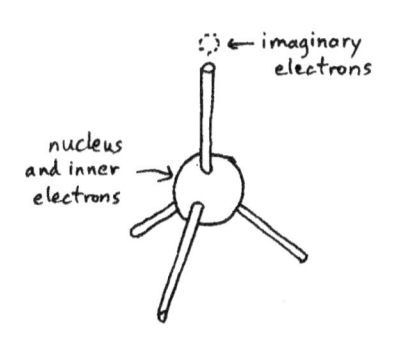

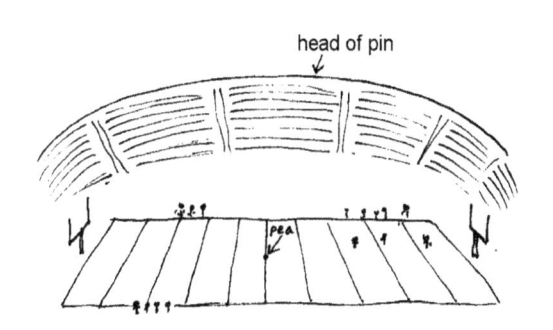

A weakness of all these models is that they do not show the relative sizes and distances between the particles. If you Imagine that the nucleus of an atom is a pea sitting on the 50 yard line inside a large football stadium. The electrons would be pin heads traveling along the outer reaches of the upper decks. It's hard to believe, but an atom is mostly empty space!!

It is the number of protons that determines what an atom is. Each element has a unique number of protons. Hydrogen has one proton, helium has two, lithium has three, beryllium has four, and so on through the Periodic Table. An atom's atomic number tells how many protons it has. Carbon's atomic number is six, so it has six protons.

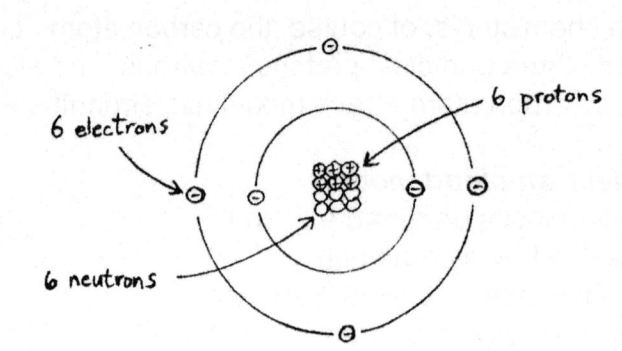

The plus signs in the protons mean they have a positive electrical charge. The minus signs in the electrons show they have a negative charge.

Since atoms must be electrically balanced, this also means that carbon has six electrons. Carbon's electrons are arranged in two layers, or shells. The first shell contains two electrons, and the remaining four are in the second shell. The fact that carbon has four electrons in its outer shell is very significant. Ideally, all atoms would like to have their outer shells filled, and, in the case of carbon, it would like to have eight electrons, not four. Like most of the smaller atoms on the Periodic Table, carbon lives by the motto: *"8 is great!"*

Electrons form pairs, with one electron spinning one way, and the other electron spinning in the opposite direction. (It's like a very simple dance.) Carbon would like each of its electrons to have a partner. So, carbon is out looking for four electron "dance partners" to fill in these empty places.

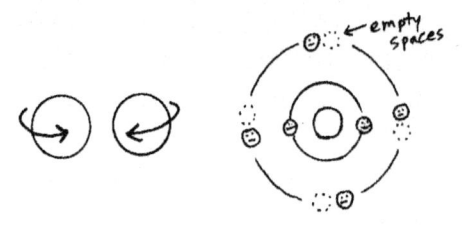

How does carbon find electrons to fill in these empty places? It borrows them from other atoms. It just so happens that there are other atoms out there that have the same problem carbon does. They have electrons without partners, too. These atoms would love to get together with carbon and share one or more electrons, in an attempt to make pairs of electrons. Let's look at a couple atoms that would like to share electrons with carbon.

Hydrogen is the smallest atom there is. It is made of only one proton and only one electron. What fun can just one electron have? The proton isn't much company. It can't do the electron dance. So, hydrogen's electron goes out looking for a partner.

Look! There's a carbon atom! It needs some partners! So hydrogen goes over to carbon and puts its electron into one of carbon's empty slots. Now we have one happy electron couple!

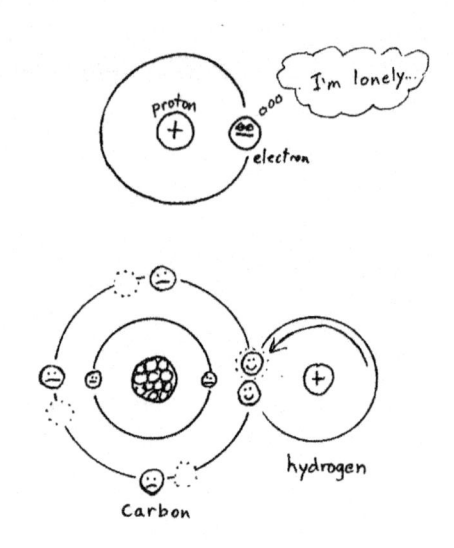

2

Then hydrogen calls up three of its hydrogen friends and tells them to come on over and fill the other three slots. Now we have a real square dance! Carbon is thrilled to have partners for its four electrons. This works out rather well!

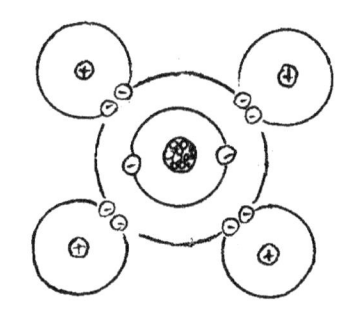

Another atom that can cooperate with carbon is chlorine. Chlorine's problem is that is has seven, not eight, electrons in its outer shell. Chlorine is out looking for a free electron that can pair up with its lonely electron. Can carbon do this? Carbon has four electrons that are looking for partners. One of those electrons could go over and fill in chlorine's empty slot. What if there were four chlorines that were all looking for partners and they were all willing to come over to the carbon and pair up with one of carbon's lonely electrons? Hey—this works out pretty well, too!

Cl   Cl
  \\ /
   C
  / \\
Cl   Cl

Here is an easy way to draw it.

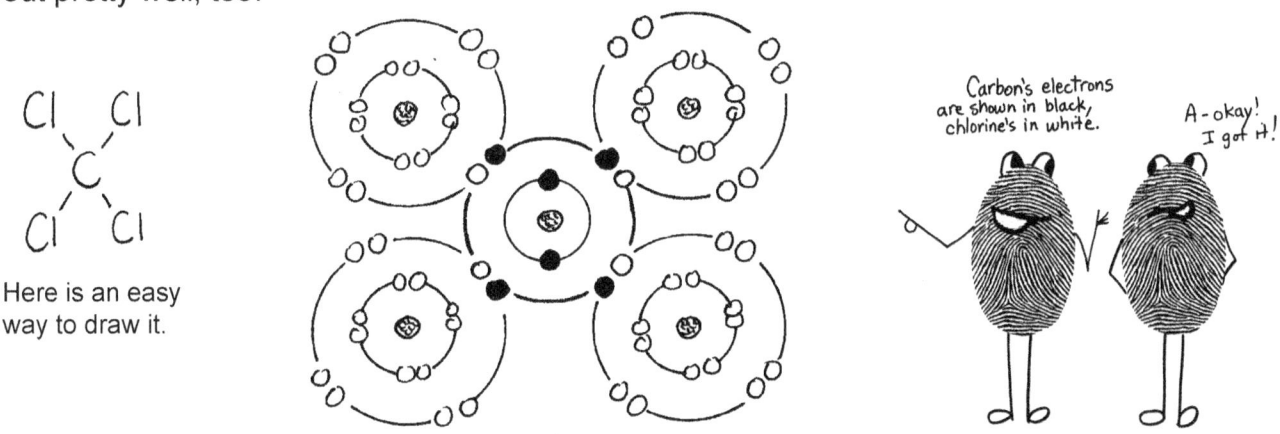

Carbon's electrons are shown in black, chlorine's in white.

A-okay! I got it!

Life is seldom perfect, even in the atomic kingdom. Sometimes things don't work out so well and carbon must adapt to unusual "dance partners." For example, sometimes carbon has to make do with only two atoms, not four. In the carbon dioxide molecule, carbon pairs up with two oxygens. Since oxygen has two free partners, two oxygens can provide a total of four partners—just what carbon is looking for. All they need to do is slide their electrons over a bit and make them match up.

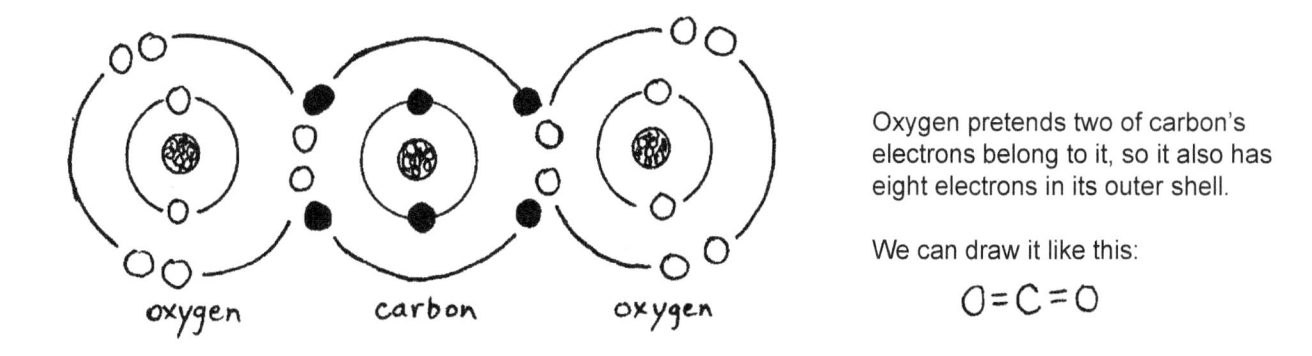

oxygen   carbon   oxygen

Oxygen pretends two of carbon's electrons belong to it, so it also has eight electrons in its outer shell.

We can draw it like this:

O=C=O

When carbon doubles up like this, we call it a **double bond.** That makes sense, doesn't it?

Carbon can also bond with itself. The only problem is that the carbon atoms on the edges will have unpaired electrons hanging off. But, nevertheless, carbon does bond with itself. The free electrons dangling on the edges usually pick up a hydrogen atom, or some other atom that happens to be in the area.

There are basically three ways that carbon bonds with itself. Each of these substances is called an **allotrope**. The first allotrope of carbon is **diamond**. Diamonds are made of pure carbon. The bonds between the carbons are very, very strong, making diamond the hardest substance on earth. Diamonds are so hard they can be used (on industrial saw blades) to cut metal and concrete. This is how the carbon atoms are linked in diamonds:

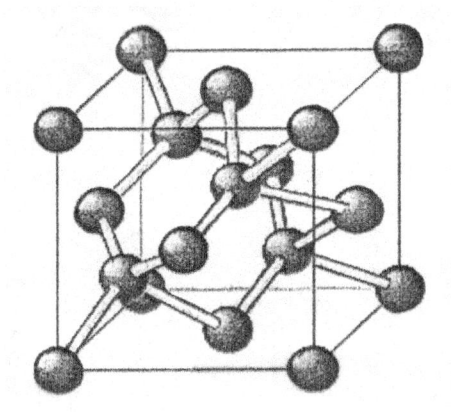

Another allotrope of carbon is **graphite**. You use graphite all the time. It is the "lead" in pencils. (Lead is not used anymore, of course, having long ago been discovered to be dangerous to our health. Graphite is now used in pencils, but the word "lead" still lingers on.) In graphite, the carbon is arranged in layers, like this:

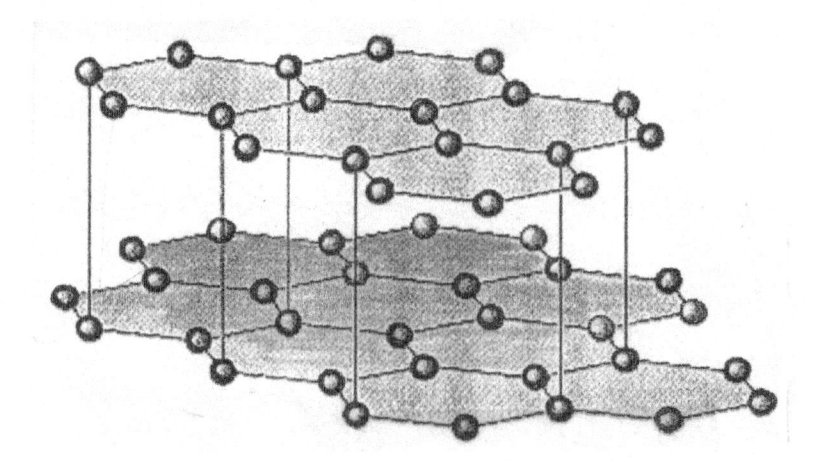

Each layer is made of hexagonal shapes. The layers are loosely bonded to each other and can slide around. This is what makes graphite feel slippery. If you rub your fingers on the end of a pencil, the slippery sensation you feel is the layers sliding back and forth. Graphite can be used as a lubricant. Some people rub a pencil on the drawer runners in dressers so that the drawers go in and out smoothly. It's hard to believe that graphite and diamonds are made of the same stuff, but if you could squeeze graphite hard enough, the atoms would rearrange themselves and form a diamond!

The third allotrope was not discovered until 1985. It was named ***buckminsterfullerene***, after the architect Buckminster Fuller, who was famous for his geodesic dome structures in the 1960's and '70's. Since the name is so long, scientists have come up with a nickname for this substance. They call the molecules ***buckyballs***.

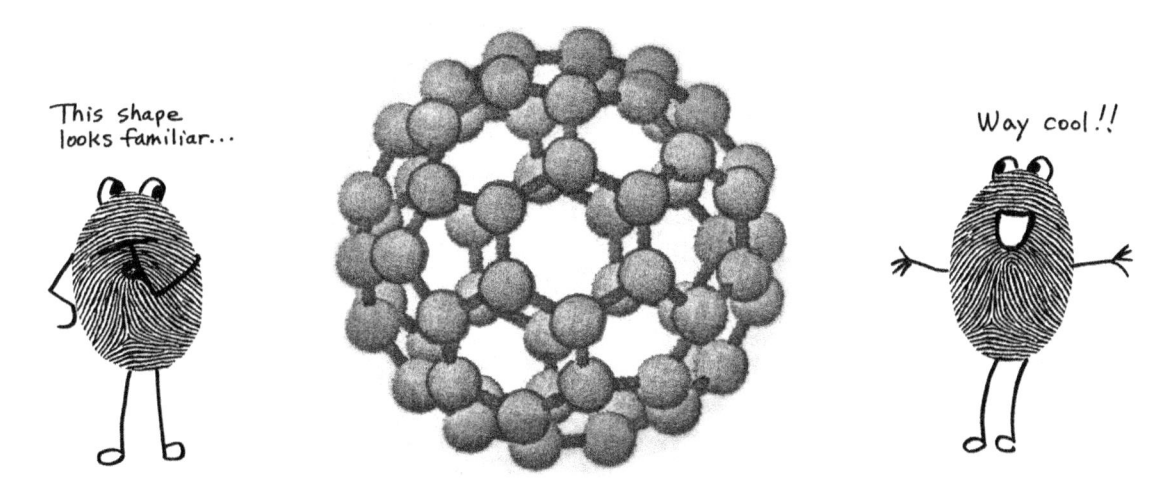

This shape looks familiar...

Way cool!!

If you think this pattern looks like a soccer ball, you are absolutely right. The pattern on a soccer ball is exactly the same as a buckyball. There are 20 hexagons and 12 pentagons, with each pentagon completely surrounded by hexagons.

What are buckyballs good for? Some scientists think they might be good for microscopic lubrication or bearings in a microscope motor. Maybe they can be used inside the human body for drug delivery (by putting the drug molecules inside the bucky balls). If you add a few potassium atoms to the buckyball, it will conduct electricity as well as metal does. A low temperatures, it becomes a superconductor.

Where can you find these weird balls? Buckyballs are a component of black soot—the kind that collects on the glass screen in front of fireplaces. Scientists don't go around collecting soot, however. They manufacture buckyballls in their labs by vaporizing graphite with a laser.

Two more forms of carbon that should be mentioned are coal and charcoal. They are made of mostly carbon, but the carbon atoms are not bonded in geometrical shapes. The scientific word for "no shape" is ***amorphous***. ("A" means "without" and "morph" means "shape.") Coal and charcoal are said to be amorphous types of carbon. There are also small amounts of other types of atoms mixed in with the carbon. Coal comes from ancient plants that were buried and put under extreme pressure. Charcoal is made by burning wood in a low-oxygen environment.

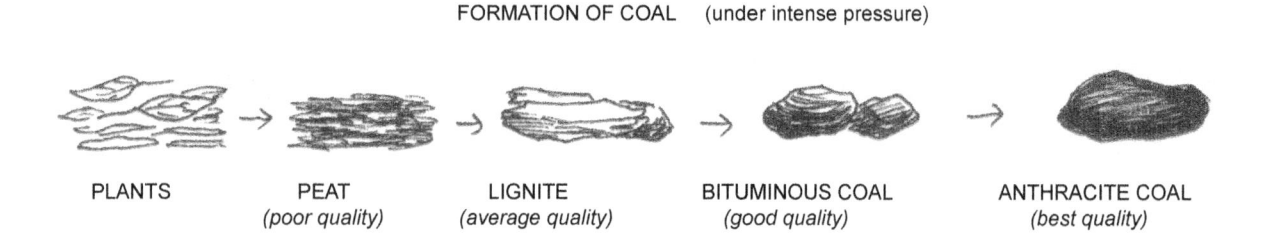

FORMATION OF COAL   (under intense pressure)

PLANTS → PEAT *(poor quality)* → LIGNITE *(average quality)* → BITUMINOUS COAL *(good quality)* → ANTHRACITE COAL *(best quality)*

Comprehension self-check

See if you can fill in the blanks and answer these questions, based on what you remember reading. If you have trouble, go back and re-read.

1) All atoms are made of three types of particles: _____, _____, and _____.
2) The three types of atomic models mentioned in this chapter are _____, _____, and _____.
3) Which model gives us the best picture of what an atom really looks like? _____
4) Which model is the best one to use when making molecule models? _____
5) Which model is the best for showing exactly what is going on with the arrangement of electrons into shells? _____
6) Which one is easiest to draw? _____
7) Which one is easiest to build out of craft materials? _____
8) If we were to make a model of an atom that was proportionately correct, our nucleus would be the size of a _____ in a _____ and the electrons would be the size of _____ traveling around the _____.
9) It is the number of _____ that make an atom what it is. This number is called the _____ number.
10) Most atoms in the top part of the Periodic Table (the smaller, non-metal atoms) live by this motto: _____.
11) If an atom does not have a full outer shell of electrons, what does it do about it? _____
_____
12) When carbon has to double up and share more than one electron with another atom, we call this a _____ bond.
13) Three substances that demonstrate how carbon atoms bond with each other in geometrical shapes are _____, _____, and _____.
14) Which one of these substances has a molecular structure than looks like a soccer ball? _____
15) Two substances that contain mostly carbon but do not demonstrate a geometric shape are: _____ and _____.

On-line Research

Find the answers to the following questions by researching the Internet.

1) What famous scientist invented the solar system model for representing atoms?

2) Diamonds sometimes contain a small number of atoms other than carbon. These other atoms are called "impurities" and they cause the diamonds to have slight tints of color. What colors can diamonds come in?

3) Who was the first person in history to make an artificial diamond?

4) What is "activated" charcoal and what it is used for?

5) Something related to coal is "coke." What is coke?

Chapter Two: Alkane Hydrocarbons

We learned in chapter one that carbon often bonds with hydrogen. When carbon bonds with just hydrogen, they form a molecule we call a **hydrocarbon**. The simplest hydrocarbon is **methane**. It consists of one carbon atom and four hydrogen atoms:

Here are three different ways of drawing the methane molecule. The one on the left is called a "structural formula." It is easy to draw, and because it uses letters to represent the atoms, you always know what the atoms are. However, it does not show the three-dimensional shape of the molecule. The one in the center, the "ball and stick" model, shows how methane really looks in three dimensions. The hydrogen atoms want to stay as far apart from each other as possible, and this "tetrahedral" shape is the result. The model on the right is called a "space-filling" model. It probably comes closest to showing us what a real methane molecule looks like, because real molecules don't have sticks separating the atoms. Space-filling models are easy to make out of clay, but are difficult to draw. We won't be seeing them very much in this book, but it is good for you to have seen a few and understand what they are.

Methane is a small, lightweight molecule that floats around in the air as a gas. You can't see it or smell it. (Gas companies must add a smelly substance to it so that we can smell gas leaks in our homes.) We sometimes call it "natural gas" because it occurs naturally in the earth, often forming in areas where oil and coal are found.

Methane burns easily in the presence of oxygen, and it burns cleanly, without polluting the air. This makes it excellent for use as a fuel, but it also makes it very dangerous for coal miners who run into pockets of methane gas as they are digging. A spark of any kind can ignite the gas and create a deadly mine fire. In the early days of mining, the miners sometimes took caged birds with them into the mines. The birds were very sensitive to the methane gas and would act strangely, or even faint, if there was methane present. By watching the behavior of the bird, the miners would have an early warning signal telling them that methane was lurking in the mine.

Some types of bacteria produce methane. Farmers know that rotting vegetation can produce both methane and heat. (Not a good combination when you don't want fire!) Fires can start spontaneously in storage silos if enough methane builds up.

Methane-producing bacteria live in our intestines, also. Yes, gas is really... gas. Healthy intestines have millions of harmless (and beneficial) bacteria living in them. We need these bacteria in our intestines. They aid in digestion and keep us healthy. When certain foods pass through the intestines undigested, the bacteria produce an extra amount of methane and hydrogen. But remember, methane has no odor. The odor we associate with intestinal gas comes from very small amounts of other substances such as hydrogen sulfide. Since methane is flammable, it is fortunate that the methane in our intestines is mixed with other gases such as nitrogen and carbon dioxide, which are not flammable. However, there is enough methane in some intestines to cause problems. Surgeons in the early days of medicine learned the hard way about the flammability of methane when sparks from their operating instruments would occasionally cause small explosions in the patients' intestines!

Let's leave that last paragraph unillustrated and move on!

Methane is the first and simplest member of a whole group of carbon compounds called **alkanes**. The second member of this group has two carbon atoms in it and is called **ethane**. This is how it looks:

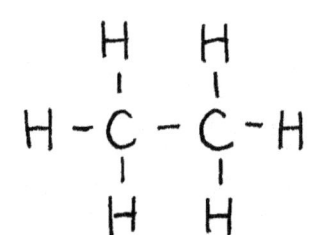

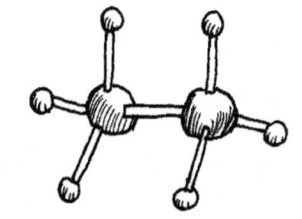

structural formula   the ball and stick model   space filling model

As you can see, ethane is made of two carbon atoms and six hydrogen atoms. We can write it like this: C_2H_6. (This is called the **empirical formula**.) Both carbon atoms have all four of their free electrons attached to another atom, so this combination works out well. Ethane is also a gas.

If another carbon atom is added on, we make a substance called **propane** (C_3H_8).

Can we stop drawing those other two models? Thanks!

Undoubtedly, you've heard of propane. You may have a propane tank outside your house, connected to a gas grill.

Add another carbon atom to the string, plus a few more hydrogens, and you have a molecule named **butane** (C_4H_{10}). Butane can be found in hand-held lighters.

```
      H   H   H   H
      |   |   |   |
  H - C - C - C - C - H
      |   |   |   |
      H   H   H   H
```

You can keep on adding carbon atoms and make the string longer and longer. You could have dozens, hundreds, thousands, or millions of carbon atoms in an alkane string. Short strings with 1 to 4 carbon atoms are gases. Strings made of 5 to 18 carbon atoms are liquids, and strings with 19 or more carbon atoms are solids.

So where do these names (methane, ethane, propane, butane) come from? What do they mean? An organization called the **International Union of Pure and Applied Chemistry (IUPAC)** decides what to name molecules and chemical compounds. Chemists all over the world need to use the same names for things so that they can discuss their work with each other. If a chemist speaks about "methanol" or "ethylene glycol," all the other chemists need to know exactly what substance he is talking about. Sometimes IUPAC decides to go with names that chemists have already been using for a while. Sometimes, IUPAC decides to change the name to something more logical. The goal is to have a naming system with rules that everyone knows, so that there is as little confusion as possible. And confusion is a distinct possibility in a science where there are millions of molecules that could be named!

The first step in naming a carbon compound is to count how many carbon atoms are in it. This is how you count carbons:

1	2	3	4	5	6	7	8	9	10
meth-	eth-	prop-	but-	pent-	hex-	hept-	oct-	non-	dec-
		(prope)	(byute)					(known)	(deck)

These are the prefixes that come before suffixes like "ane" or "ene" or "yne." In this chapter we are talking about alk*anes*, so each of these prefixes has "ane" after it. "Ane" simply means single-bonded carbons. We have seen methane, ethane, propane, and butane. We can now add pentane, hexane, heptane, octane, nonane, and decane.

You might recognize the word **octane**. This word is found on gas pumps, where they post "octane ratings." A gasoline that has an octane rating of 87 means that the gasoline is 87% octane and 13% heptane. Inside the engine, the fuels get compressed before they are ignited by the spark plug. Heptane has the unfortunate characteristic of exploding too early, before it is ignited by the spark. This causes something called "knocking" in the engine, which is not desirable. Octane can handle compression much better. So, the more octane, the better. Unfortunately, the higher the octane rating, the higher the price, also! Better things always cost more, don't they?!

Chains of 12 to 16 carbons give you kerosene fuels. 15 to 18 carbons make heating oil. 20 to 40 carbons give you paraffin waxes and asphalt. Strings of hundreds or thousands of carbons make various kinds of plastics. (Plastics have their own chapter later in the book.)

Number of carbons	Uses
1-4	natural gas (used for fuel)
5-12	gasoline, solvents
13-16	kerosene, diesel fuel, jet fuel, heating oil
17-20	lubricating oils
21--	paraffin, asphalt

All the products listed above can be made from the same raw material: **crude oil**. "Crude" just means raw or unrefined-- the natural stuff as it comes up from the ground. Scientists guess that crude oil was formed by the decomposition of plants and animals under great pressure a long time ago. Crude oil is made of alkanes.

A factory called a **refinery** can sort out the different lengths of alkanes in crude oil. The refinery uses a process called **distillation**. You may be thinking of distilled water and wondering if there is a connection. Yes, the process of distillation is similar no matter what you are distilling. **Distilling** means heating a substance until it turns to steam, then gradually cooling it.

Crude oil is heated until it turns into vapor (at 350° C), then this vapor is pumped into the bottom of a very tall tube. The temperature is hot at the bottom, and cooler at the top. The longest hydrocarbon chains turn back into a liquid (condense) onto trays at the bottom of the tube and run into pipes. The next-longest hydrocarbons liquefy at the next level up and run into those pipes, and so on, until the very shortest hydrocarbon chains, such as methane and propane, are collected at the top.

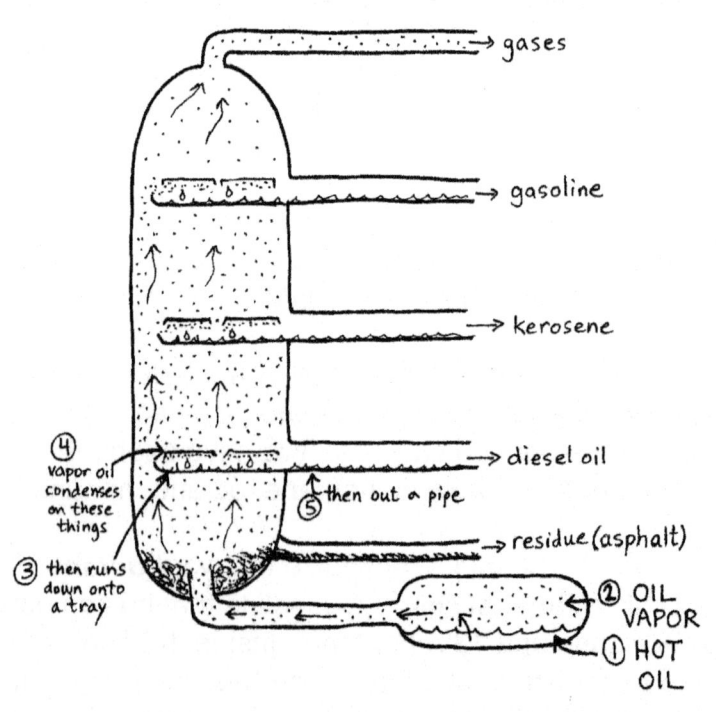

Cracking is a process by which they take medium-sized chains and break them into smaller pieces. (That's easy to remember!) Cracking is done by heating the medium-sized chains in the absence of air (and sometimes using chemicals called catalysts, which help the reaction occur). Cracking is often used as a way of producing extra gasoline, a substance which is always in demand.

Two more ideas that we need to discuss in this chapter are chlorinated hydrocarbons and isomers. Let's tackle chlorinated hydrocarbons first.

As we mentioned in chapter one, carbon can bond with an atom that is willing to share an electron. Hydrogen very often does this, but other atoms do, too. Chlorine is an atom that has only seven electrons in its outer shell—three happy pairs and one very unhappy electron that is all alone. Chlorine gladly attaches itself to carbon. Here are four examples of molecules where one or more hydrogens are replaced by chlorine:

methyl chloride   methylene chloride   chloroform   carbon tetrachloride

Methyl chloride is mainly used in making silicone substances (sealants, waterproofing materials, artificial body parts, Silly Putty). Methylene chloride is used as a paint remover. Chloroform started out as an anesthetic (putting you to sleep for surgery), but has now been replaced by safer substances. Chloroform is sometimes referred to as "knock-out gas." (Bad guys in movies soak handkerchiefs in chloroform and put them over the faces of their victims.) Carbon tetrachloride was formerly used in dry-cleaning, but is no longer used because of safety concerns. It can react with water to produce a poisonous gas.

These substances do not dissolve in water, which is a problem when they escape out into nature. **DDT** (dichlorodiphenyltrichloroethane) is famous for both its effectiveness as an insecticide (it did a great job!) and, unfortunately, its ability to destroy wildlife such as birds and reptiles (it did a great job at that, too!).

Carbon compounds can contain fluorine along with chlorine. The fluorine atom is in exactly the same state as the chlorine atom, with one unhappy, unpaired electron. Fluorine will gladly attach itself to a carbon.

These molecules are called (no big surprise here...) chlorofluorocarbons, or CFC's for short. They are used as propellants in aerosol spray cans. The CFC's don't hurt us directly because they don't react chemically with anything. The problem with them is that they diffuse up into the atmosphere where they are changed into molecules that can damage the protective ozone layer in the atmosphere. CFC's are no longer used in most countries.

One last topic remains: **isomers**. The name sounds strange, but the idea is very easy. Isomers are molecules with exactly the same number of atoms but in a different geometrical arrangement.

For example, let's look at butane, C_4H_{10}. The most obvious way to arrange the atoms is like this:

$$H_3C-CH_2-CH_2-CH_3$$

However, you could reshuffle the carbons a bit and make the molecule look like this:

It is still C_4H_{10}, butane. To differentiate it from regular butane, scientists call this "isobutane," an isomer of butane.

Here are three isomers of pentane, C_5H_{12}.

Why are isomers worth mentioning? One practical use for isomers is in gasoline. Petroleum chemists have found that branched isomers of octane actually burn better than straight octane. Branched nonane and decane are also put into gasoline. The chemists alter the straight alkanes that come from the refinery, adding chemicals that cause them to rearrange into branched isomers.

We didn't draw all the H's, but you know they are there, right?

Sad, isn't it?

Zzzzz

Comprehension self-check

See if you can fill in the blanks and answer these questions, based on what you remember reading. If you have trouble, go back and re-read.

1) The simplest hydrocarbon is called _____.
2) Three ways you can draw molecules are _____ _____, _____ _____ _____, _____-_____.
3) Methane is also called _____ gas.
4) Does methane burn easily? ____
5) Where can methane be found in our bodies? _____
6) Methane, ethane, propane, etc. belong to a group of molecules called _____s.
7) What does the IUPAC do? _____
8) Can you count to ten in carbons?
9) Where can you find octane and heptane mixed together? _____
10) Too much heptane and not enough octane causes this problem: _____.
11) Very short alkanes are _____, medium sized are _____ and longer ones are _____.
12) Raw or unrefined oil is called _____ oil.
13) A factory that processes oil is called a _____.
14) The primary method factories use to refine oil is called _____, which is heating then cooling and condensing the oil.
15) Breaking hydrocarbon chains into smaller pieces is called _____.
16) Name two other atoms, in addition to hydrogen, that will bond with carbon: _____ and _____.
17) CFC's contain these three types of atoms: _____, _____ and _____.
18) DDT was used to kill _____ but it also killed _____.
19) What was chloroform used for? _____
20) Molecules that contain exactly the same number of atoms, but in a different geometric arrangement, are called _____

On-line research

1) Where are the world's largest sources of crude oil? Name at least five places:

2) Name three US states that are known for their coal mining.

3) How long has the IUPAC been in existence?

4) What is ozone?

5) What famous scientist invented a safety headlamp for miners?

6) Did miners really take birds into mines, or is this just an "old wives' tale"?

Hydrocarbon puzzle

Here are the clues for the missing words. You have to figure out which goes where!

- A factory where hydrocarbons are processed
- The primary method factories use to process hydrocarbons
- Gasoline is mostly this hydrocarbon
- This hydrocarbon is found in handheld lighters
- This hydrocarbon is found in gas grill tanks
- This atom is the "F" in CFC's

- This is the word for hydrocarbon chains with only single bonds
- Hydrocarbons burn easily. They are highly _____.
- Chlorofluorocarbons destroy the _____ layer of the atmosphere.
- This method is used to break apart hydrocarbon chains.
- This hydrocarbon is natural gas.

"Cross one out" puzzle

1) Which one of these is not a hydrocarbon?
methane   gasoline   diesel fuel   rubbing alcohol   kerosene   asphalt   ethane

2) Which one of these has nothing to do with refining crude oil?
distillation   fermentation   condensation   evaporation

3) Which one of these is not an alkane?
propane   butane   ethyne   nonane   decane   heptane   methane   octane

4) In which one of these places will you not find natural gas?
mountain tops   grill tanks   intestines   swamps   silos   mines

5) Which one of these is not an alkane hydrocarbon?
CH_4 C_4H_{10} C_3H_8 C_2H_2 C_5H_{12}

6) Which one of these does not bond with carbon?
Chlorine   fluorine   carbon   hydrogen   helium

Chapter Three: "-enes" and "-ynes"

In chapter one, we mentioned that carbon can sometime form what we call a "double bond." Then in chapter two, we saw nothing but single bonds. Alkanes have only single bonds in them. Now we are going to look at some molecules with double, even triple, bonds in them.

What would happen if we plucked some hydrogens off an alkane? Let's try it.

STEP 1   STEP 2   STEP 3

Look at what happened—the carbons tilted themselves a bit so that their unpaired electrons matched up with each other. That seems to work out pretty well. However, we no longer have an alkane, we have an **alkene**. Alkenes are molecules similar to alknanes, except that somewhere in the molecule there are some carbons forming a double bond with each other.

The alkene shown here, in step three, is called ethylene. Ethylene gas may sound like a poisonous name, but it is a harmless gas produced naturally by ripening fruit. Yes, that bowl of fruit there on the table is giving off ethylene gas. Commercial produce growers have found that they can speed up the process of ripening by steaming their produce in ethylene. Tomatoes, especially, can be "reddened up" by exposing them to ethylene. Unfortunately, the taste does not improve as fast as the color does. Gassed winter produce may look good, but it doesn't taste like that vine-ripened summer stuff! Ethylene gas is also used as an ingredient in automobile anti-freeze (ethylene glycol) and in plastics called polyethylene. We will learn more about these plastics in a later chapter.

Can chemists change ethene back into an ethane by adding some hydrogens? Yes, they can. Here is how they write this process:

ethylene   +   hydrogen   →   ethane

Alkane molecules are what we call **saturated**. Saturated means completely full. When a liquid is saturated, it can't hold any more of whatever you are trying to stir into it.
When the job market is saturated, there are no more open jobs to be found. (When your brain is saturated, it can't hold any more information and you need recess or a nap!) When a hydrocarbon is saturated, it has all the hydrogen it can possibly hold on to. The opposite of saturated is **unsaturated**. If a hydrocarbon has some double bonds that it could open up, then it is unsaturated.

SATURATED   UNSATURATED

Now let's look at a molecule with a triple bond. If we pluck off another pair of hydrogens, carbon has no choice but to increase the double bond to a triple bond, sharing not two, but three pairs of electrons. Carbon must feel like a contortionist in an old-fashioned circus! (Contortionists are the performers that can bend their bodies in all sorts of unnatural ways.)

This molecule is the smallest member of the **alkyne** group. Alkynes all have at least one carbon with a triple bond. To really confuse you, the name of this chemical is acetylene, as in acetylene torch. Hmm... maybe IUPAC didn't get there in time and acetylene got named by someone not familiar with the ane/ene/yne naming rule.

Alkenes and alkynes have many of the same properties as alkanes. Molecules with only 2 to 4 carbons are gases, 5 to 18 carbons are liquids, and 19 or more carbons are solids. They do not dissolve in water; they float on water. (Think of an oil spill.)

Another group of molecules that ends in "-ene" is the **benzene** group. This group is also called the **aromatic hydrocarbons** because the first ones that were discovered had strong smells. Later on scientists discovered that not all members of this group have odors. But it was too late—the name was impossible to change by that point.

The discovery of the structure of benzene has a famous story attached to it. Benzene's empirical formula, C_6H_6, had been discovered in 1825 by Michael Faraday (who is more famous for his work with electricity). Chemists drew up every possible configuration they could for C_6H_6. Here are two of them:

All of the configurations contained several double and/or triple bonds. However, chemistry experiments with benzene clearly demonstrated that benzene couldn't have double and triple bonds. What was up? No one could figure it out for 40 years! Then along came a scientist named August Kekule. He worked on the puzzle long and hard until it almost drove him crazy. One night (or so goes one version of the story) he fell asleep thinking about the benzene puzzle. As he slept he dreamed that the straight molecule curved around until its ends touched, forming a ring. When he woke up he realized he had solved the puzzle in his sleep. Benzene must be a ring!

He still had some work to do on the puzzle after he woke up, however. There was still a double bond problem even with this structure. If you look at the molecule above and count the bonds attached to each carbon, you will see that there are only three. Carbona13ac always makes four bonds. What was happening? This solution was proposed:

The bonds between the carbons alternate back and forth between single and double so fast they are neither single nor double. The electrons are not tied down to any one place, but are spread around the ring. After deducing that this must be the case, chemists decided to draw the benzene structure like this:

— carbons aren't drawn, but are there, nonetheless!
— circle represents all 6 hydrogens

The benzene ring is a very stable structure. Stable molecules are generally less dangerous than unstable ones. If it were not for your liver, benzene would not be considered poisonous. Benzene would just float on through you body, not bothering with any of your cells. But when benzene arrives in the liver, the liver starts to disassemble the molecules. The liver is just doing its job. The liver is supposed to take chemicals apart and get rid of them. This time, however, disassembly is not helpful. But your liver doesn't know this, and it starts messing with benzene, disturbing the stable structure. Now, thanks to your liver, you now have an unstable, dangerous substance in your body!

If you add a CH$_3$ to one edge, you get toluene, a very useful and commonly used chemical, but one that is very nasty to your health.

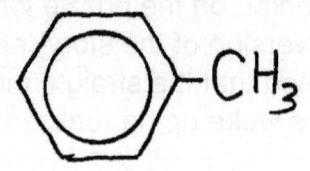

Toluene is a clear, fragrant liquid which is used as a solvent in products such as paints, varnishes, cleaning products, pesticides, adhesives and explosives. You almost certainly have products in your home that contains toluene. Toluene is a hazardous chemical, though, and must not be dumped down drains. It has been proven to cause cancer in laboratory animals. It should be disposed of at an official hazardous waste collection site. Fortunately, toluene does eventually break down, so it won't stay in the environment forever.

One interesting side note about toluene is that it is produced naturally by the tolu tree. This tree grows in South America and is tapped (like a maple tree) to get the tolu resin, which is used in all sorts of food and health products. The natives use it as a natural remedy for many different illnesses.

If you join two benzene rings together, you form naphthalene. You know naphthalene as moth balls. If you have never smelled moth balls, you're missing something—wow, are they pungent! You'll never forget that smell.

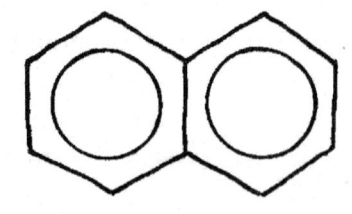

You can remember that this structure is what moth balls are made of because it kind of looks like a moth, doesn't it?

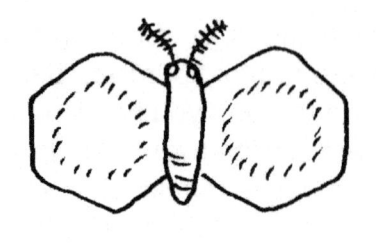

Comprehension self-check

See if you can fill in the blanks and answer these questions, based on what you remember reading. If you have trouble, go back and re-read.

1) Alkanes have _____ bonds, alkenes have _____ bonds and alkynes have _____ bonds.
2) Ethylene gas is produced naturally by _____ _____.
3) Hydrocarbons that have the maximum number of hydrogens they can possible hold are said to be s_____.
4) Hydrocarbons that have double or triple bonds that could be opened up (to allow for the addition of more hydrogens) are said to be u_____.
5) Molecules that contain at least one benzene ring are called _____ _____.
6) August Kekule solved the benzene puzzle while he was _____.
7) How many benzene rings does toluene contain? ___
8) How many benzene rings does naphthalene contain? ___
9) What household product is made of naphthalene? _____
10) What does the naphthalene molecule resemble? _____

On-line research

1) Another alkene is "xylene." What is it, and what is it used for?

2) Can you find xylene's molecular structure and draw it below?

3) Over-exposure to xylene causes these health problems:

4) What happens to xylene when it gets out into the environment?

5) Is xylene considered a carcinogen (cancer-causing chemical)?

Draw the bonds

Your job is to put all the bond lines between the letters. Here's how to do it: make sure that each carbon, "C," has four bond lines going out from it. (Hydrogens can only have one line sticking out from them.)

1.
```
   H H
H  C C  H
   H H
```

2.
```
 H   H
  C C
 H   H
```

3. H C C H

4.
```
H C C C H
  H   H
```

5.
```
    H   H
    C C
 H C     C H
    C C
    H   H
```

6.
```
  H H   H H
H C C C C C H
```

7. O C O

8.
```
   H H
H C C C C C H
   H H
```

9.
```
  H H     H H
H C C C C C C H
  H H     H H
```

10.
```
  H H H H H
H C C C C C H
  H H H H H
```

11.
```
  H H
H C C H
H C C H
  H H
```

12.
```
    H       H
    C       C
 H C   C   C H
    C   C
  H C       C H
     C   C
     H   H
```

Chapter Four: Functional Groups

Building organic molecules is a little like building with a children's construction toy. You can imagine popping sections on and off and adding new parts. If you take the end hydrogen off an alkane, you could stick on something else.

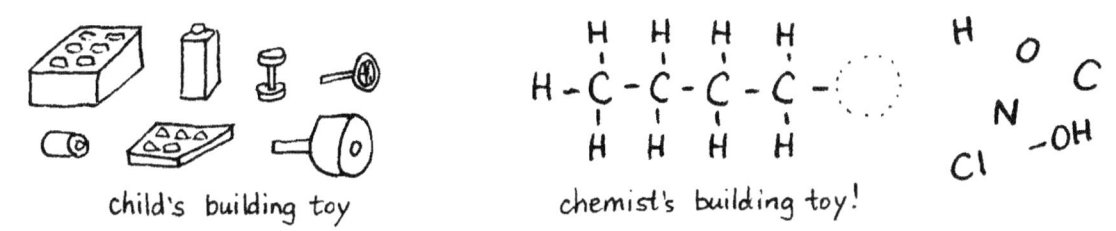

child's building toy   chemist's building toy!

What could you put on? If it were a toy you might add a red brick, or three blue beads, or a set of wheels. But since it is a molecule, your only options are things like oxygens, nitrogens, or more hydrogens. Here is a sample of some of the parts we can stick on an alkane:

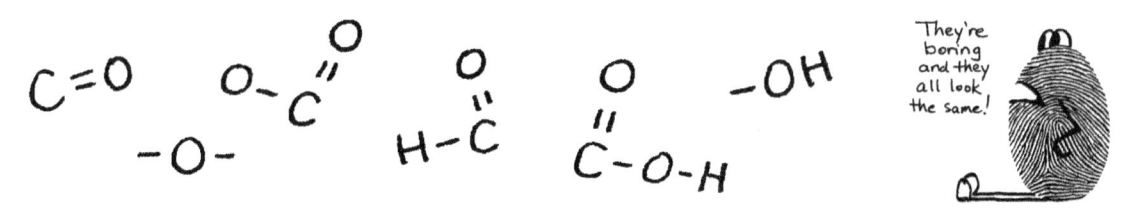

They're boring and they all look the same!

Each of these parts can turn the alkane into something totally different, just like adding wheels to a Lego block can turn it into a vehicle. Chemists don't call these things "parts;" they call them **functional groups**, because each one will make a molecule function a certain way, just like those wheels make the block function as a vehicle. These functional groups make the molecules function as things like alcohols or acids.

Here are the groups we are going to talk about in the rest of the chapter:

Name of functional group	What it looks like
Alcohol	$-OH$
Carboxylic acid	$H-O-\overset{\overset{O}{\|\|}}{C}-$
Aldehyde	$\overset{\overset{O}{\|\|}}{-C-H}$
Ketone	$-\overset{\|}{C}=O$
Ester	$-\overset{\overset{O}{\|\|}}{C}-O-$
Ether	$-O-$

I'd rather build with Legos!

Let's look at each group separately, starting with alcohol.

We will take the smallest alkane, methane, pop one hydrogen off, and stick on the functional group "OH."

This type of alcohol is called **methanol**. "Meth-" means "one," and "-ol" means it is an alcohol. Now, after telling you it is called methanol, we need to let you know that, once again, somebody in the chemistry naming department got there before the IUPAC and starting calling it "methyl alcohol." This name stuck and you will hear it called by this name, also. Not only that, but it is also called "wood alcohol" because you can make it from wood, like this:

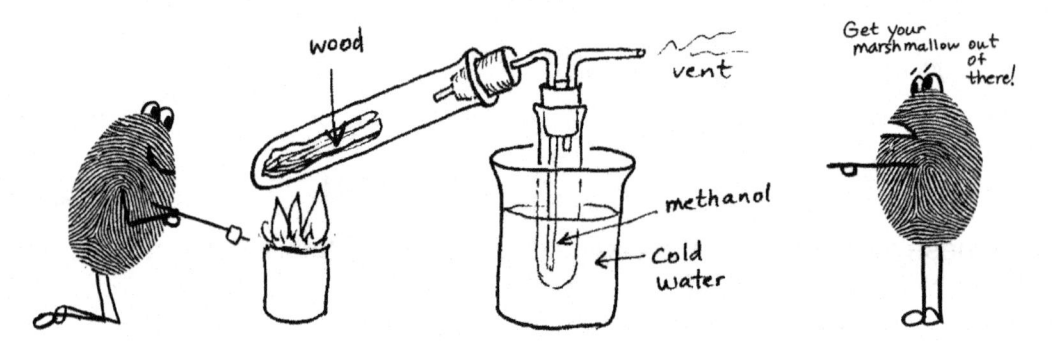

Methanol is poisonous. It is used in industry as a solvent and as an ingredient for more complex chemicals. Researchers are experimenting with it to see if it could be used as a fuel for vehicles.

Now let's take the next smallest alkane, ethane, and stick the "OH" on it.

What would this be called? If methane turned into methanol, then ethane would turn into... **ethanol**, right? Right! However, (here it comes again) chemists used to call it ethyl alcohol, and you will still hear this term used. And, just like with methanol, there is a third name. Ethanol is sometimes called "grain alcohol" because it is commonly made from the fermentation of grains or other starchy plants.

Ethanol is the alcohol in beverages such as beer and wine. Like all alcohols, ethanol is technically a poison. Consumed in small amounts, the alcohol doesn't kill; it just slows down the brain and nerves. People interpret a mild slowing down of the nervous system as enjoyable. After a certain point, however, the slowing down of the nervous system becomes dangerous, especially if the affected person is driving a car. Consuming large amounts of ethanol too quickly can cause unconsciousness, or even death.

Let's look at one more alcohol. We'll use propane as our base:

H-C-C-C-H ⇨ H-C-C-C-H ⇨ H-C-C-C-H

Since it is sticking off the middle carbon, it's an isomer of propanol, thus it is isopropanol.

The names for this substance are: isopropanol, isopropyl alcohol, and rubbing alcohol. You probably have a bottle of this in your medicine cabinet at home. It is very poisonous, which makes it excellent as a disinfectant. Nurses always rub isopropanol on your arm before giving you a shot so that the needle doesn't push germs under your skin.

Let's try another functional group. We will pop a hydrogen off a methane and stick on a COOH.

H-C(H) ⇨ H-C- ⇨ H-C-C-OH

We have made an acid called **acetic acid**, which is found in vinegar. (The Latin word for vinegar is "acetum.") **Carboxylic acids** smell foul and strong. (Okay, maybe you like the smell of vinegar, but it is a very strong smell!)

If you turn butane into a carboxylic acid, you get **butyric acid**, which is one of the foulest smelling substances there is. Rancid (rotten) butter contains butyric acid. Human body odor is partly caused by small amounts of butyric acid.

H-C-C-C-C-OH butyric acid (byu-teer'-ick)

but-yr

butter ⇕ butyr

A new reason to hate chemistry!

If you stick the COOH on just a hydrogen, you get **formic acid**, which is produced by ants. (The Latin word for ant is "formica.")

H-C-OH
formic acid

The sting you feel when an ant bites you is not from its teeth, but rather from the formic acid it injects into your skin.

The other carboxylic acids aren't things you are familiar with, so let's save your brain space for the other functional groups.

Let's do **aldehydes** and **ketones** next. If you stick the aldehyde group on a methane, you get a substance known as acetaldehyde.

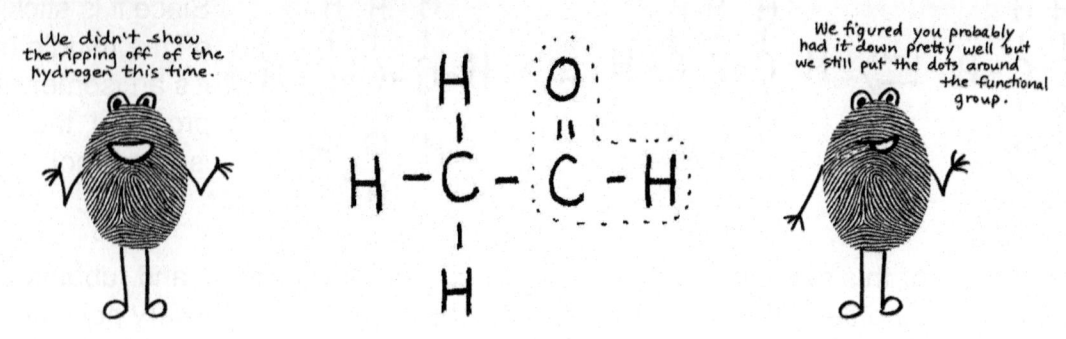

We didn't show the ripping off of the hydrogen this time.

We figured you probably had it down pretty well but we still put the dots around the functional group.

Never heard of it, right? Okay, let's do one you may be familiar with. Let's put the aldehyde group on just a hydrogen.

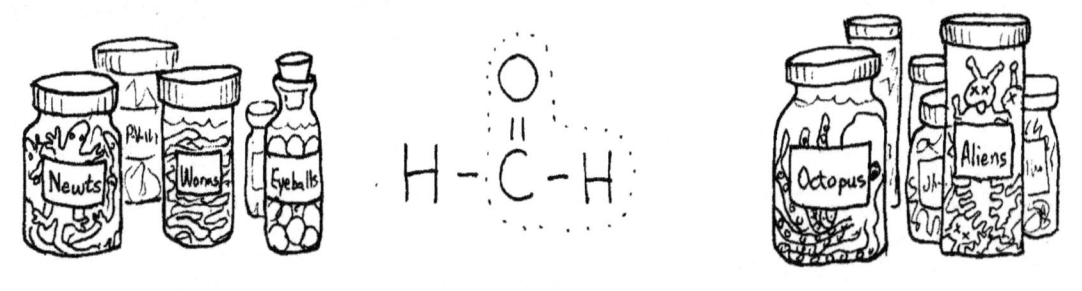

This is **formaldehyde**. It is a gas at room temperature, but can easily be dissolved into water to make **formalin**, a liquid used to preserve biological specimens in jars. Formaldehyde is used in industry to make plastics and to disinfect buildings.

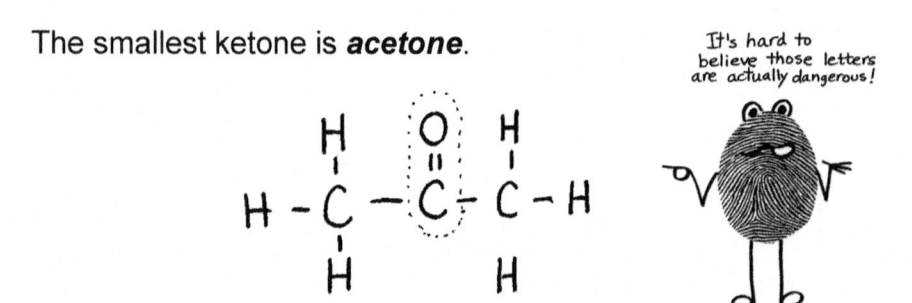

The smallest ketone is **acetone**.

It's hard to believe those letters are actually dangerous!

It is used by manufacturers of rubber, plastics, and varnishes. It is used as a varnish remover because it can dissolve dried-on varnish. One type of varnish it can remove is fingernail polish, so acetone is often the primary ingredient in fingernail polish removers. (Just as an interesting side note-- bug collectors have been known to kill bugs by putting them in a jar with a cotton ball that was soaked in acetone.)

The other ketones are also solvents used in industry. We won't bother you with their names or chemical formulas.

We've done enough stinky things; let's talk about some sweet smells. Let's look at some **esters**. The esters have pleasant, fruity smells, which is ironic because the way esters are manufactured is to combine two stinky things: a carboxylic acid and an alcohol! Two foul-smelling molecules can be combined to make some of the most delicious smells on earth!

Here is a chart showing some esters and what they smell like. The names of the esters come from the acid and the alcohol they were made from.

Name	Empirical formula	What they smell like
Methyl butyrate	$CH_3CH_2CH_2COOCH_3$	Apple
Ethyl butyrate	$CH_3CH_2CH_2COOCH_2CH_3$	Pineapple
Propyl acetate	$CH_3COOCH_2CH_2CH_3$	Pear
Pentyl acetate	$CH_3COOCH_2CH_2CH_2CH_2CH_3$	Banana
Pentyl butyrate	$CH_3CH_2CH_2COOCH_2CH_2CH_2CH2CH_3$	Apricot
Octyl acetate	$CH_3COOCH_2(CH_2)_6CH_3$	Orange
Methyl benzoate	$C_6H_5COOCH_3$	Kiwi
Ethyl formate	$HCOOCH_2CH_3$	Rum
Benzyl acetate	$CH_3COOCH_2C_6H_5$	Jasmine

Don't the names sound horrible? Speaking of horrible, our last functional group gets us back to bad smells. The last group is the **ethers**. Ethers are best known for the role they played in the history of medicine. Diethyl ether was once used to put people to sleep before surgery.

Diethyl ether caused side effects such as nausea and vomiting, and it has now been replaced by other substances, including other ethers. An ether that is important to the gasoline is known by its nickname, MTBE (its real name is long and complicated). It is put into gasoline to reduce the amount of carbon monoxide in automobile exhaust.

Some wart removers contain ether. If you want to know what ethers smell like, take a whiff of Compound W™.

There are other functional groups, also. We didn't look at the phenols or the amines and amides. We'll see the amines in a future chapter. You can study the others if you take an organic chemistry class in college.

Comprehension self-check

See how well you can remember what you read. Feel free to go back and look up the answers if you can't remember.

1) What do chemists call the "parts" that cause an organic molecule to function a certain way? _____ _____
2) Name three alcohols. (Use IUPAC names) _____, _____, _____
3) What are other names for these alcohols: _____, _____, _____
4) Which type of alcohol is found in beer and wine? _____
5) What is the functional group that makes a molecule an alcohol? _____
6) How to carboxylic acids smell? _____
7) In what room of your house would you be most likely to find acetic acid? _____
8) What animal produces formic acid? _____
9) What substance is used to preserved biological specimens? _____
10) What ketone is found in nail polish remover? _____
11) Which type of organic molecule smells good? _____
12) What does pentyl acetate smell like? _____ (We didn't really expect you to remember this one!)
13) Ethers were once used to _____.
14) An ether named MTBE is put into _____.
15) Name one functional group we'd didn't look at in this chapter: _____.

On-line research

1) What percentage of beer is actually alcohol? What about whiskey?

2) How much ethanol in your blood makes you legally drunk?

3) What is the punishment (in your state) for driving under the influence of alcohol?

4) What is denatured alcohol?

5) Name three things you can do with vinegar besides using it in cooking. (Believe it or not, there is actually a group called the "Vinegar Institute." Their website is www.versatilevinegar.org.)

Chapter Five: Combining Functional Groups

What would happen if you put more than one functional group on a molecule? What if you put a whole bunch of them all on one molecule? Would you get a jumbled mess, or would you get something useful? It could be either one, depending on what you did and how you did it. We can't possibly cover every single combination of functional groups, but we can look at some of them.

If you combine several carboxylic acids, you still have an acid, just a more complex one. Here are some examples of these more complicated acids.

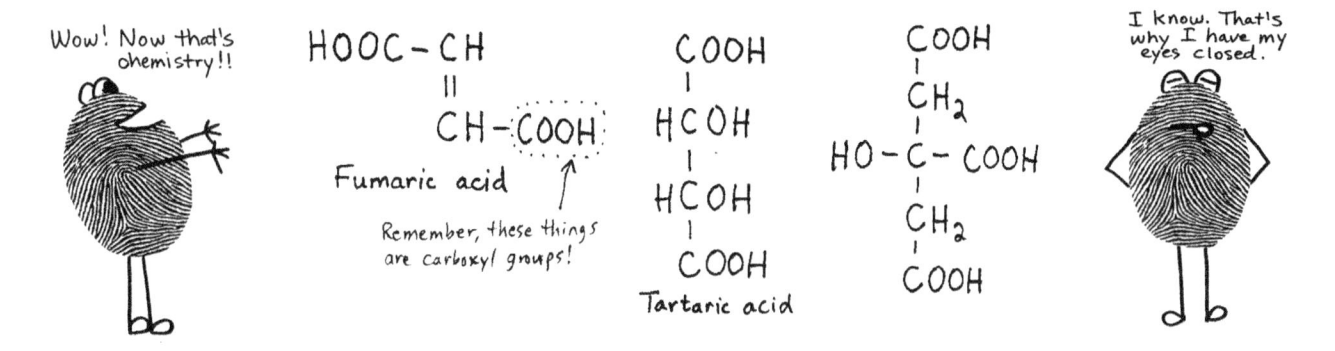

Wow! Now that's chemistry!!

HOOC-CH
  ‖
  CH-COOH

Fumaric acid

Remember, these things are carboxyl groups!

COOH
 |
HCOH
 |
HCOH
 |
COOH

Tartaric acid

COOH
 |
CH₂
 |
HO-C-COOH
 |
CH₂
 |
COOH

I know. That's why I have my eyes closed.

All three of these acids are used in cooking and food processing. Fumaric acid and tartaric acid (cream of tartar) are used along with baking soda to make breads rise. Citric acid is used in food processing to add "tartness" to the flavor or to make the chemistry of the foods more acidic. There are lots more of them, similar to these. Many are used in making plastics or paints. But you really don't want to see a bunch more molecular structure drawings, right? Good.

What happens if you combine a carboxylic acid with a benzene ring?

⬡—C(=O)—OH

You get benzoic acid, an ingredient in **sodium benzoate**, a common food preservative. You probably consume sodium benzoate just about every day. It stops molds from growing on food.

If you add another carboxyl group, you get phthalic acid, which is used in the production of paints and plastics.

NOTE:
It doesn't matter which way it is tipped ⬡ or ⬢. Whichever is better for your drawing!

⬡—COOH
  —COOH

We could go on adding acids to benzenes... but we're not. You can study them later on, if you go into organic chemistry as a career.

Here's another idea: what if you put an aldehyde on a benzene ring? What do you get?

This is benzaldehyde ("ben-zall-de-hide"). It can be made naturally by cooking down almond and apricot pits, or artificially by adding chemicals to toluene. It smells and tastes like almond and is used as artificial almond flavoring. Here's a question for the chemical philosophers (or the philosophical chemists): If the exact same substance can be produced from either a "natural" source, such as a nut, or an "artificial" source, such as chemicals in a lab, should the substance be classified as natural or artificial? That's a tricky question, isn't it? What if the manufactured substance is absolutely identical to the same substance as it is found in nature? Is H_2O (water) made in a lab the same as H_2O (water) found in nature?

Once again, we are going to leave further combinations of these two groups to your college professors. Moving right along...

What would happen if you mixed an alcohol with a carboxylic acid? Let's try it and see what happens. Let's mix glycerol with nitric acid:

glycerol (alcohol) + HNO_3 (an acid) → an ester

I'm sure glad we don't have to memorize these!

We get... an ester? Yes, an ester called **nitroglycerin**. You may be familiar with the name of this chemical. You may know that it is used to make dynamite. What you may not know is that nitroglycerin is also a medicine used to treat heart disease! Nitroglycerin causes the muscles that line the inside of blood vessels to relax. The arteries open up, more blood can get through, and blood pressure drops.

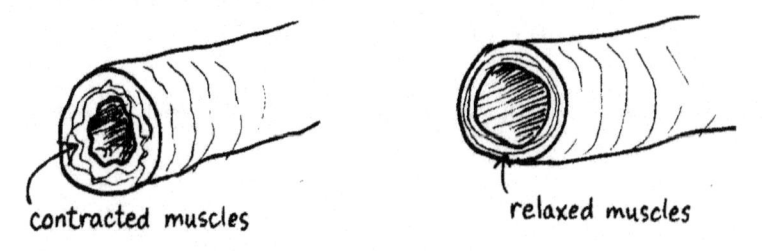

contracted muscles   relaxed muscles

An alcohol and a carboxylic acid can combine to form an ester. But can you go the other way? Can an ester be broken apart to make an alcohol and an acid? Yes, and in fact, people have been doing this for centuries, although they did not know the chemistry of what they were doing. They were simply making soap. Before the age of high-tech detergents, soap was made by heating animal fat with lye. Lye was made from wood ashes.

A fat called glycerol tristearate can be broken down into stearic acid and glycerol:

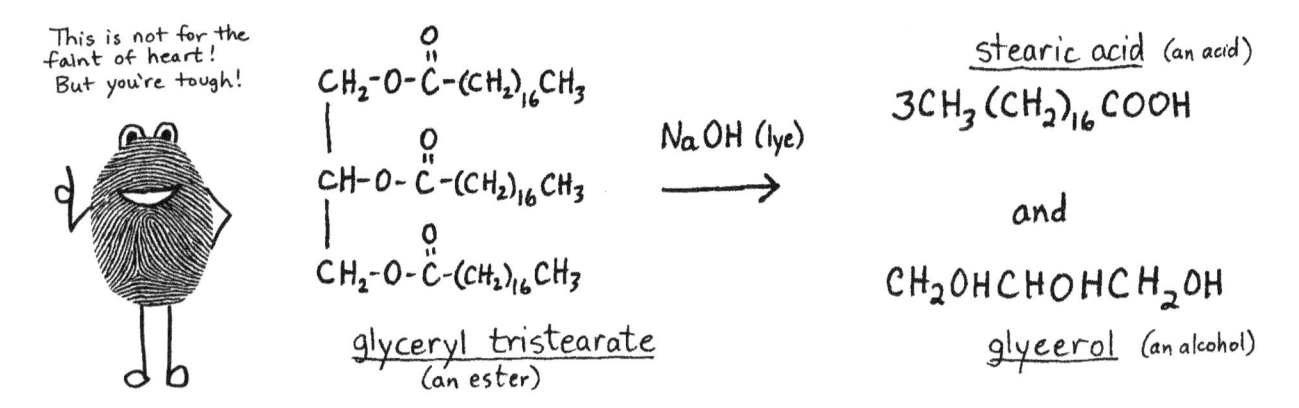

This is not for the faint of heart! But you're tough!

$$CH_2-O-\overset{O}{\overset{\|}{C}}-(CH_2)_{16}CH_3$$
$$CH-O-\overset{O}{\overset{\|}{C}}-(CH_2)_{16}CH_3 \xrightarrow{NaOH \text{ (lye)}}$$
$$CH_2-O-\overset{O}{\overset{\|}{C}}-(CH_2)_{16}CH_3$$

glyceryl tristearate (an ester)

stearic acid (an acid)
$$3CH_3(CH_2)_{16}COOH$$

and

$$CH_2OHCHOHCH_2OH$$
glycerol (an alcohol)

The stearic acid then reacts with the lye (sodium hydroxide) to form sodium stearate, a type of soap. The sodium stearate floats to the top of the cooking mixture and can be skimmed off.

$$3CH_3(CH_2)_{16}COOH + NaOH \rightarrow CH_3(CH_2)_{16}COONa$$
stearic acid   sodium hydroxide (lye)   sodium stearate (SOAP!)

So that's how you make old-fashioned soap. But how does soap work? The secret of the soap molecule is that it has two opposite ends: one end that loves oil, and one that loves water.

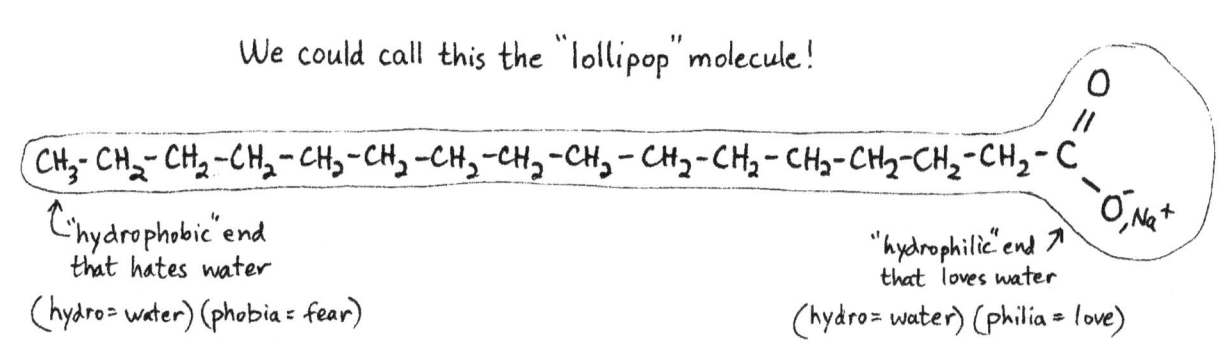

We could call this the "lollipop" molecule!

$$CH_3-CH_2-CH_2-CH_2-CH_2-CH_2-CH_2-CH_2-CH_2-CH_2-CH_2-CH_2-CH_2-CH_2-CH_2-\overset{O}{\overset{\|}{C}}-O^-,Na^+$$

"hydrophobic" end that hates water
(hydro = water) (phobia = fear)

"hydrophilic" end that loves water
(hydro = water) (philia = love)

All dirt particles are surrounded by a thin layer of oil. Since oil and water don't mix, this makes it impossible for the water to "pick up" the dirt particle and carry it away. Every time a water molecule comes close to a dirt molecule, they repel like magnets do when you try to put two north poles together. The water can't even get near the dirt.

water molecules

H_2O

close-up of water molecules

Then along comes a soap molecule. The soap's oil-loving end grabs onto the dirt molecule, and the soap's water-loving end grabs a water molecule. The water molecule follows other water molecules rushing by, and the whole chain goes down the drain.

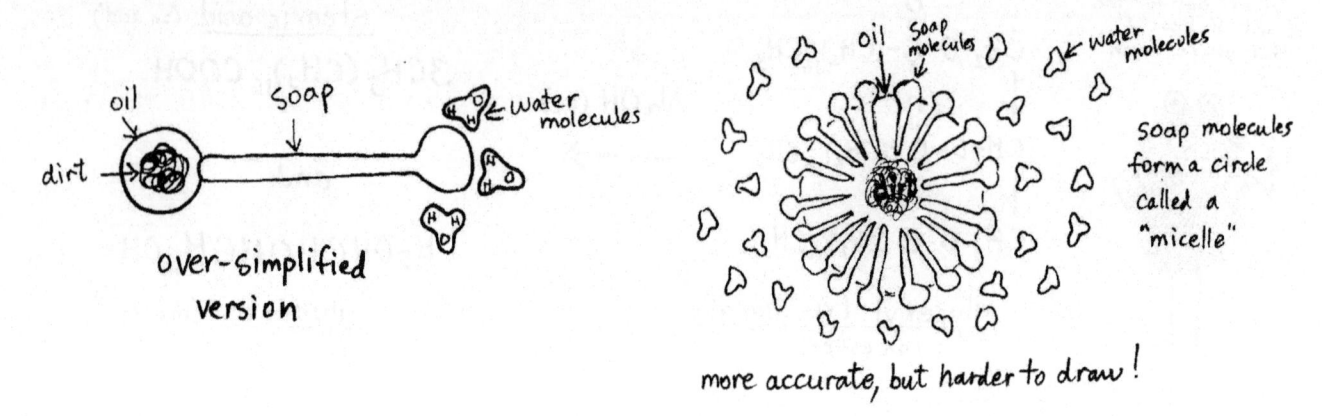

Functional groups can often be spotted hanging off the ends of lots of large molecules. We are going to take a brief look at two types of large organic molecules found in animals: prostaglandins and pheromones.

Prostaglandins were first discovered in men and were thought to have come from the prostate gland (which is only found in males). Then...oops-- they were found in females, too, and then in other parts of the body! So much for the name being appropriate. But the name stuck. Prostaglandins control many body processes, such as blood pressure, body temperature, production of stomach acid, muscle contraction, pregnancy, the menstrual cycle, inflammation, and pain. Here is a diagram of a typical prostaglandin.

You will notice that there a lot of letters missing. Where are all the carbons and hydrogens? What do the lines mean? Each line is a bond, and at each point where two lines meet, there is a carbon atom. It's invisible, but all chemists know it is there.

A double line means a double bond between the carbons. There are also a lot of invisible hydrogens, too. Each carbon must form four bonds, so if there are just two lines going out from a carbon, you know it must have two hydrogens attached to it.

Here are some other prostaglandin molecules, just so you can see what they look like:

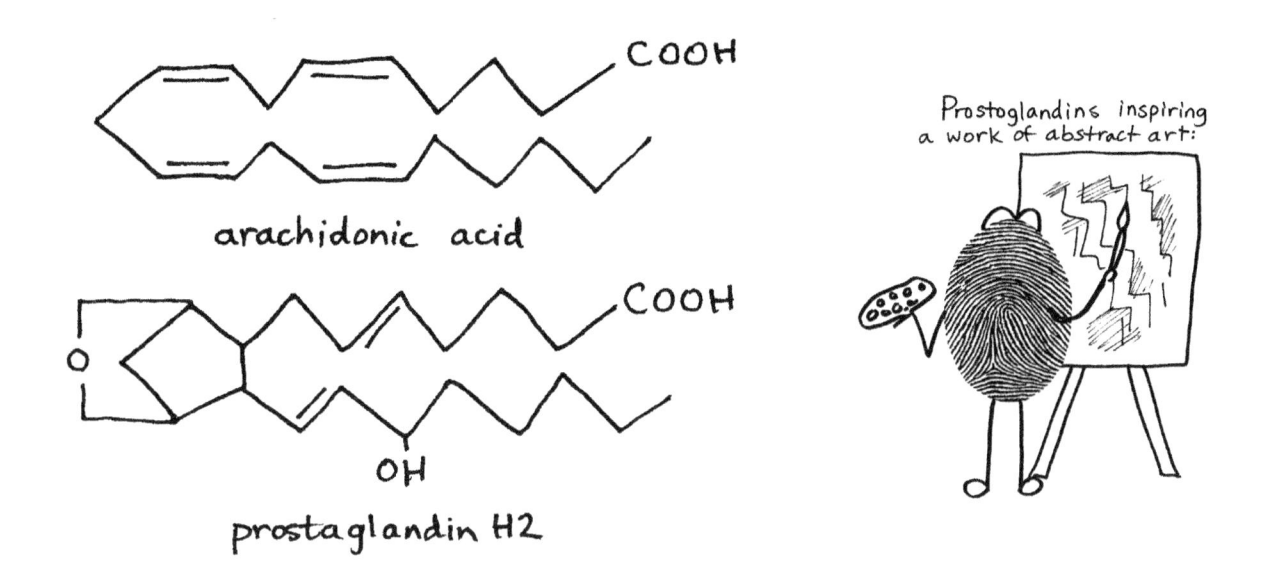

arachidonic acid

prostaglandin H2

Prostoglandins inspiring a work of abstract art:

The last type of molecule we are going to look at is a **pheromone**. Pheromones are the chemicals animals use to communicate. Animals "smell" pheromones and know what they mean. Here are some examples. Can you spot some functional groups? You might want to circle them with your pencil.

Queen bee pheromone

honey bee pheromone

house fly pheromone

musk deer pheromone

civet cat pheromone

Here are some examples of what pheromones can do:

- Ants secrete pheromones to warn of danger, to map a trail to a food source, to mark out boundaries, and to tell others what work needs to be done. Dead ants give off a pheromone that tells the other ants to carry it away. If you dab this pheromone on a live ant, its buddies will carry it off to the ant graveyard again and again, no matter how many times it returns! (It will be okay, though-- eventually the pheromone will wear off and the ant will be able to return to ant society.)
- Queen bees make pheromones to communicate to their drones.  
- Some spiders make pheromones that smell like moth mating pheromones. A male moth thinks it smells a female, goes to the place where the smell is coming from, and gets stuck in the web. 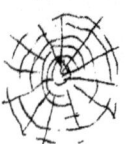
- Mammals have pheromones in their urine that lets them "mark" their territory with their scent. That's why you see them peeing on everything.
- Some plants make pheromones to attract a particular type of insect.
- Female rabbits release a pheromone that causes their babies to start nursing right away. The mother might have to flee at any moment, so the babies can't waste any time! 
- Most animals make a series of pheromones that are used in the reproductive process. They communicate things like being in heat, being pregnant, etc.
- Male deer can smell female deer from miles away. It only takes a few pheromone molecules in the air for them to detect the scent!

Scientists think humans make pheromones, too, but we cannot smell them like animals can. They may still affect our brains, though, causing changes in our behavior.

We've got a little less than half a page left. What can we do? How about if we show you a couple of ways we can alter the benzene ring? What if we removed one of the carbons and replaced it with a nitrogen?

PYRIDINE RING

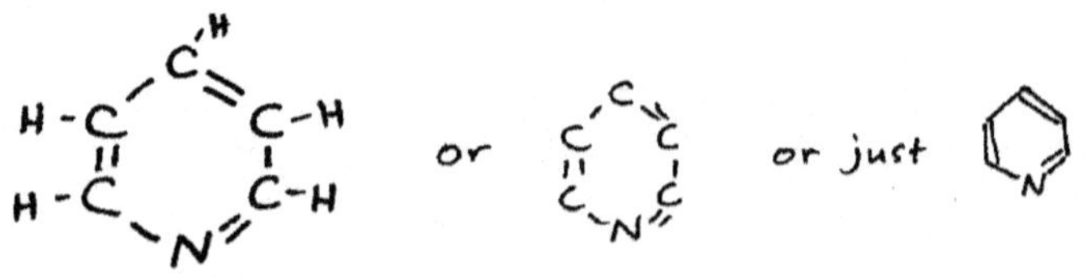

This is called a pyridine. It is found in some B vitamins and in nicotine. If you attach it to a benzene ring you get quinoline, which is made into quinine, an anti-malaria drug.

If you took away a carbon and made it a pentagon instead of a hexagon, you get something called a pyrrole ring.

PYRROLE RING

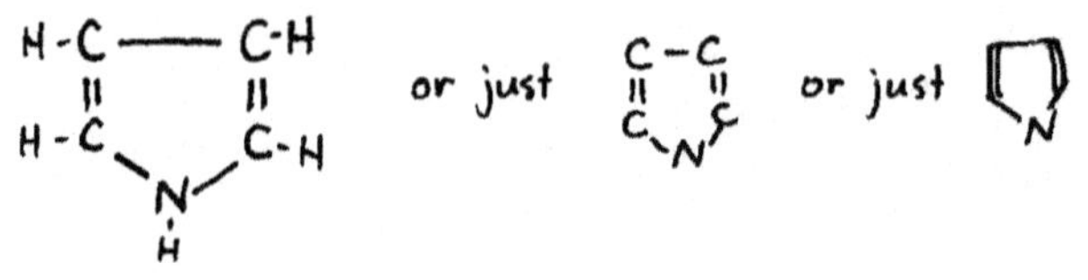

It is found lots of places: chlorophyll in plants, hemoglobin in blood, and B vitamins, just to name a few.

The story of Percy Julian

Percy Julian was born in Alabama around the year 1900. His grandparents had been slaves. Even though slavery was over, blacks in the south still were not permitted to do many things, including attending good schools. Percy had to go to a high school for blacks that had very little money, and, therefore, had no science equipment. This was devastating for an intelligent young man whose heart's desire was to become a chemist.

Percy was a hard worker, though, and managed to get into DePauw University in Indiana. Even though he had to work full-time to put himself through college, he still managed to graduate at the top of his class. Because he was black, however, no one offered him a graduate assistanceship. He had to take a job teaching and wait for an opportunity to come along.

When Harvard University offered a chemistry competition, Percy entered and won. He earned a Masters degree in chemistry from Harvard in only one year. But still, no university would hire him.

Then one of his friends found someone to sponsor him to study in Vienna, Austria. He enjoyed working there at the University of Vienna, because no one cared about the color of his skin. While in Vienna, he heard about a chemical mystery no one could solve. There was an African bean, called the Calabar bean, that produced a substance needed to cure glaucoma (an eye disease). Scientists needed a way to produce this substance artificially, without having to rely on a supply of beans.

The Calabar bean had been used in Africa in witchcraft trials. They made suspected witches swallow it, thinking that if they died they were guilty and if they lived they were innocent. What was really going on was that the toxins inside the bean would shut down the person's nervous system, causing death. If the person was lucky enough to vomit up the bean, he would survive.

Percy returned to the United States to begin working on finding a way to make this substance, called physostigmine (pronounced like "fizz-o-stig-mean"). He knew that the empirical formula for physostigmine was: $C_{15}H_{21}N_3O_2$. He figured out that part of the structural formula must have two attached rings: a benzene ring and a pyrrole ring:

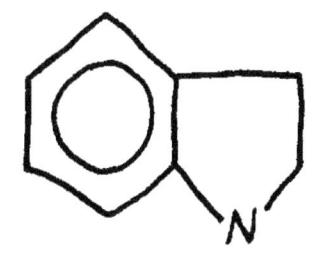

"indole"

This structure has a name of its own. It is called indole. In a diluted form it smells like orange blossoms. In a concentrated form it smells like raw sewage!

Percy could get indole from sources other than the Calabar beans, including soy beans, orange blossoms, and coal tar. So he could use indole as the base for building an artificial physostigmine molecule. Now he needed to find a way to attach the other necessary atoms to indole.

It took years of research, lots of money from a few generous donors, and help from a number of assistants, before Percy finally arrived at the solution. He knew that another team of researchers in England was working on the same thing, and had announced that they were very close to a solution. When Percy read their research report, though, he knew they were on the wrong track. Still, Percy needed to hurry, so he could be first and could claim credit for the discovery.

At last he made a sample of what he believed was pure artificial physostigmine. To determine if he was right, he needed to compare it to natural physostigmine. If the artificial substance melted at exactly 139° F, just like the natural substance did, that would prove they were identical.

They watched the test tubes nervously, waiting to see if the two substances would melt at exactly the same instant, as soon as the temperature reached 139°. Yes!! They did! Percy had made artificial physostigmine!

For this accomplishment, Percy won several prizes and honorary degrees. You'd think that now, every university in the country would want him, right? No, they all turned him down, even his alma mater, DePauw University!

Percy took a job with Glidden Company in their soy bean research department. He discovered how to make artificial hormones and the drug cortisone from soy beans. He also invented fire-fighting foam. He eventually started his own company, and ended up being a millionaire.

This story ends happily ever after, but don't forget that the reason it did was because of Percy's excellent character traits. When life was unfair to him, he did not whine and complain; he worked hard and proved himself.

Every single one of us has times in our life when we feel disadvantaged in some way. Remember Percy's example, and "percy-vere"!

Comprehension self-check

See if you can answer these questions. If you can't, go back and look up the answer.

1) Can a molecule have more than one functional group on it? _____
2) What do acids taste like? Are they sweet, sour, bitter or salty? _____
3) What does benzaldehyde taste like: peanut, almond, vanilla, or orange? _____
4) Do you think water made in a lab from hydrogen gas and oxygen gas is really water? __
   Why or why not? _____
5) Name two things nitroglycerin is good for: _____, _____
6) A carboxylic acid and an alcohol combine to form an _____.
7) Which of these is a "lollipop" molecule? soap, plastic, oil, water, acid _____
8) What does hydrophilic mean? _____
9) What does hydrophobic mean? _____
10) Does a soap molecule stick to oil or water or both? _____
11) Name some body processes that prostaglandins control: _____
_____
12) Give three examples of how animals use pheromones:
   a) _____
   b) _____
   c) _____
13) The substance physostigmine occurs naturally in : _____
14) Indole is made of these two rings: _____ and _____.
15) The way Percy knew that his substance was identical to natural physostigmine was by comparing their _____ _____.

On-line research

1) One major manufacturer of soap was the first to create soap that floated in the tub instead of sinking to the bottom. (Back in the days when everyone bathed instead of showered, this was a big deal!) Who was this and how did it happen?

2) What does a chocolate molecule look like? (Draw it in the space below.)

Word puzzle! (includes review from past chapters)

An aldehyde that tastes like almond: __ __ __ __ __ __ __ __ __ __ __
                                      42   26   1 15   58

An explosive that can help the heart: __ __ __ __ __ __ __ __ __ __ __ __
                                      41 50 53 5   30   36   57

Physostigmine cures this eye disease: __ __ __ __ __ __ __
                                      7   45   38 39

This regulates body temperature: __ __ __ __ __ __ __ __ __ __
                                 34   10 61 14 4   28   6

C_6H_{12} is this kind of formula: __ __ __ __ __ __ __ __
                                     19 51   37

Moths can smell these for miles: __ __ __ __ __ __ __ __ __
                                 16 22   20 25   59 49

Benzene with one carbon replaced with a nitrogen: __ __ __ __ __ __ __
                                                  46 18 44   33

The food preservative sodium benzoate is made from this acid: __ __ __ __ __ __ __
                                                              29 27 60   24

Hydrophilic means loving: __ __ __ __
                          3 9   13

The functional group OH makes something into an __ __ __ __ __ __
                                                   2 12 40

Benzyl acetate smells like: __ __ __ __ __ __
                            47 17 55   52

Toluene is made by this tree: __ __ __ __
                              11   48

Methyl benzoate smells like this fruit: __ __ __
                                        8

Cream of tartar (a baking ingredient) comes from this acid: __ __ __ __ __ __ __
                                                            21   31

How many bonds can carbon make? __ __ __
                                23 54

Compound W wart remover smells like this: __ __ __ __
                                          43 32

A benzene ring is made of carbon and __ __ __ __ __ __
                                     35   56

****

__ __ __ __ __ __ __ __ __ __ __ __ __ __ __ __ __ __
1 2 3   4 5 6 7   8 9 10 11 12 13 14 15 16 17 18

__ __ __ __ __ __ __ __ __ __ __ __ __ __ __
19 20 21 22 23 24 25 26 27 28 29 30 31 32 33

__ __ __ __ __ __ __ __ __ __ __ __ __?
34 35 36 37 38 39 40 41 42 43 44 45 46

__ __ __ __ __ __ __ __ __ __ __ __-__ __ __ __!
47 48 49 50 51 32 52 53 54 55 56 57 58 55 59 60 61

36

Chapter Six: Plastics

In this chapter, we will begin to combine all the stuff about "anes" and "enes" with all the stuff about functional groups. We will be able to make some really cool items!

Do you remember good old ethylene? Well, if you play construction set with a whole bunch of ethylenes, and hook about a thousand of them together to make a long chain, you get a molecule called **polyethylene**. ("Poly" means "many.")

Etheylene

Remember ethylene?

THREE WAYS OF SHOWING POLYETHYLENE:

$$\sim CH_2CH_2-CH_2CH_2-CH_2CH_2-CH_2CH_2-CH_2CH_2-CH_2CH_2 \sim$$

This is the organic chemistry symbol for "etcetera."

Don't forget – the molecule isn't flat. It has a zig-zag shape!

How do you get these ethylenes to hook together? Chemists certainly don't stick them together by hand. They use high temperatures, high pressure, and chemicals called **catalysts**. A catalyst is a chemical that helps a reaction to occur, or at least speeds it up. The catalyst is not destroyed in the process. It can be used over and over again.

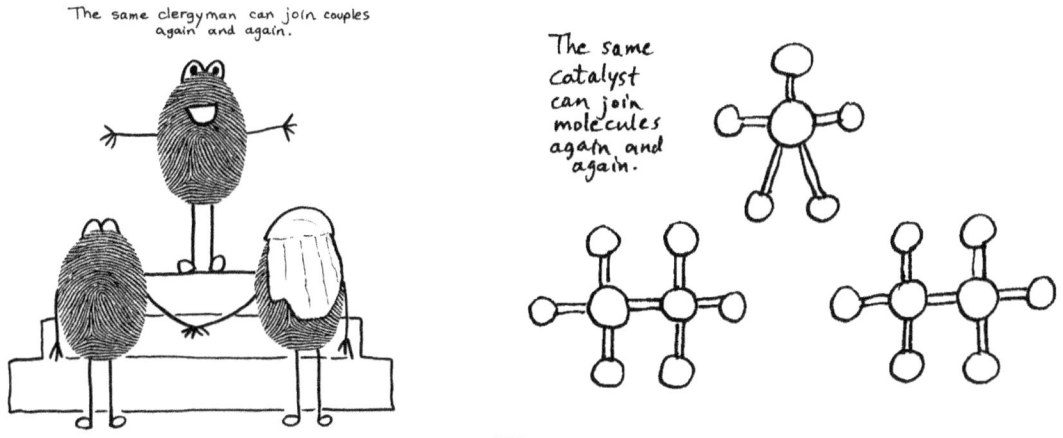

The same clergyman can join couples again and again.

The same catalyst can join molecules again and again.

What can you do with polyethylene? Almost anything! You can make bags, bottles, jugs, cups, utensils, toys, sports equipment, tubes, insulators, photographic film (the stuff no one uses anymore because we've gone digital), beauty products, fabrics, and a lot more. Polyethylene is the most common type of plastic we use everyday.

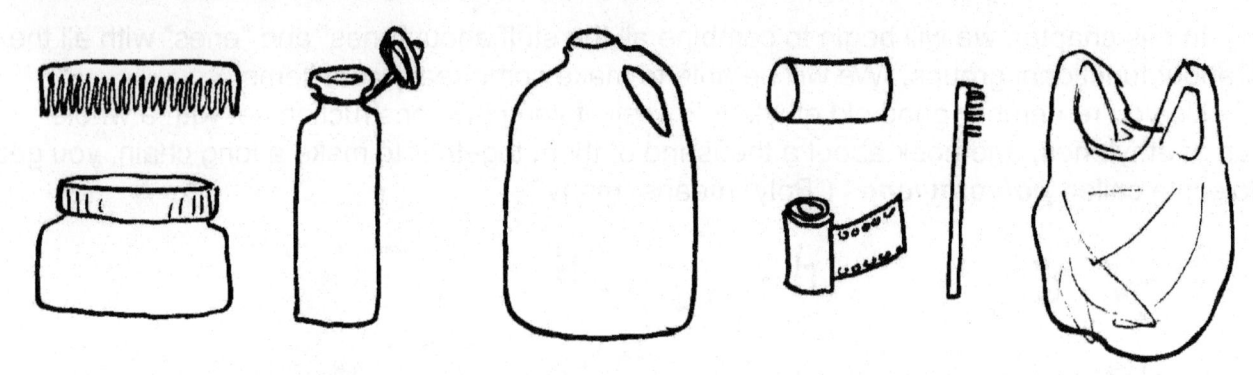

Polyethylene was invented before the start of World War II and was immediately put to use by the Allied army for insulating cables. Polyethylene was flexible and tough and could withstand both high and low temperatures, making it perfect for protecting the wires that ran into important things like radar machines.

There are basically two types of polyethylene: high density and low density. **High density polyethylene (HDPE)** is made up of long, linear chains that don't have many side branches. They can pack into an orderly crystalline structure, making high density polyethylene tough and strong and great for making things like bottle caps, toys, and milk jugs.

It didn't take a lot of talent to do that illustration!

Low density polyethylene (LDPE), on the other hand, has lots of side chains branching of the main chain. These branches prevent the molecules from packing close together.

Low density polyethylenes are more bendable and melt at lower temperatures. If you put a high density polyethylene object in boiling water, it will hold its shape. If you put a low density polyethylene object into boiling water, it will melt and become severely deformed. However, you really want bendable plastic for some things. Low density polyethylene is great for things like bags and squeeze bottles.

Polyethylene plastic is a ***thermoplastic*** polymer, meaning that it can be melted and reshaped again and again. Not all plastics are like this. (***Thermosetting*** plastics have the opposite characteristic: they are "set" into a shape the first time, and that's it.)

Thermoplastic = "re-use" it

Thermoset-it? = Forget it!

Because polyethylene can be re-shaped, it is easily recycled. For instance, old soda bottles and milk jugs can be turned into fabric (polyesters), park benches, play equipment, sports and camping gear, insulation for buildings, "bedding" for new highways, and so much more!

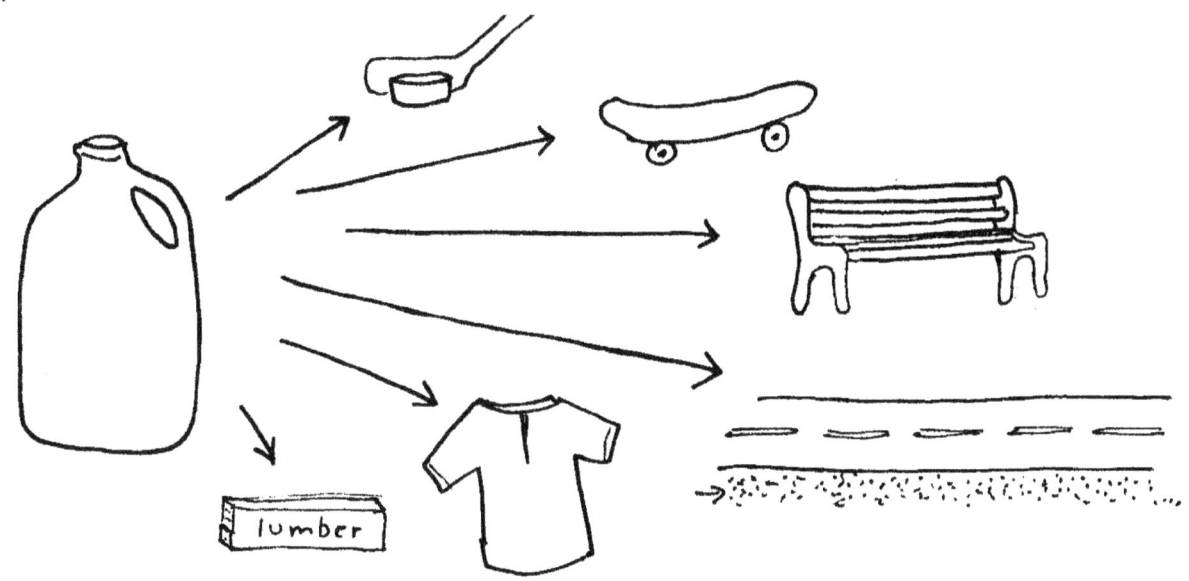

Polyethylene is just one of a whole category of molecules called ***polymers***. We already learned that "poly" means "many." "Mer" just means a molecule. (Maybe poly-olecule sounded too cutesy? Poly-moly is even worse!) Polymers are long chains of any kind of molecule. There are natural polymers as well as man-made polymers. Starches and proteins are natural polymers. We'll look at them in a later chapter.

Another man-made polymer is ***polypropylene***. The basic unit of polypropylene is propylene (or propene if you use the official IUPAC word). "Prop" means three carbons, and "ene" means there is a double bond in there somewhere. Let's draw propylene:

$$H_2C = CH - CH_3$$ (with all H's shown explicitly)

Now to make it into a polymer. We will open up the double bond and rearrange the hydrogens a bit. A propylene will attach to every other carbon atom, with hydrogens in between.

Propylene gets Rearranged

This is the "mer" (one unit of propylene)

Then join them to make polypropylene

$$\sim CH-CH_2-CH-CH_2-CH-CH_2-CH-CH_2-CH-CH_2\sim$$
$$\quad\; |\qquad\qquad\; |\qquad\qquad\; |\qquad\qquad\; |\qquad\qquad\; |$$
$$\;\, CH_3\quad\;\; CH_3\quad\;\; CH_3\quad\;\; CH_3\quad\;\; CH_3$$

Speaking of hard-shell luggage, I need a vacation from this stuff!

Polypropylene is a tough plastic suitable for molding into hard shell luggage, battery cases, and appliances. In small pieces it is good for indoor-outdoor carpets.

Hey-- let's do a crazy experiment! Let's attach one of those nifty benzene rings onto a polyethylene chain. What will happen?

I think they look like icicles.

They remind me of wasp nests – or maybe bird houses.

Yikes! We've made **polystyrene**! We've helped to pollute the world! Add some air bubbles and we've got Styrofoam to throw into landfills: disposable hot beverage cups, fast food plates, padding inside appliance and toy boxes, packing "peanuts," etc. Of course, Styrofoam is wonderful when you want things insulated and padded. That's why they make it. It does a great job.

Airhead!

Look who's talking, foam face!

picnic plates

custom protection for appliances

What will happen if we add some chlorine molecules to polyethylene?

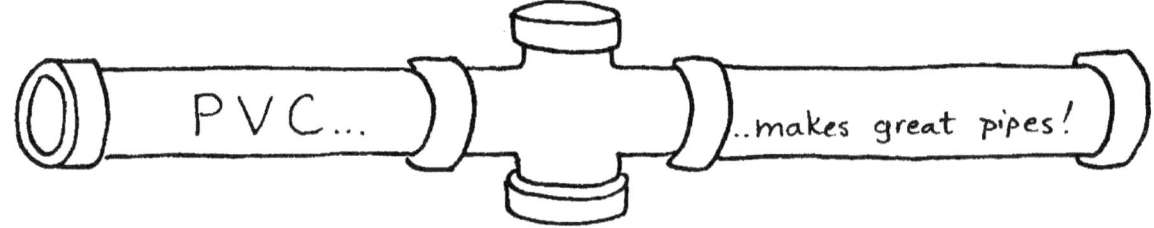

$$\sim CH_2CH-CH_2CH-CH_2CH-CH_2CH-CH_2CH-CH_2CH \sim$$
$$\qquad\;\;|\qquad\quad\;|\qquad\quad\;|\qquad\quad\;|\qquad\quad\;|\qquad\quad\;|$$
$$\qquad\;\;Cl\qquad\;\;Cl\qquad\;\;Cl\qquad\;\;Cl\qquad\;\;Cl\qquad\;\;Cl$$

PVC... ...makes great pipes!

Chemists call this **polyvinyl chloride**. It's perfect for many things. You can make it into artificial leather. You can make it into pipes that will never rust. You can make it into unbreakable clear bottles, floor tiles, shower curtains, plastic wrap, toys, hardware parts-- it's amazingly useful!

This is fun! Let's mess up polyethylene some more. Let's add fluorine instead of chlorine. We'll adapt the ethylene molecule first, by putting flourines on instead of hydrogens. That'll shake things up! What will happen?

[Structure of polytetrafluoroethylene: a chain of carbons each bonded to two F atoms]

We've made... Teflon! Teflon is used for many things, but the one which you are probably familiar with is the coating on non-stick frying pans.

Here's a clever idea: can we replace three hydrogens with one nitrogen? Nitrogen can make three bonds. Three hydrogens should be equal to one nitrogen. Let's pop off three H's and stick on an N and see what happens.

[Structure of polyacrylonitrile: carbon chain with alternating H and CH-CN substituents]

Wow! We've created something you artsy-craftsy people will like. This substance is called polyacrylonitrile (don't even bother trying to remember it, let alone pronounce it!). But it makes great yarn, and is a key ingredient in many paints.

Save the elephants!

Once upon a time, people used ivory to make things like piano keys and billiard balls. Since ivory comes from elephant tusks, and elephants do not go around giving away their tusks, the use of ivory necessarily involves killing elephants. This is not good, needless to say.

You're not taking MY tusks, pal!

So a contest was held to see who would be the first to come up with an ivory substitute. An American inventor named Wesley Hyatt found a way to soften cellulose nitrate by treating it with ethyl alcohol and camphor. (Cellulose is the "stuff" that plants are made of. When it is treated with nitric acid, it forms cellulose nitrate.) This new material, celluloid, could be shaped into smooth, hard billiard balls. This was also wonderful for the billiard table industry, because since these new balls were much less expensive than ivory ones, an average-income family could now afford a billiard table.

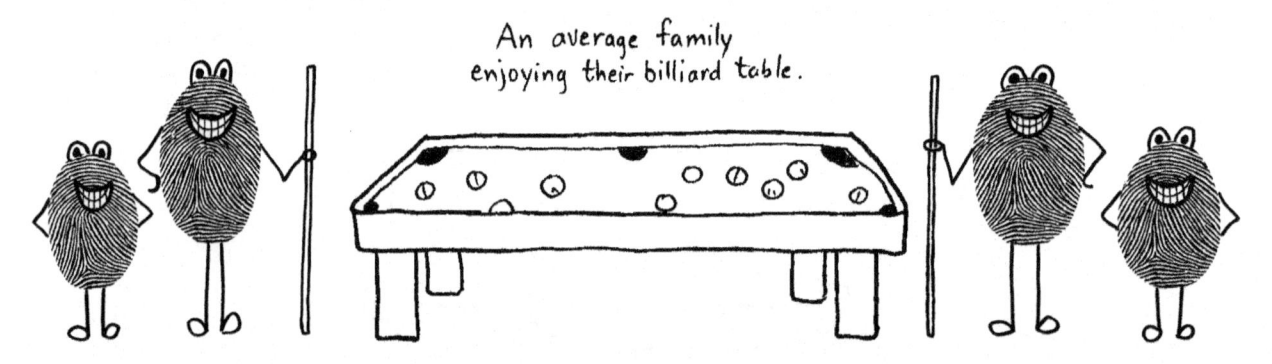

An average family enjoying their billiard table.

Celluloid was also used in the brand new film industry, just getting started in the early twentieth century. The movie industry became known as the "celluloid industry."

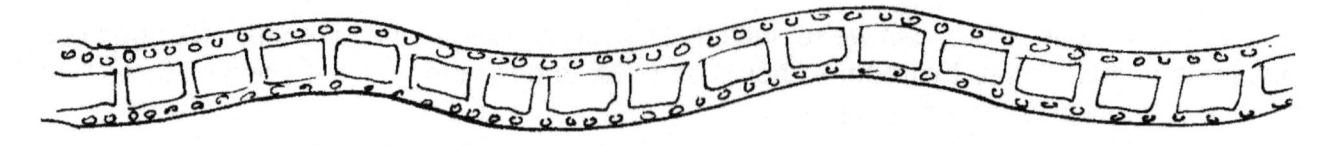

Celluloid had the unfortunate characteristic of being highly flammable, however. Cellulose nitrate is also used to make smokeless gunpowder. Fires in theatres, started by the ignition of the film, caused hundreds of deaths. As soon as a safer substance became available, celluloid was abandoned. Today, cellulose acetate is used instead of cellulose nitrate.

Ooops...

Save the lac bugs!

Once upon a time, people used a tiny bug called a lac to make shellac, a substance that was painted onto surfaces such as wood to give them a shiny finish. As you can imagine, it took an awful lot of lac bugs to make enough shellac to varnish even a small picture frame!

Then along came Leo Baekeland. He came to the United States from his homeland of Belgium. After achieving great success in the photographic film industry, he used his riches to set up his own research laboratory. Leo put his lab to work trying to find a substitute for shellac.

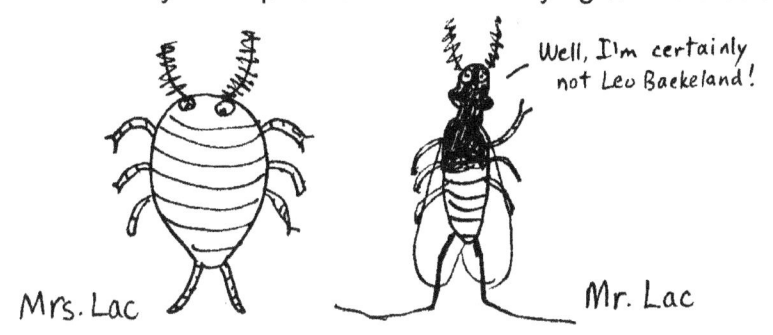

One of the experiments he tried was mixing carbolic acid with formaldehyde. Other chemists had warned him about this experiment, but he did it anyway. When the mixture cooled, it turned into a hard solid that simply would not come out of the test tube. No matter what anyone tried, the substance could not be dissolved. Lots and lots of glassware had to be pitched at Leo's lab!

One day, Leo got to thinking that a substance that could not be dissolved by anything might actually be useful. He came up with a way to shape it into practical things like bowls. A bowl that would hold harsh chemicals and not dissolve would be helpful in chemistry labs. He knew he was on to something, so he decided to give his new substance a name: Bakelite. This was the world's first plastic.

Bakelite was soon used for many purposes. One of the more well-known uses was for telephones. (You know—those black phones that sat on office desks for decades.) Bakelite is still used today for things like light switches and pot handles.

Comprehension self-check

You know what to do by now, right?

1) What does "poly" mean? _____
2) A chemical that helps a reaction occur without itself being consumed is a _____.
3) The most common type of plastic we use today is _____.
4) The two kinds of polyethylene are _____ _____ and _____ _____.
                                    (Don't use abbreviations.)
5) What do HPDE molecules look like? _____
6) What do LDPE molecules look like? _____
7) Which one will melt more easily, HDPE or LDPE? _____
8) What kind of things do they use LDPE for? _____
9) Is polyethylene a thermoplastic or a thermosetting plastic? _____
10) Which kind can be reused again and again? _____
11) Which one of these is the IUPAC name? propylene / propene
12) What kind of plastic is used to make Styrofoam? _____
13) What does PVC stand for? _____
14) Why is celluloid no longer used? _____
15) Did Baekeland ever find a way to manufacture artificial shellac? _____

On-line research

1) Is shellac toxic? What else is it used for besides varnishing wood?

2) What product did Leo Baekeland invent that earned him a million dollars?

3) Where is the Bakelite Museum?

4) What is nylon and how is it made?

Review

Section 1: "Who Am I"?

A	B	C	D	E	F	G	H
Crude Oil	methane	chloroform	carbon tetrachloride	isomer	CFC's	acetic acid	methanol

___ 1) Burning me puts nothing but carbon dioxide and water into the air, so they say I burn "cleanly."

___ 2) Scientists suspect that I might be damaging the Earth's ozone layer.

___ 3) I am a heavy liquid that is used in fire extinguishers and in dry cleaning of clothes.

___ 4) My name means "same parts." I have many twins who are identical to me and yet have different shapes.

___ 5) My nickname is "black gold."

___ 6) I can put people to sleep.

___ 7) I would be methane, except that one of the hydrogens has been replaced with an OH functional group.

___ 8) I am the active ingredient in vinegar.

Section 2: Matching

___ 9) propane

___ 10) butene

___ 11) butyne

___ 12) ethanol

___ 13) naphthalene

___ 14) soap molecule

___ 15) acetic acid

___ 16) prostaglandin

Section 3: You respond

17) What does hydrophobic mean? _____

Name two ways animals use pheromones:

18) _____

19) _____

20) A carboxylic acid and an alcohol combine to form an _____.

21) Can you put more than one functional group on a molecule? _____

22) What does methane smell like? _____

23) Aromatic hydrocarbons are molecules that contain at least one _____ _____.

24) Formic acid is made by this member of the animal kingdom: _____

25) Formalin is used to _____.

Section 4: True or False

___ 26) Esters are toxic.

___ 27) Animals can smell pheromones.

___ 28) Nitroglycerin is explosive.

___ 29) Nitroglycerin is used in heart medication.

___ 30) Lye is used to make soap.

___ 31) Ethers smell good.

___ 32) Ethers are used as artificial food flavorings.

___ 33) Ethanol is the type of alcohol found in beer.

___ 34) Acetone is toxic.

___ 35) Naphthalene is toxic to moths.

___ 36) Ethylene gas is toxic.

___ 37) Alkanes contain only single bonds

___ 38) Soap contains fat.

Section 5: Draw

Draw a benzene ring without using any letters. (2 pts.)

Chapter Seven: Rubber and Silicones

Polymers occur everywhere in nature. Remember, the word "polymer" doesn't mean manmade, it only means a very long chain. The natural world is full of polymers. The first one we are going to look at is rubber.

Natural rubber was discovered in Central and South America hundreds of years ago by the native peoples who lived there. Certain trees oozed a milky substance that we now called *latex*. They used latex for making flexible containers, shoes, and balls, and for waterproofing. When the Europeans came to the Americas, they were fascinated with it and sent samples back home to Europe. One of these samples came into the hands of a scientist named Joseph Priestly, who is famous for discovering oxygen. He found that the strange ball could rub off pencil marks, so he began calling it a *rubber*. More and more people acquired "rubbers" to erase their mistakes, and the name stuck even though many other uses were found for this substance

Natives make slashes in the trunks and let the latex sap run out into buckets, similar to collecting maple sap.

The world's first rubber processing factory was set up in Paris in 1803. The factory didn't actually make rubber from scratch, of course; it just processed the latex imported from Central and South America. The "raw" latex rubber had to be mixed and chopped to make the polymer chains a bit shorter. In 1823 Charles Macintosh began using latex rubber to make waterproof fabrics. Some people still use the word "macintosh" when referring to a raincoat.

In 1823, Charles Goodyear accidentally discovered a way to improve rubber. Up until now, rubber had the unfortunate characteristic of adapting to the climate: it got gooey in the heat and brittle in the cold. Goodyear dropped hot sulfur onto the rubber and found that this cured the gooey/brittle problem. The addition of sulfur made the rubber resistant to the effects of both heat and cold. He called his accidental invention "vulcanization." (Vulcan was the Roman god associated with volcanoes, which emit a lot of hot sulfur.) Vulcanized rubber opened up whole new industries, such as the manufacturing of tires.

Poor Goodyear died in poverty. He never got to see tires with his name on them!

I like this page- not a chemical formula in sight anywhere!

The demand for latex rubber benefited countries like Brazil. In fact, Brazil decided that it would not allow the latex trees to be taken out of the country to be grown elsewhere. Despite this law, seeds from these trees were smuggled to England, and from there were taken to Sri Lanka and Indonesia, where plantations of latex trees were started. In time, these plantations produced so much latex that they became the world leaders in latex production, just as Brazil had feared.

To understand Charles Goodyear's accidental invention (vulcanization), we need to take a close-up look at the rubber molecule. Since it is a polymer, it must have individual "mer" units. It does. The "mer" is called *isoprene*.

ISOPRENE

It's not really that much more complicated than ethylene. Well, okay, just a little. But not too much. To make rubber, we need to attach a bunch of these isoprenes together:

Now we need to back up the focus a bit, so that we can't see the letters any more. We'll just draw rubber polymers like this:

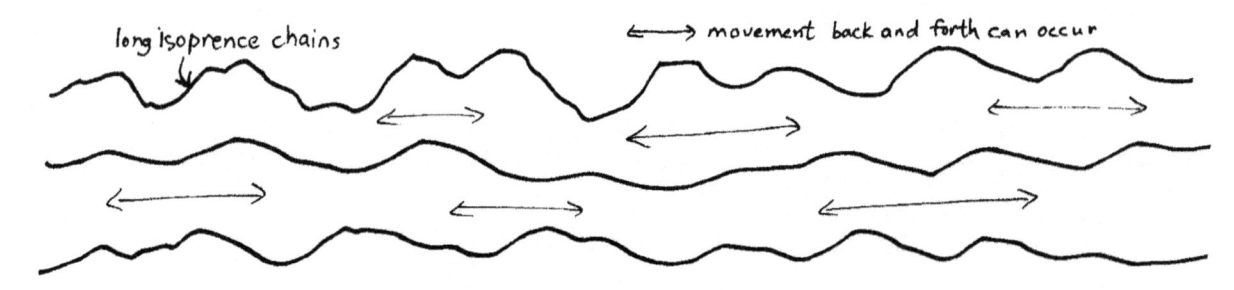

The chains are not attached to each other and can slip back and forth. The slipping around of the chains is what causes natural rubber to be too soft. What happens in vulcanization is that the sulfur atoms connect the chains together at various points. Scientists call this *cross-linking*. The cross links stop the polymers from slipping. They also cause the rubber to snap back to its original shape after being stretched. (Materials that stretch and snap back are called *elastomers*.)

During World War II, Japan blocked the Allied countries from receiving shipments of latex rubber from Indonesia. (No tires, no military vehicles!) America responded by trying to find a way to make synthetic (manmade) rubber. This search led to the discovery of other polymers such as Neoprene. After much experimenting, scientists finally found a way to make polyisoprene (artificial rubber) from petroleum. Today, 60% of all rubber comes from petroleum refineries, not latex trees.

We all know that rubber bands stretch; they are elastomers. Many fabrics stretch. Balloons stretch. But there are other things in our everyday life that contain elastomers, and we don't even know it. One surprising place you meet elastomers is in paint. Water-based latex paints contain rubber elastomers that make the paint flexible after it is dry. Chemists are always trying to improve the durability of the elastomers in paint so that we don't have to re-paint things so frequently.

Another type of natural latex rubber is "chicle" (pronounced: "huckle"). The chemical formula for chicle is very similar to rubber. Chicle comes from the sap of the sapodilla tree in Central and South America. The natives there liked to use chicle as chewing gum. In the 1800's, Americans began to investigate this natural rubber to see if it might be good for something. Nope. It was terrible as rain gear and even worse for tires. One day an inventor popped a piece in this mouth, and... thus began America's obsession with chewing gum. Food scientists discovered ways to add flavorings and colorings to make chewing gum even more enjoyable. Chewing gum was sold in vending machines (in the New York subway) as early as 1888.

Chiclets™ gum is named after chicle.

Bubble gum was not invented until 1906, by a man named Frank Fleer. His invention came on the market in 1926 with the name "Dubble Bubble." Bubble gum is not just chicle. It is a synthetic polymer similar to chicle, but with much better elasticity. Plain old chewing gum just doesn't let you blow huge bubbles like bubble gum does.

Humans have always been chewing "gum." The ancient Greeks chewed mastiche (mas-teek-uh), from the mastic tree. Ancient Mayans chewed chicle. Native Americans in North America chewed spruce sap, and passed the habit on to the settlers. The settlers improved the sap by adding beeswax. But nothing compares to modern chewing gum!

Even though we are studying carbon chemistry, we are going to look briefly at a polymer that is not based on carbon. It just seems to fit in so nicely that it is a shame not to mention it. This polymer is based on a chain of silicon and oxygen atoms, instead of carbon.

$$-O-Si-O-Si-O-Si-O-Si-O-Si-$$

(Can stick anything here)

The reason silicon can replace carbon as the core of a polymer is because it can make four bonds, just like carbon can.

Silicones can be oily, rubbery, or solid, depending upon how long the polymer chains are. Some silicon polymers are excellent for waterproofing. Raincoats and umbrellas are often coated with silicon polymers. Silicon oils are used as lubricants (you may have WD40 around your house) and as fluid in hydraulic pumps. Polishes for cars and shoes often have a silicon base. The most famous silicon polymer is probably "Silly Putty."

Remember that we told you that during World War II scientists began searching for a way to make synthetic rubber? One of these scientists was James Wright, who worked for General Electric in Connecticut. One of the experiments he tried was mixing boric acid with silicone oil. It didn't make rubber. But it did make a most intriguing substance. What could it be used for? He couldn't think of a use for it, so he sent samples to other scientists and asked them to see if they could find something it was good for. After several years, not a single scientist had come up with a use for the stuff! Then a creative toy manufacturer got a sample of it and decided it was just fine the way it was. Pop it in a plastic egg and sell it for a couple bucks. And thus, Silly Putty™ was born. It still doesn't have a practical use, but it's fun to play with!

Why does Silly Putty™ come in eggs? No reason - but it's a 50-year tradition!

Silly Putty™ is actually a very thick liquid. Scientists would say it is a **viscous** substance. There's your vocabulary word for the day. A substance with low viscosity is very runny, like milk or water. A substance with high viscosity is thick, like syrup. Silly Putty™ is even thicker than syrup. It is so viscous that it will take hours, even days, to drip off a table!

Wow! It does drip!

Don't forget that silicon polymers really don't belong in this book! Their chain is based on silicon, not carbon.

Comprehension self-check

1) Where were latex rubber trees first discovered? _____
2) What did the natives do with the rubber? _____
3) Where did the name "rubber" come from? _____
4) Who was the first person to use rubber raincoats? _____
5) Who discovered how to "vulcanize" rubber? _____
6) What element is used to vulcanize rubber? _____
7) What does vulcanization do to the quality of the rubber? _____
8) Rubber trees were smuggled out of Brazil and planted in: _____
9) Why were rubber trees not planted in England? (The text doesn't tell you this, just use common sense about plants and geography.) _____
_____
10) What is the "mer" in rubber polymers? _____
11) Vulcanization causes the polymers in rubber to _____
12) Polymers that stretch and snap back are called _____
13) The word "synthetic" means _____
14) How many bonds can silicon form? _____
15) Name three things that silicon polymers are good for (other than Silly Putty™).
_____
_____
_____

16) This word means a very thick, liquid texture: _____
17) Put these substances in order, from low to high viscosity (in your opinion): ketchup, vegetable oil, maple syrup, water, Silly Putty™, shampoo, petroleum jelly (Vaseline)
_____

18) Does temperature affect viscosity? (Think about warm maple syrup.) _____
19) Does Silly Putty™ contain carbon? _____
20) Is SIlly Putty™ a polymer? _____

On-line research

1) Visit **dubblebubble.com.** Take a virtual tour of the gum factory, read gum stories, learn more gum history, and more!

2) Visit **sillyputty.com**. It's a cool site with lots of activities, trivia, contests, and more.

"1-800-4REVIEW"

All the words in this search have to do with rubber. In fact, they are all written in this chapter somewhere. The word bank is in code, but it isn't a straightforward "number-to-letter" correspondence—that would be too easy. Instead, we've invented a code that will require you to do some critical thinking. The numbers correspond to letters on a phone pad. So the number 2 could be either A, B, or C.

Good luck! You'll need it! (Oh, all right. We'll give you one letter in each word.) Write the word above the numbers when you figure it out.

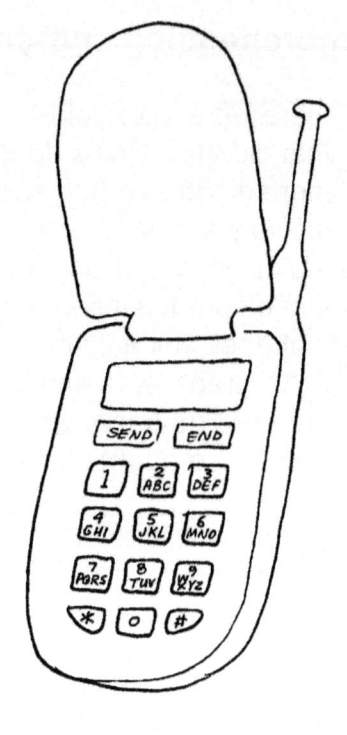

ELASTOMER
35278663R

POLYMER
765963R

LATEX
528E9

RUBBER
R82237

CHICLE
244C53

GUM
486

ISOPRENE
4767736E

VISCOUS
847C687

SULFUR
7U5387

BRAZIL
2R2945

SAPODILLA
S27634552

CROSSLINK
C76775465

PRIESTLY
P7437859

GOODYEAR
466D9327

MACINTOSH
62246T674

VULCANIZATION
8U5226492846N

INDONESIA
4N3663742

```
Y U J F U T G K W Y R I P C F V C B H D G U M T R X W C
L Q E V Y U Y G Z B P H I N D O N E S I A A M O R I S Y
Q J L D H D M W A L K U H Q E Y Z Q P O L Y M E R G W Y
L X A V N P Y N J U M O L I Y F C V H R I S O P R E N E
N K S Y W T J L K H W Y A G Z E D N V U E Z U Y D E E C
U F T M C K R K S O L L T S T S M F I K Q H G E U P P O
J W O Y M E E A J J K J E M R N B M S Y I U X V H H O R
R U M N T Y X T R L R W X M G F Z C C G H A R R U F E H
X F E K F O H K X Q V R L A I I S V O U H V U D Q B V J
G L R P R I E S T L Y E Z C W R L K U C T H B T Y H L N
V U L C A N I Z A T I O N I F H M P S O C R G Y Y F R P
F Z G A E J M C H I C L E N W Q B G C O R M K P K R F S
L Y O Q R H H G E A V S X T Q P Q P K Y O Y B G E U I Q
H V O S A P O D I L L A E O A Y X H B W S I M A L B C W
E L D A R H V G I Q X S S S H X E N N G S A H N W B W D
F A Y V H T U S J R U T I H T Y E J Y U L R F P P E H R
V H E I K H E Y V E B R A Z I L D O P G I B S W M R H D
G S A W C S M H Z Y J C D U K Q W A U Q N V K T O S Y X
A V R J O H J Z O H Q M C R U N A G K X K F P U R J A E
W X O L V S U L F U R D N R X V B N Z T B L Q T H F J Z
```

Chapter Eight: Carbohydrates

Almost everything we eat is a carbon compound-- everything from candy and cookies to vegetables and meats. Even vitamins have carbon as their base. (Minerals, however, are not carbon-based. They are made of other elements.) In this chapter, we are going to look at the "sweetest" of these groups: the **carbohydrates**.

As you can guess from the name (remembering that "hydro" means water, and water is H_2O), carbohydrates are made of carbon, hydrogen, and oxygen. The smallest carbohydrate molecules are the simple sugars, known in the world of chemistry as **monosaccharides** (**mono** means "one," and **saccharide** ("*sack-a-ride*") means "sugar"). A simple sugar molecule can look like a straight line, or it can curve around to make a circle. The circle form is more common.

Look- it's an aldehyde!

I was told this is glucose.

Glucose is not only the most common sugar, but is also the most common chemical compound in the natural world. It is the sugar that your cells use to get energy. The cells tear apart the glucose sugar molecule to release energy stored in it. How did the energy get there in the first place? Plants used energy from the sun, plus water and carbon dioxide to make glucose.

PLANTS DO THIS: CO_2 (carbon dioxide) + H_2O (water) + energy $\Rightarrow$ $C_6H_{12}O_6$ (glucose) + O_2 (oxygen)

ANIMALS DO THIS: O_2 (oxygen) + $C_6H_{12}O_6$ (glucose) $\Rightarrow$ energy + H_2O (water) + CO_2 (carbon dioxide)

The glucose molecule is transferring the sun's energy to your cells!

The cells in your body need a constant supply of glucose sugar. Glucose must be in the blood all the time so that any cells that need energy can grab a glucose. After you eat, of course, there is lots of sugar available. (You'll have to wait until a little later in the chapter to learn how your body breaks apart the carbohydrates into individual glucose sugars. Hang in there a minute and finish this train of thought first.) Right after a meal, your cells have more glucose than they can use. But what happens between meal times? What if you don't eat all day? How do your cells survive? The answer is that the body was designed with a glucose storage system.

Have you ever seen strings of onions or other dried vegetables hanging from the rafters in old-fashioned kitchens? This method of food storage is a good picture of how your body saves glucose molecules for later use. Your body strings up glucose molecules and stores them in your muscles and liver. These strings are called **glycogen**.

Some of the glucose molecules from your food get used right away, and others get stored as glycogen. When the amount of glucose in the blood gets too low, your body gets out those glycogen strings and starts taking them apart and putting the glucose molecules into the blood.

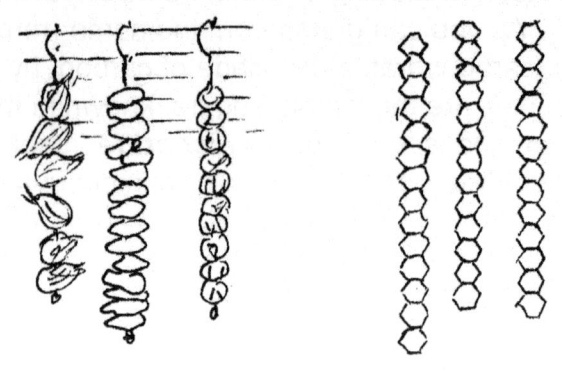

strings of dried fruits and vegetables

strings of glucose molecules

So what would happen if your body could not make these strings? You'd have way too much glucose in your blood for a while, then it would get all used up and you'd have no sugar at all in your blood. This is what the disease called **diabetes** is all about. A hormone called **insulin**, made by your pancreas, tells your body to start making strings. It's like the supervisor on the job, telling the workers what to do. If there isn't any insulin, strings don't get made. In diabetes, the pancreas does not make enough insulin, and diabetics have to put insulin into their blood using a hypodermic needle. They must constantly test the amount of glucose in their blood to make sure it doesn't get too high or too low. Diabetics must tell their body when to start making glycogen strings.

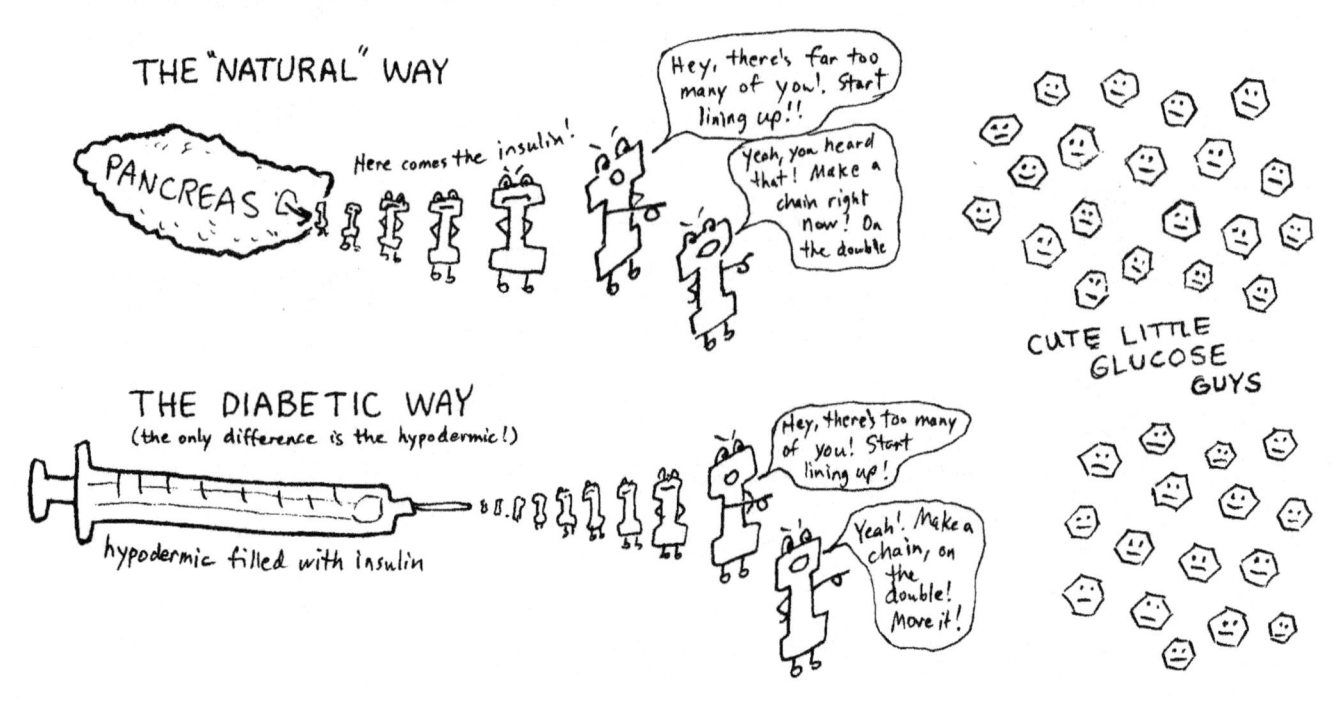

THE "NATURAL" WAY

PANCREAS — Here comes the insulin!

"Hey, there's far too many of you! Start lining up!!"

"Yeah, you heard that! Make a chain right now! On the double"

THE DIABETIC WAY
(the only difference is the hypodermic!)

hypodermic filled with insulin

"Hey, there's too many of you! Start lining up!"

"Yeah! Make a chain, on the double! Move it!"

CUTE LITTLE GLUCOSE GUYS

54

You may have heard of another type of diabetes, called "type 2 diabetes." It is similar to the original "type 1" diabetes in that it is a problem with insulin. However, "type 2" can, in a large part, be prevented, whereas the original "type 1" kind is something you are born with (which is why it is sometimes called juvenile diabetes). We hate to be the deliverer of bad news, but one of the things that leads to type 2 diabetes is consistently eating too much sugar. Bummer, right? Wouldn't it be nice if we could live on cookies and candy? They taste so good! We don't want to limit the number of sweets we eat. It's just not fun. Let's look at what goes on when we eat lots of sugar.

Remember that insulin's job is to tell your body to get those extra glucose molecules into strings and store them away.

Well, what if the job is so big, that the insulin just can't keep up? Your body could send out even more insulin to shout the message even louder.

What happens if there are still lots of glucoses floating in your blood stream. Your body could try sending out even more insulin messengers.

But, alas, the job is still too big. And worse yet, the blood is getting tired of hearing all this nagging going on all the time and stops listening. There just isn't enough insulin available to get all those glucoses stored away. You now have two problems: high blood sugar, *and* high insulin! This is called ***insulin resistance***. So then what? What harm can this do? Try high blood pressure, heart disease, stroke, depression, confusion, fatigue, kidney problems, osteoporosis, blindness... do we need to go on?

It's a hard choice, though, isn't it? We all love sweet tastes. The good news is that you don't have to completely give up sweets. You just need to keep them under control. Mom is right. You need to eat your veggies and save the candy for special occasions. Even better news is that as you start to reduce the amount of sugar you consume, you will find that you are more sensitive to sugar-- it won't take as much of it to please your taste buds. You can cut down the amount of sugar in your recipes and they'll taste just as good. Isn't the body amazingly adaptable?!

Another way our bodies cope with too much sugar is to store it as fat. The body can only store a certain amount of sugar as glycogen. If you eat way too much sugar, your body only stores some of it as glycogen (for between meal snacks) then turns the rest into fat, for long term storage (in case of famine). We'll look at fat in the next chapter.

What would happen if you did not eat any carbohydrates? Your body would have to look elsewhere for glucose molecules. The next place the body goes is to protein and fat. Your body can take apart protein and fat molecules and make glucose molecules out of the spare parts. This is a lot harder than just breaking down starches, though. If given a choice, the body will always choose to use carbohydrates first. However, if it is not given carbohydrates, it has no choice but to begin using fats and proteins. This is the idea behind the Atkins diet. If you cut way back on the number of carbohydrates you eat, you can force your body to starting using fat, including the fat you have stored in, and on, various parts of your body, most notably around the waist and hips.

Getting back to sugar molecules, let's look at another simple sugar that is almost identical to glucose. Can you spot the difference?

You would think that your cells would be able to tear apart **galactose** since there is almost no difference between it and glucose. Nope. To use galactose, your body must first turn it into glucose. More extra work for your poor body...

One last simple sugar: ***fructose***. Fructose is the sugar found in fruit. It is the sweetest of all the sugars.

Now let's start building with sugars. If we put two monosaccharides together we get a ***disaccharide*** (***di*** means "two"). Let's try those two sugars that are almost identical: glucose and galactose.

Lactose is the sugar found in milk. You probably don't think of milk as being sweet. Lactose may not be as sweet as the sugar you sprinkle on your cereal, but it is still a sugar.

Now let's pick up that train of thought that we left hanging on the second page of this chapter. We said the cells of your body can only use glucose for energy, right? So that means that to use the glucose in lactose, your body must disconnect the two sugars. Your body makes a particular enzyme that that is able to split lactose into glucose and galactose. ***Enzymes*** are a type of catalyst. They help a reaction to occur without themselves being changed by it. The enzyme that breaks apart lactose is called ***lactase*** (note the ending: "-ase" instead of "-ose").

People whose bodies do not make this enzyme cannot properly digest milk. They are said to be "milk intolerant." (Note: This is not the same as a milk allergy.) If lactose gets into the lower intestines without having been disassembled into glucose and galactose, it can cause diarrhea. Fortunately, you can buy milk with lactase already in it. (No one should have to eat a chocolate brownie without a glass of milk!)

Let's put glucose together with fructose.

GLUCOSE + FRUCTOSE → SUCROSE

I love this molecule!

This is **sucrose**. Good old table sugar! That wonderful stuff you can sprinkle on your cereal, put into fudge recipes, and mold into all kinds of candies. Once again, to be able to use the glucoses in sucrose, your body must tear apart the two sugars. And just as lact<u>ose</u> is broken down by lact<u>ase</u>, suc<u>rose</u> is broken down by suc<u>rase</u>. You're seeing a pattern here, right? The breaker-downer always has the same name as the sugar except that it ends in "–ase" instead of "–ose."

Just as a side note, part of the tearing apart process requires water molecules. Have you ever noticed that eating sweets can make you thirsty? There's a reason behind that thirst. Your body is telling you to get some water down there so it can tear apart those sucrose sugars. Your body puts a water molecule between the sugars.

Another disaccharide is **maltose**: two glucose molecules stuck together.

We really got lazy on this drawing! You know there are letters around everywhere. But chemists often simplify like this.

GLUCOSE + GLUCOSE → MALTOSE

Maltose glasses?!

Maltose is not commonly found in nature. It is present in germinating grain seeds, such as wheat and barley. Malt sugar is part of the beer brewing process.

What if we connect more than two monosaccharides? How many could we connect and what would we get? As you may be able to guess, a long string of sugar molecules would be a sugar polymer, or **polysaccharide**. One type of polysaccharide is called starch. Starch is just a whole string of glucose molecules.

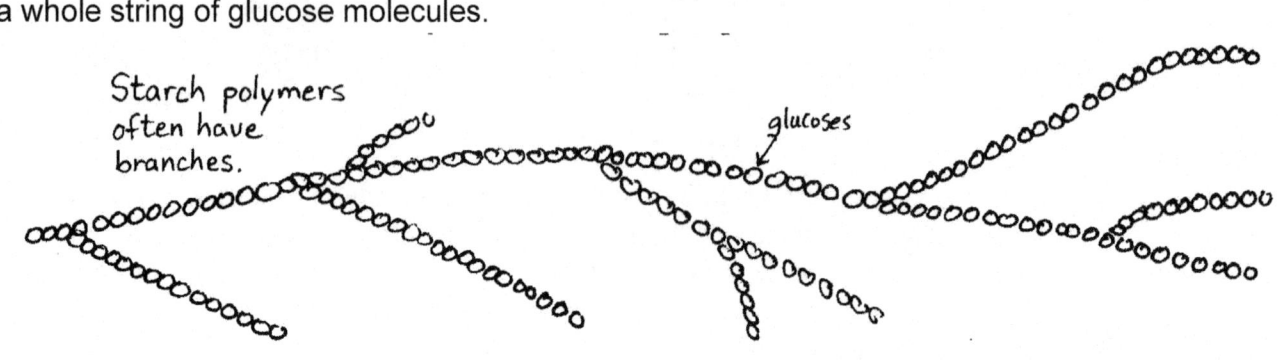

Starch polymers often have branches.

glucoses

Starches can have anywhere from hundreds to thousands of glucose molecules. Now, if you are an attentive reader, you may be wondering how we can say a string of glucose molecules is called starch, when we just said that your body strings up glucoses and we call these strings glycogen.   The answer is that glycogen is a type of starch.   Starch is the larger category. All glycogens are starches, but not all starches are glycogens. Scientists sometimes call glycogen "animal starch." Just like glycogen is energy storage for animals, starch is energy storage for plants. (Only we can use theirs, but they can't use ours. One of the inequalities of life, eh?) Plant starch is mainly found in seeds and roots. We make flour by grinding up seeds from certain plants, such as wheat or oats.

Starch is found in foods like bread, crackers, pasta, rice, and potatoes. When you eat these foods, your body gets busy breaking apart the polymers into individual glucose molecules that can go into your blood stream. The longer the chain, the longer it takes for your body to break it apart. A very long chain can keep providing fresh glucose molecules for many hours. This is why potatoes "stick with you" longer than a handful of crackers. Starches with very long chains are called **complex carbohydrates**.

There are other things you can do with starch, besides eat it. For example, starch can be used as a natural fabric stiffener.   In the days before permanent press fabrics, starching and ironing were a regular part of doing laundry. Starch was squirted onto shirt collars, for example, to keep them sticking up and looking crisp.

Do you remember that there is a simple sugar that looks almost exactly like glucose, yet is unusable to our body? Galactose is almost identical, except that two atoms on one end are switched top and bottom.   The last carbohydrate we will look at is another case where two things look very similar and yet the small difference makes all the difference. The polymer on the top is starch. The one on the bottom is **cellulose**. Can you spot the difference?

Cellulose is the "stuff" plants are made of. The very slight difference is in the way they are attached. The link between them is at a slightly different angle. Big deal, right? Amazingly enough, this miniscule difference between them means that we can digest starch, but not cellulose. If we eat a leaf or a stem, it passes right through our digestive system. You'd starve to death if you ate only grass.

Cellulose is not bad for us, though. In fact, eating cellulose can help our intestines by pushing food through at a fast pace. If food sits and gets stuck, we call it constipation. This is an unpleasant feeling, as anyone who has been constipated can tell you. Cellulose is sometimes referred to as **fiber** or **roughage**. Nutritional experts are always telling us to get enough fiber in our diets.

So how does a cow live on just grass? A cow must be able to digest cellulose, right? Wrong! No animal in the world can digest cellulose. The secret is that these vegetarian animals rely on bacteria living in their digestive system. Certain types of bacteria can break down cellulose. The grass the cow eats is eaten by the bacteria living in the cow's rumen (the first of four stomachs). The bacteria tear apart the plant cells, releasing the nutrients inside. When the bacteria die, they are digested and used by the cow's system. The cow gets more nutrition from digesting bacteria than it does from the grass! We don't think of a cow as living on bacteria, do we? It's shocking!

A COW'S STOMACHS

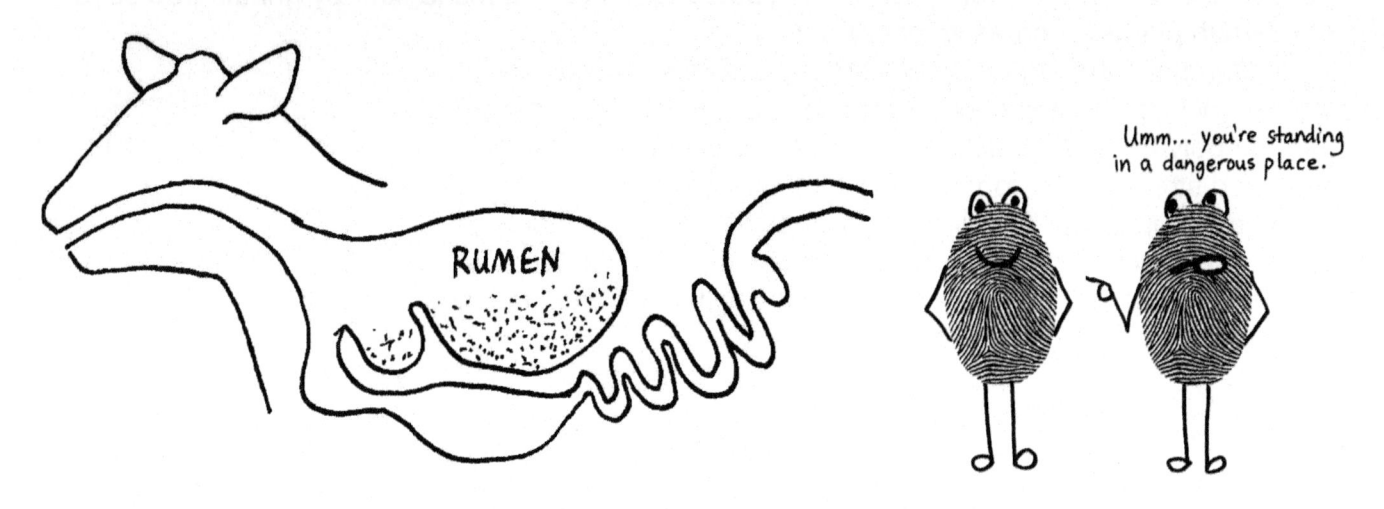

Cellulose is what plants are made of. Without cellulose there would be no alpine forests, no swaying fields of grain, no tree swings. Well, you could have the swing, just not the tree. Cellulose is a part of our life in ways other than nutrition. The two biggest uses we have for it are lumber and paper.

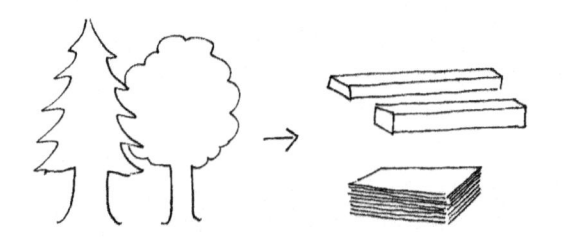

Cellulose can sometimes be used to replace plastic polymers, making products completely biodegradable. For instance, many companies are using packing "peanuts" made of starch, not Styrofoam. After you receive the package, you just dump the peanuts into the sink, dissolve them with hot water, and flush the harmless residue right down the drain. They don't sit in a landfill and you don't have to worry about recycling them.

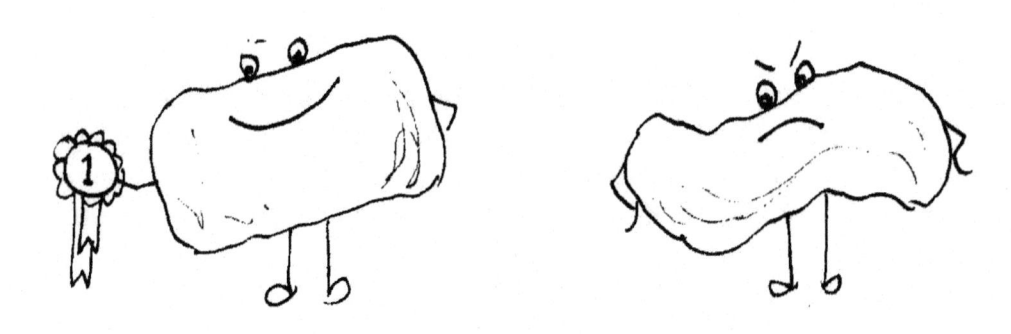

"Oops! I discovered a sweetener..."

Saccharin *("sack-a-rin")* was discovered by accident in 1879 by a chemist named Fahlberg. He spilled an unknown chemical on his hand and didn't bother to wash up before dinner (not a recommended lab procedure!). He noticed the bread he was eating was unusually sweet and by tasting residues on his clothes and hands (not a recommended lab procedure!), figured out that the sweetness had come from the chemical. He later named this chemical saccharin. By 1907, saccharin began to be used as a sugar substitute. In the 1960's it was widely used by the soft drink industry for "diet" sodas. Two sweeteners that contain saccharin are "Sweet 'N Low" and "Sugar Twin."

Despite the controversy over whether saccharin is safe for human consumption, the overall evidence suggests that it is safe. Studies of the human population (as opposed to lab rats) have never found any solid evidence that saccharin is unsafe.

Aspartame was discovered by accident in 1965 by a chemist named Schlatter. He was working on a project aimed at discovering new treatments for stomach ulcers. One of the steps in the process was to make something called: aspartyl-phenylalanine methyl ester. He accidentally spilled some on his hand and later licked his finger as he reached for a piece of paper (not a recommended lab procedure!). He noticed a sweet taste and decided to test the chemical to see if it would sweeten his coffee. It did, and the rest, as they say, is history.

Cyclamate was discovered in 1937 by a chemist named Sveda, working at the University of Illinois. While working on making a fever-fighting drug, he was smoking a cigarette (doubly not a recommended lab procedure!). He noticed a sweet taste on his cigarette and realized he had gotten cyclamate on it. He was the first one in the lab to taste the chemical they were working with, so he gets credit for the discovery.

Sucralose was discovered by accident in England. A British sugar company was doing research on sucrose. They were adding chlorine molecules to the sucrose. They sent samples of this chlorinated sugar to one of their employees for testing. This particular employee was not a native English speaker and he misunderstood what they wanted. He thought they wanted it "tasted" instead of "tested." Well, he tasted it, and found out that this substance is about a hundred times as sweet as regular sugar.

Comprehension self-check

1) What are carbohydrates made of? _____, _____, and _____.
2) What does the word saccharide mean? _____
3) What are the two shapes a monosaccharide can have? _____ or _____
4) Glucose provides your body with _____, which originally came from the _____.
5) What is glycogen? _____
6) When does your body need glycogen? _____
7) What does insulin do? _____
8) What is it called when your body does not make enough insulin? _____
9) What can cause type 2 diabetes? _____
10) What can be the results of having high blood sugar all the time? _____ _____ _____
11) After your body can't store anymore glucose as glycogen, it starts storing it as ____.
12) If you don't give your body carbohydrates, where does it get glucose? _____ _____ _____
13) Galactose is almost identical to _____.
14) Which is the sweetest of all sugars? _____
15) If you put two monosaccharides together you get a _____.
16) The sugar found in milk: _____ The enzyme that tears it apart: _____
17) People who do not make the above enzyme are called _____ _____.
18) The correct name for table sugar is _____. It is made of these two simple sugars: _____ and _____.
19) Two polymers made of glucose sugars are: _____ and _____.
20) One of these (in 19) is not digestible by animals. Which one? _____
21) When cellulose is a part of our diet, we often call it _____ or _____.
22) What is a polysaccharide? _____
23) Name something you can do with starch besides eating it: _____
24) "Sweet 'N Low" and "Sugar Twin" are made of this artificial sweetener: _____
25) How were most artificial sweeteners discovered? _____

On-line research

1) Name three more ruminants (who have a "rumen" stomach, like the cow, and depend upon bacteria living in the stomach to digest the plant they eat).

2) Name a monosaccharide that was not mentioned in this chapter. (It helps if you include the word "list" in your key words.)

3) What are the symptoms of diabetes? What do doctors look for?

If you would like to see the inside of a ruminant stomach, go to: arbl.cvmbs.colostate.edu/hbooks/pathphys/digestion/herbivores/rumen_anat.html

Chapter Nine: Fats

Fats belong to a class of molecules called **lipids**. Lipids are substances that will not dissolve in water. Why not? For the answer we need to go back to those "lollipop" molecules we saw when we learned about soap. Remember that one end loves water and the other end hates water.

$$CH_3-CH_2-CH_2-CH_2-CH_2-CH_2-CH_2-CH_2-CH_2-CH_2-CH_2-CH_2-CH_2-CH_2-CH_2-CH_2-CH_2-C\overset{O}{\underset{O^-Na^+}{\lessgtr}}$$

↖ hydrophobic   ↑ We can write all 11 of these CH_2's as: $(CH_2)_{11}$ hydrophilic ↗

However, and this is a big however, "lollipops" like this never occur all by themselves in the natural world. In the manufacturing of soap, these "lollipops" are forced to stay apart from each other so that they can hold onto dirt with one side and water with the other. The element sodium is forced to stick to the end of the "lollipop." The sodium comes from the lye, but where do the "lollipops" come from? You may remember that the main ingredient in soap is fat. Isn't it strange that the very thing we want to scrub off our hands (fat or grease) is the very thing we need in order to clean them?!

Here is a typical molecule of fat:

$$CH_2 - OCCH_2(CH_2)_{11}CH_3$$
$$|$$
$$CH - OCCH_2(CH_2)_{11}CH_3$$
$$|$$
$$CH_2 - OCCH_2(CH_2)_{15}CH_3$$

Those look like lop-sided lollipops.

Look more like golf clubs to me.

There are three "lollipops" held together at one end by a "clamp" called glycerol. The "clamp" covers the would-be-water-loving end so it cannot attach to water. Thus, this molecule will not mix with water (which is another way of saying it will not dissolve in water). In soap making, you must force the glycerol to let go of the three "lollipops" so that they can be free to attach to water molecules.

$$CH_2 - \quad Na^+ \,\!\!\bar{\,\,}OCCH_2(CH_2)_{11}CH_3$$
$$|$$
$$CH - \quad Na^+ \,\!\!\bar{\,\,}OCCH_2(CH_2)_{11}CH_3$$
$$|$$
$$CH_2 - \quad Na^+ \,\!\!\bar{\,\,}OCCH_2(CH_2)_{11}CH_3$$

← reverse this left for right and compare to the "lollipop" at the top of the page

The distinguishing feature of lipids is that they don't dissolve in water. But you already know this from your experiences in everyday life. You've seen oil droplets keeping to themselves in the salad dressing, you've seen hamburger grease floating in the dishpan, and you've noticed that grease won't wash off your hands without soap. If you want to dissolve a lipid, you must use nasty substances like gasoline or carbon tetrachloride.

Lipids include fatty acids, steroids, cholesterol, hormones, and vitamins A, D, E and K. The only one of these we are going to take a closer look at is fatty acids. You've probably already heard the term fatty acids, as fats and fatty acids seem to be in the news a lot nowadays. Just the word "fatty acid" is enough to make you not want to eat too many of them. But what are they, and what do they do? Here is a typical fatty acid:

You've studied functional groups, so, being the excellent chemistry student you are, you will be able to look at this molecule and exclaim, "Hey, look! There's the acid functional group: COOH! That means it's an acid!" Yes, that COOH hanging off the end classifies it as an acid. Now look at the long hydrocarbon chain. If that COOH were not on the end, what would this molecule be? Just an alkane, right? That COOH is the difference between drinking coconut oil and gasoline!

Here are some common fatty acids and where you will find them:

Name	Formula	Where found	# carbons
Butryic acid	$CH_3CH_2CH_2COOH$	butter	4
Caprylic acid	$CH_3(CH_2)_6COOH$	coconut oil	8
Palmitic acid	$CH_3(CH_2)_{14}COOH$	palm oil	16
Stearic acid	$CH_3(CH_2)_{16}COOH$	beef tallow (fat)	18
Oleic acid	$CH_3(CH_2)_7CH=CH(CH_2)_7COOH$	olive oil	18
Linoleic acid	similar to oleic, but 2 double bonds	oybean oil	18
Linolenic acid	similar to oleic, but 3 double bonds	fish oils	18

Undoubtedly, you noticed on the chart that the fatty acids starting with olive oil have double bonds in them. (You did notice, right?) What does the double bond mean, and what can it do? Stretch your memory back to the earlier chapters, and remember that a double bond means that the molecule could take on more atoms if it had to. A molecule with a double bond is unsaturated. That double bond can open up and let two more atoms attach (usually hydrogen, but not always). The fats in the chart that have only single bonds are **saturated fatty acids**. They can't take on anymore hydrogens.

The fats that have double bonds are called **unsaturated fatty acids**. Those double bonds could be forced to open up and accept some hydrogens. If a fatty acid contains multiple double bonds, it is called **polyunsaturated**.

So that's what a fatty acid is. Now, what does it do? Your body uses fatty acids as a raw material to manufacture cell membranes, hormones, and prostaglandins. Let's look at just one of these: cell membranes. The membrane is the outer layer around all your cells. We might want to call it a "wall" except that scientists reserve the term "cell wall" for the outer layer in plant cells. Plant cells have a true cell wall, whereas animal cells have just a membrane that separates the inside from the outside.

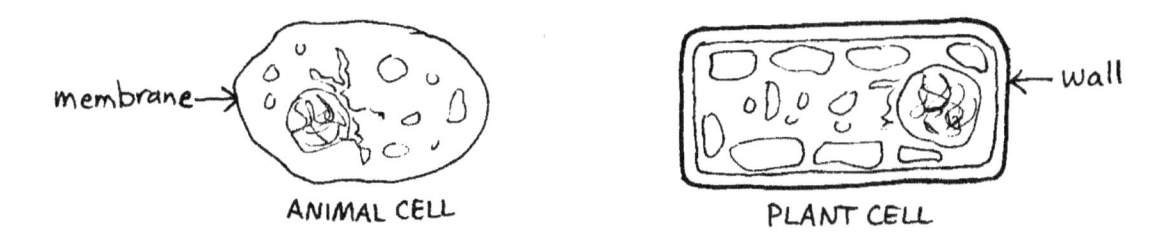

What is the outer membrane made of? "Lollipops"! Yes, it is made of a double layer of "lollipop" molecules with their water-hating tails turned inward facing each other. At certain intervals there are "doors" that can let things in and out of the cells.

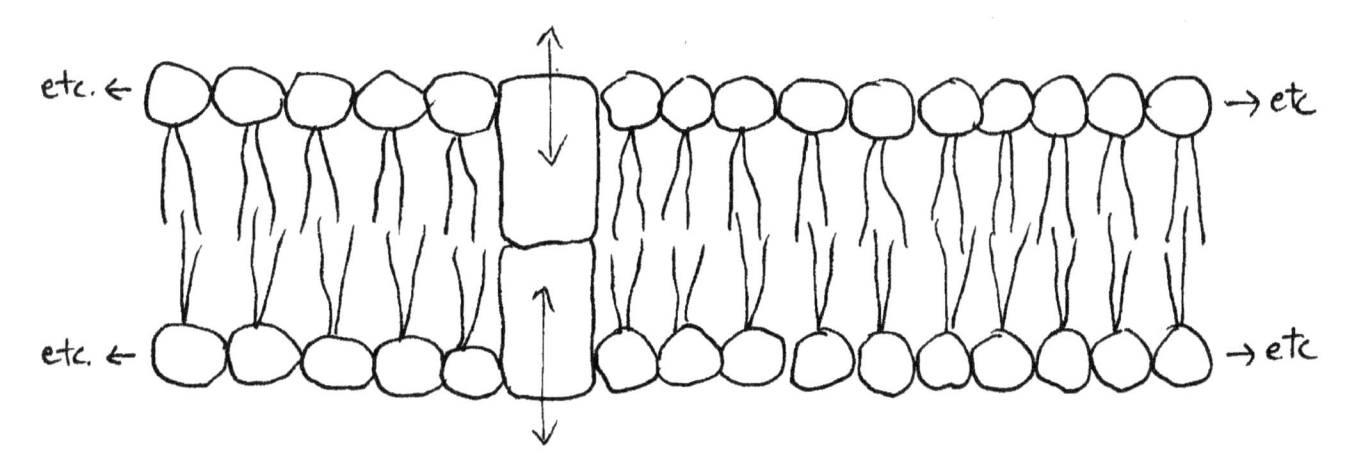

Your body is constantly making new cells. Old cells wear out and are replaced. When you get injured, your body must manufacture new cells quickly. The food you eat gives your body the raw materials it needs to build new cells. Your body can make some of the fats, but there are certain fats your body cannot make. These are called the **essential** fatty acids, because they are essential to your diet. The only way your body will can get these fats is for you to put the correct foods in your mouth and swallow. (Okay, you can chew before you swallow.) These essential fatty acids include the oils found in olive oil, soybean oil, and fish oils. You need to think about what you are eating and make sure you supply your body with what it needs to maintain good health.

One kind of fat that is in the news a lot nowadays is **trans fat**. The Latin root word "trans" means "across." So what is "across" about these fats? A picture is better than a description:

Here is a normal fat molecule, called "cis" fat:

Here is a "trans" fat molecule:

Trans fatty acids are isomers of the normally occurring cis fatty acids. Your body's enzymes can break apart the cis fat, but not the trans isomer. Since your body cannot process trans fat, it floats around in your blood creating havoc. Along with saturated fats, trans fat can help to clog your arteries making it hard for the blood to get through. That's not the kind of help you need!

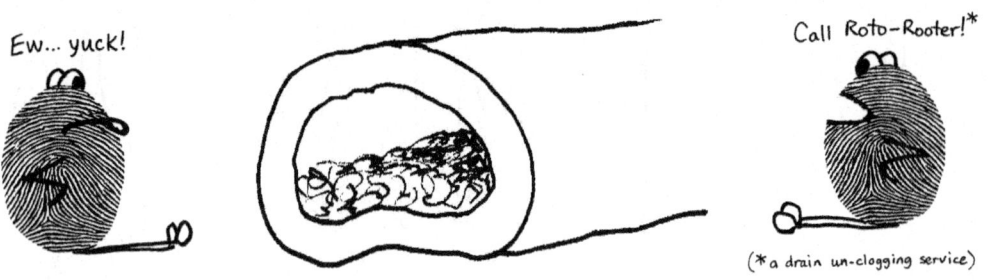

So where does this trans fat come from? There's a short story behind the answer. One problem with saturated fats (like butter) is that they go rancid (bad) easily. For instance, crackers made with saturated fats will begin to taste bad within weeks or months. Stores like to carry products that will stay saleable for a long time. Products need to be able to sit in a warehouse for a while, then on a store shelf for a while, then on your shelf for a while. Who knows how long that could be?! Food scientists found that unsaturated fats last much longer. The only problem with them is that they are runny—the wrong texture for baking with. They then discovered that if they forced these unsaturated fats to take on more hydrogen atoms, the texture of the fat improved for baking. Now they had great texture and great shelf life.

Great solution, until it was later discovered that the hydrogenating process created these trans fat isomers, which are bad for you. The good news is that food scientists are now discovering ways to prevent trans fats from forming, and many new "no trans fat" products are showing up in stores every day. Products now bear large labels proclaiming: "NO TRANS FAT!" A good rule of thumb is to stay away from products that contain "partially hydrogenated" vegetable oils.

We can't leave the subject of fats without mentioning *cholesterol*. Cholesterol is a soft, waxy substance found all throughout your body and floating in your blood. This might sound alarming, but it is not only normal, it's necessary. Cells use cholesterol to make things like cell membranes and hormones. The body makes its own supply of cholesterol, so you don't really need to eat it, but a small amount of cholesterol is part of a normal balanced diet.

Like the other fats, cholesterol is not a problem unless there is too much of it. When there is too much, it's a huge problem (though recent research has suggested that cholesterol on its own is not so much of a problem--it's when it's mixed with other fats such as the infamous "trans" fat). You may have heard about the two kinds of cholesterol: the good kind (HDL) and the bad kind (LDL). There really aren't two kinds of cholesterol. Cholesterol is cholesterol. These two substances, HDL and LDL, are proteins that carry cholesterol. You could think of them a serving trays on which the cholesterol sits. HDL stands for high-density lipoprotein. Your body makes this kind of protein to carry cholesterol away and keep the blood clean. (HDL is a "Hero.") LDL stands for low-density lipoprotein. This kind of protein is the villain; it keeps circulating cholesterol in your system. (LDL is a "Low-Down Loser.")

Fat tastes so good; it's so easy to eat too much of it! The smell and taste of deep-fried foods is almost impossible to resist. When you eat at restaurants, it is almost impossible to control the fat in your food. When cooking and eating at home, many experts recommend using olive oil when frying and baking, eating lots of fish, and avoiding shortening if possible.

We all know that our bodies make and store fat. We hear lots of talk about the dangers of being too fat. So fat is bad, right? Would we be healthier without it? Why do we have it, then? Is it good for anything? Surprisingly, you couldn't live without fat cells! The energy stored as glycogen in your liver and muscles can only get you through about one day. If you don't eat for more than one day (like when you have the stomach flu) your body must tap into some of the fat reserves. It gets out those fat molecules and tears them apart, releasing energy. If you don't eat for a very long time and you deplete all your fat supplies, the body then starts using protein for energy. Unfortunately, the place your body gets protein is from your own muscles. This is the beginning of true starvation.

Fat has other important jobs, too. In the abdomen, it cushions and protects your vital organs, such as your heart, liver, and kidneys. Fat tissue fills in the spaces around your intestines and attaches them to each other so they don't slide around too much. Fat insulates the body against cold. It gives the body a pleasing shape. So we can't equate the word "fat" with the word "bad." Fat isn't bad; it's essential. It just needs to be kept in balance with everything else.

Comprehension self-check

1) Fats belong to a class of molecules called _____. They will not _____ in water.
2) In soap, the element _____ is forced to stick on the end of a fat molecule.
3) The "clamp" that holds three fatty acids together is called _____.
4) A fatty acid looks like a _____ chain with this functional group on it: _____
5) A saturated fat has all (single/double) bonds.
6) An unsaturated fat has at least one _____ bond.
7) A polyunsaturated fat has many _____ bonds.
8) What part of an animal cell is made of "lollipop" molecules? _____
9) The outer layer of a plant cell is called a _____.
10) Fatty acids your body cannot make are called _____ fatty acids.
11) Essential fatty acids can be found in these types of oil: _____, _____, _____
12) What does "trans" mean in Latin? _____
13) Your body can break apart ____ fat, but not _____ fat.
14) Saturated fats _____ easily.
15) Scientists began to hydrogenate unsaturated oils (force them to take on more hydrogens) in order to make them _____.
16) An unfortunate result of hydrogenation is to produce _____.
17) Can your body make cholesterol? _____
18) Why, then, do you eat it? (Think of foods that contain cholesterol, and how they taste.) _____
19) Which kind of cholesterol (protein, really) is the good one? ____ The bad one? ____
20) Name three helpful things fat does in your body: _____, _____, _____

On-line research

1) When you have your cholesterol checked, you get three numbers: LDL level, HDL level, and total cholesterol count. Write in numbers that would be good to get:

      HDL: LDL: Total cholesterol:

2) Can you find the recommended weight for someone of your age and height?

3) What is the Atkins diet and why is it so different from all other diet plans?

Chapter Ten: Proteins

The last category of edible carbon-based polymers is **protein**. Protein is what bodies are made of. Each kind of living cell—skin, muscles, nerves, hair, blood, teeth, feathers, hooves, etc.—is made of its own kind of protein. Plants are made of cellulose, animals are made of proteins.

A protein has a string of carbons as its structural base. It also has hydrogens and oxygens, similar to carbohydrates. But proteins have an element we have not yet seen in any other polymers in this book: **nitrogen**.

Actually, I remember seeing N in a plastic polymer.

Yeah, you would remember something like that!

Since proteins are polymers, what are their "mers"? Individual units of protein are called **amino acids**. There are 20 different amino acids. Here are a few of them:

Glycine

$$CH_2-COO^-$$
$$|$$
$$^+NH_3$$

Lysine

$$H_3\overset{+}{N}CH_2CH_2CH_2CH_2-CH-COO^-$$
$$|$$
$$NH_2$$

Glutamine

$$H_2N-\overset{O}{\overset{\|}{C}}-CH_2CH_2-CH-COO^-$$
$$|$$
$$^+NH_3$$

Cysteine

$$HS-CH_2-CH-COO^-$$
$$|$$
$$^+NH_3$$

Look-- cysteine contains a sulfur, too!

Tyrosine

$$HO-\bigcirc-CH_2-CH-COO^-$$
$$|$$
$$^+NH_3$$

Tryptophan

$$CH_2-CH-COO^-$$
$$|$$
... $^+NH_3$
NH

Look-- I couldn't care less about the dumb sulfur!

Phenylalanine

$$\bigcirc-CH_2-CH-COO^-$$
$$|$$
$$^+NH_3$$

Proline

$$CH_2-CH_2$$
$$CH_2 \quad \quad C-COO^-$$
$$^+NH_2 \quad H$$

Notice the little plus and minus signs next to some of the N's and O's. These are very important. They are the places where the amino acids can stick to other amino acids. The positive charges stick to negative charges, just like opposite ends of magnets attract. Or maybe like elephants-- trunk to tail, trunk to tail, trunk to tail...

The attractive force than holds two amino acids together (with negative joined to positive) is called a ***peptide bond***. Think of amino acids as strange-looking elephants with positive tails and negative trunks. If we force one elephant to drop an oxygen from its trunk, and another elephant to drop two hydrogens from its tail, they will join, leaving a water molecule behind in the process.

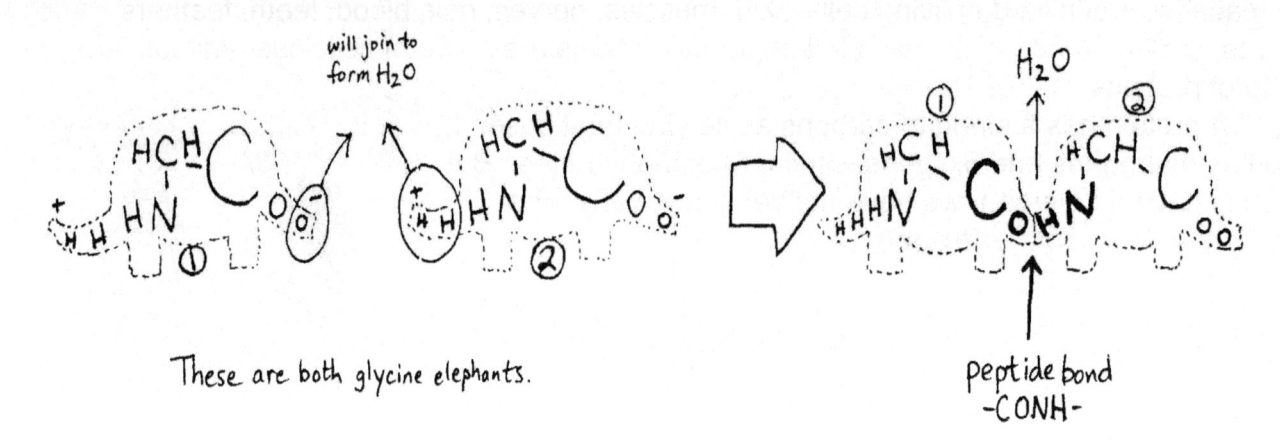

These are both glycine elephants.

peptide bond —CONH—

Notice that the trunk of the lead amino elephant and the tail of the one in the rear still have their electrical charges and will therefore be able to connect with more amino elephants.

A small chain of amino acids is called a ***polypeptide***. When the chain gets really long we call it a ***protein***.

glycine — alanine — valine — tyrosine — histidine — serine — glutamine — arginine

They stopped drawing elephants. Now they look like beads or something. I liked the elephants better!

You know, amino acids don't look like either elephants or beads. They look like complicated molecules, and are way too hard to draw all the time!

Proteins are different from carbohydrates and fats because they contain information. The order in which the amino acids are strung together means something. A certain pattern will cause the molecule to function a certain way in the body. A blood protein called hemoglobin has the formula $C_{3032}H_{4816}O_{780}N_{780}S_8Fe_4$. But uou can't just take 3032 carbons, 4816 hydrogens, 780 oxygens, 780 nitrogens, 8 sulfurs, and 4 irons and throw them together and expect to get hemoglobin. These elements are arranged into a unique pattern. If an amino acid gets out of place, the hemoglobin will not function correctly. For instance, a disease called sickle cell anemia occurs when one out of every 300 amino acids is in the wrong place. The order is crucial.

The human body contains about 30,000 types of proteins. Each protein is made of thousands of amino acids which must be in exactly the right order. This fact poses a huge problem for the theory of evolution. The probability of all of our 30,000 proteins occurring by chance is as good as zero.

But it gets more complicated! Not only is the sequence unique, but so is the way the protein strand "crumples up." Each protein folds or twirls or bunches up to form a unique shape.

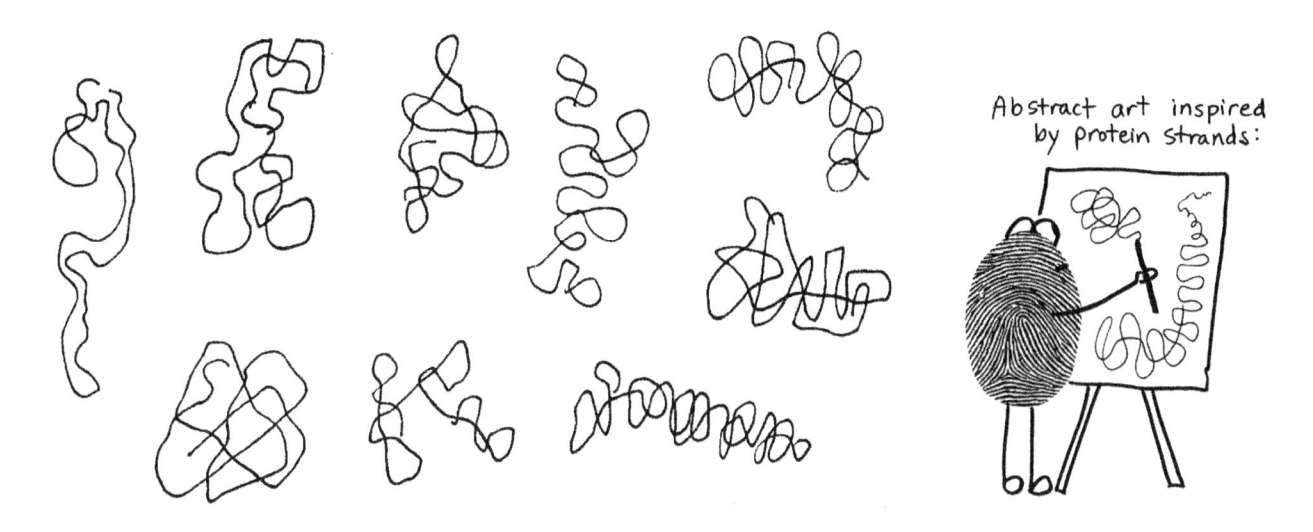

Abstract art inspired by protein strands:

The shape of the protein will determine its job in the body. Most of our body chemistry depends on what scientists call the "lock and key" principle. The proteins are designed to fit into certain receptacles that are the reverse shape. Enzymes are a good example of this. In this example, the shape of the enzyme allows it to break apart a molecule.

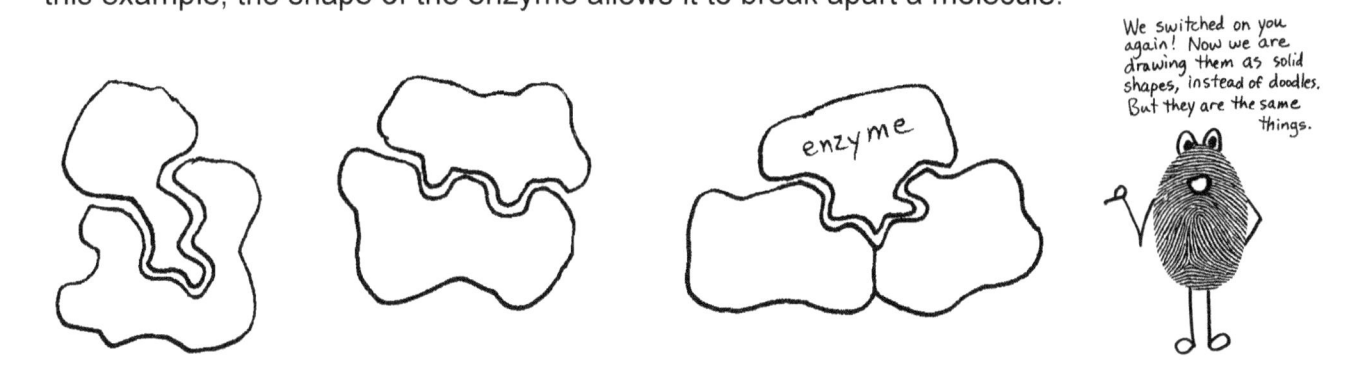

We switched on you again! Now we are drawing them as solid shapes, instead of doodles. But they are the same things.

There is also a place on the enzyme that can be used to prevent the enzyme from working. The body can send an "inhibitor" to bind to this site, making the enzyme the wrong shape, thus preventing it from working.

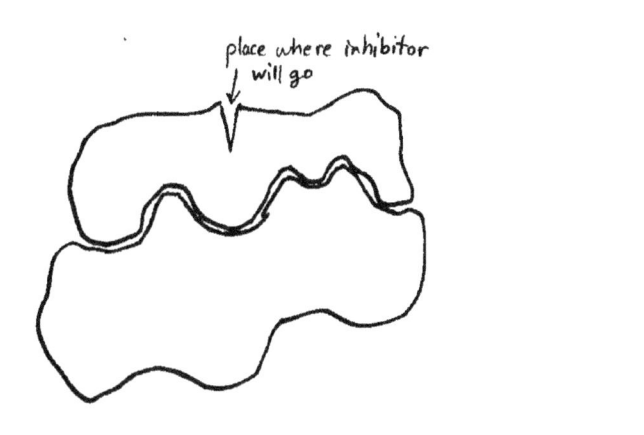

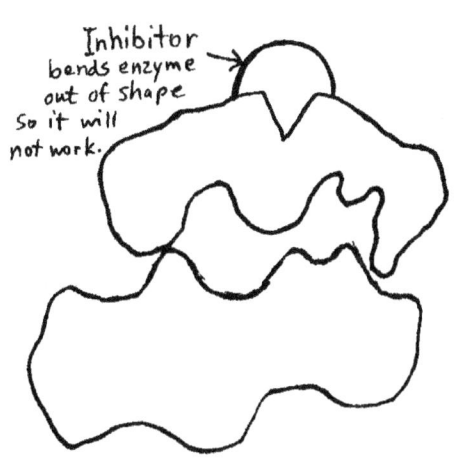

place where inhibitor will go

Inhibitor bends enzyme out of shape so it will not work.

Another shape proteins often take is called a *helix*. Proteins in wool, hair, and muscles take on this shape.

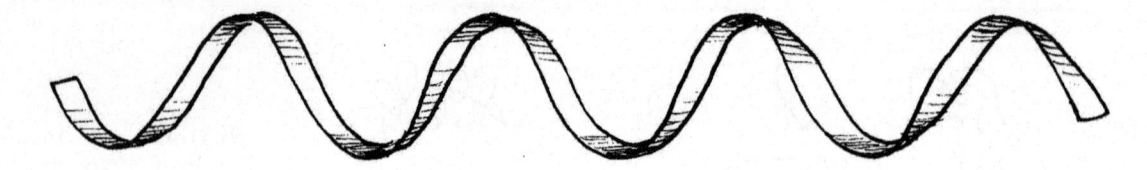

The most famous helix-shaped protein is **DNA, deoxyribonucleic acid**. This protein's job is to store information, like a library. Let's build some DNA.

First, we need a monosaccharide. Remember the simple sugars glucose, galactose and fructose? They aren't the only simple sugars in the world. One that we didn't mention in the chapter on sugars because we were saving it until now, is **ribose**. Ribose, minus one oxygen atom, is called **deoxyribose**. ("De" meaning "without, or taken away," and "oxy" being an abbreviation for "oxygen.") Can you spot the missing oxygen on deoxyribose?

ribose

deoxyribose

Ribose is used to make RNA, which is very similar to DNA. In this chapter, we are just going to build DNA, so we'll be using the deoxyribose sugar. Besides this sugar, we need two more things: a phosphate and a base. Here is a phosphate:

It looks simple in comparison to a lot of molecules we've seen in this book! Just a phosphorus, four oxygens, and a hydrogen. Nothing to it!

The base is the most complicated of the three ingredients, because there are four kinds of bases. This is where the nitrogen atoms come in.

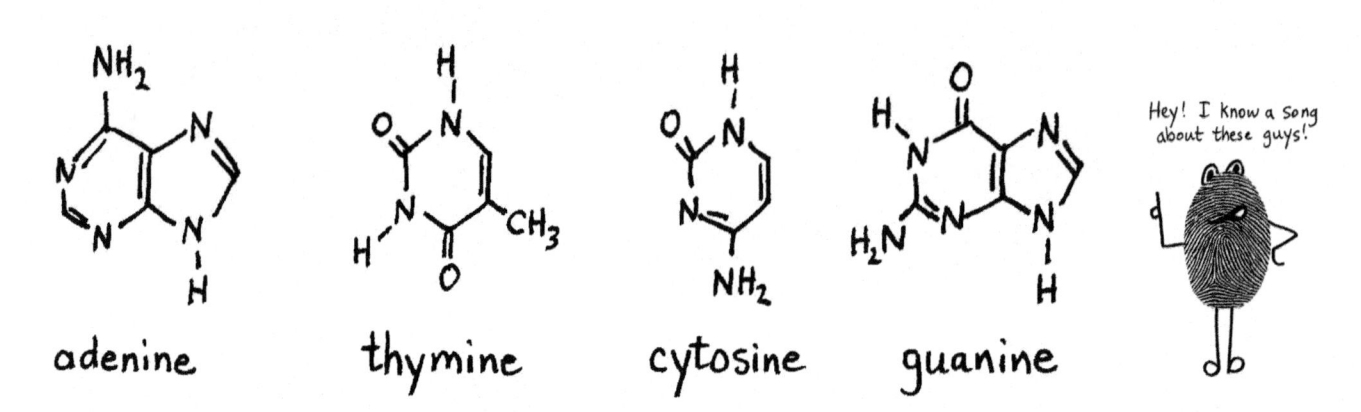

adenine   thymine   cytosine   guanine

Hey! I know a song about these guys!

72

Now let's put our three pieces together. We'll have to take off two OH's on the sugar, in order to stick the phosphate and base on.

These three units stuck together are called a **nucleotide**. The nucleotides can form a polymer, like this:

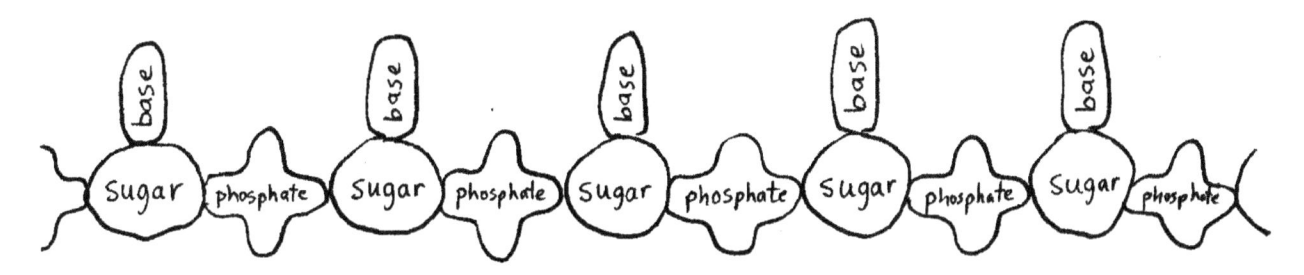

The last step is to take two of these long polymers and match them up, side by side.

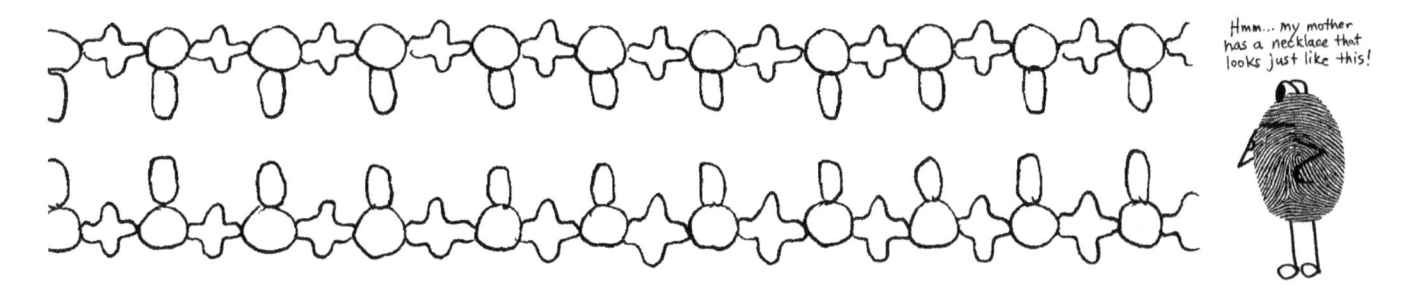

The only tricky part is that adenine must always be paired with thymine, and cytosine must always be paired with guanine. (Remember, the straight letters go together, and the round letters go together.)

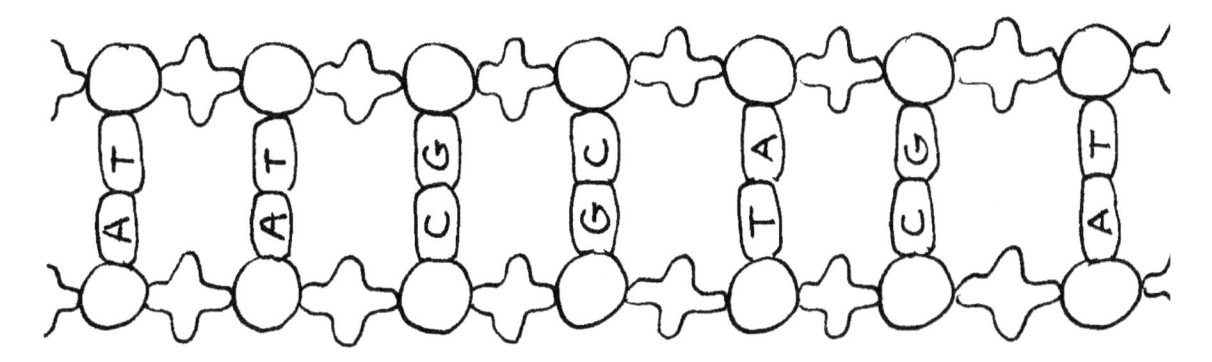

Now we have something that looks like a ladder. The rungs are pairs of bases, and the side rails are made of alternating sugars and phosphates. The last thing we need to do is give our ladder structure a little twist.

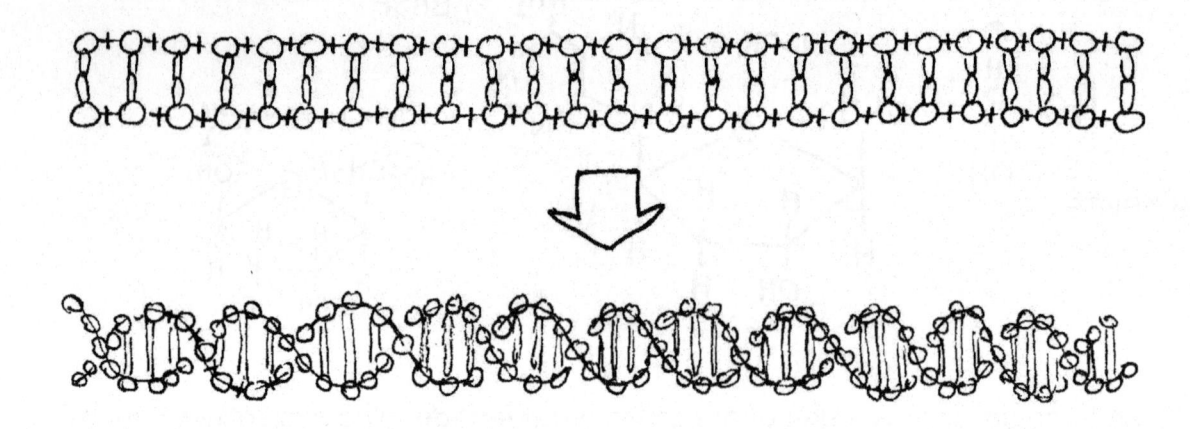

This shape is called a **double helix**. (Each side of the ladder is a single helix, so together they form a double helix.) The discovery of the shape of DNA was one of the landmark scientific discoveries of all time. Strange as it may seem, scientists knew about the information contained in DNA long before they actually knew what it looked like. Then, in 1953, **James Watson and Francis Crick** announced to the world that they had figured out the structure of the DNA molecule. They had used principles of physics, chemistry, and mathematics, along with X-ray diffraction experiments and ball-and-stick models. For their excellent work they were awarded the Nobel prize in 1962.

Now for the grand finale of the chapter! We are going to see how those amino acids are related to DNA. Bases come in sets of three. Three bases form a code for one amino acid. For example, CGC always means arginine, and GGC always means glycine. (There are even combinations that mean "stop" just like a period in a sentence!)

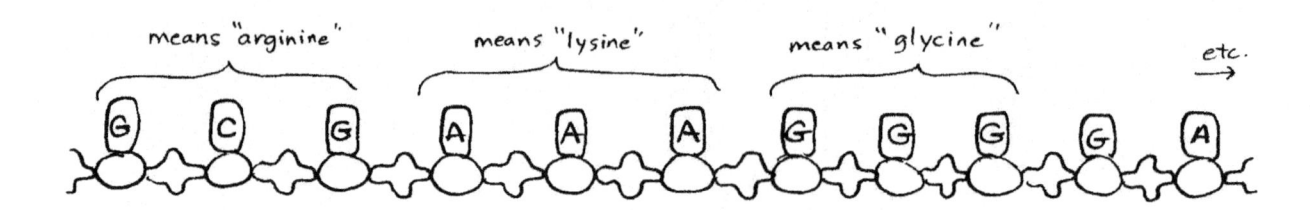

The pattern of these triplet sets tells how to assemble a certain protein using amino acids. (You'll remember that proteins are polymers made of amino acids.)

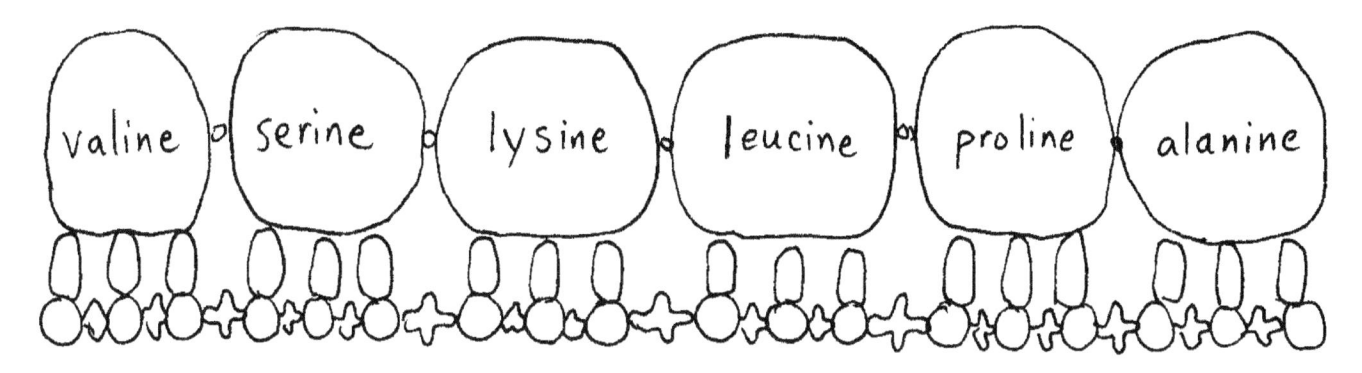

valine — serine — lysine — leucine — proline — alanine

Certain manufacturing sites in your cells "read" this information from the DNA and "learn" how to make a particular protein. Each cell is programmed to make just one kind of protein.

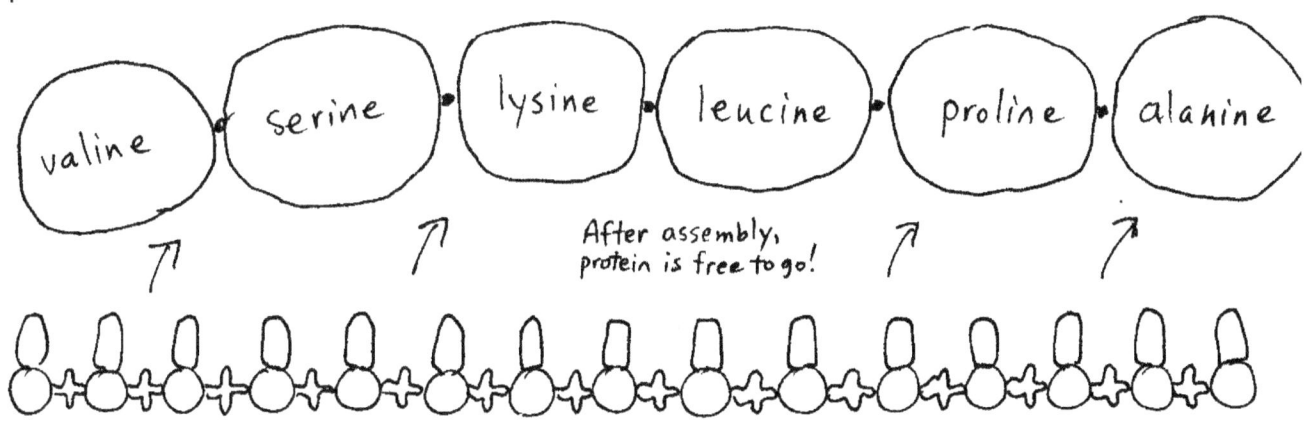

valine — serine — lysine — leucine — proline — alanine

After assembly, protein is free to go!

After these long chains of amino "beads" are complete, your cells then curl them into helix shapes, or fold them into pleated ribbons. Then those helices and ribbons get folded again, this time into complex shapes you can't describe with words. Each amino acid has characteristics (electrical, chemical, physical) that cause it to "like" or "dislike" other amino acids or other substances such as water. As each amino acid moves toward things it "likes" and away from things it "hates" the protein acquires a unique shape.

The shape of a protein is what determines what job it will do. On page 71 we saw that enzymes have shapes that fit into other molecules, like a key fits into its lock. The shape has to be exact. Other proteins act like messengers. Some provide transportation for other molecules. The shape of muscle proteins allows them to slide back and forth, causing movement. Antibody proteins have shapes that allow them to bind to foreign invaders so they can be destroyed.

There are millions of different types of proteins in your body, so DNA contains an incredible amount of information! If you uncoiled your DNA, it would be about 6 feet long. Big deal, right? That doesn't seem very long. But remember, the thickness would still be microscopic. If we increased the size of the DNA so that it was as thick as a piece of thread, the length would then be over 100 miles!

Comprehension self-check

1) Plants are made of _____, animals are made of _____.
2) Proteins are polymers made of individual units called _____ _____.
3) Unlike carbohydrates and fats, proteins contain the element _____.
4) Amino acids are acids so they must have this functional group: _____.
5) The attraction that holds two amino acids together is called a _____ bond.
6) Small chains of amino acids are called _____.
7) Another way proteins are different from carbohydrates and fats is that they contain _____ _____.
8) The protein's "secret code" is the unique arrangement of its _____ _____.
9) The shape of a protein will determine _____.
10) A type of protein that acts as a catalyst is called an _____.
11) How do you stop an enzyme from working? _____ _____ _____.
12) Proteins of wool, hair and muscles take this shape: _____.
13) What three parts do you need to make DNA? _____, _____, and _____.
14) What does DNA stand for? _____.
15) What does deoxy- mean? _____.
16) What is ribose? _____.
17) What elements are in a phosphate? _____, _____, and _____
18) Name the four bases: _____, _____, _____, and _____
19) When ribose, a base, and a phosphate are stuck together, they make a _____
20) Who discovered the shape of DNA? _____.
21) Three bases form a code for one _____ _____.
22) One cell makes this many types of proteins: _____.
23) If you uncoiled the DNA in one of your cells, how long would it be? _____
24) Remember, a protein is a polymer made of _____ _____.
25) Where does information come from? (in your own words) _____ _____.

On-line research

1) What is the name of the enzyme made in your stomach that breaks apart the peptide bonds in proteins?

2) Can you find the name of the cell organelle that builds protein chains? Is it inside or outside the nucleus of the cell?

3) Who was Gregor Mendel and what did he do that is relevant to this chapter?

Chapter Eleven: Carbon Oxides and the Carbon Cycle

In chapter one, we stared out with just the carbon atom. It was so easy. By chapter ten we were looking at DNA, the most complicated molecule in the universe! Let's end our study by going back to something relatively simple: carbon attached to just one or two oxygens. We'll start with a carbon and two oxygens: **carbon dioxide**.

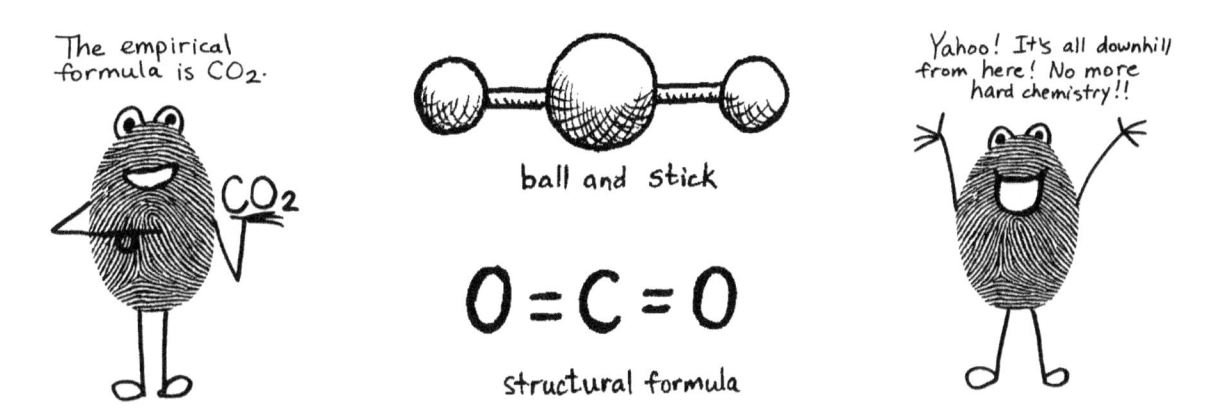

The empirical formula is CO_2.

ball and stick

$$O = C = O$$
structural formula

Yahoo! It's all downhill from here! No more hard chemistry!!

Refreshingly, simple, isn't it? No functional groups, no glycerol clamps, no hydrophobic tails, no complicated geometry. The only tricky thing about it is that the bonds between the atoms must be double bonds, because carbon must have four bonds coming from it.

Carbon dioxide is a natural part of our world. Animals make it, and plants use it. Carbon dioxide and oxygen are traded back and forth from animals to plants.

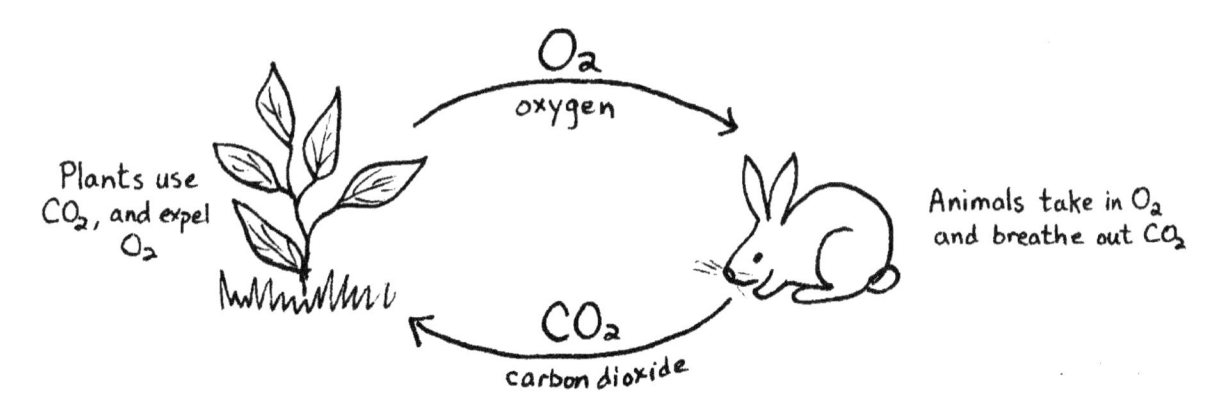

Plants use CO_2, and expel O_2

O_2 oxygen

CO_2 carbon dioxide

Animals take in O_2 and breathe out CO_2

Animals are not the only source of carbon dioxide, however. The Earth itself produces large amounts of it. Volcanoes belch out huge amounts of carbon dioxide. There are natural carbon dioxide vents at various points around the globe that put out as much as 200 tons of it every day. Mt. Etna, in Italy, produces 35,000 tons per day. Researchers from Penn State estimate that between Naples and Florence, there are over 150 vents, each producing hundreds of tons of carbon dioxide per day.

Some scientists estimate that human activities, such as the burning of fossil fuels, may put as much as 25 billion tons of carbon dioxide into the air each year. These scientists also estimate that the plants and oceans of earth can remove 15 billion tons per year. If these estimates are correct, that leaves a 10 billion ton surplus of carbon dioxide each year. Many people are concerned that this increase of CO_2 levels in the atmosphere could contribute to the gradual warming ("global warming") of the earth due to the ability of CO_2 to trap heat in the atmosphere. This is called the "greenhouse" effect. It is a very controversial subject, and one that deserves truly scientific study, unaffected by politics. Some people claim that politicians are all too eager to use this topic to accomplish their political goals. We're not going to delve any deeper. You can study this topic on your own.

The next molecule we are going to look at is carbon with only one oxygen: **carbon monoxide**.

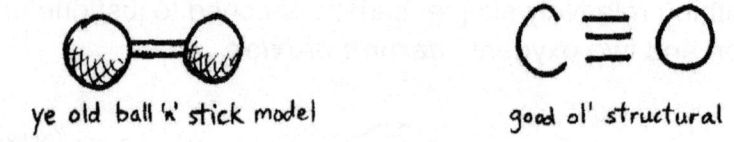

ye old ball 'n' stick model

$C \equiv O$

good ol' structural

How can this be? Carbon must have four bonds, and oxygen can only form two bonds. How does it take on three? Truthfully, chemists can't fully understand it or explain it.

Sometimes it is drawn like this:

$\overset{\ominus}{C} \equiv \overset{\oplus}{O}$

However it is drawn or explained, it's an anomaly. That means it's an exception to the rules. It shouldn't exist, but it does.

Carbon monoxide is often a byproduct of the combustion of fossil fuels. When octane (gasoline) is burned in engines, the chemical formula is something like this:

$$2\ C_8H_{18} + 25\ O_2 \rightarrow 18\ H_2O + 16\ CO_2$$
octane   oxygen   water   carbon dioxide

No carbon monoxide is formed in this reaction. The problem comes when there is not enough oxygen on the left side of the equation. What if there aren't 25 oxygens available for every two octanes? Some of those carbon dioxides end up with only one oxygen, making them into carbon monoxide.

$$2\ C_8H_{18} + 23\ O_2 \rightarrow 18\ H_2O + 12\ CO_2 + 4\ CO$$
octane   not enough oxygen   water carbon dioxide carbon monoxide

Carbon monoxide is bad stuff. Because carbon needs to have four bonds, it's out to fix the problem, not matter the cost. One thing carbon monoxide loves to bond with is the hemoglobin in your blood. It adores that iron atom sitting in the middle of your hemoglobin.

Oh, no! He's moving in on my territory!

Hellooo, iron! Wanna go for a ride with me?

Help! I need oxygen!

A cell calling to hemoglobin from off-stage.

The only problem is that the iron atom has a job: transporting oxygen to your cells. But the CO doesn't care. It comes and attaches itself to the hemoglobin anyway. So off goes the hemoglobin to make its delivery to one of your cells. When the cell, which is desperately in need of oxygen, reaches out to take the oxygen off the hemoglobin, it finds... carbon monoxide?!! "I can't use this stuff!" the cell complains. "Go back to the lungs and get an oxygen for me!" The hemoglobin goes back to the lungs, but the carbon monoxide just won't get off! It's stuck! Crisis!

When this happens to a lot of your hemoglobin cells, it is called carbon monoxide poisoning and it can kill you. Since carbon monoxide has no smell, you can't rely on your nose to tell you if you are experiencing high levels of carbon monoxide. You don't know it's there until you start feeling sleepy. But feeling sleepy is not always unpleasant, so you don't immediately sense danger. Then you fall asleep and never wake up.

Since carbon monoxide can also be a byproduct of combustion in devices that heat homes, many homes are now equipped with carbon monoxide detectors. These devices work like smoke detectors, emitting a loud beeping noise.

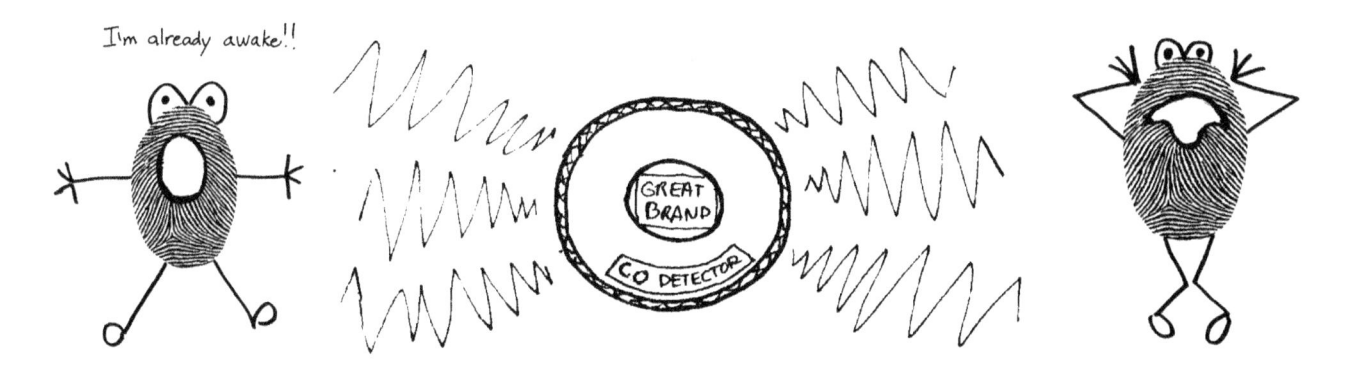

When carbon combines with three oxygens, we call it the **carbonate ion**, written like this: CO_3^{2-} and drawn like this:

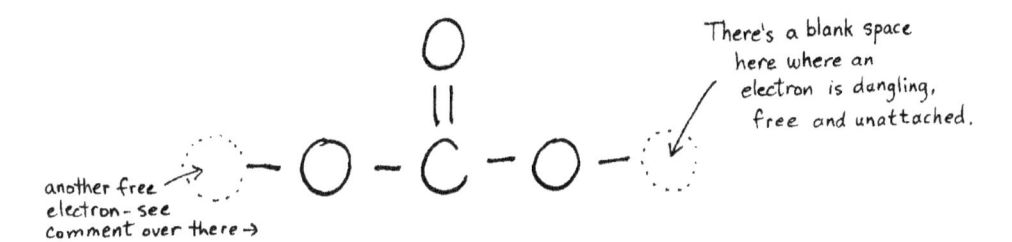

Carbon is happy, but two of the oxygens are not. Oxygen atoms need to make two bonds. These two oxygens have electrons dangling, unbonded. Since electrons have a negative electrical charge, these two unbonded electrons give this molecule an electrical charge of negative two. That's what the 2- means when we write CO_3^{2-}.

An atom or molecule with an electrical charge is called an ion. CO_3^{2-} is called the carbonate ion, and is found in all sorts of places. The carbonate ion can "clean up" unwanted mineral ions from water. Water with too many mineral ions is called "hard' water and can cause problems in water pipes. (Notice the 2+ on magnesium. This means a positive electrical charge of 2. It's the exact opposite of CO_3, which means they are a perfect match for each other.)

$$Mg^{2+} + CO_3^{2-} \rightarrow MgCO_3$$

You will find the carbonate ion in the kitchen, too. Baking soda is the common name for the chemical compound called sodium bicarbonate: $NaHCO_3$. It's job in a recipe is to react with an mild acid, producing gas bubbles (carbon dioxide!) which make the food rise when baked, produced a light, fluffy texture.

with baking soda

without baking soda

In geology, the carbonate ion shows up in limestone, which is made of calcium carbonate, $CaCO_3$. Limestone caves are a fascinating display of what carbon dioxide and calcium carbonate can do. Carbon dioxide in the air dissolved in rainwater, forming carbonic acid, which then seeped into the ground. As the carbonic acid penetrated into areas of limestone, it dissolved away areas of the stone, creating caverns and tunnels.

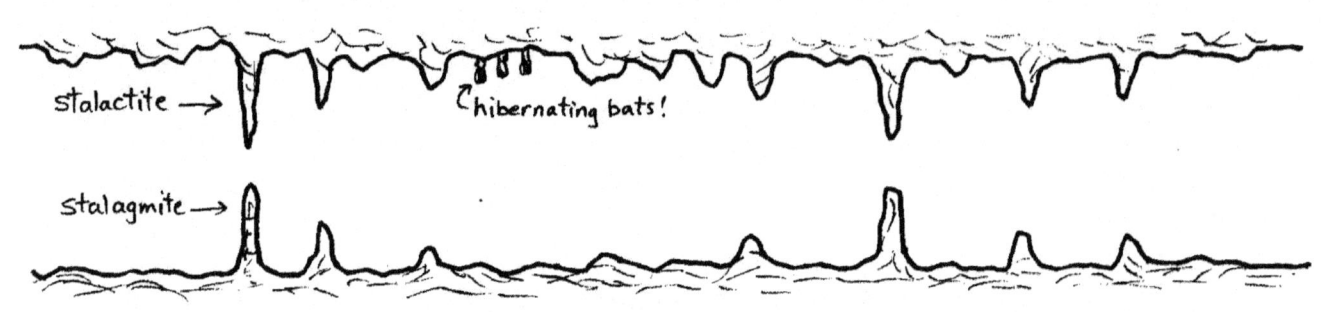

stalactite →

hibernating bats!

stalagmite →

The stalactites and stalagmites are reverse examples of the dissolving process. Water, saturated with calcium carbonate, evaporates and leaves behind deposits of calcium carbonate.

The famous white cliffs of Dover (on the southern coast of England) are another geological example of calcium carbonate.

In the ocean, calcium carbonate is found in seashells and coral. It is the "stuff" that these structures are made of. Chemically, there is not much difference between limestone and seashells.

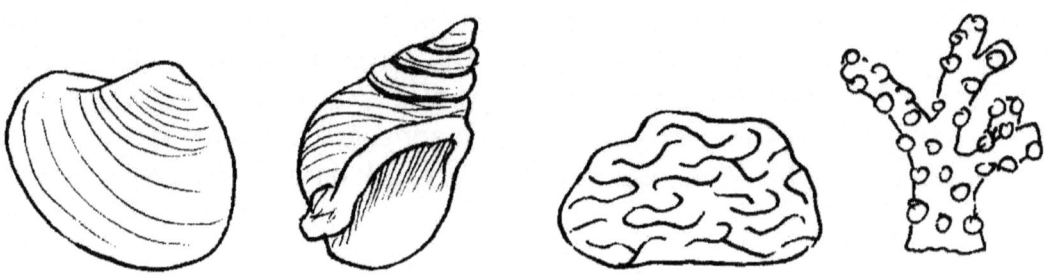

I think this is my favorite page of the whole book!

In biology, we find calcium carbonate in egg shells.

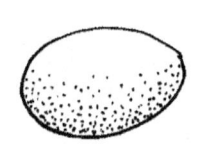

80

This chemical similarity in such an array of seemingly unrelated things is a good introduction to our last topic: ***the carbon cycle***.

A carbon atom is a carbon atom, no matter where it is found. A carbon atom found in an eggshell is the very same as a carbon atom found in polyethylene plastic or in DNA. In fact, a carbon atom can switch from one molecule to another. When a plant takes in CO_2, it tears this molecule apart and uses the carbons and oxygens separately. It puts the carbon atom into a glucose molecule. So the very same atom that was floating around in the atmosphere as carbon dioxide ends up in a molecule of sugar!

From there, the carbon travels around through animal bodies being converted into various starches or proteins. When the animal or plant dies, bacteria decompose the body and take the carbon out of the sugar and make it into either carbon dioxide or methane.

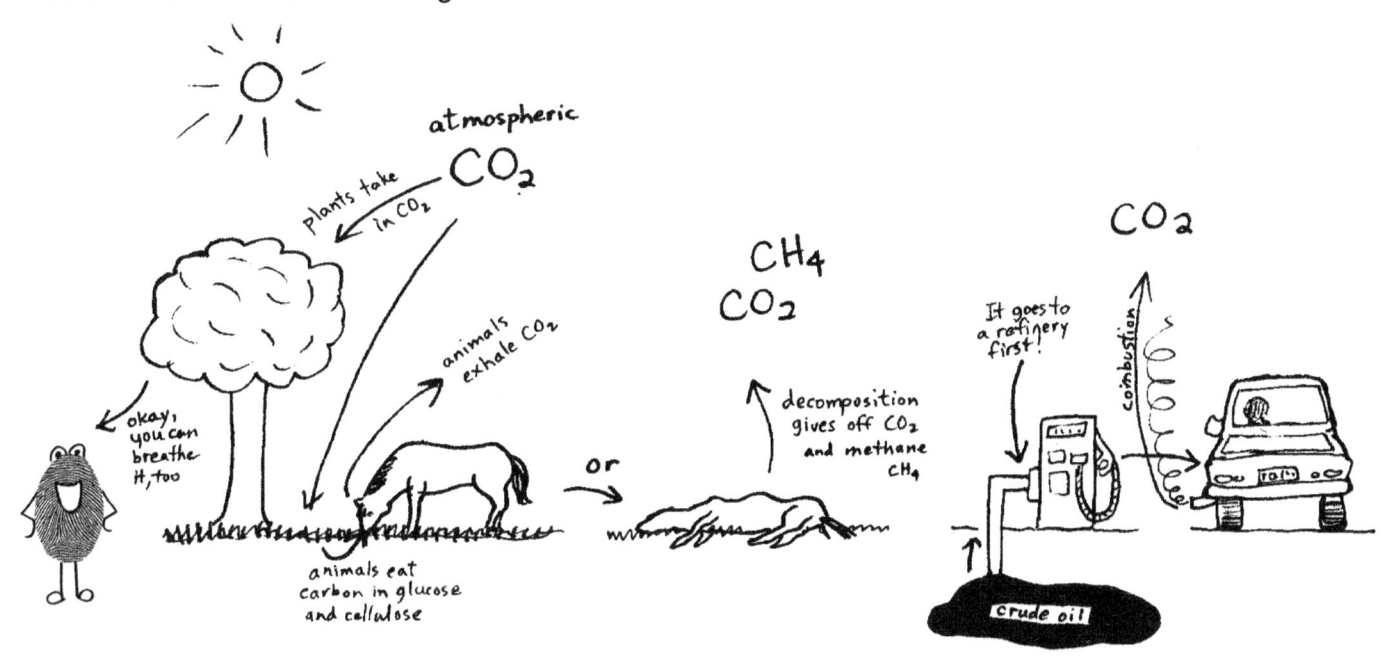

The carbon dioxide is ready to start the whole cycle again, being taken in by a plant and converted to glucose. The methane could be collected and used as cooking fuel, or it could be used as a raw material to manufacture plastics.

In the ancient past, decomposition, along with extreme pressure, caused the carbons from ancient plants and animals to turn into hydrocarbon chains. Crude oil was once proteins and carbohydrates in living organisms. This part of the carbon cycle has not happened recently. Scientists speculate that it could happen again, given the right circumstances, so it is technically included as part of the carbon cycle.

The carbons found in petroleum are put back into the atmosphere by combustion. Remember the formula we just saw? It said that octane reacts with oxygen to produce water and carbon dioxide.

$$2 C_8H_{18} + 25 O_2 \rightarrow 18 H_2O + 16 CO_2$$

Not all petroleum is used for fuel. Some of it goes to plastics industries. As you know from previous chapters, crude oil is the raw material used to make paints, plastics and nasty solvents. Some lucky carbon atoms end up as milk jugs and plastic toys. What is their fate? Sometimes they get recycled, but a lot end up in landfills.

Comprehension self-check

This is the last round of questions!

1) CO_2 is _____ _____.
2) What kind of living organism needs CO_2? _____
3) What kind of living organism produces CO_2? _____
4) Name two non-living sources of CO_2: _____, _____
5) Some scientists are concerned that increasing levels of CO_2 in the atmosphere are producing _____.
6) CO is _____ _____.
7) Most CO is produced by _____.
8) CO can poison you by bonding to your _____ molecules.
9) What is the first symptom of CO poisoning? _____
10) CO_3 is called the _____ ion.
11) CO_3 has an electrical charge of _____.
12) Name two geological examples of calcium carbonate: _____
13) Where is calcium carbonate found in the ocean? _____
14) Plants take the carbon atoms out of CO_2 and put them into _____.
15) Carbon atoms in petroleum go through combustion and end up in the _____ as _____

On-line research

1) When carbon dioxide is made so cold that it turns into a solid, it is called _____ The temperature at which this happens is ____ °C (____°F)

2) Name five countries where you will find limestone caves:

3) Draw a very simple diagram illustrating what "the greenhouse effect" means:

Bibliography

These are the books I read to learn about organic chemistry. (I did not copy anything out of these books. Everything written in this curriculum is my own writing.)

<u>Chemistry for Changing Times</u>, 8th edition, by John W. Hill and Doris K. Kolb, published by Prentice-Hall, Inc., Upper Saddle River, NJ. © 1998, ISBN 0-13-741786-1 (General chemistry textbook intended for high school or for college non-science majors.)

<u>Chemistry of Carbon Compounds</u>, 3rd edition, by David E. Newton, published by J. Weston Walch, Publisher, Box 658, Portland, Maine 04104.
© 1994, ISBN 0-8251-2487-5 (Organic chemistry text intend for advanced placement high school or entry level college.)

<u>Contemporary Chemistry; A Practical Approach</u>, by Leonard Saland, published by J. Weston Walch, Publisher, Box 658, Portland, Maine, 04104. ©1986, ISBN 0-8251-1799-2 (Leonard Saland is the chairman of the Physical Science Dept. at Louis Brandeis High School in New York.)

Penn State Earth and Mineral Sciences bulletin, Volume 66, 1997. (Article on research into Italy's carbon dioxide vents.)

"Hands-On Plastics," a scientific investigation curriculum put together by the American Plastics Council, 1801 K Street NW, Suite 701-L, Washington D. C., 20006. (Reference for experiment on identifying types of plastics.)

I also used websites quite a bit. Here are the main ones I read, listed in order of how much I used them. I highly recommend going to them yourself!

www.Howitworks.com (one of my favorites!)
www.Chemed.chem.purdue.edu
www.Encyclopedia.com
www.Infoplease.com
www.chemistry.uakron.edu/genobc
www.elmhurst.ude/~chm/vchembook
www.medic8.com/healthguide/articles/exerciseanddiabetes
www.nexusresearchgroup.com/fun-science/fun.sci.htm
http://arbl/cvmbs/colostate.edu/hbooks/pathphys/digestion
www.post-gazette.com (for almond cookie recipe)

Answer Key

ANSWERS

PAGE 6:

Comprehension self-check:
1) protons, neutrons, electrons
2) electron cloud model, solar system model, ball and stick model
3) electron cloud
4) ball and stick
5) solar system
6) solar system
7) ball and stick
8) pea, football stadium, pinhead, upper decks
9) protons
10) atomic
11) It tries to borrow or share electrons with another atom (or atoms).
12) double bond
13) diamond, graphite, buckyball
14) buckyball
15) coal and charcoal

On-line research:
1) Niels Bohr
2) blue, green, pink/purple, and various shades of yellow (including canary yellow, fancy yellow)
3) The information we found said that a team of Swedish scientists did it on Feb. 16, 1953, but never got credit for it. The credit usually goes to GE employee Tracy Hall, on Dec. 16, 1954.
4) Activated charcoal has been treated with oxygen in order to open up spaces between the carbon atoms. This increases the number of bonding sites available for molecules to stick to. It is used in filters because the carbon atoms will catch and keep molecules that pass through.
5) Coke is charcoal that has been baked in a low-oxygen environment, in order to purify the carbon. Just like charcoal is made from wood, coke is made from charcoal. Coke will produce even more heat than charcoal, and is used in the production of steel.

PAGE 13:

Comprehension self-check:
1) methane
2) structural formula, ball and stick, space-filling model
3) natural
4) yes
5) intestinal tract
6) alkanes
7) International Union of Pure and Applied Chemistry
8) meth, eth, prop, but, pent, hex, hept, oct, non, dec
9) gasoline
10) knocking in the engine
11) gases, liquids, solids
12) crude
13) refinery
14) distillation
15) cracking
16) Chlorine, bromine, and fluorine are the ones we have in mind.
17) chlorine, fluorine, carbon
18) insects, birds, fish, other animals
19) make people unconscious
20) isomers

On-line research:
1) Saudi Arabia, Iraq, Iran, Kuwait, Qatar, Libya, Nigeria, United Arab Emirates, Algeria, Indonesia, Venezuela, Russia, Mexico, United States, and countries around the North Sea such as Norway and the UK.
2) Pennsylvania, West Virginia, Illinois, Indiana, Kentucky, Ohio, Colorado, Utah, Montana, Texas, Wyoming
3) Since 1919
4) Ozone is made of three oxygen atoms. In the atmosphere it helps to stop ultraviolet radiation from reaching the surface of the earth.
5) Humphry Davy
6) Yes, they really did!

PAGE 14:

Hydrocarbon puzzle answers, from top to bottom: methane, refinery, distillation, fluorine, octane, cracking, alkane (or butane), propane, flammable, ozone, butane (or alkane)

"Cross One Out"
1) rubbing alcohol, 2) fermentation, 3) ethyne, 4) mountain tops, 5) C_2H_2, 6) helium

PAGE 19:
Comprehension self-check:
1) single, double, triple
2) ripening fruit
3) saturated
4) unsaturated
5) aromatic hydrocarbons
6) sleeping
7) one
8) two
9) moth balls
10) a moth

On-line research:
1) Xylene is a colorless, sweet-smelling, flammable liquid that is made from petroleum, as well as occurring as a by-product of forest fires. It is used as a solvent or as an ingredient in the paint, varnish, rubber, and leather industries.
2) Xylene's molecular structure could be any of these isomers:

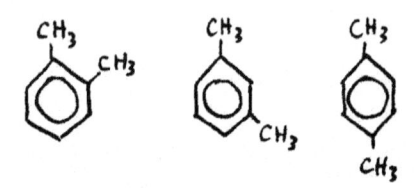

3) High levels of exposure to xylene causes neurological symptoms such as headaches, dizziness, confusion, muscle fatigue, difficulty breathing. It can also cause irritation to eyes, nose, throat, and lungs. It has not been found to cause cancer.
4) Xylene evaporates quickly into the environment. In the air it is broken down by sunlight. In water and soil, it is broken down by microorganisms.
5) No.

PAGE 35:
Comprehension self-check:
1) yes
2) sour
3) almond
4) yes
5) dynamite, heart medicine
6) ester
7) soap
8) "water-loving"
9) "water-fearing"
10) both
11) blood pressure, body temperature, stomach acid, muscle contraction, pregnancy, menstruation, inflammation, pain, and many more not mentioned in this chapter.

PAGE 26:
Comprehension self-check:
1) functional groups
2) methanol, ethanol, isopropanol
3) methyl alcohol (wood alcohol), ethyl alcohol (grain alcohol), isopropyl alcohol (rubbing alcohol)
4) ethanol
5) -OH
6) foul and strong
7) kitchen
8) ant
9) formalin
10) acetone
11) esters
12) banana
13) put people to sleep
14) gasoline
15) phenols, amines, amides

On-line research:
1) Up to 6%. Whiskey can be as high as 90% (180 proof) but is general more like 45% (90 proof). Wine is generally 6-15%. These are just general figures, and could vary slightly.
2) .08 -.10
3) This will depend upon your state and the level of blood alcohol.
4) Ethanol (grain alcohol) that is being manufactured for scientific or industrial purposes and must have foul-tasting chemicals added to it to make sure no one will drink it. (Because of financial concerns, not health concerns.)
5) There are a multitude of uses related to cleaning, sanitizing, laundry, and dyeing.

12) any of the examples on page 32
13) the Calabar bean
14) benzene ring, pyrrole ring
15) melting points

On-line research:
1) An employee of the Ivory soap company accidentally left the mixing machine on over the lunch hour. When he came back the mixture was all frothy, but he went ahead and poured the mixture into the molds. After these bars had been sold and used, people started writing to the company asking about the "floating soap." The company investigated what had happened and this story came to light.
2) The chocolate molecule:

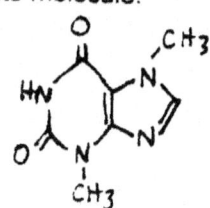

PAGE 36:
The joke is: "How long was the gypsy moth fooled by the pheromone trap?
Punch line is "Just pheromone-ment!"

PAGE 44:
Comprehension self-check:
1) many
2) catalyst
3) polyethylene
4) low density and high density
5) long chains with no side branches
6) long chains with lots of side branches
7) low density
8) bags and squeeze bottles
9) thermoplastic
10) thermoplastic
11) propene
12) polystyrene
13) polyvinyl chloride
14) It was flammable.
15) no

On-line research:
1) No. Coating fruits and vegetables; used for shiny coating on medicine tablets, chocolates and playing cards; used as ingredient in wax, rubber, and cosmetics; used to coat dental molds; used as a hat stiffener; once upon a time used for phonograph records. You may find more uses that are not on this list!
2) Photographic paper called Velox. He sold this invention to Kodak in 1899 for a million dollars.
3) Somerset, England. (bakelitemuseum.co.uk)
4) Nylon was invented to be a replacement for natural silk. Nylon has similar chemistry to silk, because it contains a functional group called "amide." The process of making nylon is very similar to how a spider spins its silk. As the liquid polymer is extruded, upon contact with the air, it hardens into a very strong and thin fiber. Artificial nylon is also "spun" by extrusion into very thin fibers.

PAGE 45:
Section 1: Who Am I?
1) B 2) F 3) D 4) E 5) A 6) C 7) H 8) G
Section 2: Matching
9) G 10) C 11) A 12) D 13) E 14) H 15) B 16) F
Section 3: You respond
17) "fear of water" or "water-hating"
18) and 19) Name any of the facts listed on page 32
20) ester
21) yes
22) no smell, nothing
23) benzene ring
24) ant
25) preserve biological specimens
Section 4: True or False
26) F 27) T 28) T 29) T 30) T
31) F (Esters smell good, ethers smell bad.)
32) F (Esters are used as flavorings, not ethers.)
33) T 34) T 35) T
36) F (It is produced by ripening fruit!)
37) T
38) T
39-40) The benzene ring without any letters:

PAGE 51:
Comprehension self-check:
1) South and Central America
2) The same thing we do with it: water-proofing, rubber balls, rubber containers.
3) Joseph Priestly used it as an eraser, to rub off pencil marks.
4) Charles Macintosh
5) Charles Goodyear
6) sulfur
7) Makes it stay flexible in the cold (doesn't get brittle), and helps it not to melt in the heat.
8) Indonesia and Sri Lanka
9) The climate in England is not suitable for growing tropical plants.
10) isoprene
11) cross-link
12) elastomers
13) man-made
14) four
15) water-proofing, lubricants, polishes, hydraulic fluid
16) viscous
17) Our opinion is: water, vegetable oil, maple syrup, shampoo, ketchup, Vaseline™, Silly Putty™
18) It sure does!
19) no
20) yes

PAGE 52:
"1-800-4REVIEW"

ELASTOMER 35278663R
POLYMER 765963R
LATEX 528E9
RUBBER R82237
CHICLE 244C53
GUM 486
ISOPRENE 4767736E
VISCOUS 847C687
SULFUR 7U5387
BRAZIL 2R2945
SAPODILLA S27634552
CROSSLINK C76775465
PRIESTLY P7437859
GOODYEAR 466D9327
MACINTOSH 62246T674
VULCANIZATION 8U5226492846N
INDONESIA 4N3663742

PAGE 62:
Comprehension self-check:
1) carbon, hydrogen, oxygen
2) sugar
3) chain, ring (circle)
4) energy, sun
5) stored glucose
6) when the glucose in the bloodstream is gone
7) tells the body to make glucose into glycogen
8) diabetes (type 1)
9) overeating sugar for a long period of time
10) high blood pressure, heart disease, stroke, depression, confusion, fatigue, kidney problems, osteoporosis, blindness
11) fat
12) fat and protein
13) glucose
14) fructose
15) disaccharide
16) lactose, lactase
17) milk intolerant, or lactose intolerant
18) sucrose, glucose and fructose
19) starch and cellulose
20) cellulose
21) fiber, roughage
22) a string of many simple sugars
23) stiffening fabrics, making craft projects
24) saccharin
25) by accident

On-line research:
1) sheep, goats, llamas, alpacas, camels
2) ribose, erythrose, threose, glyceraldehydes, dihydroxyacetone, 2-deoxyribose (Ribose was the one we had in mind, because it will show up in chapter 10.)
3) frequent urination, excessive thirst or hunger, weight loss, fatigue, irritability, blurry vision

PAGE 68:
Comprehension self-check:
1) lipids, dissolve
2) sodium
3) glycerol
4) hydrocarbon chain, acid (COOH)
5) single
6) double
7) double
8) cell membrane
9) wall
10) essential
11) olive, soybean, fish
12) across
13) cis, trans
14) spoil, go rancid
15) have a better texture for baking
16) trans fat
17) yes
18) It tastes good!
19) HDL, LDL
20) store energy, cushion and protect organs, insulate against cold, look nice under the skin

On-line research:
1) HDL: Over 60 is good, LDL: Under 100 Total: Less than 200.
2) Answers will vary.
3) Atkins diet is based on eating protein and fat and very little carbohydrate. Most diet plans recommend low-fat, whereas Atkins tells you to eat fat.

PAGE 78:
Comprehension self-check:
1) cellulose, protein
2) amino acids
3) nitrogen
4) COOH
5) peptide
6) polypeptide
7) information
8) amino acids
9) function in the body
10) enzyme
11) an inhibitor
12) helix
13) sugar, base, phosphate
14) deoxyribonucleic acid
15) without oxygen
16) a sugar
17) phosphorus, oxygen, hydrogen
18) adenine, thymine, cytosine, guanine
19) nucleotide
20) Watson and Crick
21) amino acid
22) one
23) 6 ft (approximately)
24) amino acids
25) From intelligence.

On-line research:
1) pepsin
2) ribosomes, outside the nucleus
3) Gregor Mendel was a monk who lived in the 1800's and experimented with pea plants. He discovered the science of heredity (genetics).

PAGE 84:
Comprehension self-check:
1) carbon dioxide
2) plants
3) animals
4) volcanoes, carbon dioxide vents, cars, factories, you may think of others
5) global warming (greenhouse effect)
6) carbon monoxide
7) combustion of fossil fuels
8) hemoglobin
9) feeling sleepy
10) carbonate
11) -2
12) Dover's white chalk cliffs, caves and cave formations, you may think of more
13) shells, corals, sea water
14) glucose
15) air carbon dioxide or carbon monoxide

On-line research:
1) dry ice
2) United States, most of the European countries, lots of the Caribbean countries, and Asian countries such as China, Cambodia, Vietnam. You may find others.
3) Diagram of greenhouse effect:

Teacher's Section

Lots of extra activities and experiments!

Chapter One Activities

Activity 1.1: Building carbon's allotropes

Background information

The different shapes pure carbon can take (diamond, graphite, buckyballs) are called **allotropes**. Other elements have allotropes, too. Sulfur, for instance, can be found in two different crystal shapes.

You will need:
- One box of Jujubes™ candies
- Two boxes of toothpicks (round or square, not flat)

Note: If you can't find Jujubes, you can use small jelly beans. (Gummy bears and marshmallows are not recommended.) Jujubes are good to work with because they are small and hard. The small size keeps the structures from being too heavy, and the hard texture keeps the toothpicks in place. A box of Jujubes contains about 300 candies, which is more than enough to make all three models. (You could probably make two of each model, if the graphite and diamond ones are of modest size.) You will need to buy the sturdier type of toothpick with the square or round center, not the flimsy flat ones. (If you are purchasing for a group, allow three boxes of toothpicks for every one box of Jujubes, four boxes if you anticipate enthusiastic builders who will want large models.)

Instructions:

Diamond: Make sure that each carbon atom is connected to four others. The geometry will emerge naturally as a result.

Graphite: You can make several sheets of hexagons, then put them on top of each other, or you can make a flat sheet of hexagons and just build upwards on top of it.

Buckyball: Start by making 12 pentagons. Each pentagon will contain 5 candies and 5 toothpicks. A buckyball contains 60 carbon atoms, and since 12x5=60, you will not need any more candies. Now use just toothpicks to begin making each pentagon completely surrounded by six hexagons. A pentagon can't touch another pentagon.

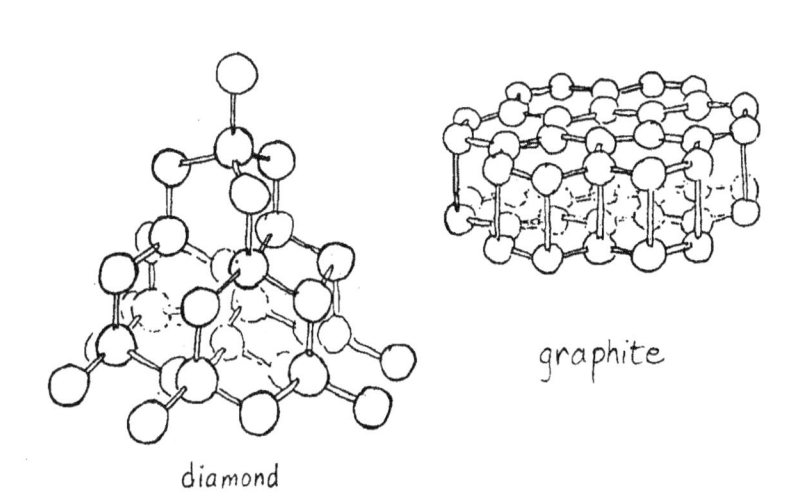

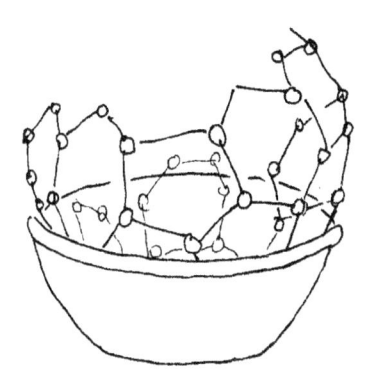

diamond

graphite

A bowl is a big help when making the buckyball!

Activity 1.2: Organic molecules card game

Background information
The molecules you will make in this game may or may not be actual molecules found in nature. There are so many organic molecules out there that, chances are, your molecules will be at least very similar to real ones.

Here is what the letters stand for: H=hydrogen, C=carbon, O=oxygen, N=nitrogen, Cl=chlorine, Br=Bromine, F=fluorine. Notice how many hydrogen cards there are in the game. 90% of all atoms in the universe are hydrogen!

The lines on the cards represent electrons that the atom would like to share with another atom.

You will need:
- to photocopy the playing card patterns onto card stock, then cut them apart into individual squares.

Note: The game can accommodate 2-6 players. If you have more than six students and decide to make more than one copy of the game, you may want to consider making each set of cards a different color. If all of your sets are the same color, there is a high likelihood that cards will get placed into the wrong deck and you will end up with one set having too many cards and another too few, and the only way to straighten them out being to painstakingly count all the cards and compare each set to the original patterns. Life is too short to spend time counting cards. Make your sets different colors.

Instructions
Give each player 5 cards. The rest go in a draw pile. Put one of the carbons (with no double bonds) face up to be the starter card. The players take turns laying down cards, trying to get rid of all their cards. The first player to get rid of all their cards wins. HOWEVER, the last card he lays down MUST complete a molecule in order to win the game. If a player lays down his last card on an incomplete molecule, he must then draw another card. He may not lay this new card down immediately, but must wait until his next turn to play it.

The lines represent bonds. You must match single bonds to single bonds and double bonds to double bonds. The molecule is complete when no bonds are "left hanging." Each bond (line) must have an atom attached to it.

Notice on the double bond O that there are dotted lines. This is so you can turn the card caddy-corner and match the double bond with two single bonds.

If a player cannot lay down a card, he must take one from the draw pile. He may lay this card down immediately if he can do so.

If a molecule is finished and all players are still holding cards, simply begin another molecule. Remember, you must use a single bond carbon (four lines) to begin a new molecule.

In order to win the game, a player must lay down his last card *as the final atom in a molecule*.

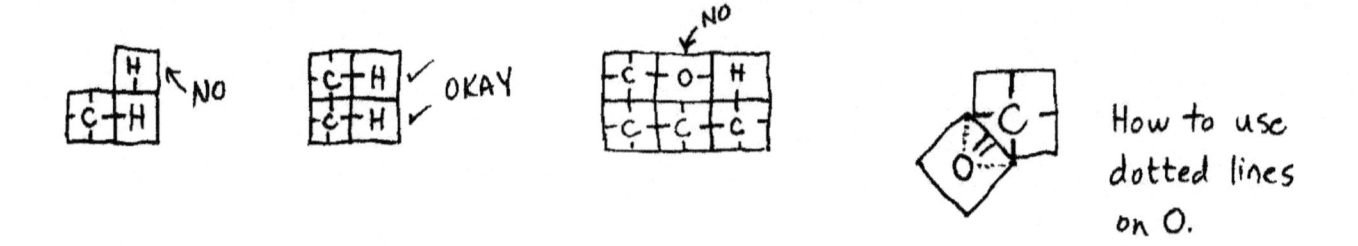

92

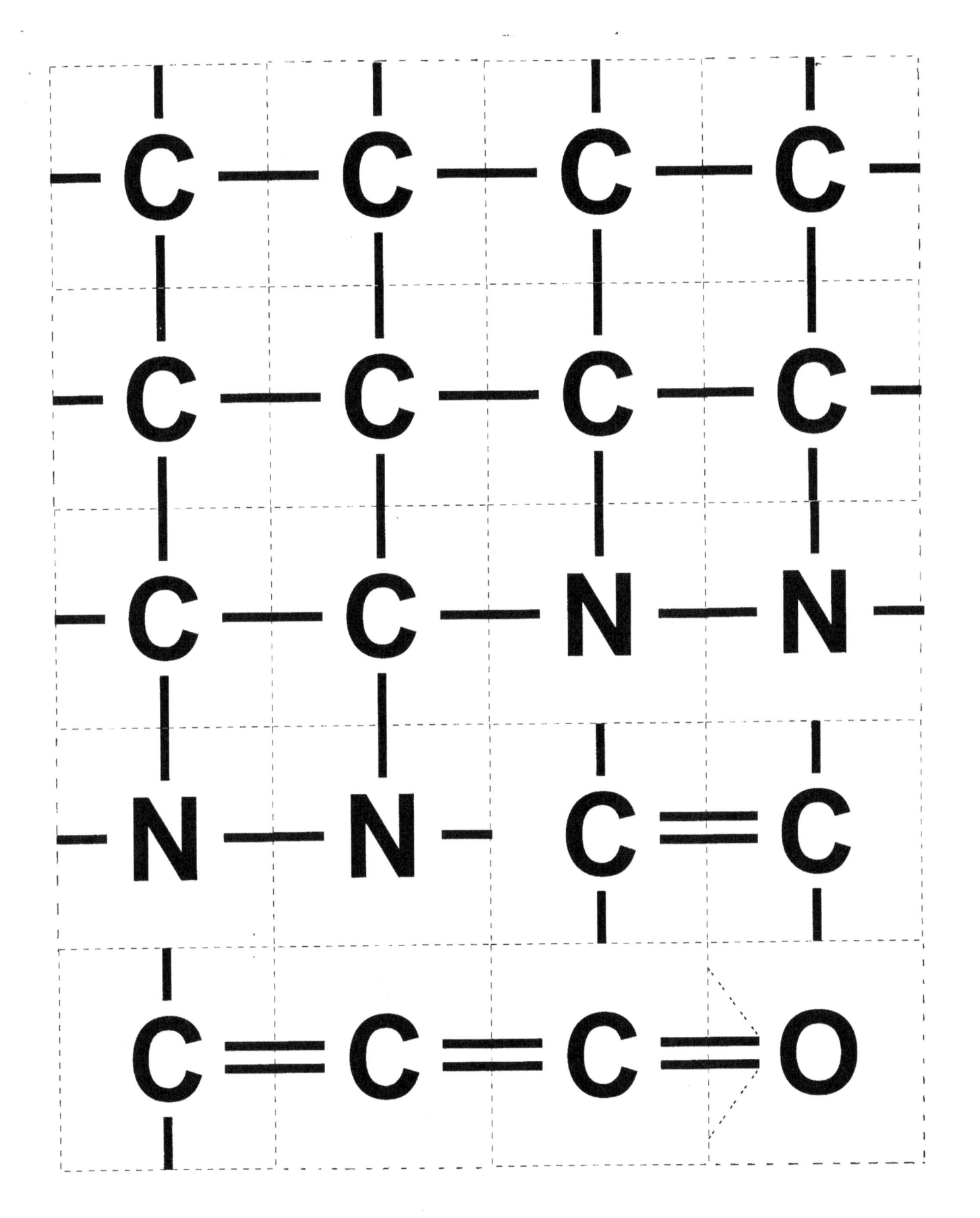

Make one copy (per game) on card stock.
If you are making mulitple copies of the game, make each game a different color (so you can easily tell which cards belong to which set).

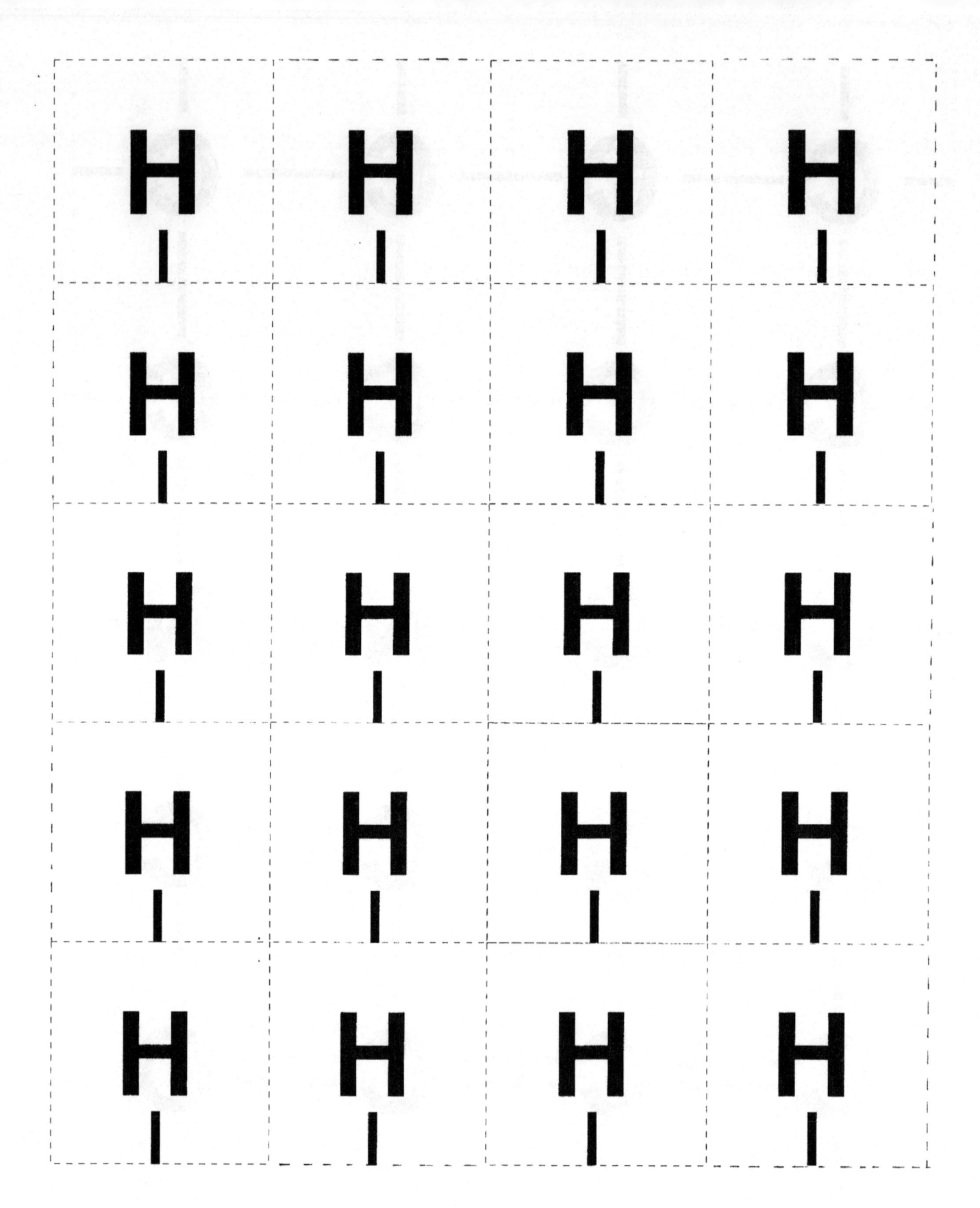

Make one copy (per game) on card stock.
If you are making mulitple copies of the game, make each game a different color (so you can easily tell which cards belong to which set).

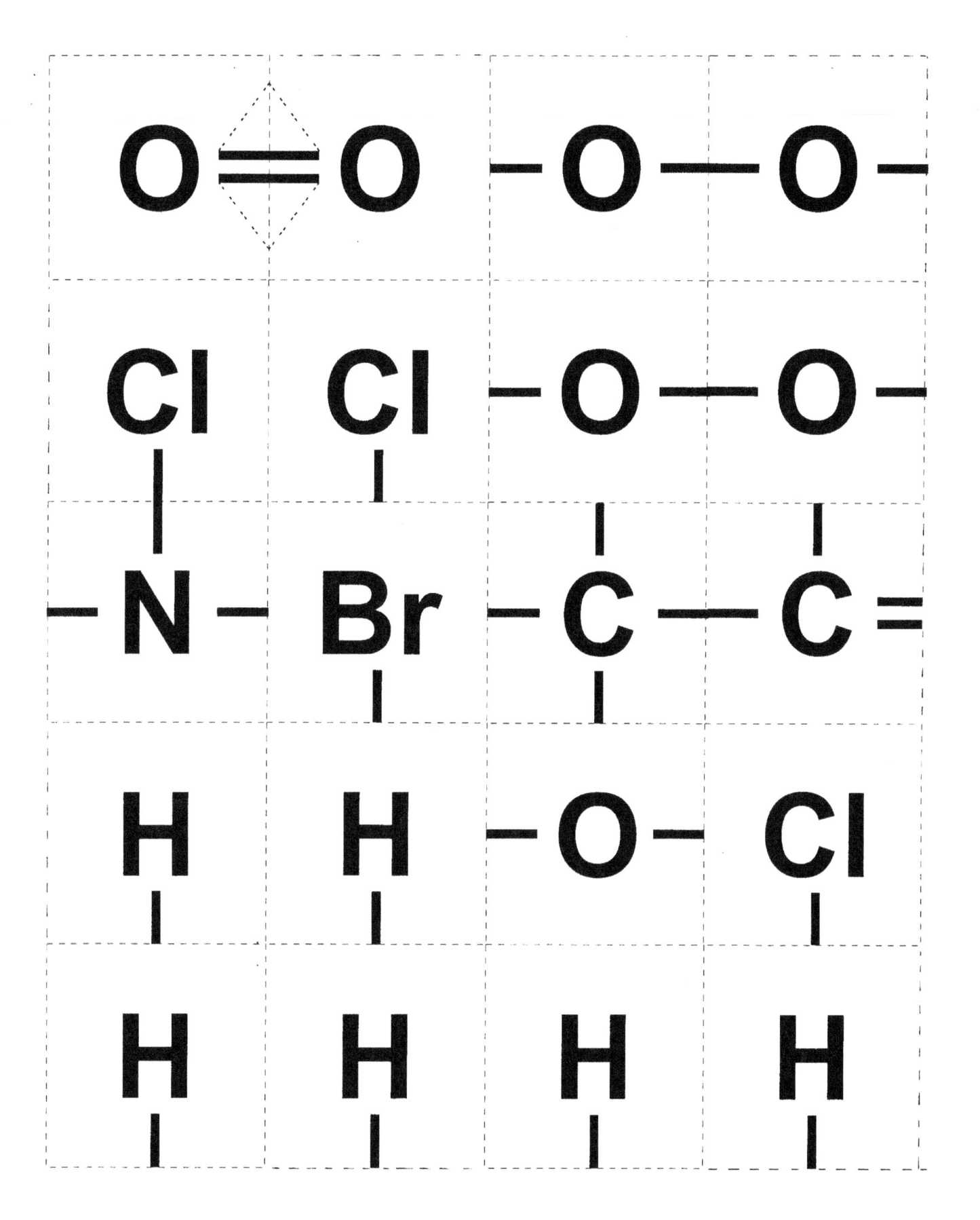

Make one copy (per game) on card stock.
If you are making mulitple copies of the game, make each game a different color (so you can easily tell which cards belong to which set).

Activity 1.3: Burning contest

Background information

Ancient people learned that if they burned wood in a low-oxygen environment they could make a black fuel that would burn longer than wood and produce more heat with less smoke.

You will need:
- charcoal briquette
- block of wood same size as briquette
- matches
- lighter fluid
- marshmallows to toast, if you want to compare quality of heat
- a safe place to do the burning

Instructions

Burn a charcoal briquette and a piece of wood the same size and compare the duration of burning and the quality of heat.

Can you re-light the charcoal you made from the wood? Why not?

Activity 4: Take a tour of a coal mine

Take a (virtual) tour of a coal mine! Log on to www.youtube.com and search for "coal mine tour." You'll get lots of options.

Chapter Two Activities

Activity 2.1: Practice Counting 1-10 Carbons

Background information

Learning to count carbons isn't any harder than counting to ten in Spanish or French. Actually, it is easier because you don't have to worry about your accent. Also, several of the prefixes are the same, or similar, to words you use in math.

You will need:
- The list in chapter two

Instructions

Practice counting a few times. Practice without looking. Practice tomorrow once or twice, and a few times the day after. Bet it won't take you long to rattle them off like a pro! Here's an additional idea: Use the tune of "One Little, Two Little, Three Little Indians" and sing these words:

Meth- little, *eth-* little, *prop-* little carbons,
But- little, *pent-* little, *hex-* little carbons,
Hept- little, *oct-* little, *non-* little carbons,
Dec- little carbon atoms.

Would you like to know more? Here is a list if you would like to continue on counting carbons. You can put "-ane" after each one to name alkanes.

11	undec-	the alkane would be "undecane"
12	dodec-	the alkane would be "dodecane"
13	tridec-	etc.
14	tetradec-	
15	pentadec-	
16	hexadec-	
17	heptadec-	
18	octadec-	(If you want a much longer list, there are some
19	nonadec-	available on-line. Just use a search engine.)
20	eicos-	
21	henicos-	
22	docos-	
23	tricos-	
24	tetracos-	
25	pentacos-	
26	hexacos-	
27	heptacos-	
28	octacos-	
29	nonacos-	
30	triacont-	
31	hentriacont-	
32	dotriacont-	
33	tritriacont-	
34	tetratriacont-	

Activity 2.2: Build some alkanes

You will need:
- Long paper strips (any colors) cut in two lengths, the shorter length being half the length of the longer one.
- Scotch tape or stapler

Note: You may want to keep these chains (hang them up if you have a classroom, store them carefully if you don't) so that you can use them for the "Polymer Party" on the last day of class.

Instructions

You will be making paper chains similar to the standard type made for parties, only these will be scientific models, as well. We suggest that you use just two colors in your chain, one for carbon and one for hydrogen. To use lots of colors, make lots of chains! Use this drawing as your pattern:

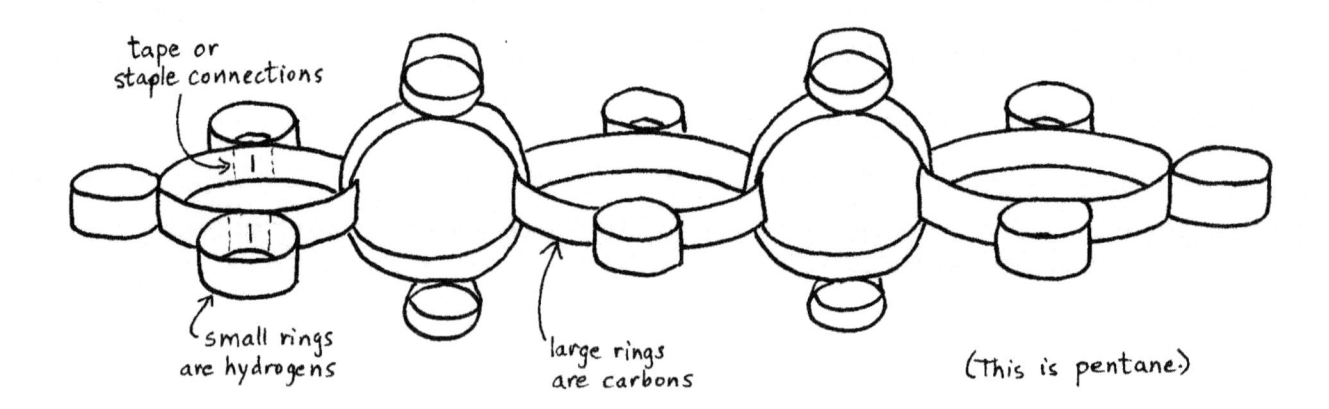

You can make the chains as short or long as you want to. Try to name the alkanes as you make them. Don't forget to put a hydrogen on the ends. Each carbon atom should be connected to four other atoms.

Activity 2.3: Build some isomers

You will need:
- Some of the cards from the card game you played in chapter one. You will need all of the H and C cards, plus a couple others (you will be using the backs of these cards, so it doesn't matter which ones you choose)
- A pencil

Instructions

Start by putting out one carbon card. Attach hydrogens. Can you make any isomers of this molecule? *(No.)*

Now lay out two carbons connected to each other. Add the hydrogens. Are there any other ways you could arrange this molecule? *(No.)*

Now add another carbon so you have a chain of three. Add the hydrogens. Are there any other ways you could arrange this molecule? Remember, you have to use all of the atoms and the bonds have to match up correctly. *(You could put the three carbons into an L shape instead of a straight line.)*

Now add a fourth carbon to the chain. Put hydrogens around. Can you rearrange these cards to form a different shape? *(Yes, the carbons could go into a T. They could also go in a "circle," that is, a square circle.)* This circular structure has a special name: cyclobutane. Can you make cyclopentane and cyclohexane?

Continue on like this. You may need to make some "spacers" using a pencil on the back of the other cards:

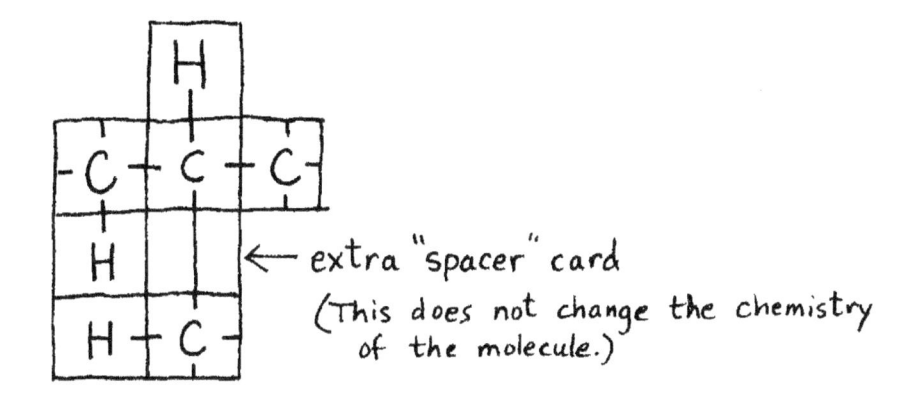

← extra "spacer" card
(This does not change the chemistry of the molecule.)

You should have enough cards to make molecules up to decane. (Remember from the text that isomers of octane, nonane, and decane are what gasoline is made of.)

If you are working in a class, you could divide up into teams that would work on one alkane each, or you could set it up as a contest to see who could come up with the most isomers or who could rearrange the molecule the fastest.

Activity 2.4: Make marbled paper using alkanes

Background information:
 Paint thinners are usually made of petroleum distillates—liquids that were distilled from petroleum at a refinery. They are about 9-16 carbons long. One of the basic properties of alkanes is that they do not mix with water; they float on the surface. We can use this property of alkanes to help us make a beautiful decorative paper.

You will need:
- Paint thinner
- One or more colors of oil-based paint (such as you would use to paint a house or a piece of outdoor furniture)
- A 9x13 pan with an inch or so of water in it
- Sheets of paper
- Some paper cups and spoons for mixing
- Plastic fork

Instructions:
 Pour a few spoonfuls of paint into a cup and add just enough paint thinner to make the paint runny. Take a plastic fork, dip it in the paint mixture, and splash some drops lightly onto the surface of the water. (If you want to use more than one color, repeat this process with as many colors as you will use.) When you have your color droplets on top of the water, take the fork and swirl them around. When the pattern looks nice, take a sheet of paper and lay it on the surface of the water for just a second, then pull it up. The paint will instantly adhere to the paper transferring the beautiful pattern onto it. Lay the paper out to dry. When it is dry, you can draw on it, or use it in a craft project. (It might be so beautiful, though, that you may want to frame it as art!)

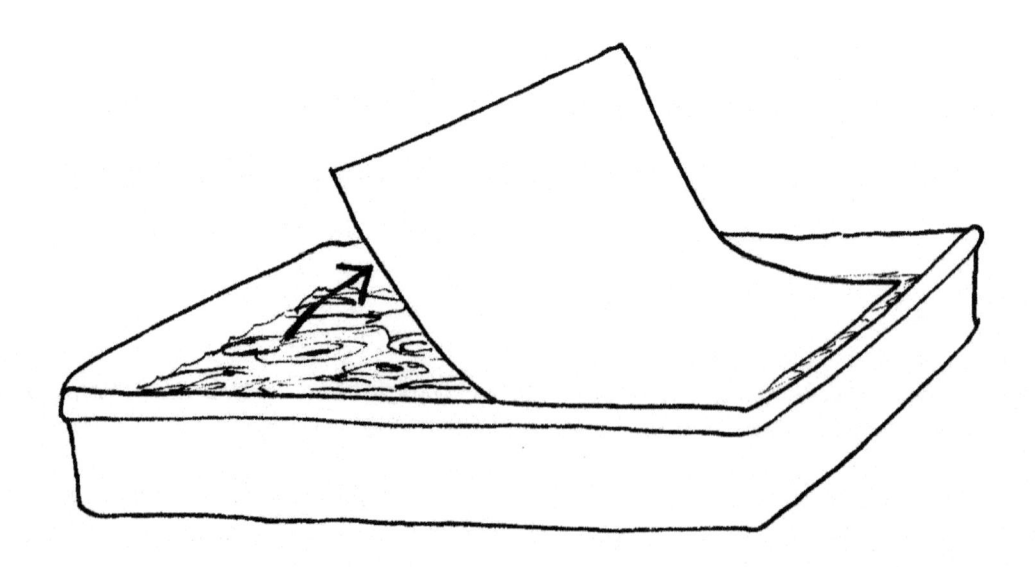

Chapter Three Activities

Activity 3.1: Toluene scavenger hunt

Background information:
What kind of activities can you do after a chapter about dangerous chemicals?! Here's one that is safe.

You will need:
- A location with places you can look for cans of solvents, paints, etc. A basement or garage is perfect.

Instructions:
Can you find a product that contains toluene? Look at the labels on cans in a workshop or garage or cleaning closet and see if you can find one that contains toluene. Are there any warnings on the container? What do they say?

Activity 3.2: Smell an alkene (safely)

Background information:
The fumes from naphthalene and paradichlorobenzene are toxic to moths. They are not exactly good for people, either, but one sniff from a distance won't hurt you. To kill moths, the clothing container needs to be air-tight so that the fumes build up enough to kill the moths. Clothes that have been stored in moth balls need to be aired out before they are worn. Being exposed to the fumes for a long period of time isn't healthy.

You will need:
- A moth ball or similar product that contains naphthalene or paradichlorobenzene.

Instructions:
Smell from a safe distance, not with your nose right on the moth balls. (It is never wise to put your nose right up to, or right over, a substance you've not had experience with before!)

Activity 3.3: Burning contest: Alkane versus Alkene

Background information:
All hydrocarbons can be used as fuel. Do they all burn the same?

You will need:
- A propane torch
- An acetylene torch
- A few pennies (other metal objects if you wish, such as an aluminum can)
- Pliers
- Hotpad

Instructions:

Don't go out and buy these items. If you don't have them or can't borrow them, just skip this activity.

Compare the ability of each torch to melt the penny. Be patient; it may take a minute or two, but you should get observable results. The acetylene torch burns at a much higher temperature and can soften the penny. The propane torch will turn the penny gray, but won't melt it.

Obviously, extreme supervision is required for this activity. However, it's especially worth doing if you have a group of boys. They'll love it.

Actvitity 3.4: The Benzene Ring Dance

You will need:
- The soundtrack from the CD
- A "boombox" to play the CD
- A space large enough to accommodate 12 people moving around quite a bit
- 12 people (you could possibly adapt the dance to six people who are holding balls or something to represent hydrogens)

Instructions:

You must assign 6 people to be carbons and 6 to be hydrogens. Have the carbons stand in a circle with about three feet of space in between them. The hydrogens will stand on the outside of the ring, with each hydrogen touching the back of a carbon.

Make a carbon ring.

Add hydrogens for each carbon.
Hydrogens touch the back of their carbons.
(6 carbons, 6 hydrogens)

The soundtrack on the CD will give you:
A) an introduction
B) 64 beats for one time through the whole dance
C) 64 beats for a second time through the whole dance
D) an ending

The dance itself consists of 64 beats divided up into four 16-beat sections. The four sections go like this:

1) 16 beats of going clockwise. (The whole ring rotates together.)
2) 8 beats for the hydrogens to go inside the carbon ring, then 8 beats to come back out again.
3) 8 beats for each carbon and hydrogen "couple" to swing their partner one direction, then 8 beats to go in the opposite direction.
4) 16 beats for the "couples" to promenade counterclockwise.

Here are illustrations and further explanations of each of the four parts of the dance:

1) 16 beats of going clockwise. The whole ring rotates together. Time it so that the 16 beats rotates the ring one time and everyone gets back to approximately where they started.

2) 8 beats for the hydrogens to go inside the carbon ring. If they can get inside in 4 counts, you could have them remain standing inside the ring for counts 5, 6, 7, 8 and clap their hands to these beats. So it would be 1, 2, 3, and 4 for going in and then clap, clap, clap, clap. Then there are 8 beats for going back out. You can do the same clapping routine on beats 5, 6, 7, 8, if you wish.

Hydrogens go inside ring.

Here are the hydrogens inside, clapping 5, 6, 7, 8.

→ Then, back out, the same way you went in.

3) 8 beats for the "couples" to swing their partner. Then 8 beats to swing the other way.

This shows one particular couple swinging the other way, for the other 8 beats.

3) 16 beats for the "couples" to promenade. The promenade should be timed so that after 16 beats everyone is approximately where they started.

Chapter Four Activities

Activity 4.1: Play the "Functional Group" Game

You will need:
- Copies of the pages that follow. Card stock is best if you can get it.

Instructions:
Cut out the two game board sections and assemble as indicated. Cut apart your colored cards. This game will accommodate up to four players. There should be four sets of molecule cards, each one printed on a different color. Each player chooses a different color.

The game can be played with 2, 3, or 4 players. It is similar to tic-tac-toe. The goal is to get three of your colored cards in a row. You will notice that the game board is the same from any direction. Each player can see the words right-side-up.

Each player shuffles their own stack of molecule cards, puts them facedown in a "draw" pile, then takes three cards off the top. Players should not let the other players see their cards.

The first player chooses one of the cards in his hand and puts it down inside the correct functional group square. He then draws another card from his stack so that he once again has three cards in his hand. The next player can put a molecule on a square (in the correct functional group, of course), or, if he happens to have a card of the same functional group as the first player did, he can lay down his card right on top of the first player's card. He then draws another card from his pile, to keep three cards in his hand. The play continues thus, with each player laying down one of his three cards, then drawing a card from his pile and adding it to his hand so that he is holding three cards at all times. Since you can lay cards on top of other cards, you might get quite a stack of cards on any one square by the end of the game!

The first person to get three of their color in a row wins. Pretty simple! The more you play, the more familiar you will become with functional groups.

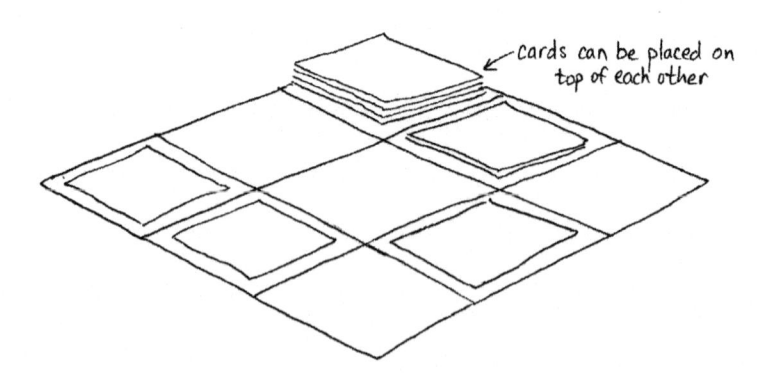

COPY ONTO WHITE PAPER (one sheet per game)

ALKENES
double-bonded carbons — C=C

ALKANES
only single bonds — C-C

ALKYNES
triple-bonded carbons — C≡C

CARBOXYLIC ACIDS
$-\overset{O}{\underset{\|}{C}}-O-H$

ALCOHOLS
-OH

ALDEHYDES
$-\overset{O}{\underset{\|}{C}}-H$

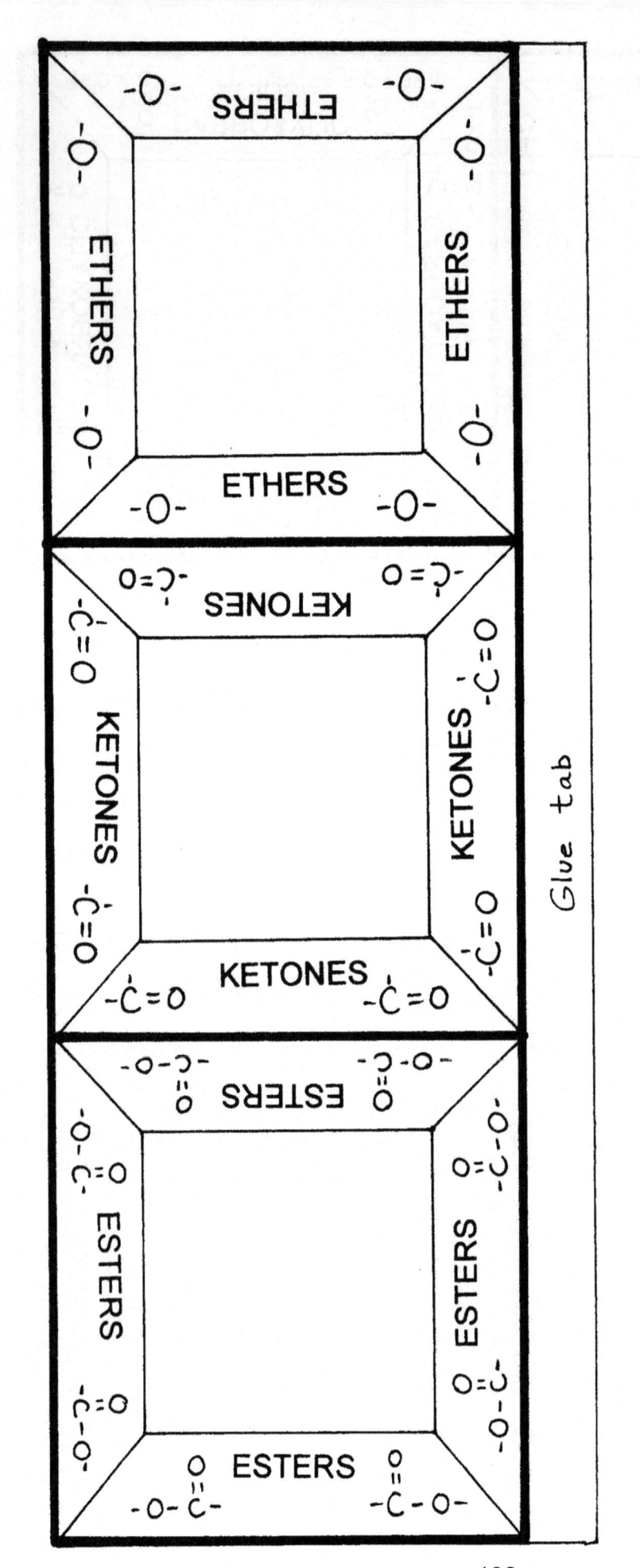

To assemble game board:

overlap and glue

COPY ONTO WHITE PAPER
(one sheet per game)

Game board template with three panels (ETHERS, KETONES, ESTERS) and a glue tab, showing functional group symbols: $-O-$ for ethers, $-\overset{|}{C}=O$ for ketones, and $-\overset{O}{\overset{\|}{C}}-O-$ for esters around each panel.

Alkanes	H–C(H)(H)–H (methane)	H–C(H)(H)–C(H)(H)–C(H)(H)–H (propane)	(branched alkane structure)
Alkenes	H₂C=CH₂	H₂C=C=CH₂	Cl₂C=CCl₂
Alkynes	H–C≡C–H	H–CH₂–C≡C–CH₂–H	F–C≡C–Cl
Alcohols	H–C(H)(OH)–C(H)(OH)–H	CH₃CH₂CH(OH)CH₃	CH₃CH₂CH(OH)CH₃
Ethers	CH₃–O–C(CH₃)(CH₃)–CH₃	H–CH₂–O–CH₂–H	CH₃–O–CH₃

4 COPIES ON COLORED PAPER (one each of four different colors)

Aldehydes	H–C(=O)–H	CH$_3$–C(=O)–H	CH$_3$CH$_2$–C(=O)–H
Ketones	CH$_3$–C(=O)–CH$_3$	CH$_2$–C=O / CH$_2$–CH$_2$ (cyclobutanone: CH$_2$–CH$_2$ ring)	CH$_3$CHCH$_2$–C(=O)–CH$_3$
Esters	H–C(H)(H)–C(=O)–O–C(H)(H)–H	CH$_3$CH$_2$CH$_2$COOCH$_3$	CH$_3$COOCH$_2$CH$_2$CH$_3$
Carboxylic acids	H–C(H)(H)–C(=O)–O–H	H–C(=O)–O–H	O=C–O–H / H–C–H / H–O–C–C(=O)(O–H) / H–C–H / H–O–C=O
Bonus cards	Cl–C(Cl)(Cl)–Cl	CH$_3$CH$_2$OH	Cl–C(H)(H)–H

4 COPIES ON COLORED PAPER
(one each of four different colors)

Activity 4.2: An experiment using isopropanol

You will need:
- rubbing alcohol
- water
- a thermometer (two thermometers will make the experiment go faster)

Instructions:
Read the temperature on the thermometer. Now dip the thermometer in water and back out again. Blow gently on the thermometer until the water has evaporated. Read the temperature on the thermometer. Wait until the thermometer has reached room temperature again. Now dip the thermometer into the alcohol and back out again. Blow until evaporated. Read the temperature. Is there a difference? The alcohol molecules are able to evaporate more quickly that the water molecules. Evaporation takes heat away from the object, cooling it down.

Activity 4.3: An experiment with acetic acid

Background information:
Acids are often used in the dye industry as ***mordants.*** A mordant is a chemical that makes the dye adhere (stick) to what it is dying, whether it be fabric or, in this case, eggs. You will see how much difference a mordant can make.

You will need:
- water
- vinegar
- four eggs (hard boiled is great, but regular will work, also)
- four cups (large enough to hold one egg)
- four spoons
- food coloring (just one color)
- some paper towels

Instructions:
Each cup will be filled 2/3 full with liquid, but the proportion of water to vinegar will be different in each cup.
Cup #1: just water
Cup #2: water with one tablespoon vinegar
Cup #3: half water, half vinegar
Cup #4: just vinegar
Put six drops of food coloring in each cup. Stir. Put one egg in each cup. Wait about 10-15 minutes. Take the eggs out and observe.
The results should be something like this:
Cup#1: very light color
Cup#2: very good, strong color
Cup #3: good color, but surface of egg bubbly and not so nice, dye comes off just a little
Cup #4: good color, but surface of egg terrible; dye comes off

Cup #2 will be the obvious winner; a good strong color, and the surface of the egg is nice and smooth. Of course, chemists have figured this out already and that's why the instructions on Easter egg dyes tell you to add a spoon of vinegar. The vinegar (acetic acid) acts as a mordant to help the color stick to the egg.

Activity 4.4: An experiment with acetone

Background information:
This experiment is listed on many science websites and generally the directions say that you can do the experiment with nail polish remover. However, the nail polish removers available in the stores in my area did not contain enough acetone to make this experiment work. I found pure acetone in the paint department of WalMart. Acetone should also be readily available in any hardware store.

You will need:
- acetone (you'll need acetone for an experiment in chapter 6, also)
- packing peanuts (the Styrofoam kind, not the biodegradable starch kind)

Instructions:
Apply the acetone to the packing peanuts and watch the results. They should shrink and melt immediately. Six drops of acetone can completely melt down one packing peanut. The acetone breaks down the polystyrene polymer molecules. (More on polystyrene in the next chapter...)

Activity 4.6: Taste-test some esters

You will need:
- artificially flavored candy

If you are doing this unit with a class and need a "sweetener" to help them love doing chemistry, this is a good excuse to hand out candy!

(Disclaimer: There is no way to know the exact names of the artificial flavors and whether they fall into the category of esters, as seen in this chapter, without contacting the company that makes them and talking to the chemists.)

Chapter Five Activities

Activity 5.1: An experiment with soap and surface tension

Background information:
    Water molecules stick together. They are polar, which means they have a positive end and a negative end. The positive ends of the molecules are attracted to the negative ends of other water molecules, and the result is that they stick together. This creates something called "surface tension," which can hold up very light objects.

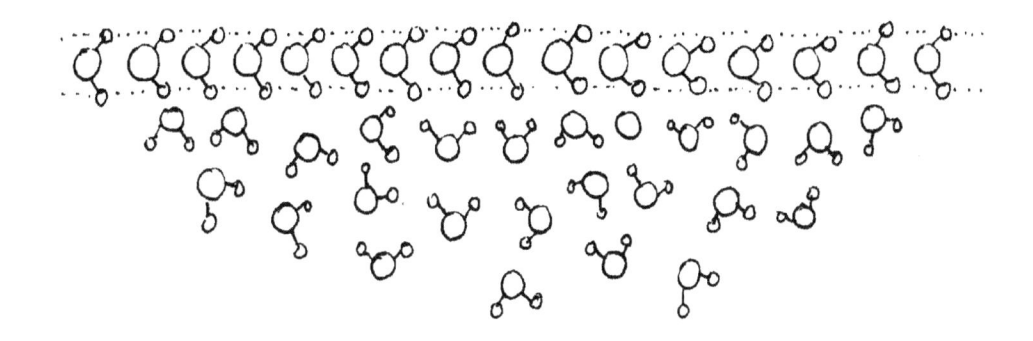

You will need:
- Soap
- Pepper
- Bowl
- Water
- Paper clip

Instructions:
    Fill the bowl with water. Sprinkle pepper on the surface. The pepper should be spread out evenly across the surface. Now smear a small amount of soap on one finger and lightly touch the surface of the water in the center of the bowl. What happens to the pepper? *The pepper should move away from your finger. The pepper might even start to sink. The soap has destroyed the surface tension on top of the water. Those "lollipops" interfere with the attraction between the water molecules.*
    Rinse the bowl and try the same thing with the paper clip. Can you make the paper clip float on the surface of the water? If you are patient, you should be able to make it float. The paper clip is light enough that it should not break the bonds between the water molecules on the surface (the surface tension). Now put your soapy finger in. What happens?

Activity 5.2: Make homemade soap (glycerin soap)

Background information:
You don't need a lot of fancy equipment or hours of time to make glycerin soap. Glycerin soap is very easy to make. You can buy kits that are microwavable. You just add scent, color, and decorations, and pour into a plastic mold. You can buy molds, or you can use plastic containers from around your house. Even plastic packages (such as batteries or small toys come in) will work as molds.

You will need:
- Glycerin soap making supplies from your local craft store

Instructions:
Follow the instructions that come with the soap making kit.

Activity 5.3: Enjoy some benzaldehyde

Background information:
Many "artificial" flavorings are identical to their "natural" counterparts. Benzaldehyde manufactured in a lab is indistinguishable from "natural" benzaldehyde found in almonds. It's the exact same stuff! Here is a recipe that uses both "natural" and "artificial" benzaldehyde. This recipe is called Almond Demasiado (meaning "too much" in Spanish).

You will need:
- 1 ½ sticks unsalted butter
- 1 ¾ cups flour
- ¾ t. baking soda
- ¼ t. salt
- ½ cup loosely packed brown sugar
- ¼ cup granulated sugar
- 7 ounce package almond paste or marzipan, grated
- 1 large egg, plus one large egg yolk
- 1 T. almond extract
- 1 cup salted almonds, chopped
- 1 cup blanched slivered almonds

Instructions:
Melt butter over low heat and set aside to cool slightly. Place oven racks at top and lower middle positions and preheat oven to 325. Stir together flour, baking soda, salt. Set aside.

Beat together butter and sugars. Beat in the marzipan, and then the egg, egg yolk, and almond extract. Add dry ingredients (but not the nuts) and beat with mixer on lowest speed until just combined. Fold in the nuts.

Drop blobs (2 T.) of dough onto parchment-covered cookie sheets, no more than 8 per sheet. Bake for 6-8 minutes, then reverse cookies sheets (top and bottom racks) and bake for another 6-8 minutes, until just barely golden and slightly puffed.

Remove cookies and allow to cool on sheets for 10 minutes before transferring them to cooling racks.

Chapter Six Activities

Activity 6.1: Recycling relay

Background information:

Have you ever noticed those numbers (nside triangles made of arrows) on the bottoms of plastic containers? Those numbers are a code that the plastic industry uses to help sort plastics for recycling. The numbers correspond to the chemistry of the plastics. The first line gives the letter abbreviation, the second line gives the chemical name for the plastic, and the third line gives just a few examples of where you might find this type of plastic. You may find lots of other examples in your own plastic collection.

- PET (or PETE)
  Polyethylene terephthalate
  Soft drink bottles, peanut butter and salad dressing jars

- HDPE
  High density polyethylene
  Milk jugs, grocery bags, detergent bottles, toys

- PVC
  Polyvinyl chloride
  Clear food packages, shampoo bottles

- LDPE
  Low density polyethylene
  Bread bags, frozen food bags, grocery bags

- PP
  Polypropylene
  Ketchup bottles, yogurt and margarine containers, medicine bottles

- PS
  Polystyrene
  VCR/CD cases, coffee cups, plastic utensils, meat trays, fast food boxes

Most communities now have recycling programs that offer consumers the convenience of curb-side pick-up. The consumer does not have to sort their materials. They just toss them all into one bin and set it out for pick-up. In this activity, you will be playing the part of the recycling company who comes and gets the items from the bin and has to sort them out correctly.

You will need:
- a variety of plastic containers
- two recycling bins (or medium sized boxes if you don't have recycling bins)
- pages with the recycling numbers printed on them (large enough to see from a distance)
- optional: eight boxes or other containers in which to put each type of plastic
- a large enough space to run a relay race

Instructions:
Here is a suggestion for how to set up your relay race area:

Racers may only take one plastic item at a time. First team to empty their bin (and sort them correctly!) wins.

Activity 6.2: Sorting plastics using chemical analysis

Background information:
Each type of plastic has unique chemical characteristics. In this lab you can use these characteristics to figure out what an unknown plastic is made of.

You will need:
- a sample of each type of plastic (numbers 1-6)
- some plastic samples that are not labeled (small pieces are fine)
- corn oil
- acetone
- isopropyl alcohol
- a 3-inch piece of 20-gauge copper wire (exact length and gauge not crucial)
- some medium-sized beakers or glass jars
- small ceramic plate or dish
- an alcohol burner (the kind used to keep food warm at receptions) (they are inexpensive and easily purchased at any rental store, or even at WalMart)
- tongs and pliers
- plastic spoons
- stirring rod (wooden stick will do)
- a hot plate (or some other way to boil water)
- water in a small pan or Pyrex jar (so it can be boiled)
- safety goggles

SAFETY NOTE: You must keep the acetone away from the area where you are doing the flame test. Acetone is highly flammable.

Instructions:

Set up six "test stations":
- **The water test**: a jar or glass half-filled with room temperature water
- **The copper wire test**: an alcohol burner and the piece of copper wire. If your wire is insulated, strip only about a half an inch from one end. If it is not insulated, you might want to provide a hot pad to hold the wire with.
- **The acetone test**: a small glass jar or beaker half-filled with acetone (you may want to keep a lid on it when not in use)
- **The heat test**: a container of boiling water (continuously boiling) and a pair of tongs which with to hold a plastic sample for immersion into the water
- **The alcohol test**: a jar or glass half-filled with alcohol
- **The oil test**: a jar or glass half-filled with corn oil

Here is the logical path to follow to identify the plastics. First try it with the known samples, to see if you get the results you should. Then try it with a mystery sample.

1) The water test. Put the plastic in the water and try to push it under. If it sinks, go to step 2). If it floats, go to step 5).
2) The copper wire test. Take the copper wire and heat the end in the alcohol burner until it is red hot. Touch the plastic so that a bit of the plastic sticks to the hot wire. Put the wire back in the flame so the plastic sample gets burned. Watch the color of the flame as the plastic burns. If the flame is green, your plastic is #3, polyvinyl chloride. If the flame is orange, go to step 3).
3) The acetone test: Use tongs or pliers to lower the plastic sample into the acetone. Hold it there for about half a minute. Bring it back up, dab it off, and squeeze it to see if it has been softened by the acetone. (You may even want to scratch it with your fingernail to see if some plastic scrapes off.) If the acetone softened the plastic, the plastic is #6, polystyrene. If the plastic did not soften, go to step 4).
4) The heat test: Use tongs to put the plastic sample into the boiling water for about half a minute. Remove plastic and squeeze to see if the boiling water soften it. If it did soften, your plastic is #1, polyethylene terephthalate (PET or PETE). If it did not soften, this plastic is part of a category not covered by the numbers 1-6. There are other types of plastic out there!
5) The alcohol test: Put the sample in the alcohol and see if it floats. If sinks, your plastic sample is #2, high density polyethylene (HDPE). If it floats, go to step 6).
6) The oil test: Put your sample in the corn oil and see if it floats. Push it down a bit and see if it pops back up. If your sample sinks in the oil, it is #4, low density polyethylene (LDPE). If it floats in the oil, it is #5, polypropylene.

Clean-up: All materials can be flushed down the drain except the acetone. Pour unused acetone back into the container it came from.

Activity 6.3: A polymer that absorbs water

Background information:
Super-absorbency diapers use a polymer called polysodium acrylate. From the name, you can see that this polymer contains many sodium atoms. Remember that the "lollipop" molecule had a sodium on one end—the end that attracted water molecules. The sodium atoms on this polymer do the same thing—attract water molecules. The water molecules come over and cling to the sodium atoms on the polymer, adding a lot more mass to the polymer.

In this experiment, you will see just how much mass the water can add to the polysodium acrylate molecule.

You will need:
- A super-absorbency disposable diaper (any size or brand)
- Water
- A one-cup measure

Instructions:
Before you begin, take a guess as to how many cups of water your diaper can absorb. Then fill your one-cup measure and slowly pour it on the diaper. Give it a little time to sink in. Fill your cup again and slowly pour over the diaper. Did the diaper absorb both cups of water? Keep doing this until your diaper will not absorb any more water.

When we did this experiment, we found that a little tiny size 1 (next up from newborn) diaper would absorb at least 7 cups of water!

You may want to discuss afterwards the significance of this experiment to water safety for babies. Note that they now make special diapers for wearing under bathing suits. These "Swimmies" do <u>not</u> contain polysodium acrylate, for obvious reasons!

You may want to try this experiment again, but using salt water to simulate ocean water. How safe are these diapers at the beach?

Activity 6.4: Another diaper experiment

You will need:
- A super-absorbent disposable diaper
- A pair of scissors
- A plastic baggie
- Optional: food coloring
- A paper cup

Instructions:

Carefully cut open the middle of the inside of the diaper (the part that would be right where the action is!). Remove a section of this cotton filling and put it in the baggie. Shut the baggie and then gently shake the baggie to agitate the cotton, causing a powder to sift to the bottom of the bag. This powder is the polymer. Remove the cotton fibers, leaving the powder.

Put a small amount of the powder into the cup and add some water. Observe results. You can add a drop of food coloring if you want to. Keep adding a little water at a time and observe.

Now take a blob of the gel and examine it carefully. (Don't worry, it is non-toxic.) Look for any crystals. Leave this blob on the plate for several days and let it dry out. What happens?

Activity 5: Product testing

Background information:

All large plastic manufacturers have full-time staff devoted to testing and re-testing their products. The plastics are stretched, boiled, bent, hammered, etc. to determine their limits. The testers can find out exactly how many pounds of pressure it takes before a certain plastic tears or bends, or how many degrees of heat it can take before it begins to soften. The company can let the consumer know the limits of the product so that they don't go over safety limits and endangered lives.

Here are some examples of very practical questions that testing can answer. What would happen to a plastic flotation device that was left out in the heat of the sun for days on end? How many pounds of pressure can a heavy plastic safety helmet withstand? How many hours of baby-chewing can a plastic toy withstand before the edges become ragged or sharp? How many children can safely ride on a tire swing suspended by a nylon rope? How many pounds of groceries can a plastic bag hold before it splits and dumps the food on the ground? The goal of the plastics manufacturer is made a product with as little plastic as possible, but without sacrificing any durability or safety.

You will need:
- some plastic products for testing: identical items of different brands (for example, three or more brands of plastic wrap)
- various testing devices depending upon how you want to test your product (for example, if you want to smash, you'll need a hammer)
-

Instructions:

Determine what quality you will test for. With plastic grocery bags or plastic wrap you might want to test for strength or ability to stretch. With a yogurt carton you might want to test how much pressure it can take and still pop back into shape.

Before you begin, think about these questions.
- Why are the qualities you have chosen to test important to the consumer?
- What is the consumer looking for in this product?
- Are there multiple factors that determine the suitability of this product? (For example, is being stretchy just as important as being strong?)
- What could happen if the product did not have these qualities?

Set up a testing method that gives consistent results each time. This might take some adult supervision. The test must be "fair" every time, so that the results will be as accurate as possible. (For example, if you test how much of a load a bag can carry, use objects that are of the same weight to load down the bag. It will then be a fair comparison if you say that one bag held eight cans and one held ten. If the cans are of different sizes and weights, the results will not be valid.) Help the students think through the validity of the testing they have designed.

Conduct your tests and determine which product is the winner.

Activity 6.6: "The Plastic Song"

You will find the audio tracks on the CD (or as mp3 files, if you have the digital download). There are two tracks, one with the vocals and one without (so you can sing it yourself!).

The Plastic Song

(to the tune of "Big Rock Candy Mountain")

I'm proud of my collection, it's not toy cars or dolls;
I don't like coins or bottle caps, or stamps or baseball cards.
I'm proud to be the owner of many fine works of art;
     they are very lightweight,
     when the fall they don't break,
     can be made in any shape,
     come in clear and opaque,
and I dearly love my plastic!

I fell in love with plastic when I was just a kid,
I filled my shelves and closets with bottles, bags and lids.
I filled my head with knowledge and learned how plastic's made;
     it comes from oil
     then the oil they do boil
     making liquid and gas
     which then do pass
to the factories that make plastic.

I know that plastic's made of polymers so miniscule.
The <u>poly</u> part means many, the <u>mer</u>'s a molecule.
The <u>mer</u>s and made of atoms, with carbon at the core;
     a polymer's a chain,
     a very long chain,
     a molecular train
     that can take a lot of strain,
and polymers make up plastics.

I've noticed little numbers on my plastic works of art;
I know they're for recycling (if I have a change of heart!)
The names that match these numbers-- they mostly end in -<u>ene</u>:
     like polyethylene
     and polypropylene
     and polystyrene
     but the one with chlorine
is polyvinyl chloride.

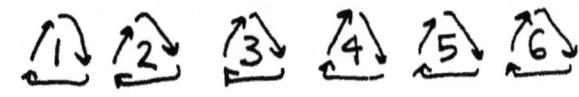

     So come to my home
     where you can roam
     in my Styrofoam
     and I'll let you take home
a precious piece of plastic!

Chapter Seven Activities

Activity 7.1: Skit about Charles Goodyear

You will need:
- The following skit. Make copies for each student if you are doing it with a group.

Instructions:
Your options:
- You can simply read the skit as extra reading material to learn more about Charles Goodyear.
- You can use it as "Readers' Theater" and have students read the various parts out loud without acting it out.
- You can perform the skit without props, using only pantomime.
- You can perform the skit with props.

Activity 7.2: Skewer a balloon

Background information:
Balloons are made of elastomer polymers. The molecules are very long and are all tangled together. If you break them suddenly, the balloon will pop. However, if you slowly and gently push the polymers out of the way, you can create a hole without popping the balloon.

You will need:
- Several balloons (at least 9 inch diameter)
- A wooden skewer (like a shish-kabob stick; fairly thin, and pointed at one end)
- Petroleum jelly (Vaseline)
- penny

Instructions:
Inflate the balloon and tie it shut. You might want to under-inflate it just slightly. Lubricate the skewer. Gently insert the sharp end of the skewer in the end of the balloon. Use a twisting motion. Push the skewer through the middle and out the other side.

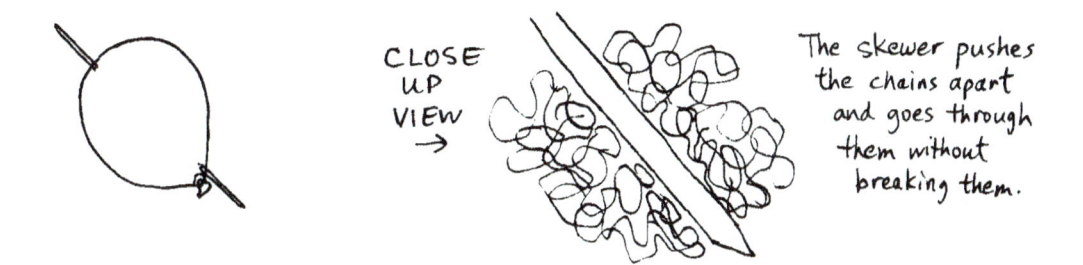

CLOSE UP VIEW →

The skewer pushes the chains apart and goes through them without breaking them.

Here is something else you can try with another balloon. Put a penny inside before inflating balloon. Push skewer in just one end, pull skewer out. Turn hole downwards so the penny covers the hole on the inside. Now turn the balloon around. Does the penny stay on the hole? The air pressure should keep it in place.

CHARLES GOODYEAR
Inventor of vulcanized rubber

Speaking parts: narrator, Charles Goodyear, a company president, Charles' wife, a prison guard, a friend
Non-speaking parts: police, Goodyear children (who can be cut out entirely if you want to keep the cast small)
Props: something to simulate a rubber bottle, a pot and a spoon to stir it with, something to simulate a fishing pole, paper plates to be the family dishes, a stack of books, a box or envelope with a construction paper "medal" in it

Production note: Directions are not given for when actors and props are to be on and off the "stage" area (you certainly don't need a stage!). The director can suggest the appropriate comings and goings on and off the stage area as he/she sees fit. You may want the narrator on stage all the time, or on only when lines are being read. It is up to the director's discretion. Feel free to add or subtract little details to make the performance more your own, also!
****

NARRATOR: Charles Goodyear was born in Connecticut in the year 1800. As a child, gum elastic fascinated him. He once found a rubber bottle and marveled at its wonderful mysterious properties.

CHARLES: (examining the bottle) Wow! This stuff is wonderful and mysterious!

NARRATOR: Charles' father sold farming tools to farmers. Charles learned a lot about tools and later he moved to Philadelphia where he opened his own hardware store. Charles was great with tools but he was terrible with managing money and soon his store went bankrupt.

CHARLES: I'm not very good at running a hardware store, but I really love tools. What can I do? I know! I'll become an inventor!

NARRATOR: Charles declared himself a professional inventor and went off to New York to try to interest the Roxbury India Rubber Company in his design for an improved valve for their life preservers.

CHARLES: Hello, Mr. Company President, Sir. Could I interest you in my latest invention? It's a new and improved valve for your life preservers.

MR. PRESIDENT: Valves, shmalves! What I need around here isn't a new valve, it's new and improved rubber! This stupid rubber is so tricky to work with that sometimes I think we're fools to make life preservers out of it! Rubber seems to turn into sticky goo when it's hot and get hard as stone when it's cold!

NARRATOR: Charles Goodyear suddenly saw his life's challenge before him: to improve rubber.

CHARLES: (Rising to his feet with a dreamy look in his eyes) God has chosen me to improve rubber as a gift to the world!

NARRATOR: Charles went home to his wife with his happy news.

CHARLES: Honey, I have a new career: improving rubber!

WIFE: But Charles, you don't know anything about chemistry and you don't have any money to buy supplies.

CHARLES: (grandly) That doesn't matter!

NARRATOR: Suddenly there was a knock on the door. It was the police who had come to arrest him for being in debt. It was common back in those days for someone to be put in prison for being in debt.
 (Charles is dragged off to prison.)
In prison, Charles began working on his new rubber project. In a kitchen in a small building on the prison grounds he began blending rubber with everything he could think of, hoping one of these things would improve the consistency of the rubber. He tried ink, oil, various chemical, and even soup and cream cheese!

PRISON GUARD: Here is your lunch, Mr. Goodyear, sir.

CHARLES: Terrific! Just what I need! Maybe this peanut butter will be the answer I'm looking for! (Charles stirs it into his rubber mixture.)

NARRATOR: After several years of experimenting both at home and in his prison workshop, he finally discovered that nitric acid seemed to cure the stickiness problem, so that the rubber could withstand extreme heat without turning into goo. Charles was able to start a factory to produce this new rubber, but unfortunately, a financial panic struck the city and his factory went bankrupt. With no money to pay the rent on his house, Charles had to move his family into his empty factory on Staten Island. Their only food was whatever they could catch by fishing in the harbor.

CHARLES: (While fishing with his kids) Things aren't so bad, are they, kids? There's nothing like nice fresh catfish for dinner. Someday I'll get my lucky break and we'll look back on this and laugh.

NARRATOR: Charles Goodyear's lucky break came one day when he was experimenting with mixing sulfur in with the rubber. By accident, he dropped a lump of this sulfur and rubber mix onto a hot stove.

CHARLES: Oops! Oh no! It'll melt down and stick onto the stove and it will take hours to get it scraped off!

NARRATOR: But to his surprise, the lump of rubber did not melt onto the stove. It charred and turned tough, like leather. He decided to test this tough rubber in the cold.

CHARLES: I think I'll set this rubber outside in the snow and see what happens. (He opens a pretend door and pantomimes putting it in the snow)

NARRATOR: To his great delight, the rubber remained soft and flexible even in the cold.

CHARLES: (Pretends to get his rubber back out of the snow and bring it inside. Then he examines it and finds it flexible.) I've done it! This rubber stayed flexible even in the cold. Now I've solved both the hot AND the cold problems! I think I'll called my invention: vulcanized rubber. You know, after the Greek god, Vulcan, who lived down inside a volcano. Get it? Volcanoes are hot, my stove is hot....

WIFE: Yes, that sounds wonderful! You've done it! Good for you, Charles. But, how are we going to find more money to keep your research going?

CHARLES: We'll have to sell some things.

WIFE: Here's all of our dishes, They might be worth something. And here, take the children's school books. I'll just teach them without any books.

CHARLES: Honey, you're terrific.

NARRATOR: So Charles kept his research going until he discovered the exact formula for making the perfect rubber. Charles, however, was also successful at financially ruining himself and he made the mistake of allowing other companies to begin manufacturing rubber products before he had received his patent for the rubber discovery. He went to court to try to stop people from copying his method of vulcanizing rubber, and ended up paying his lawyer every last penny he had. This is what one of Charles' friends said about him:

FRIEND: If you meet a man who has on a rubber cap, a rubber coat, a rubber vest, rubber shoes, and is carrying a rubber wallet with no money in it, that's Charles Goodyear!

NARRATOR: Charles had to borrow money to go to London to display his new rubber inventions. Millions of people came from all over Europe to see this new rubber, but poor Charles stayed poor.

Napoleon III, of France, was so impressed by his invention that he awarded Charles the cross of the Legion of Honor award. But.... the medal had to be delivered to the prison because that's where Charles was again.

PRISON GUARD: A package for you, Mr. Goodyear.

CHARLES: (opens package) Wow, it's a medal from Napoleon III. I'm sure this is the beginning of a new start to my life. I can see it now... rubber boats, rubber bands, rubber clothes, self-inflating rubber beds, rubber wheelbarrow tires, rubber dog houses.......

NARRATOR: Charles Goodyear never did manage to make any money on his invention. He died a poor man and left his family with huge debts. But as Charles always said:

CHARLES: The advantages of a career in life should not be estimated exclusively by the standard of dollars and cents. The only cause for regret is when one man sows, and <u>no one</u> reaps.

Activity 7.3: Use a polymer to demonstrate that heat is molecular motion

Background information:
Molecules are always in motion. It may seem strange to think of the molecules in a table or chair as moving around, but they are. The more motion there is, the more heat there is. If you put a heater next to a chair and warmed it up, you are causing the molecules in the chair to move faster. Weird, eh? How fast are the molecules moving in a red hot piece of steel? How fast are the molecules moving in a piece of ice?

If the molecules in an object are moving around, that means heat is present. If something causes those molecules to suddenly stop moving, the heat energy that was there is released into the environment around it. In this experiment, you will be stopping and starting the motion of molecules. You will be able to feel the resulting increase and decrease in temperature.

You will need:
- A large rubber band, as wide as possible
- A plastic grocery bag

Instructions:
Put the rubber band to your upper lip or your forehead and feel the temperature. Keep the rubber band against your skin and stretch it quickly. You should feel a substantial change in temperature. Now let the rubber band shrink back down quickly. How long did it take for the heat to disappear?

Now try the same thing with a piece of plastic bag. The bag should produce even more heat than the rubber band.

Here is a picture of what is going on. You can demonstrate this for the students using a piece of string or yarn with some kind of balls attached (even marshmallows strung on).

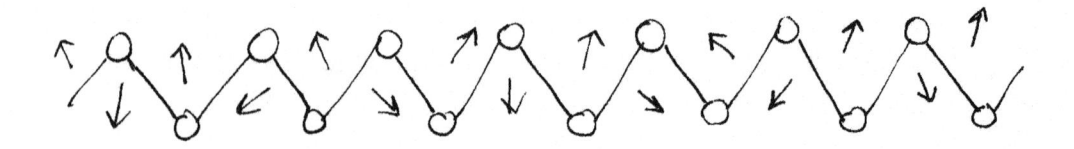

The polymer molecules are in motion. Therefore, they are not stretched out tight. They have to have room to move around. And where there is motion, there is heat. When you stretch the rubber band, you make them do this:

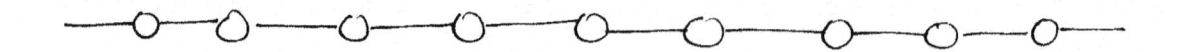

Can they move around if they are kept in this position? No, not very much. All the motion (heat) they had in them had to leave. You felt this release of heat on your skin. When you let the rubber band relax, you are allowing heat to go back in. You felt heat leave your skin and go back into the rubber band.

Activity 7.4: Cross link some polymers to make "slime"

Background:
This is similar to what Charles Goodyear did when he vulcanized rubber. In this experiment, you will cause polymers to cross-link. Instead of rubber, we will use polyvinyl acetate and polyvinyl alcohol, and instead of sulfur we will use borax.

You will need:
- Elmer's regular white glue (which is polyvinyl acetate)
- Elmer's gel glue (which is polyvinyl alcohol)
- Borax powder (available in laundry section of grocery store)
- Glycerin (optional)
- Food coloring (optional)
- Plastic cup
- Stirring stick of some kind

Instructions:
Dissolve the borax powder in water until no more will dissolve. If you want to color your slime, add food coloring to the borax water.

Put four parts Elmer's white glue and one part borax solution into a cup and stir well. The borax molecules will cross-link the glue molecules and completely change the texture, turning it into the ever-popular "slime."

Now try the other glue. Dilute the gel glue first, by adding two parts water to one part glue. Stir well to get the lumps out. (Letting it sit awhile might help, too.) Mix four parts gel glue solution to one part borax solution. Stir well. If you want to make this slime more gooey, add glycerin (quarter teaspoon glycerin for every half cup slime).

Compare the slimes. How are they the same? How are they different?

This is what is happening:

Regular glue:

Polyvinyl acetate:
~CH−CH$_2$−CH−CH$_2$−CH−CH$_2$~
       | | |
    O−C−CH$_3$ O−C−CH$_3$ O−C−CH$_3$
       ‖   ‖   ‖
       O   O   O

Borax molecules: B(OH)$_4$ B(OH)$_4$ B(OH)$_4$

Polyvinyl acetate:
       O   O   O
       ‖   ‖   ‖
    O−C−CH$_3$ O−C−CH$_3$ O−C−CH$_3$
       | | |
~CH−CH$_2$−CH−CH$_2$−CH−CH$_2$~

Gel glue:

Polyvinyl alcohol:
~CH−CH$_2$−CH−CH$_2$−CH−CH$_2$~
     | | |
    OH   OH   OH

Borax molecules: B(OH)$_4$ B(OH)$_4$ B(OH)$_4$

Polyvinyl alcohol:
    OH   OH   OH
     | | |
~CH−CH$_2$−CH−CH$_2$−CH−CH$_2$~

The B(OH)$_4$ molecules are attracted to the "O" and "OH", which is shown by dotted lines

⌢ signifies attraction

127

Activity 7.5: What percentage of a piece of chewing gum is rubber?

You will need:
- A piece of gum
- A scale than can measure in increments of 1/10 ounce.

Instructions:
Weigh the piece of gum in the wrapper. Then chew the gum for a while, but don't throw the wrapper away. Place the chewed gum back on the wrapper and weigh again. Put the second number over the first to make a fraction. Turn the fraction into a percent. This is the percentage of your gum that is rubber. All (or almost all) the rest of the weight was sugar.

Activity 7.6: Experiments with Silly Putty

Background:
Just another reminder: Silly Putty™ doesn't rightly belong in this book on carbon compounds! You might want to remind the students of this again.

This experiment is all about viscosity. Silly Putty™ is a good example of something with a very high viscosity. Like all liquids, it drips and runs. It just does it very slowly. But you can't force it to drip or spread out faster than it wants to! Unlike low viscosity liquids, the polymer chains can be snapped if pressure is applied quickly.

You will need:
- Silly Putty™ or other brand silicon putty (the same stuff, but cheaper)
- Heavy books
- Hammer
- Time
- Optional: mass of tangled yarn to represent putty polymer molecules

Instructions:
First test: Hit the putty with a hammer. What happens? It should be impossible to squash it with the hammer. Hard as you hit, it will resist you and bounce the hammer right back. After you have hit it with the hammer several times, feel the temperature of the putty. Is it warm? You have put energy into the putty and stirred up the molecules.

Second test: Put a book on the putty and wait. Over the course of minutes or hours, the putty will flatten. If you can, leave the book on it overnight and see how flat the putty will become.

Third test: Roll the putty into a perfectly round ball, then let it sit for a while. If you can let it sit for a day or two, you will see it go very flat.

Fourth test: Pull the putty apart quickly. You should be able to snap the blob in half very cleanly. The polymer molecules need time to untangle as you stretch the putty. Just imagine pulling quickly on a knot of tangled hair. Ouch! You need time to straighten out and untangle the hairs. It's the same with the putty molecules. They need time to sort themselves out. (You can demonstrate this with the mass of tangled yarn.)

Fifth test: Get the putty to drip. Stick a blob on the side of a bookcase or refrigerator, or drooping over the edge of a table. Wait as long as you can. Days are good, weeks are even better. We've heard a report of a blob of Silly Putty taking over a month to drip to the bottom of a frig! That's viscosity for you!!! (For a quick demo of dripping putty, stretch it out into a fairly thin string and watch for about 5 minutes. How thin can it get?)

Optional demo: Use the tangled mass of yarn to represent the polymer molecules. If you pull quickly on the mass what happens? If you patiently pull little by little, can you get it to stretch farther than when you pulled quickly?

Activity 7.7: Compare Silly Putty™ and bubble gum

You will need:
- Your Silly Putty
- A piece of bubble gum

Instructions:
Chew the gum so that it has the consistency of the putty (soft and gooey). Try doing the Silly Putty activities with the gum. Have a stretching contest. Which can string out farther without breaking?

NOTE: Warn students that both Silly Putty and bubble gum make a mess when they get stuck to things like clothes and carpets.

Chapter Eight Activities

Activity 8.1: Taste a starch being turned into sugar

Background information:
Your mouth makes an enzyme that immediately begins breaking down some starches. The starches are broken into simple sugars even before they reach your stomach. You can taste this transformation into sugar.

You will need:
- A plain cracker (a soda cracker or oyster cracker)

Instructions:
Put a bite of the cracker (or a whole cracker if it is small) into your mouth but do not chew. Let it sit in your mouth until it dissolves. Observe the difference in taste as it sits in your mouth. It should begin to taste a little sweet. Don't expect it to taste sweet like a piece of candy tastes sweet. The cracker is being broken down into glucose, which doesn't taste as sweet as the sucrose in candy.

Now do a quick comparison. While that mildly sweet taste is still in your mouth, pop another piece of cracker in. Does the fresh cracker taste at all sweet? This comparison is usually quite striking.

Activity 8.2: Test for starch

Background information:
Iodine molecules just happen to react with starch in a way that produces a dark color. Iodine does not have this effect on other types of food. We can use this fact to test for the presence of starch in foods. (This test is sometimes used on paper money to check for counterfeiters who may have used a paper with greater starch content than the paper used by the US mints.)

You will need:
- Iodine (No longer available at most pharmacies—you may have to order from a science catalog. We suggest:
- A variety of substances to test for starch (crackers, pasta, fruit, vegetables, meat, cheese, etc.) You only need a very small amount of each.
- An eyedropper (although you could get along without it if you had to)

Instructions:
Drop one or two drops of iodine onto a food. If it turns dark purplish-black, it contains starch.

Activity 8.3: Artificial sweetener taste test challenge

You will need:
- A packet of saccharin (Sweet 'N Low™ or Sugar Twin™)
- A packet of sucralose (Splenda™)
- A packet of aspartame (Nutrasweet™)
- A packet of regular white sugar (sucrose)

- A packet of Kool-Aid™ drink mix
- Several drinks sweetened with one of these sweeteners (these will be your mystery substances)
- Water
- Small paper cups (bathroom size is fine)
- Plastic spoons

Instructions:
Each student should receive four little cups. Put each packet of sweetener into a cup and label the cups. Add some water and stir. Taste each one carefully. Are they all sweet? (Some people perceive saccharin as bitter, not sweet.) Is there a difference in actual taste, not just sweetness? Add a sprinkle of Kool-Aid flavoring and taste them all again.

Now for the mystery substances. Pass out samples of the sweetened drinks. (Do not let the students see the bottles you poured from.) Have the students taste the sweetened drinks and try to guess which sweetener is in them. They may want to sip the original samples a few more times for comparison.

Activity 8.4: Is milk sweet?

Background information:
We don't think of milk as being sweet, but it has lots of lactose sugar in it. People who cannot break apart the lactose into simple sugars are said to be "milk intolerant." Lactaid™ milk has the lactase enzyme mixed right into the milk, so it's been "predigested" for you. Sounds gross, but it isn't. It's just splitting apart a sugar into smaller sugars. That's not gross. Glucose tastes a little sweeter than lactose, so would this "predigested" milk taste sweeter than regular milk?

You will need:
- A sample of regular milk (any kind—1%, 2%, whole)
- A sample of Lactaid™ milk (or other brand made for lactose intolerants) Try to make sure both milks have the same fat content (1%, 2%, whole) so that you are only comparing the sweetness and not the overall quality of the milk.

Instructions:
Taste the milk. What do you think? Is one sweeter?

Activity 8.5: Glycogen tag game

Background:
This game simulates what happens in the bloodstream. The adult in charge is a bit like the insulin, which tells the glucoses to start joining into a line.

You will need:
- A large space in which to play tag
- Optional: boundary markers if you need to contain the game in a certain area
- Optional: strips of tough fabrics (12-15 inches in length) You can also have players just hold hands to form a line. (With mixed-gender middle school groups, we highly recommend the fabric strips. This greatly eases any social awkwardness of sensitive students.)

Instructions:

Each player represents a glucose molecule. Each player receives a fabric strip to hold in one hand. This will be the bonding site. The object of the game is to be the last glucose to get added to the glycogen.

The adult in charge must choose one player to start the game as "It." At the signal "Go!" the person who is "It" must try to tag one of the other glucose molecules. When successful, that second molecule joins to the first, holding onto the bonding site strip. Now these two are "It" together, and must try as a team to tag another molecule. When successful, there will now be three glucoses in the string. We are starting to form a glycogen string! This three-molecule glycogen must try to tag a fourth glucose. The game goes on like this until there is only one person who has not been tagged. You can declare this person the winner, or you can just declare the game over when this last person is tagged.

Note: The adult in charge may have to make on-site rulings about fair moves. You can choose to allow tagging from both ends of the glycogen string, or not, depending upon which will work better in your situation. Will you allow the string to loop around itself and get twisted up? The game can get complicated, but very entertaining!

Activity 8.6: Learn more about carbohydrates

There is so much more you can learn about carbohydrates! This is a huge topic, and we just barely touched on it in this chapter. If you would like to learn more about carbs and sugars, we suggest one good place to get information and experiments:

www.exploratorium.edu/cooking

The Exploratorium is a hands-on science center in San Francisco. It was one of the first hands-on science museums in the country, and remains one of the best. With the invention of the internet, they have expanded their services so that you can "visit" their museum virtually. They've even recorded some of their live programs so that you can benefit from them. Cool! Their site is well worth visiting again and again.

Chapter Nine Activities

Activity 9.1: Test for fat content

You will need:
- Brown paper (from a paper lunch bag)
- Foods that may or may not contain fat (Make sure to include some of their favorite snack foods!)

Instructions:
This is a very simple, yet effective, test for fat content in foods. You simply rub the food on the brown paper. Rub for a half minute or so. (Some foods may take a little longer to soak in.) Now observe the brown paper. Is there a grease mark? Hold it up to a light. Does the spot let light through?
The darker the spot and the more light it lets through, the more grease that food contains.

Activity 9.2: Cake testing

Background information
Why do we put fat such as butter or oil into baked goods? What does margarine do in a cake? It doesn't provide sweetness or flavor. It doesn't make it rise. What does fat do in recipes? This experiment will let you investigate the role of fat in baked goods.

You will need:
- Flour
- Sugar
- Baking powder
- Eggs
- Milk
- Vanilla
- Shortening
- Butter
- Vegetable oil (any kind)
- Margarine
- Cooking utensils and access to oven

Instructions:
Here is the cake recipe, minus the fats:
 1 ½ c. flour
 ¾ c. sugar
 ½ t. baking powder
 ¾ c. milk
 1 egg
 1 ½ t. vanilla
 1/3 c. of one of these fats: shortening, oil, butter, margarine

Make the recipe four times, each time adding one of the fats. You can make them as cakes or as cupcakes. You can cut the recipe in half or in fourth if you want much smaller cakes.   Bake at 375 for 25-30 minutes for a cake, 15-20 minutes for cupcakes. (They are done when a toothpick comes out clean.)

NOTE: You must try to make sure that all the cakes bake at the exact same temperature for the exact same amount of time. You want the only comparison between the cakes to be the difference in the types of fat.

Do a taste-test comparison after the cakes cool. What difference is there in the textures of the cakes? Which one do you prefer?

Activity 9.3: Insulating property of fats

Background information:
In the text, we mentioned that one important job fat does in the body is to provide insulation from cold. Animals like polar bears, seals, and whales have large amounts of body fat. In this experiment you will see how insulated fat can be.

You will need:
- Shortening (and/or butter or margarine)
- Ice water

Instructions:
Put a layer of shortening (or butter or margarine) on the index finger of one hand. The index finger on the other hand will remain clean. Now put both index fingers into the ice water and leave them there for a while. How much longer can your insulated finger stand the extreme cold?

Activity 9.4: Learn more about fats and foods

If you would like to learn more about fats and get some more recipes to try, log on to:

www.exploratorium.edu/cooking

Chapter Ten Activities

Activity 10.1: Watch an animation of protein synthesis

The manufacturing of proteins in your body is an incredibly complicated procedure. This chapter only introduced the topic! If you would like a little more information about protein synthesis, try out some of the videos posted on the Basement Workshop YouTube channel: YouTube.com/eejm63. Click on the "Cells" playlist, then on the videos that have the word "transcription" in them. There are also some videos on Watson and Crick and Rosalind Franklin. (These DNA videos were posted to supplement the "Cells" curriculum, but they fit in nicely with this one, too.)

Activity 10.2: DNA song

You will need:
- The DNA Song audio track on the CD (or the digital audio file if you have the digital version)

Instructions:
Here is a song that will help you remember the basics of DNA. Hopefully, the song will tumble around in your brain for a while and repeat itself over and over again at odd moments of your day, reinforcing this information. (NOTE: A "music video" version of this song is available on the Basement Workshop channel at YouTube.com/eejm63. It's in the "Cells" playlist. Look for the molecule picture.)

Deoxyribonucleic acid,
Watson and Crick worked together with Franklin,
Learned its shape from X-ray diffraction,
Double-helix DNA.

Adenine, thymine, cytosine, guanine,
Adenine, thymine, cytosine, guanine,
Adenine, thymine, cytosine, guanine,
Make the rungs of DNA.

> James Watson (an American) went to England to work with Francis Crick. They both got help from English scientist Rosalind Franklin, an expert in the field of X-ray crystallography.

Activity 10.3: Experiment with an enzyme

Background information:
Remember from the text that enzymes are catalysts for chemical reactions. That is, they help a reaction occur without themselves being used up. Enzymes are very specific. They only work on the substrates (molecules) they were designed for. Each reaction in your body has its own enzyme. Your body makes a lot of enzymes!

This experiment uses an enzyme found in the stomach of calves. Calves live on milk in the first stage of their life, just as all mammals do. However, a calf's digestive system is a little different than your own, since cows have four stomachs. This enzyme is found in the fourth stomach. The enzyme's job is to "coagulate" milk. This means that the proteins stick together and form clumps.

Hundreds of years ago, humans discovered how to use this enzyme (from the stomachs of their freshly butchered calves) to make foods such as cheese and puddings. Nowadays, you don't have to butcher a calf to get this enzyme; it is available in the grocery store as little dry tablets. The enzyme itself is called **rennet**, and the brand name it is sold under is called Junket™. (Just like Kleenex™ is a brand name for facial tissues.)

You will need:
- Rennet tablets (brand name: Junket™)
- Milk
- Soy milk (readily available in grocery stores now, in the milk section)
- Water
- Some kind of fruit juice
- Eight little bowls

Instructions:
Pour a little of each liquid into the bowls. The temperature will be right out of the refrigerator. Now warm some of each liquid to lukewarm (body temperature—when you stick your finger in, it will seem neither cold nor hot). Pour a little of each warmed liquid into a bowl. Now you will have eight bowls. Four of them cold, four of them warm. Add half a Junket™ tablet to each. Crush the tablet and stir. Let them sit for half an hour. Check them every five minutes to see what is (or is not) happening.

Now observe the bowls. Are any of the liquids coagulated? Compare the milk dishes. Did the temperature of the milk affect the amount, or rate, of coagulation?

Enzymes work best at body temperature. Why would this be so?

An interesting side note is that Tofu is made by coagulating soy milk with magnesium sulfate.

Activity 10.4: Make a milk dessert using rennet

Instructions:
Many delicious desserts can be made using rennet. Why not prepare a recipe and taste the results? There may be recipes on the Junket™ box (or package insert), or you could search for some recipes on the internet.

Activity 10.5: Make glue using a milk protein

Background information:
This is a recipe that goes back hundreds of years, just like the rennet recipes. It was discovered that a protein in milk, called **casein**, could be used for jobs where you wanted something to stick, such as glue or paint. The addition of an acid to the milk allows the casein to be isolated. What happens to the milk in this experiment is similar to the coagulation in the rennet experiment, but the protein here will not be as spongy or fluffy in texture. The solid curds in this experiment are technically an "acid precipitate." (If you want a very detailed explanation of the chemistry, go to this web address: www.accessexcellence.org/AE/AEPC/IFT)

You will need:
- A cup of milk
- ½ teaspoon vinegar
- Stove or microwave (and pan or bowl, accordingly)
- Muslin cloth (a woven fabric)
- Borax
- Spoon and plate

Instructions:
Add the vinegar to the milk and stir. Heat, but do not boil, until the curds and whey appear. Pour off the whey (liquid) and put the curds into the cloth. Squeeze out extra liquid. Dump out curds and let them dry thoroughly. Grind the dry curds into a powder and add a little Borax powder. This "glue powder" can be stored indefinitely. When you are ready to make glue, just add a little water to the powder.

Activity 10.6: Watch the "Biuret test" being performed

Background information:
The Biuret test is the test for the presence of proteins. If a chemist wants to know if any proteins are present in a certain solution, he can do this test to find out. If there is protein in the solution, it will turn blue. Cool, eh?

You could do this test yourself if you have copper sulfate and sodium hydroxide. However, there is a German University website that does this experiment for you so all you have to do is watch. No mess, no clean up!

Instructions:
Go to this address:

http://www.uni-regensburg.de/Fakultaeten/nat_Fak_IV/Organische_Chemie/Didaktik/Keusch/D-Video-e.htm

Click on Biuret test. (You may want to click on the explanation first, before you watch the video clip.) If the site address fails, you may want to search for either "Regensburg chemistry" or "Biuret test demonstration."

NOTE: If you have the chemicals, and would like to do this test yourself, you can place a pea-sized sample of a food on a dish and add 1 ml of sodium hydroxide, then 5 drops copper sulfate. Light blue means no protein. Very dark blue (almost purple) means protein is present.

Chapter Eleven Activities

Activity 11.1: Carbon cycle board game

You will need:
- copies of the following pages (on card stock, if possible)
- a die

Set-up instructions:
Copy the following pages onto card stock. If card stock is not available, paper will do. You can print them using the CD copy of the curriculum that came with this book, or you can carefully cut the pages out of the book and use them. (If you want to print a copy of the game and don't have a color printer, just print in black and white.

Cut the sections apart like this:

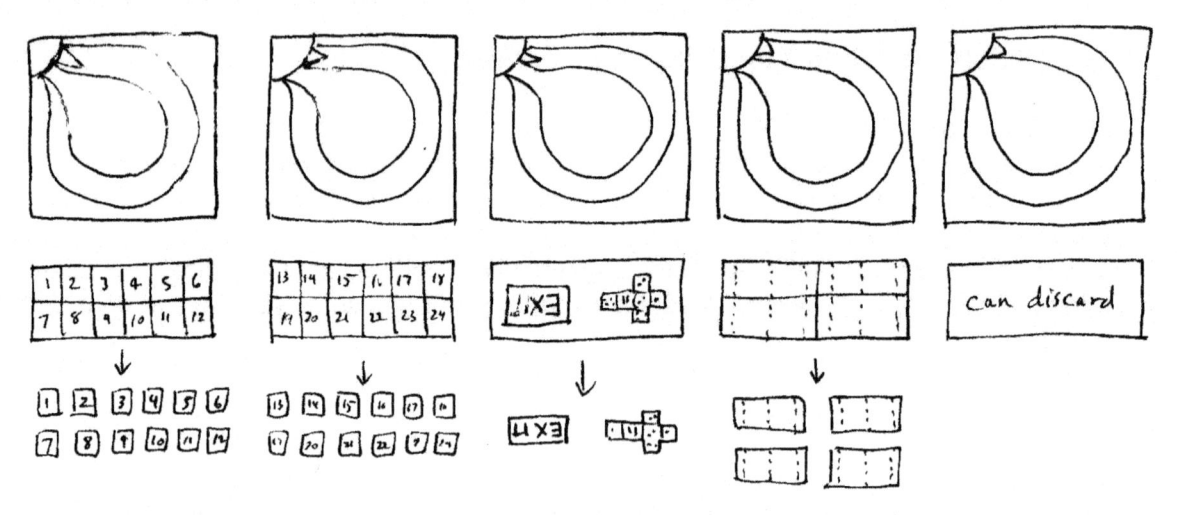

The empty circle is for you to make up your own cycle, if you wish. The circles are interchangeable. You could even make copies of the blank circle and make four of your own cycles!

Four square pieces with the circles in them should be taped together so that the "atmospheric CO_2" circle is in the middle, as shown on right.

The circles are interchangeable and can go in any order.
Cut out the EXIT sign and have it ready to use when the game begins. Cut apart the numbered rectangles, shuffle them, and put them in a pile, face down. If you don't have a die handy, you can put together the paper die. Any die you have around the house will be fine. For tokens (the things you hop around the board) you can use any little objects you have around the house, or you can cut out and put together the paper tokens provided. Assemble them like this:

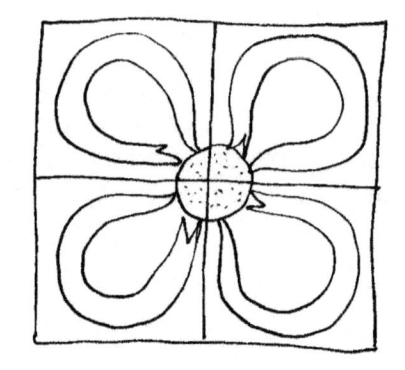

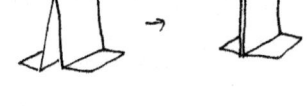

How to play:

All tokens start in the center circle. Draw the first numbered card off the number deck and put the EXIT sign on the space that has that number next to it.

The object of the game is to get off the board and out of the carbon cycle. (Your token represents a carbon atom.) You can only get off if you land on the EXIT in an exact number of hops. For example, if you roll a three, your count of "one, two, three" must land you exactly on the EXIT, and not past it.

You will notice that the spaces on the board are in the shape of arrows. You must follow the direction of the arrows as you move. In other words, in each circle you move clockwise. There are two ways you can play:

1) MODULAR: When you get back to the center, you count the center as one space, then you may keep going into any other circle. You can go back into the one you just came from, or you can go into another one. It's your choice. This will result (usually) in a shorter game, time-wise.

2) SEQUENTIAL: You can follow the numbers and do the circles in order. This will result (usually) in a longer game.

In either game, whenever anyone rolls a 6 (or rolls "Draw Card" if you are playing with the paper die) they take the top card from the number pile. They then move the EXIT card to that space. Thus, the EXIT card will be constantly moving during the course of the game.

Activity 11.2: Fun with sublimation of dry ice (a three-part experiment)

Background information:

You will remember from the text that dry ice is solid carbon dioxide. When something sublimes, it goes straight from its solid phase to its gaseous phase. In the first part of this experiment, you will see just how much gas is packed into solid dry ice.

You will need:
- A chunk of dry ice
- A gallon size zipper-seal baggie
- A cup of hot water
- Optional: a few drops of dishing washing detergent
- Some small candles
- Optional: a ruler or small board to use as a ramp

Instructions:

PART ONE: Chip off a small piece of dry ice (about the size of a marble) and put it inside the baggie. Zip it tight. Wait. Gradually the carbon dioxide will sublime and become a gas. The amount of gas inside the baggie will increase until the baggie is popping at the seams. It might even pop open if the pressure gets to much. More likely, it will leak in a very unexciting way.

PART TWO: Put a small piece of dry ice in a cup of hot water. This will speed up the sublimation so much that the gas will pour into the air, creating what looks like "smoke." Students are fascinated by this even if they've seen it before. Notice how this cold steam goes down as it pours out. It is colder than the surrounding air, and cool air sinks. Light a candle, hold the cup at least six inches above the flame, and pour. The carbon dioxide will put out the flame. If you want to do something more spectacular, put a series of small and/or short candles down a ramp, and pour the carbon dioxide from the top of the ramp. The gas will flow downwards, putting out the candles one by one.

PART THREE: Put a piece of dry ice into the cup of water and add a few drops of dish detergent. Observe some great bubble formations!

SAFETY NOTE: Dry ice is much colder than regular ice. It will burn your skin. Use mittens or hot pads when handling it. Do not let it touch your skin.

Activity 11.3: Help the carbon cycle along

You will need:
- A piece of chalk or limestone
- Vinegar
- A cup

Instructions:

Put the chalk or limestone in the cup and add a spoon a few spoons of vinegar so the sample is just barely covered. Wait and observe. You should see bubbles forming. These bubbles are carbon dioxide. The acid in the vinegar is reacting with the $CaCO_3$ of the limestone or chalk to form calcium acetate (which you can't see because it dissolves in the vinegar), water (which you can't see because it dissolves in the vinegar), and... carbon dioxide. Since the carbon dioxide is a gas, it bubbles to the surface of the liquid. (Or the bubbles may stick to the sides of the sample for quite a while.)

The carbon in the limestone or chalk has been freed to be atmosphere carbon dioxide. And you did it! You help move carbon through a stage of its cycle!

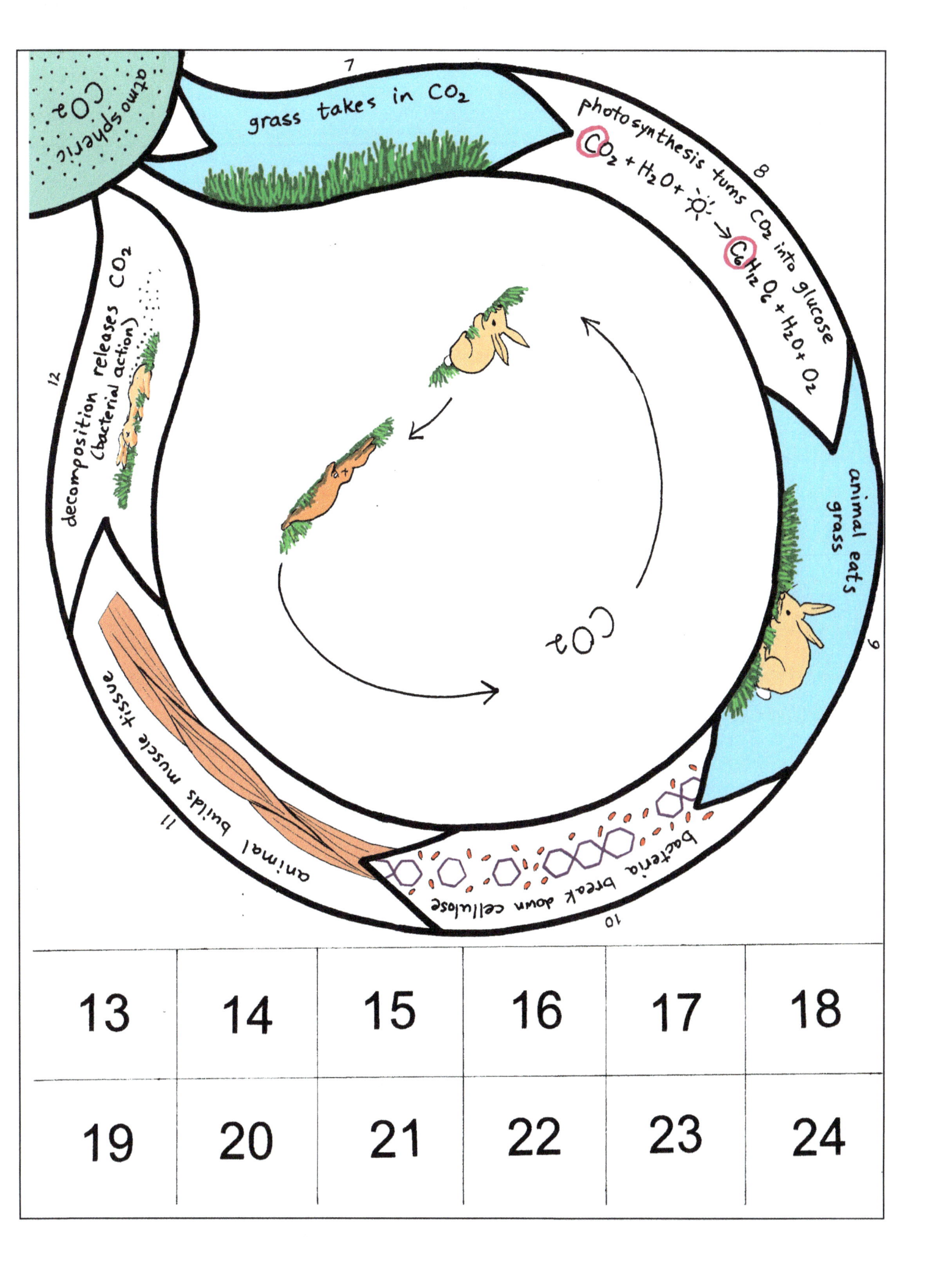

- 7. grass takes in CO₂
- 8. photosynthesis turns CO₂ into glucose
  $$CO_2 + H_2O + \text{☀} \rightarrow C_6H_{12}O_6 + H_2O + O_2$$
- 9. animal eats grass
- 10. bacteria break down cellulose
- 11. animal builds muscle tissue
- 12. decomposition releases CO₂ (bacterial action)

atmospheric CO₂

13	14	15	16	17	18
19	20	21	22	23	24

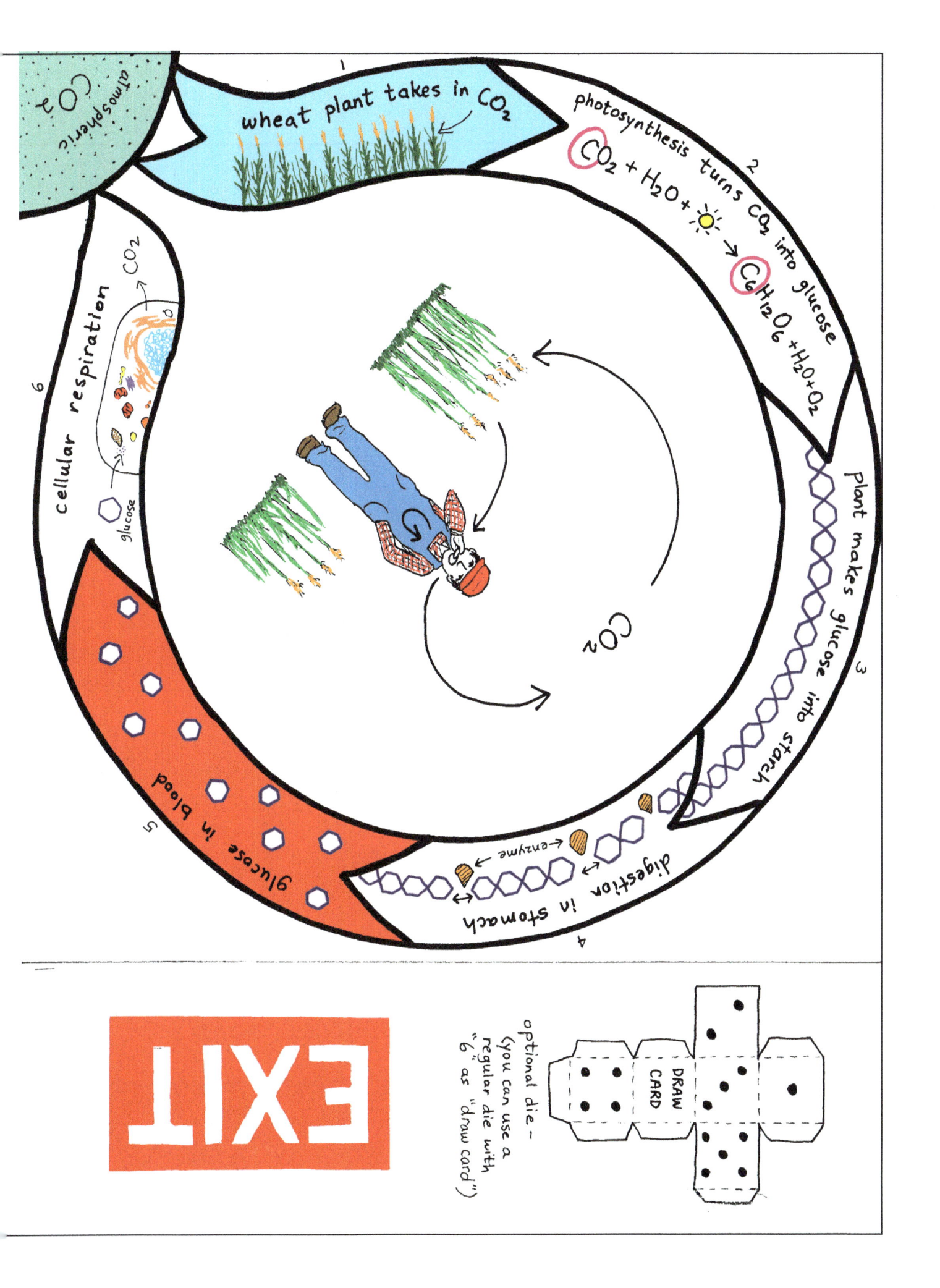

atmospheric CO_2

1. wheat plant takes in CO_2

2. photosynthesis turns CO_2 into glucose
$CO_2 + H_2O + \text{☀} \rightarrow C_6H_{12}O_6 + H_2O + O_2$

3. plant makes glucose into starch

4. digestion in stomach ← enzyme

5. glucose in blood

6. cellular respiration — glucose → CO_2

CO_2

EXIT

optional die – (you can use a regular die with "6" as "draw card")

DRAW CARD

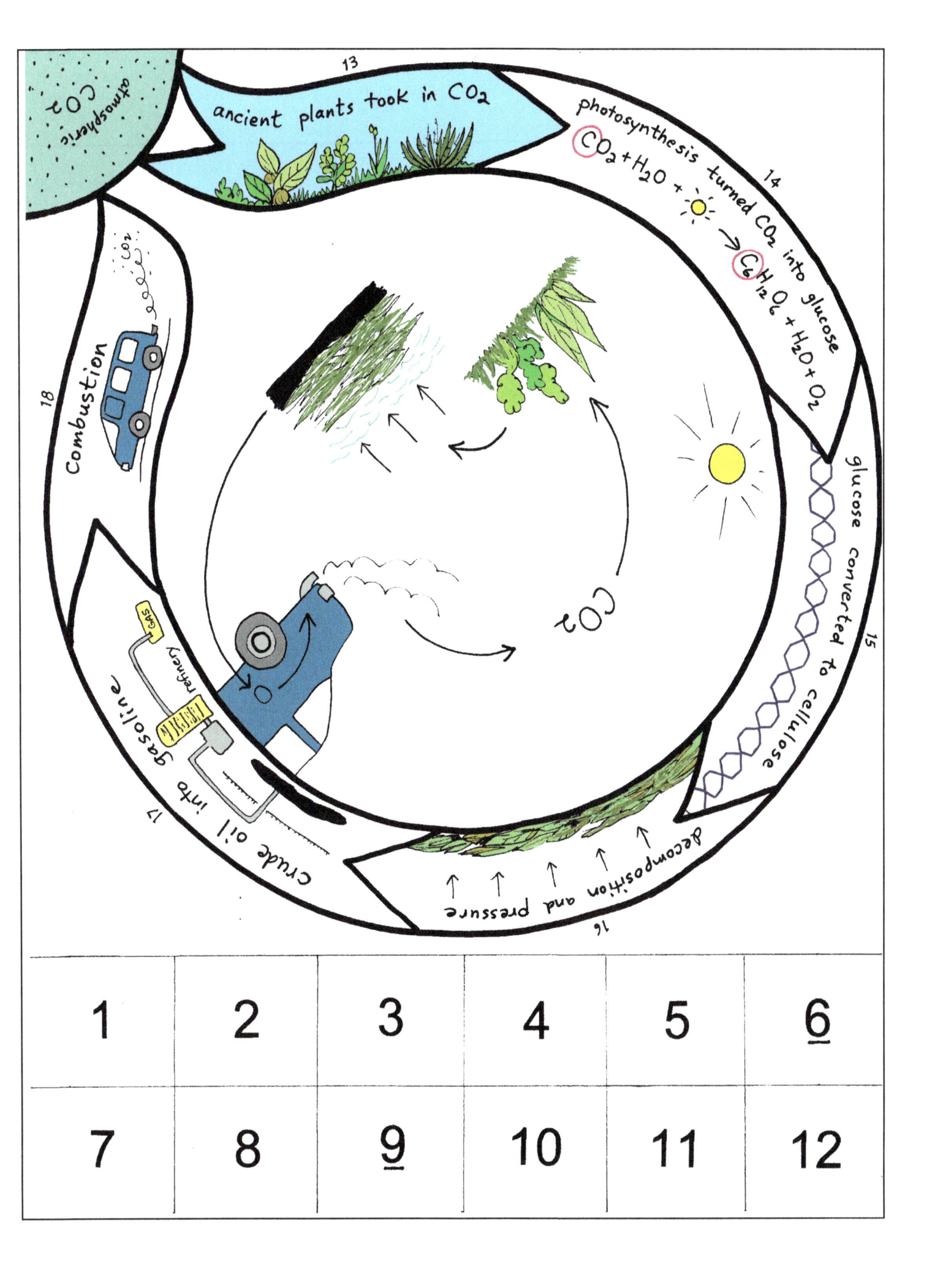

- atmospheric CO_2
- 13: ancient plants took in CO_2
- 14: photosynthesis turned CO_2 into glucose — $CO_2 + H_2O +$ ☀ → $C_6H_{12}O_6 + H_2O + O_2$
- 15: glucose converted to cellulose
- 16: decomposition and pressure
- 17: crude oil into gasoline
- 18: Combustion

1	2	3	4	5	6
7	8	9	10	11	12

19. atmospheric CO_2

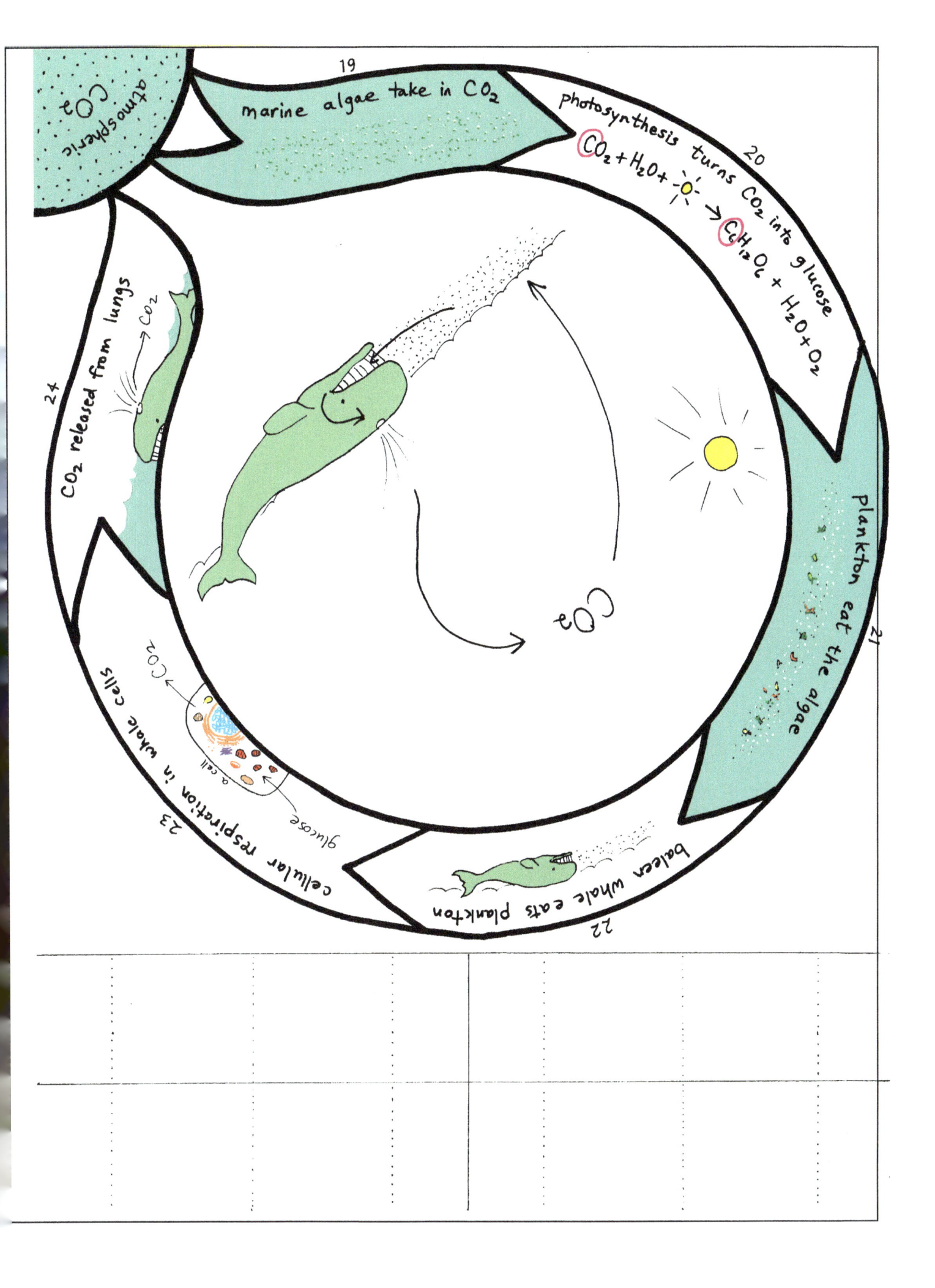

20. photosynthesis turns CO_2 into glucose
$CO_2 + H_2O + \text{☀} \rightarrow C_6H_{12}O_6 + H_2O + O_2$

marine algae take in CO_2

21. plankton eat the algae

22. baleen whale eats plankton

23. cellular respiration in whale cells
glucose → CO_2 (a cell)

24. CO_2 released from lungs

atmospheric CO_2

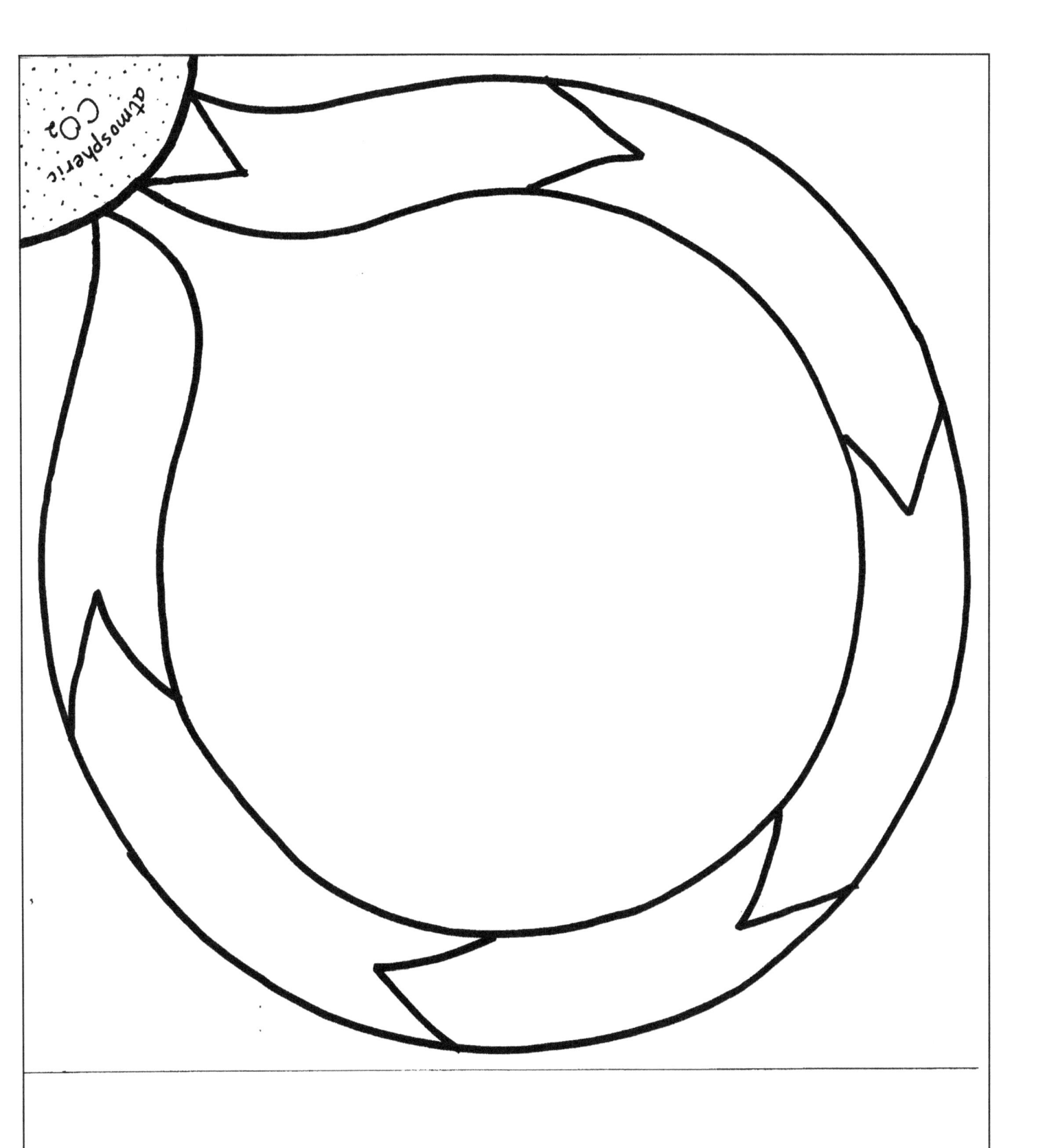

This extra page is provided so that you can draw your own carbon cycle circle(s). Replace one or more of the original squares with your own squares.

Polymer Party

Here is a great way to end your study of carbon chemistry. Throw a polymer party! It's a fun way to review.

Decorating Ideas:

- **Hydrocarbon paper chains from chapter one**
  If you saved your paper chains, hang them up.
- **Popcorn strings**
  Review the fact that corn is made from starch, which is made of strings of glucose molecules. Your popcorn string could be a model of starch or glycogen.
- **Balloons with skewers through them**
  They'll want to do this again, we bet! Or, you can use regular balloons. (Some of our resource information claims that you can string together balloons with yarn, using skewers as needles. We haven't tried it.)

Snack ideas:

- **Anything made of starch, cellulose, fat, or protein is a polymer!**
Most snack foods you would normally have at a party would be examples of polymers. You might want to label the foods with how many calories they contain, or what they are made of, or what kind of polymer they represent. You could also have a thoughtful analysis of the snacks before they are consumed and ask which ones contain polymers and which ones do not. For example, would fruit juice contain polymers? Very few, if any. Water and sugar are not polymers. There might be some cellulose molecules floating in the juice (especially with apple cider). This would be a good pre-eating exercise. Analysis will take critical thinking, and accurately applying what they have learned.

Game Idea #1: Polymer "Pass the Parcel"

You will need:
- Two small gifts (They can be anything, but how about something related to organic chemistry? A bar of soap? A box of chewing gum? A chocolate bar?)
- Odds and ends of wrapping paper
- Tape and scissors
- A photocopy of the next page
- Some kind of music and a way to play it (how about the plastic song?)

Instructions:
In this classic "parlor game," a gift-wrapped package is passed around from person to person while music is played. (Someone who is not watching the game controls the music.) When the music stops, the package also stops. Whoever has the package unwraps it. They will find another layer of wrapping paper underneath. The music begins again and the package begins going from hand to hand again. Each time the music stops, whoever has the package will unwrap it. If there is still wrapping paper on it, the game continues. The game is over when someone finally unwraps the last layer, revealing the gift. This person keeps the gift.

In this variation of the game, the person who has the gift when the music stops must read the question out loud and attempt to answer it. If they get it right, they may unwrap the gift. If they can't answer correctly, the music goes back on and the gift starts circulating again.

Preparation ahead of time:

Photocopy the following sheet with the questions on it, and cut out the questions. There are two sets of questions for two separate gifts. Assign one set of questions to each gift. Wrap the gift once and tape question 10 to it. Then wrap the gift again and tape question 9 to it. Continue like this until you have wrapped the gift ten times, and question number one is taped to the outside of the gift. Wrap the other gift the same way with the other set of questions.

This is a great way to recycle wrapping paper or use scraps that are otherwise unusable!

Answers to questions:

1a) wax, 2a) isopropyl alcohol, 3a) chlorine, fluorine, carbon, 4a) ethene, 5a) literally, "water-fearing," but "water-hating" is also a good answer, 6a) something with the same exact chemical formula, but with a different shape, 7a) dynamite, heart medicine, 8a) ester, 9a) soap, 10a) meth, eth, prop, but, pent, hex, hept, oct, non, dec.

1b) sulfur, 2b) isoprene, 3b) LDPE, 4b) elastomers, 5b) thermoplastic, 6b) ivory, 7b) carbon and fluorine, 8b) catalyst, 9b) polystyrene, 10b) bubble gum and Silly Putty™

General review questions:

1a) Which of these hydrocarbons is longest in length:
natural gas, liquid gasoline, or wax?

2a) Which one of these is not a hydrocarbon:
kerosene, isopropyl alcohol, or diesel fuel?

3a) Chlorofluorocarbons contain what three elements?

4a) Which one of these contains a double bond:
ethane, ethene, or ethyne?

5a) What does hydrophobic mean?

6a) What is an isomer?

7a) Name two things nitroglycerin is used for.

8a) An acid and an alcohol combine to form an _____.

9a) What is sodium stearate?

10a) Can you count to ten in carbons?

Polymer questions:

1b) What element is used to vulcanize rubber?

2b) Which one of these is found in nature?
Polypropylene, polystryrene, or isoprene?

3b) Which of these will melt at lower temperatures:
LDPE or HDPE?

4b) Polymers that stretch and snap back are called _____.

5b) Which one of these can be melted and re-shaped?
    Thermosetting plastic or thermoplastic

6b) Celluloid was invented to replace what natural resource?

7b) What are the two elements that make Teflon?

8b) A chemical that helps a reaction occur without itself being consumed is called _____.

9b) Which one of these plastics contains a benzene ring?
    Polypropylene, polystyrene, or polyvinyl chloride

10b) Name the very popular products invented by Frank Fleer and James Wright.

Game idea #2: Bubble blowing contest

You will need:
- One piece of bubble gum for each contestant
- Make-shift calipers:

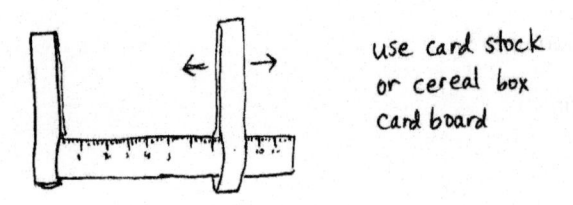

use card stock or cereal box card board

Instructions:
   This is very straightforward: the person who blows the biggest bubble wins. You might want to put students in pairs, and have them take turns blowing and measuring.
   You may want to talk about calipers ahead of time and how they are used to measure thickness. Calipers are used in many industries. Some calipers are very finely graded and can measure things as thin as a sheet of paper.
   Let the contestants have a certain amount of time (two minutes?) to chew and soften their gum. Then start blowing! The person with the calipers should be right ready to measure. The person chewing can use a signal (such as "thumbs up") when they think they have their maximum bubble and want to measure it. Have the calipers all the way open, put the zero marker on one side of the bubble and then quickly and carefully (so as not to damage the bubble) bring the other marker flush with the other side of the bubble. Even if the bubble bursts right then, don't worry, you still have your measurement if the marker hasn't moved.

Game idea #3: Chemical Concentration

You will need:
- Photocopies of the following pages
- These ten words written (in large letters!) each on a separate piece of paper: polyethylene, polypropylene, polystyrene, polyvinyl chloride, Teflon, isoprene rubber, musk deer pheromone, prostaglandin, soap, benzene ring
- Sixteen sheets of opaque paper (construction paper will work well, or any other heavyweight paper) with the numbers 1-16 written on them, one number per paper. Make the numbers very large and easy to see.
- A blank wall or other large vertical space
- Tape
- The sticky, rubbery stuff you use to put up posters (You can substitute a small piece of tape, but don't blame us for any damage to the wall.)

Instructions:

Preparation: Before the students enter the room, put the eight molecules and the eight words on the wall in a square, in random order. Cover them with the numbered papers, with the numbers going in order, and just tape the top of these sheets, so that the number papers can be lifted, like a flap, to look underneath.

under the numbers will be either a word or a chemical formula

Half of these have words under them, half have formulas.

Divide the players into two teams. The teams take turns calling out two numbers. (Make sure the players on each team take turns calling out letters.) Those two numbers are lifted to reveal what is underneath. If they match, the flaps stay up. If not, the flaps go back down. The team that gets the most matches wins. It's up to you whether you want to play that if you get a match you get to go again. Just decided ahead of time and announce the rules accordingly.

$$-\underset{\underset{F}{|}}{\overset{\overset{F}{|}}{C}}-\underset{\underset{F}{|}}{\overset{\overset{F}{|}}{C}}-\underset{\underset{F}{|}}{\overset{\overset{F}{|}}{C}}-\underset{\underset{F}{|}}{\overset{\overset{F}{|}}{C}}-\underset{\underset{F}{|}}{\overset{\overset{F}{|}}{C}}-\underset{\underset{F}{|}}{\overset{\overset{F}{|}}{C}}-\underset{\underset{F}{|}}{\overset{\overset{F}{|}}{C}}-\underset{\underset{F}{|}}{\overset{\overset{F}{|}}{C}}-\underset{\underset{F}{|}}{\overset{\overset{F}{|}}{C}}-\underset{\underset{F}{|}}{\overset{\overset{F}{|}}{C}}-\underset{\underset{F}{|}}{\overset{\overset{F}{|}}{C}}-\underset{\underset{F}{|}}{\overset{\overset{F}{|}}{C}}-$$

$$CH_3-CH_2-CH_2-CH_2-CH_2-CH_2-CH_2-CH_2-CH_2-CH_2-CH_2-CH_2-CH_2-\underset{O^- \ Na^+}{\overset{O}{\overset{\|}{C}}}$$

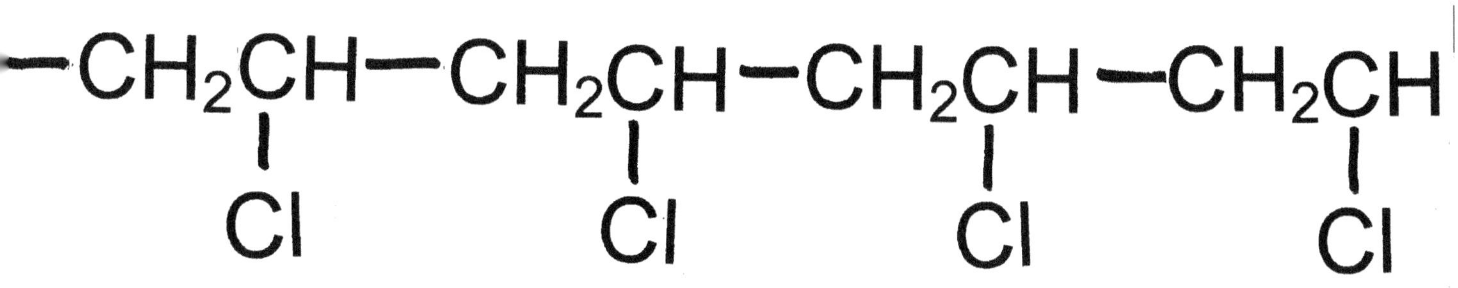

CH2CH
CH2CH
CH2CH
CH2CH
Cl
Cl
Cl
Cl

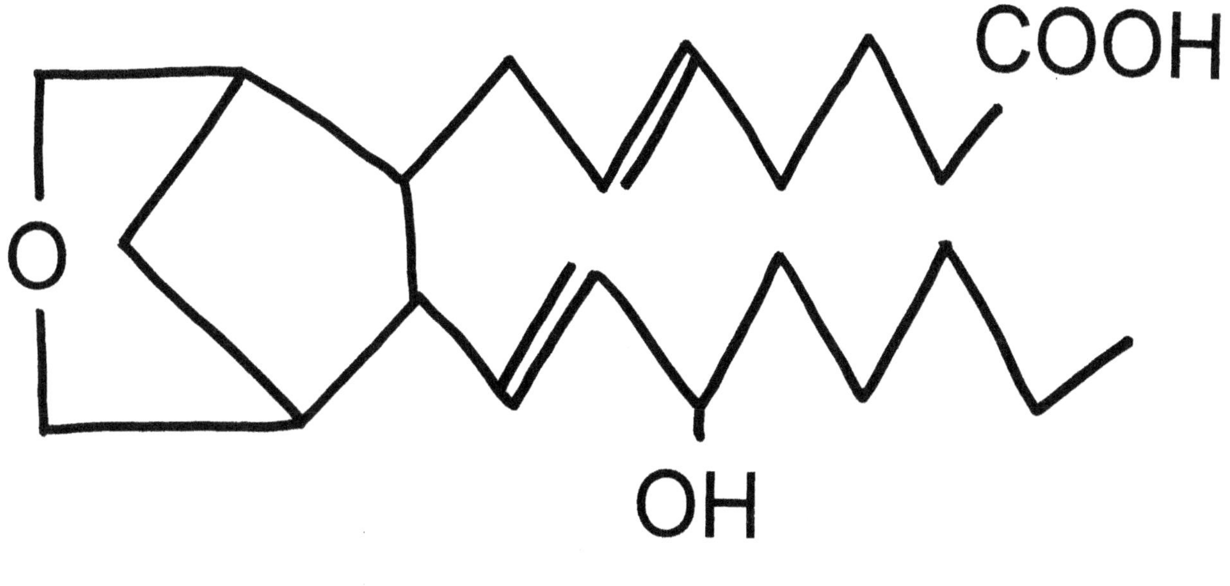

COOH
O
OH

H₂CH—CH₂CH—CH₂CH—CH₂CH—

(each CH bearing a phenyl ring)

—CHCH₂—CHCH₂—CHCH₂—CHCH₂—CHC—
    | | | | |
    CH₃   CH₃   CH₃   CH₃   CH₃

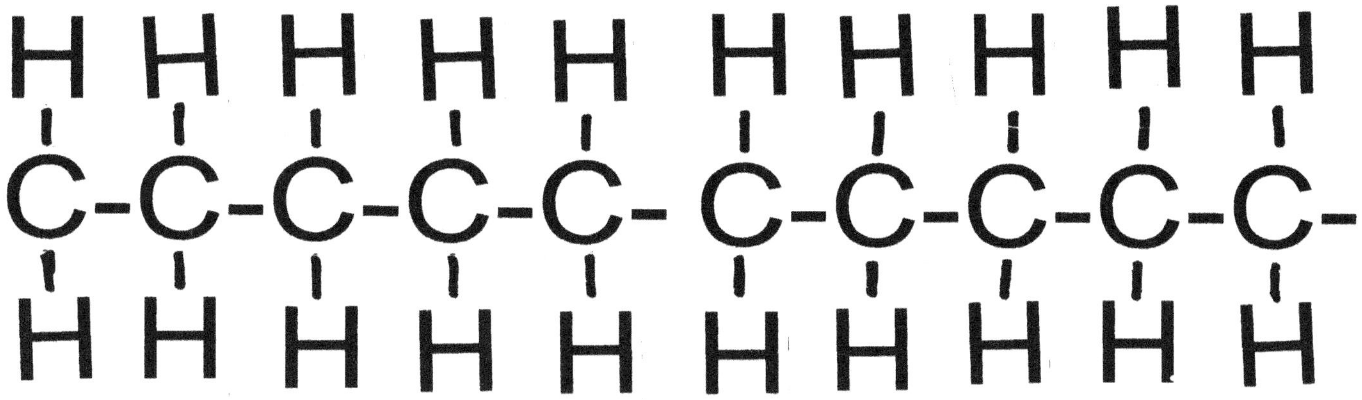

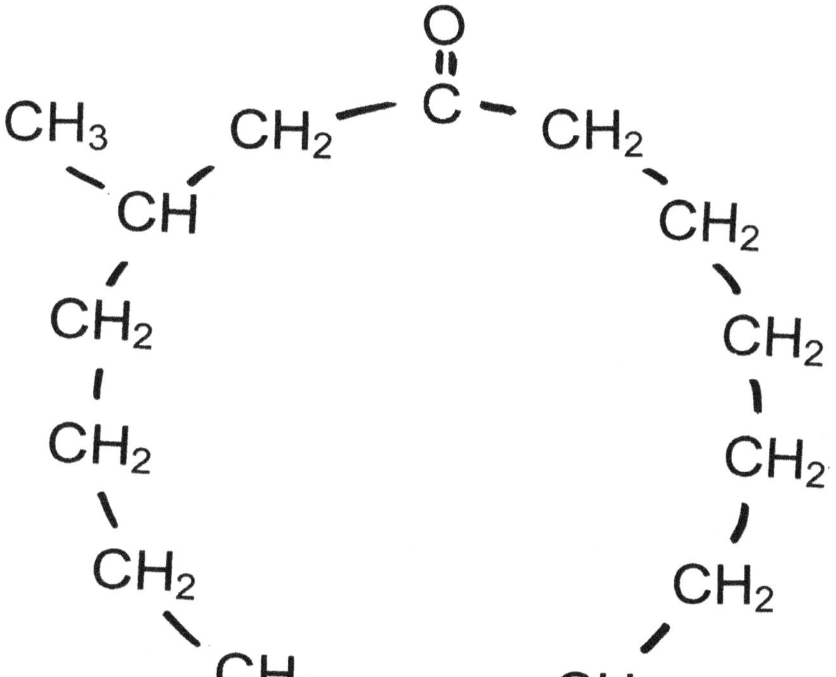

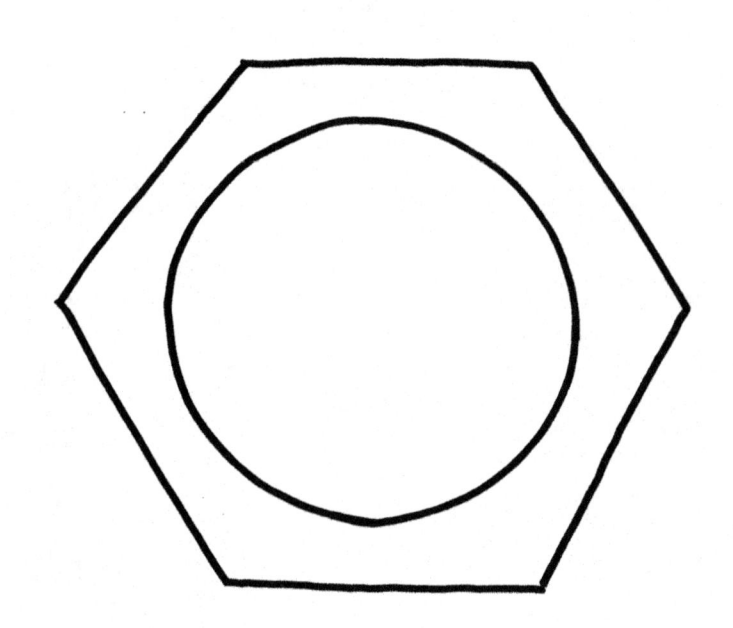

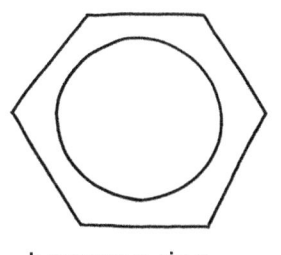

benzene ring

isoprene

musk deer pheromone

prostaglandin

polypropylene

polystyrene

PVC polyvinyl chloride

Teflon

polyethylene

soap

KEY

Bibliography

<u>Chemistry for Changing Times</u>, 8th edition, by John W. Hill and Doris K. Kolb, published by Prentice-Hall, Inc., Upper Saddle River, NJ. © 1998, ISBN 0-13-741786-1 (General chemistry textbook intended for high school or for college non-science majors.)

<u>Chemistry of Carbon Compounds</u>, 3rd edition, by David E. Newton, published by J. Weston Walch, Publisher, Box 658, Portland, Maine 04104.
© 1994, ISBN 0-8251-2487-5 (Organic chemistry text intend for advanced placement high school or entry level college.)

<u>Contemporary Chemistry; A Practical Approach</u>, by Leonard Saland, published by J. Weston Walch, Publisher, Box 658, Portland, Maine, 04104. ©1986, ISBN 0-8251-1799-2 (Leonard Saland is the chairman of the Physical Science Dept. at Louis Brandeis High School in New York.)

Penn State Earth and Mineral Sciences bulletin, Volume 66, 1997. (Article on research into Italy's carbon dioxide vents.)

"Hands-On Plastics," a scientific investigation curriculum put together by the American Plastics Council, 1801 K Street NW, Suite 701-L, Washington D. C., 20006. (Reference for experiment on identifying types of plastics.)

I also used websites quite a bit. Here are the main ones I read, listed in order of how much I used them.

    www.Howitworks.com (one of my favorites!)
    www.Chemed.chem.purdue.edu
    www.Encyclopedia.com
    www.Infoplease.com
    www.chemistry.uakron.edu/genobc
    www.elmhurst.ude/~chm/vchembook
    www.medic8.com/healthguide/articles/exerciseanddiabetes
    www.nexusresearchgroup.com/fun-science/fun.sci.htm
    http://arbl/cvmbs/colostate.edu/hbooks/pathphys/digestion
    www.post-gazette.com (for almond cookie recipe)